OXFORD WORLD'S CLASSICS

THE ROMANCE OF THE ROSE

GUILLAUME DE LORRIS probably lived in the first half of the thirteenth century, but nothing certain is known about him. JEAN DE MEUN completed the *Romance of the Rose*. He also translated into French the *De Consolatione Philosophiae* of Boethius and the Life and Letters of Abelard and Heloise. He died *c*.1305.

FRANCES HORGAN held a research fellowship at Fitzwilliam College, Cambridge from 1983 to 1987. Since then she has combined translating and teaching with bringing up her three children.

OXFORD WORLD'S CLASSICS

For almost 100 years Oxford World's Classics have brought readers closer to the world's great literature. Now with over 700 titles—from the 4,000-year-old myths of Mesopotamia to the twentieth century's greatest novels—the series makes available lesser-known as well as celebrated writing.

The pocket-sized hardbacks of the early years contained introductions by Virginia Woolf, T. S. Eliot, Graham Greene, and other literary figures which enriched the experience of reading. Today the series is recognized for its fine scholarship and reliability in texts that span world literature, drama and poetry, religion, philosophy and politics. Each edition includes perceptive commentary and essential background information to meet the changing needs of readers.

OXFORD WORLD'S CLASSICS

GUILLAUME DE LORRIS
AND
JEAN DE MEUN

The Romance of the Rose

Translated with an Introduction and Notes by
FRANCES HORGAN

OXFORD
UNIVERSITY PRESS

Oxford University Press, Great Clarendon Street, Oxford OX2 6DP
Oxford New York
Athens Auckland Bangkok Bogotá Buenos Aires Calcutta
Cape Town Chennai Dar es Salaam Delhi Florence Hong Kong Istanbul
Karachi Kuala Lumpur Madrid Melbourne Mexico City Mumbai
Nairobi Paris São Paulo Singapore Taipei Tokyo Toronto Warsaw
and associated companies in Berlin Ibadan

Oxford is a registered trade mark of Oxford University Press

Published in the United States
by Oxford University Press Inc., New York

First published as a World's Classics paperback 1994
Reissued as an Oxford World's Classics paperback 1999

British Library Cataloguing in Publication Data
Data available

Library of Congress Cataloging in Publication Data
de Lorris, Guillaume, fl. 1230.
[Roman de la Rose. English]
The Romance of the Rose / Guillaume de Lorris and Jean de Meun ;
translated and edited by Frances Horgan.
p.   cm.—(Oxford world's classics)—Includes bibliographical references.
1. Romances—Translations into English.   2. Courtly love—Poetry.
I. de Meun, Jean, d. 1305?   II. Horgan, Frances.   III. Title.   IV. Series.
841'.1—dc20   PQ1528.A24713   1994   93–5112
ISBN 0–19–283948–9

1 3 5 7 9 10 8 6 4 2

Printed in Great Britain by
Cox & Wyman Ltd.
Reading, Berkshire

PREFACE

This translation of the *Romance of the Rose* is the second into modern English prose, the first being that of Charles Dahlberg (Princeton, 1971). It is based on the edition of Felix Lecoy (Paris, 1965–70), to which the line numbers refer. I have tried to provide a translation which is both accurate and readable, i.e. which is useful to the student while remaining accessible to the general reader. I have frequently and inevitably fallen short of both these aims, but in so far as I have succeeded, I am indebted to Professor Peter Rickard, who has generously read and commented upon the entire text. His erudition has saved me from many errors; those that remain are of course my own.

I would also like to thank Sarah Kay for her comments on the Introduction, Gillian Evans for some thoughts on thirteenth-century theology, my husband for initiating me into the mysteries of word-processing, and finally my mother-in-law, whose kindness in taking care of my children has allowed me the necessary time to complete this task.

F.M.H.

CONTENTS

INTRODUCTION

The *Romance of the Rose* is the product of two authors and two generations. The first 4,000 lines were written between 1225 and 1230 by Guillaume de Lorris, the remainder by Jean de Meun between 1269 and 1278.

This much can be stated with reasonable certainty, although we should bear in mind that the only evidence for Guillaume's authorship of the first part of the romance, and for the period of forty years which elapsed between the composition of the two parts, is supplied by Jean de Meun himself in his continuation (l. 10496 ff.). Beyond this we know nothing whatsoever about Guillaume, and little about Jean, who seems to have spent the latter years of his life in Paris and to have died there in 1305. The *Romance of the Rose* is not the only work by Jean de Meun to have survived: in addition to three translations (of Vegetius' *De re militari* (On Warfare), Boethius' *De consolatione Philosophiae* (The Consolation of Philosophy), and the letters of Abelard and Heloise), two poems (a *Testament* and a *Codicile*) are attributed to him in most of the manuscript sources.

This is the extent of our information concerning the lives of the two authors whose work was among the most influential of all medieval texts. A best seller in its day (well over 200 manuscripts have survived, compared with 84 of the *Canterbury Tales*), it was read, quarrelled over, printed, moralized, and admired until the mid-seventeenth century, edited and re-edited from 1735 onwards, and has in recent years been the subject of a vast and daunting body of critical study.

The tale is told in the first person, and purports to be an account of a dream experienced by the narrator 'five years ago or more'. A young man falls asleep in the month of May, and dreams that he is walking along a river bank when he sees a beautiful garden surrounded by a high wall, on the outside of which are portraits of such hideous creatures as Envy, Avarice, Poverty, and Old Age. Lady Idleness admits him through a tiny wicket gate, and tells him that the lord

of the garden is called Pleasure. The young man finds Pleasure
and his fair companions, and is invited by Courtesy to join
in their dance. Later, as he explores the garden, with its
abundance of plants and song-birds, he comes upon the spring
of Love, where Narcissus had met his death. At the bottom
of the spring are two crystals, each of which reflects half of
the garden. Gazing into the spring, the young man sees the
reflection of a rose-bud, whereupon the God of Love, who
has been stalking him through the garden, shoots five arrows
at him and takes him prisoner. The young man does homage
to the God of Love and swears to obey his commandments.
In return, the God will give him Hope, together with three
other gifts: Pleasant Thoughts, Pleasant Conversation, and
Pleasant Looks.

Left alone and sorrowful, the Lover sees another young
man coming towards him: this is Fair Welcome, the son of
Courtesy, who allows him to pass through the hedge surrounding the roses and gives him a leaf. Immediately, however, a hideous peasant called Rebuff rushes out and bellows
at the Lover to go away and never come back.

Alone once more, the Lover is visited by Reason, who
descends from her tower to urge him to abandon his folly,
only to be angrily spurned. Friend proves to be a more
congenial companion, and his advice to the Lover to employ
diplomacy meets with some success: with Venus' help, Fair
Welcome is persuaded to allow the Lover to kiss the rose-
bud. Once again, there is immediate consternation, and the
upshot is that Jealousy builds a square enclosure, and within
the enclosure a tower, in which Fair Welcome is imprisoned
under the watchful eye of an old woman, while the Lover
remains disconsolately outside.

It is at this point that Guillaume's narrative breaks off, and
the tale is taken up by Jean de Meun. Although Jean's contribution to the romance is approximately four times the
length of Guillaume's, the plot can be summarized quite simply, and is to some extent a duplication of the plot of the first
part. Reason, descending from her tower once again, exhorts
the Lover to abandon the God of Love, and offers herself as
mistress in his stead. Once again she is spurned, though

perhaps with a little more reluctance, and the Lover turns to
Friend for counsel. Friend gives more or less the same advice
as before, although at much greater length. He counsels the
Lover not to shrink from employing deception, bribery, and
violence to gain his ends, and warns him against marriage.

After an unsuccessful conversation with Wealth, who will
not allow him to take the path of Lavish Giving, the Lover
decides to follow the advice of Friend and placate the guardians of the Rose. Eventually, the God of Love reappears and
summons his barons to attack the Castle of Jealousy. Among
the barons are the unlikely figures of False Seeming and
Constrained Abstinence, whose presence the God of Love
will tolerate provided they serve him faithfully. In response
to the god's request, False Seeming reveals that he is a liar
and a hypocrite, and that his preferred home is among the
mendicant friars.

False Seeming and Constrained Abstinence then strangle
Evil Tongue and cut out his tongue. Together with Courtesy
and Largesse, they capture the Old Woman, who persuades
Fair Welcome to accept the gift of a chaplet of flowers from
the Lover and at the same time urges him to learn from her
mistakes and sell himself to the highest bidder.

The Old Woman then admits the Lover into the presence
of Fair Welcome, but just as he is about to pluck the rose,
Rebuff, Fear, and Shame drive him away once again and
imprison Fair Welcome with a triple lock. The Lover cries
for help, and the God of Love launches his attack, but his
barons are defeated and he is forced to send for help to his
mother, Venus. Venus arrives in her chariot, and she and the
God of Love swear before the whole army to defeat Chastity.

Meanwhile, Nature is in her forge, labouring to perpetuate
the species. She is greatly distressed because of a fault she has
committed, and makes her confession to her chaplain, Genius.
God has given the universe into her charge, and everything
in it obeys her laws, everything, that is, except for mankind.
Most of man's sins are God's concern, not hers, but one sin
is Nature's particular concern: man's refusal to co-operate
with her in the perpetuation of the species by making proper
use of the 'tools' with which she has supplied him. She

therefore dispatches Genius to excommunicate the enemies of the God of Love, and to grant a plenary pardon to all who strive to do her 'work', provided they make a good confession. Genius hastens to the army, and the God of Love dresses him up as a bishop. Skating neatly round the question of clerical celibacy (let the theologians sort that one out!), he urges the barons to 'plough' vigorously as their forefathers did, and to make sure they plough a straight furrow if they do not want their purses, hammers, styluses, and ploughshares to be torn off. If they do this, and then make a good confession, they will come to the park of the Good Shepherd, which is as far above the garden of Pleasure as truth is above fiction.

Emboldened by this sermon, the barons decide to attack. Venus shoots her fiery arrow through a tiny aperture set between two pillars and sets fire to the castle. Rebuff, Fear, and Shame take to their heels, and the Lover, who has now become a pilgrim, is able to introduce his staff into the aperture and finally to pluck the rose. Dawn breaks, and the dreamer awakes.

It will be apparent even from this sketchy outline that we are dealing with an allegorical text. Although the romance, and particularly Guillaume's contribution, can be read on a simple, literal level, it clearly 'means' something else. Both poets tell us this explicitly, and both promise explanations which never materialize. Since, unlike the author of *The Name of the Rose*, neither Guillaume de Lorris nor Jean de Meun has supplied us with a commentary, we must rely on our own resources to uncover the 'meaning' of their text. And since the text as we have it is the work of two authors separated by a period of forty years, we are bound, at least initially, to think of it as two texts.

Guillaume's poem is, at least in part, an allegorical account of the progress of a love affair. A young man encounters the most beautiful woman he has ever seen (the dreamer sees the reflection of the rose), falls in love with her (is wounded by the arrows of the God of Love), and undertakes to conduct himself according to the conventions of courtly love, or *fin' amors* (does homage to the God of Love). His advances are alternately welcomed (Fair Welcome allows him into the rose-garden and gives him a leaf) and discouraged (Rebuff drives him away). Part of him knows that his behaviour is foolish (the advice of Reason), but love is stronger than reason, and the poem ends, in courtly fashion, with the Lover's appeal to the Lady not to forget him, in spite of the obstacles that separate them.

Many elements (the May-morning setting, the first-person narrative, the mood of intense subjectivity, the use of sacred imagery to describe secular passion) link the poem to the tradition of the courtly love-lyric. This has prompted some critics to suggest that the apparently unfinished state of Guillaume's text is its intended form, since the ending as we have it, in which the Lover continues to love his lady from a distance, is characteristic of certain forms of early troubadour poetry, and it would in any case be the height of uncourtliness for a poet to address a poem to his lady in which Love actually captured the castle.

Guillaume himself is at pains to stress the didactic aspect of his work. He introduces it as 'The Romance of the Rose, in which the whole art of love is contained', and insists, when he comes to the commandments of the God of Love, that 'anyone who aspires to love should pay attention, for the romance now improves'. Clearly, Guillaume is situating his text in the tradition of treatises on the theory of love, most notably exemplified in the Middle Ages by the twelfth-century *De arte honeste amandi* (The Art of True Love) of Andreas Capellanus. His poem can be read as a kind of textbook, in which the Lover's adventures illustrate the theoretical manual for courtly lovers dictated by the God of Love.

The lesson is communicated in the form of a dream vision, a device often used as a vehicle for didacticism in Latin literature, both classical and medieval. This is the first time it occurs in amorous poetry, and Guillaume seems to be using it as a way of authenticating his narrative. He cites the fourth-century Latin author Macrobius, whose commentary on Cicero's *Dream of Scipio* enjoyed immense popularity in the Middle Ages, in support of his claim that this is a prophetic dream, and that everything in it came true, exactly as the dream predicted. Perhaps he means that his poem is autobiographical, and that the lady to whom it is dedicated, 'who is so precious and so worthy of being loved that she ought to be called Rose', is the heroine of the romance, the rose-bud 'so beautiful that . . . all the others seemed worthless in comparison'.

However, in his *Commentary* Macrobius divides dreams into five different categories, and identifies the erotic dream, which this surely is, as an insomnium or nightmare not worth interpreting. Are we reading Guillaume too simply? Certainly, the sunlit, courtly world of the garden of Pleasure is not presented unambiguously. At its centre, the spring of Narcissus threatens death and madness. Among its trees and flowers stalks the somewhat sinister figure of the God of Love, with his traps and nets. The rose-garden is surrounded by a hedge of nettles and briars, and piercing thorns grow from the stem of the rose itself. Moreover, all the Lover's actions are condemned by Reason, the daughter of God, whose advice is spurned.

Many critics have thought that Guillaume's intention was in fact to condemn what he related, and have used iconographical evidence to support this point of view: for example, the comb and mirror carried by Idleness are the traditional attributes of Luxuria, or lust.[1] It is true that Guillaume frequently invites us to read his text ironically, but the irony is of the most enigmatic kind, and is substantially attenuated by the characterization of the Lover as an innocent, trusting child who has yet to learn that Love deceives. We are apparently being asked not so much to condemn the Lover as to indulge his youthful folly.

With the appearance of Jean de Meun, we move from the court to the University, from the dreamlike stillness of the garden of Pleasure, where a lover's courtship of his lady takes the form of a series of encounters with allegorized aspects of her personality, to an atmosphere of robust academic debate in which the subjective allegories give way to a set of loquacious, pugnacious characters, most of whom are drawn from earlier philosophical works.

[1] See in particular John V. Fleming, *The Roman de la Rose: A Study in Allegory and Iconography* (Princeton, NJ: Princeton University Press, 1969).

The first of these is Reason. For Guillaume, she had been the voice of reason in the Lover himself, concerned exclusively with his particular predicament and easily silenced by the voice of desire. Jean de Meun's Reason is quite a different proposition. In the course of a staggeringly long speech of around three thousand lines, she discourses on love in its various forms (carnal desire, 'natural' love, friendship, 'pure' love, etc.), on the proper attitude to Fortune and wealth, the question of what constitutes true nobility, the relative merits of love and justice, and the nature of language. In support of her arguments she cites both classical texts and contemporary history. Her aim is to win the Lover away from his allegiance to the God of Love, and to that end she offers herself as his mistress. Needless to say, she fails. The prospect of being like Socrates holds no charms for the young man, whose mind is on much lower things. He cares not three chick-peas for Socrates (what lover ever did?), and he finds Reason's speeches wearisome.

Reason, we might say, is all talk. Certainly the Lover thinks so, and she herself represents herself as the giver of names on God's behalf, the first recipient of the God-given gift of speech. How ironic it is that in the course of her extended discussion with the Lover, communication breaks down completely. The young man totally fails to understand her: when she talks of pure love (l. 4567) he hears only hatred (l. 4615); when she talks of the castration of Saturn and the condition of mankind in the age of Jupiter, he hears only an uncourtly word ('testicles'). Unfortunately for Reason, the world has changed. No one speaks 'properly' nowadays, and language has become opaque, an impediment, rather than an aid, to understanding. In such a world, it is no surprise if Reason's discourse falls on deaf ears.

Having dispatched Reason, the young man turns for counsel to Friend, another character whom Jean de Meun takes over from Guillaume de Lorris. Here he finds advice which is a great deal more to his taste. Jean de Meun's Friend has recognizably the same role as his predecessor, but developed in the direction of a cynicism which effectively explodes the courtly courtesies of the original. In Guillaume's poem, Friend had advocated a little harmless cajolery, and advised the Lover to 'get round' Rebuff by promising never to do anything to upset him. But now, it seems, there are no depths of hypocrisy and insincerity to which the Lover should not be prepared to stoop in pursuit of his goal. Deception, bribery, time-serving, false promises, all are acceptable as means to this end. And it is Friend who quotes the indictment of marriage pronounced by the Jealous Husband, perhaps the best-known of the many examples of apparently anti-feminist writing in this text.

For some critics, the speech of Friend is an indication that Jean's *Rose* should be read as an 'anti-Guillaume', and that, whereas Guillaume intended his work to be an 'art of courtly love', Jean's intention was to offer a thoroughgoing critique of courtly love. Further evidence in support of this view is found in the speeches of the Old Woman, Nature, and, above all, Genius, who explicitly condemns the garden of Pleasure as unstable and corruptible, and the spring of Narcissus as bitter and poisonous.

This kind of view ignores the ironies already implicit in Guillaume's text (even Guillaume has Friend advise the Lover to lie to Rebuff), and also makes the fundamental mistake of supposing that Jean de Meun himself is speaking directly through his characters. In fact, the speech of the Jealous Husband is at several removes from the author: the Lover quotes Friend, who in his turn quotes the Jealous Husband. Clearly, any attempt to isolate the author's own point of view must be made with extreme caution. Paradoxically, and ironically, it is the next speaker, False Seeming, who becomes Jean de Meun's most unambiguous spokesman.

The arrival of False Seeming is a considerable shock, both for the God of Love and for the reader. For the God of Love because, as a proven traitor, who has perjured himself on countless occasions, he has no place among the noble barons of the army, and for the reader because, under the name of Religious Hypocrisy, he had specifically been excluded from Guillaume's garden. Furthermore, as a self-confessed liar, he presents the God of Love and the reader with rather a tricky problem: how do you interpret the words of a liar who says he is telling the truth? Persuaded by his barons of the need to accept the services of False Seeming, the god puts this very problem to him. He asks how he can be sure that the traitor will keep his word, since it is against his nature, and False Seeming replies simply: 'You must take the risk.'

The God of Love is also concerned to know how False Seeming can be identified in the world, and here the traitor, although unwilling to answer for fear of reprisals, is rather more helpful. 'You will certainly not be able to tell by my habit which people I am living with,' he says, 'and I will not reveal it to you by my words, however simple and mild they are. You must look at my actions, if your eyes have not been put out, for if people do not act as they speak, they are certainly deluding you.' Whited sepulchres of this kind are to be found everywhere, but above all, it seems, in the orders of mendicant friars, among whom False Seeming is most at home.

And now the author temporarily raises the allegorical veil to launch a direct attack upon the mendicant orders. We are abruptly precipitated into the world of thirteenth-century University politics, where a bitter dispute raged between the secular masters of the University of Paris and the friars who had obtained teaching positions but were unwilling to co-operate with the seculars over certain matters of University policy. The chief opponent of the friars was Guillaume de Saint-Amour, whose treatise *De periculis novissimum temporum* (On the Perils of the Last Days), from which most of False Seeming's arguments are taken, was condemned by the Pope in 1256 and led to Guillaume's exile from France until his death in 1272.

There is little doubt that False Seeming is speaking here on the author's behalf. The very choice of the name, False Seeming, which first appeared in a poem by Rutebeuf on the same subject, is an indication of Jean's intention to make a contribution to an ongoing debate. The attack is of the bitterest kind: the friars are characterized as wolves in sheep's clothing, whose cloak of holy poverty conceals a rapacious desire for gain. They care nothing for the poor, but penetrate the homes of the rich and powerful, whose confessors they become. In short, they are the servants of Antichrist, and await his coming.

No one likes a supergrass, but everyone admits he has his uses. The God of Love is prepared to put up with False Seeming, provided he turns Queen's evidence and serves him loyally, which he does by duly disposing of Evil Tongue. In the same way, the reader, observing that, for once at least, False Seeming's deeds do correspond with his words, is forced to put aside his natural distrust and accept the traitor as a reliable witness.

False Seeming's revelations concerning the ubiquitousness of hypocrisy had been anticipated by Friend. Further confirmation is now supplied by the Old Woman, whose advice to Fair Welcome is a kind of mirror-image of that given by Friend to the Lover. A young woman, if she is sensible, will bear in mind that all men are faithless, and will therefore make it her business to fleece her lovers of everything she can. Nor will she remain faithful to just one man, for, as Friend has already pointed out, marriage is against her nature. A good deal of practical advice is given concerning the conduct of amorous affairs, amounting, in fact, to an art of love, although scarcely one that Guillaume would have recognized.

Unfortunately for the Old Woman, her own disregard for these precepts during her life has brought her to her present wretched condition. Like Friend, whom Unrestrained Generosity had reduced to poverty, she preaches the message: 'Do as I say, not as I do' (an ironic echo of the gospel according to False Seeming). The speeches of Friend, False Seeming, and the Old Woman form a kind of triptych in which the world is revealed as a loveless place, and mankind as vicious, rapacious, and hypocritical. But it is time to leave the world and ascend into the heavens, where Nature is busy in her forge.

If Reason is all talk, Nature is pre-eminently a woman of action. As God's deputy, she toils ceaselessly to preserve the species by forging new individuals. Just now, however, events on earth have moved her to rest awhile from her labours and make her confession to her chaplain, Genius. And what is this confession about? Almost everything, apparently: theology, philosophy, astronomy, meteorology, optics, visions . . . the list is endless, and tends to distract us from Nature's main subject. Her repeated cry of 'let's get back to the point', i.e.

to our survey of the whole of creation, is ironic in a way that anticipates Pathelin's proverbial sheep. Man is Nature's subject, and the whole of her 'confession' can be read both as an affirmation of the 'glorious freedom of the children of God' and as a condemnation of man's wilful misuse of that freedom. Man alone among created things has reason. It was given to him not by Nature but by God himself, and it brings with it both freedom and responsibility. The whole of creation obeys Nature's laws, because it has no choice (and Nature gives us a brief glimpse of the chaos that might ensue if animals, for instance, did have a choice in the matter). But man is different: he is free to commit unnatural acts, to kill or castrate himself, and he bears the full responsibility for his actions (a large part of Nature's discourse is devoted to disposing of the traditional scapegoats: planetary influences, divine predestination, the work of demons).

How, then, has he used his freedom? Nature knows that this is none of her business: it was not she who gave man his reason. But everything else that he has comes from her, and so she is involved in his shame. Womanlike (how could she be other than true to her own nature?), she can no longer keep silent and launches into an impassioned denunciation of human conduct. This comes as no surprise: what other judgement is possible on a world which kneels before False Seeming while eagerly awaiting the advent of Antichrist?

Most of man's sins are offences against God, and God will exact retribution in his own good time. But one sin is Nature's particular concern: it is that man has failed to make proper use of the 'tools' with which she has supplied him; in other words that he has not co-operated with Nature in her long struggle to ensure the survival of the species by fathering children. This is a crime against Nature rather than against God; indeed, it is not clear whether in God's eyes it is a crime at all.

A vigorous debate concerning the virtue of chastity seems to have taken place in the thirteenth century. Writers considering the question 'whether simple fornication is a mortal sin' sometimes suggested that it was not, because it is a natural act and a natural act is not a sin. Thomas Aquinas, in his *Contra Gentiles* (Against the Gentiles), had argued that men should not be entirely chaste, because if they were, the human race would die out.

When Nature sends her priest, Genius, to excommunicate the enemies of the God of Love and give absolution to all who do her 'work', she seems to be endorsing this view. Genius's sermon is apparently intended not so much to convince his audience of the need to indulge freely in sexual intercourse (he is, after all, preaching to the converted!) as to reassure them that in doing so they will not be excluding themselves from salvation.[2] He does not say that frequent sex is the key to heaven, merely that it is not a barrier. He says that those who use their 'tools' will not be 'prevented' from entering heaven, will not be 'reproached'. He talks of pardons, of taking the burden of these sins upon himself, of making a good confession to God afterwards. In other words he offers a defence, albeit a burlesque one, of the thesis that fornication is not a mortal sin because it is a natural act and necessary for the continuation of the species.

But Genius is a selective reader. The writers who argued that fornication was a natural act and therefore not a sin did so merely as a prelude to refuting their own arguments. Aquinas made a distinction between the individual and the species and pointed out that the species would be preserved if some individuals were fruitful and multiplied while others devoted themselves to the things of God. And the proposition 'Quod simplex fornicatio utpote soluti cum soluta non est peccatum' (that simple fornication, freely consented to by both parties, is not a sin) was one of 219 formally condemned by Bishop Etienne Tempier in 1277.

Here we are on holy ground, and Genius cannot follow. As Nature's priest, he shares both her authority and her limitations. Nature has already admitted that she cannot understand phenomena which contravene her laws, which are 'unnatural' in the first sense of the word. For the most part, such phenomena can be dismissed as mere delusion (storms and tempests are not the result of demonic activity) or are

---

[2] This is not to deny that Genius spends most of his time urging the barons to procreate—as 'god and master of the organs of reproduction', he is bound to do so.

generally agreed in the Middle Ages to be evil (Genius's cruellest punishments are reserved for those who indulge in what he thinks of as sexual perversions). But when it comes to the ways in which God chooses to deal with his creatures, then Nature, by her own admission, has nothing to say. She cannot comprehend the Incarnation, for example, for according to her laws, it is impossible for anything to be born of a virgin.

Genius is in exactly the same position with respect to the virtue of chastity. He is unwilling to give up without a fight: if chastity is the best way to salvation for some, then it must be so for all, but if all men were chaste, then the race would die. But in the end, he is forced to admit his incompetence in this area: 'I know no more about it. Let theologians come and theologize about it: they will never reach a conclusion.'

Genius is not the type to be troubled by scruples. The fact that his robes are borrowed and his authority deficient matters not a scrap. He has a sermon to preach, and with Bishop Tempier nowhere in sight, he need pull no punches. In an extraordinary discourse which combines coarse, fabliau humour with passages of intense lyrical beauty, he urges his little flock to make full use of their ploughs and styluses, and assures them that, provided they make a good confession to almighty God, they will still be admitted to the park of the Good Shepherd.

This is indubitably the stuff to give the troops, who all cry: 'Amen, amen! To the assault without delay!'—better not delay, in case Bishop Tempier or Thomas Aquinas should appear over the horizon to raise the siege. And it does the trick: Fear, Shame, and Rebuff are routed, and the Lover succeeds in impregnating the rose, so Nature is satisfied.

What are we to make of it all? Can the *Romance of the Rose* be read as a single poem whose two authors are united in their support of the Lover, or ought we to read it as two texts fundamentally opposed to one another? Does Jean de Meun's Genius condone courtly love in the guise of euphemized fornication, or denounce it as sterile and unnatural? Or are the two authors in fact united in their condemnation of courtly love? These are difficult questions to answer, the more so since, in this most elusive of medieval texts, the authorial voice can scarcely be heard above those of the characters. Perhaps one reason for the continuing fascination exercised by this somewhat daunting work is that there are as many ways of approaching it as there are readers.

SELECT BIBLIOGRAPHY

Editions

Le Roman de la Rose, ed. Felix Lecoy (3 vols.; Paris: Champion, coll. CFMA, 1965–70)

Le Roman de la Rose, ed. Daniel Poirion (Paris: Garnier Flammarion, 1974)

Studies

Lewis, C. S., *The Allegory of Love* (Oxford: OUP, 1936)

Tuve, Rosemond, *Allegorical Imagery: Some Mediaeval Books and their Posterity* (Princeton, NJ: University Press, 1966)

Fleming, John V., *The Roman de la Rose: A Study in Allegory and Iconography* (Princeton, NJ: Princeton University Press, 1969)

Luria, Maxwell, *A Reader's Guide to the Roman de la Rose* (Hamden, Conn.: Archon, 1982)

Arden, Heather M., *The Romance of the Rose* (Boston: Twayne, Twayne World Author Series, 1987)

Kay, Sarah, *The Romance of the Rose* (London: Grant and Cutler, forthcoming)

The Romance of the Rose

CHAPTER 1

THE GARDEN OF PLEASURE

Some say that there is nothing in dreams but lies and fables; however, one may have dreams which are not in the least deceitful, but which later become clear. In support of this fact, I can cite an author named Macrobius, who did not consider that dreams deceived, but wrote of the vision that came to King Scipio.* Whoever thinks or says that it is foolish or stupid to believe that a dream may come true, let him think me mad if he likes; for my part I am confident that a dream may signify the good and ill that may befall people, for many people dream many things secretly, at night, which are later seen openly.

In my twentieth year, at the time when Love claims his 21 tribute from young men, I lay down one night, as usual, and fell fast asleep. As I slept, I had a most beautiful and pleasing dream, but there was nothing in the dream that has not come true, exactly as the dream told it. Now I should like to recount that dream in verse, the better to delight your hearts, for Love begs and commands me to do so. And if any man or woman should ask what I wish this romance, which I now begin, to be called, it is the *Romance of the Rose*, in which the whole art of love is contained. The matter is fair and new; God grant that she for whom I have undertaken it may receive it with pleasure. She it is who is so precious and so worthy of being loved that she ought to be called Rose.

It seemed to me that it was May, five years ago or more; 45 I dreamed that it was May, the season of love and joy, when everything rejoices, for one sees neither bush nor hedge that would not deck itself for May in a covering of new leaves. The woods, which are dry all winter long, regain their greenness; the very earth glories in the dew that waters it, and forgets the poverty in which it has spent the whole winter; this is the time when the earth becomes so proud that it desires a new dress, and is able to make a dress so lovely that there are a hundred pairs of colours in it. The grass, and the flowers, which are white and blue and many different colours, these are the dress that I am describing, and in which the earth takes pride. The birds, silent during the cold, harsh, and bitter weather, are so happy in the mild May weather, and their singing shows the joy in their hearts to be so great that they cannot help but sing. It is then that the nightingale strives to sing and make his noise, and the parrot and lark are glad and joyful; it is then that young men must seek love and merriment in the fair, mild weather. The man who does not love in May, when he hears the birds on the branches singing their sweet and touching songs, is hard of heart indeed. I dreamed one night that it was that delightful season, when everything is excited by love, and as I slept, it seemed to me that it was already broad daylight. I rose from my bed at once, put on my shoes and washed my hands, then took a silver needle from its dainty and charming case and began to thread it. I felt like going out of the town to hear the sound of birds singing among the bushes in this new season. Lacing up my sleeves,* I set off alone, rejoicing and listening to the birds, who were singing with all their might because the gardens were coming into flower.

103   Light of heart, gay, and full of happiness, I bent my steps towards a river which I heard murmuring close by, for I knew no better place to amuse myself than on its banks. The water fell swiftly and abundantly from a nearby hill; it was clear and cold as a well or a spring, not quite so great as the Seine, but wider. Never before had I seen that stream, which was so beautifully situated, and I gazed on the delightful spot with pleasure and happiness. As I cooled and washed my face in the clear, shining water, I saw that the bed of the stream was all covered and paved with gravel. The fair, broad meadow descended to the water's edge, and the morning was clear and calm, bright and mild. Then I set off through the meadow, wandering happily downstream, keeping to the river bank. When I had gone a little further, I saw a large and extensive garden, entirely surrounded by a high, crenellated wall, which was decorated on the outside with paintings and carved with many rich inscriptions. I gazed with pleasure at the images

and the paintings on the wall, and I shall tell you what they were like, as far as I can remember.

Right in the middle I saw Hate, who seemed indeed to 139 foment rage and anger; her image was angry and quarrelsome and most vile in appearance, not well attired but looking indeed like a woman wild with fury. Her ill-natured and frowning face had a snub nose, and she was filthy and hideous, hideously wrapped in a towel. Beside her on the left was another figure, of a different shape, whose name I read above her head; she was called Cruelty. Then, looking to the right I saw an image called Baseness, not unlike the other two in form and kind. She seemed indeed an evil creature, wild and cruel, an immoderate and insolent scandalmonger. The man who could create such an image knew well how to paint a portrait; it seemed a most villainous thing. She seemed to be full of abuse, a woman incapable of honouring others as she ought to. Covetousness was painted next, she who entices men to take and to give nothing in return and to heap up great possessions, who causes many to lend money at interest because of their burning desire to win and amass possessions; she it is who prompts thieves and scoundrels to steal, a most wicked and sinful act, for in the end many of them are inevitably hanged. It is she who causes men to take and steal other men's goods, to rob and defraud them (and there is no credit in such acts); it is she who makes all tricksters, and false litigants have often, through their lying talk, robbed young men and maidens of their rightful inheritance. The hands of this image were bent and grasping, and rightly so, for Covetousness is always trying furiously to steal what belongs to others, and directs her efforts to nothing but seizing their possessions. Covetousness is too fond of other men's goods.

By the side of Covetousness was seated another image: it 195 was called Avarice. The image was ugly and dirty and in a miserable state, thin, wretched, and green as a chive. So pale was she that she looked ill; she seemed a creature dying of hunger, living on nothing but bread kneaded with strong, bitter lye. As well as being thin, she was poorly dressed: her tunic was old and torn, as if it had been among dogs; it was poor and threadbare and covered in old patches. Beside her, on a thin little clothespole, hung her cloak and a dark woollen tunic. Her cloak was trimmed not with miniver but with shaggy, heavy, black lamb, a poor, shabby affair. Her dress was certainly ten years old, but Avarice is loath to hurry where clothing is concerned. For you may be sure that she would have been very much grieved if she had worn this dress out, and if it had been worn and ragged, she would not have made another until she was in grave need or want of a new one. Avarice held a purse hidden in her hand, which she tied up so tightly that it would have taken her a very long time to remove anything from it, but she had no interest in doing that; her only desire was to take nothing from the purse.

235 Envy was portrayed next, who never in her life laughed or enjoyed anything except when she saw or heard tell of some great trouble. Nothing pleases her so much as evils and misfortune. When she sees some great calamity befall a good man, the sight gives her much pleasure; she rejoices greatly in her heart when she sees some great family ruined or disgraced; and when someone achieves honour through his own abilities and prowess, this is what wounds her most of all, for I assure you that she must needs be angry when good things happen.

253 Envy is so cruel that she is loyal neither to man nor to woman, nor has she any close relative with whom she is not at odds, for in truth, she would not wish good fortune to befall even her father. Be assured, however, that she pays very dearly for her malice, for when men do well, she suffers such grief and torment that she is almost destroyed. Her cruel heart so tears her in pieces that God and men are revenged upon her. Envy never stops heaping blame upon worthy men: I think that if she knew the best and noblest man alive, whether here or beyond the sea, she would still find fault with him, and if he were so well bred that she was unable entirely to discredit or destroy him, she would still try at least to diminish his worth, and through her gossip to undermine his honour.

279 Then I saw that Envy's image had a very ugly expression: she would look askance and scowl at everything, and she had the very bad habit of never looking anyone directly in the eye, but would always close one eye in disdain, for she burned

and melted with rage when she saw anyone who was worthy or good or fair, or whom men loved or praised.

Close by Envy on the wall was a painting of Sorrow. It was quite apparent from her complexion that she was greatly tormented in her heart, and she seemed to be afflicted with jaundice; Avarice was not nearly so pale and thin as she, for the sadness and distress and troubled thoughts which she suffered night and day had made her turn quite yellow, thin, and pale. No living thing ever endured such torment or felt such distress as she seemed to do. I do not think that anyone could have done anything for her that would have pleased her, nor would she have wished at any price to be comforted or to abandon the grief in her heart: her heart was exceedingly sad and her grief deep and intense. She seemed indeed to be very sorrowful, for she had not been slow to scratch her own face, nor did she value her dress, for in her great rage she had torn it in many places. Her hair was all unbraided, and lay straggling about her neck, for she had plucked it in her anger and bad temper. And I assure you truly that she wept most bitterly, and that no one, however hard-hearted, could have seen her without feeling great pity for her, for she struck and tore at herself and beat her hands together. The sorrowful wretch was completely occupied with her grief; she had no interest in making merry, in dancing or treading the measure, for you may be sure that he whose heart is grieved has no desire for either. No one who grieved could bring himself to be joyful, for joy and grief are opposites.

Old Age was pictured next, who was at least a foot shorter 339 than she used to be, and so childish in her dotage that she could scarcely feed herself. Her beauty was quite spoiled, and she had become very ugly. All her head was white and bleached, as if with blossom. If she had died, her death would not have been important or wrong, for her whole body was dried up and ruined by age. Her face, once soft and smooth, was now quite withered and covered in wrinkles. Hair grew in her ears, and she had lost all her teeth, for she had not a single one left. She was so extremely aged that she could not have gone eight yards without a crutch. Time, which hurries on, day and night, without resting or pausing, and which leaves us and flees away so stealthily that it seems to us always to be standing still, but does not stop there at all, nor ever halts in its progress, so that one can never think of what the present time is—ask any learned clerk—for before one had thought of it, three seconds would already have passed; time, which cannot linger but always advances, never turning back, like water which always flows downhill, never a drop going back the other way; time, which outlasts everything, even iron and the hardest substances, for time spoils everything and devours it; time, which changes everything, which nourishes everything and causes it to grow and which also wears everything out and rots it away; time, which made our ancestors old, which ages kings and emperors, and which will age all of us, unless death claims us early; time, which has total power to make men old, had aged her so grievously that in my opinion she could no longer prevent herself from entering her second childhood, for I think indeed that she had no more strength or force or wit than a year-old child. Nevertheless, she had, as far as I know, been wise and sensible in her prime; I think, however, that she was wise and sensible no longer, but had completely lost her reason. I remember that her body was well clothed and covered in a fur-lined cloak. She was warmly clad because otherwise she would have been cold, for, as you know, it is the nature of all old people to be cold.

405   The image that was represented next certainly looked like a hypocrite, and her name was Religious Hypocrisy. She it is who secretly, when no one is paying attention, will fearlessly commit any crime. Her appearance inspires compassion, for she is simple and gentle of face, and seems a saintly creature, but there is no wickedness under heaven that she does not meditate in her heart. The image made in her likeness resembled her closely, being simple of bearing and shod and clothed like a nun. In her hand she held a psalter, and you may be sure that she worked very hard at her sham prayers to God and to the saints, both men and women. She was not glad or joyful but outwardly intent above all on doing good works, and she had put on a hair shirt. I assure you that

she was not fat, but seemed worn out by fasting, and her colour was deadly pale. The gate of heaven was forbidden to her and her kind, for the Gospel says that these people grow gaunt of face in order to be praised in the town, and for the sake of a little vain glory which will rob them of God and his kingdom.

The last to be portrayed was Poverty, who could not have 439 produced a single penny were she to have been hanged for it, not even by selling her dress, for she was stark naked. If the weather had been a little inclement, I think she would have died of cold, for she had nothing but a skimpy old sack covered in dreadful patches, which was her tunic and her cloak. She had nothing else to put on, and ample opportunity for shivering. She was a little apart from the others, crouching huddled in a corner like a wretched dog, for the poor, wherever they may be, are always shamed and despised. Cursed be the hour in which a poor man was conceived, for he will never be well fed, or well clothed, or well shod, and he is neither loved nor favoured.

I gazed intently on these images, which, as I have said, were 461 painted in gold and azure all along the wall. The wall, which was high and formed a square, served instead of a hedge to enclose and fence off a garden where no shepherd had ever been. This garden was most beautifully situated, and I would have been very grateful to anyone who had been willing to take me inside by way of a ladder or staircase, for it is my opinion that no man ever saw such joy or such delight as were in that garden. The place was not too scornful or ungenerous to shelter birds; never was there a place so rich in trees nor in singing birds, for there were three times as many birds as in the whole kingdom of France. The harmony of their moving songs was most beautiful to hear; the whole world must rejoice at it. For my part, I was filled with such joy when I heard it that not for a hundred pounds, if the way in had been open, would I have failed to enter and see the birds assembled there (may God preserve them!) merrily warbling love's dances and his delightfully joyful and agreeable melodies.

When I heard the birds singing, I strove with great distress 495 to discover by what device or trick I might enter the garden.

But I could find no place to get in, for I assure you that I did not know if there were any opening or pathway or place by which one might enter, nor was there a living soul there to show me, for I was alone. I was tormented by anguish, until at last I remembered that it was completely unheard of for so beautiful a garden to have no door or ladder or opening of any sort. Then I set off in great haste, skirting the enclosure and the wall that surrounded it on all sides until I found a very cramped, small, and narrow little door. No one could enter any other way. I began to knock at the door, for I did not know where to look for any other entrance. I knocked and pushed hard, listening frequently to see if I could hear anyone coming. Then the gate, which was made of horn-beam, was opened by a most lovely and beautiful maiden: her hair shone fair as a burnished bowl, her flesh was more tender than a young chick, her forehead radiant and her brows arched, her eyes not set too close together but widely and properly spaced, her nose straight and well formed, and her eyes as bright as a falcon's.

532   To excite the desire of the featherbrained she had sweetly scented breath, a pink and white face, a little, full-lipped mouth, and a dimpled chin. Her neck was well proportioned, her flesh softer than fleece and free from spots or sores: no woman from here to Jerusalem had a finer neck; it was smooth and soft to touch. Her throat was white as snow freshly fallen on the branch, her body well formed and slender. There was no need to search in any land for a more beautiful female form. She had a charming gold-embroidered chaplet; no maiden ever had one more elegant or unusual. I could not describe it properly if I took all day. On her gold-embroidered chaplet she had a garland of fresh roses, in her hand she held a mirror, and she had arranged her hair very richly with rich braid. For the sake of greater elegance she had sewn up her two sleeves, and in order to prevent her white hands from becoming brown, she wore white gloves. She had a tunic of rich Ghent green, edged all round with braid. You could tell from her finery that she had very little to do. When she had combed her hair carefully and decked herself out in her fine clothes, her day's work was done. She

spent her time in a happy and carefree manner, being troubled or anxious over nothing except attiring herself nobly. When this well-dressed maiden had opened the gate for me, I thanked her heartily and asked her her name and who she was. She was not too proud or too haughty to reply. 'Those who know me call me Idleness,' she said. 'I am a rich and powerful lady, happy especially in one thing, that I have no care but to enjoy and amuse myself, and to comb and braid my hair. I am the most intimate friend of Pleasure, the charming and elegant owner of this garden, who had the trees brought here from Alexander's lands* and planted in the garden.

'When the trees had grown, Pleasure commanded that the wall you have seen be built all around, and that the images painted on the outside be set there; as you saw just now, they are neither elegant nor charming, but sad and mournful.

'Pleasure and his followers, who live in joy and happiness, often come to amuse themselves and enjoy the shade of this place. Indeed, Pleasure is doubtless already there, listening to the song of the nightingales, thrushes, and other birds. He enjoys himself there and relaxes with his followers, for he could never find a finer spot or a fairer place in which to enjoy himself. And I assure you that Pleasure's companions, whom he takes with him in his train, are the fairest people to be found anywhere.'

When Idleness had recounted this, and I had listened carefully to everything, I said to her: 'Lady Idleness, you may be quite sure that since handsome and charming Pleasure is already in the garden with his followers, I will not, if I can help it, be robbed of the chance of seeing that assembly this very day. I must see it, for I believe that the company is fair and courteous and well instructed.'

Then, without another word, I entered the garden by the door that Idleness had opened for me, and, once inside, I grew happy, gay, and joyful; indeed I assure you that I truly believed myself to be in the earthly paradise, for the place was so delightful that it seemed quite ethereal. In fact, as I thought then, there is no paradise so good to be in as that garden, which gave me such pleasure. Many songbirds were

gathered throughout the garden: in one place were nightingales, in another jays and starlings, and elsewhere were great
flocks of wrens and turtledoves, goldfinches and swallows,
larks and titmice. In another place were assembled calandra
larks, tired from the effort of outdoing one another in song;
there were blackbirds and thrushes, trying to sing more loudly
than all the other birds, and elsewhere parrots and many birds
throughout the groves and woods where they lived, taking
pleasure in their lovely singing.

659   These birds that I am describing to you did most excellent
service. They sang as though they were heavenly angels, and
you may be sure that when I heard the sound I rejoiced
greatly, for never was so sweet a melody heard by mortal
man. So sweet and lovely was that song that it seemed not
to be birdsong, but rather comparable with the song of the
sea-sirens, who are called sirens because of their pure, sweet
voices.* The birds were intent on their singing, nor were they
inexpert or ignorant, and I assure you that when I heard their
song and saw how green everything was I grew very joyful,
and had never been so happy as I then became.

The place was so very charming that I was filled with great
joy, and then I knew and understood clearly that Idleness had
served me well by admitting me to this delight. It was right
for me to be her friend, for she had opened for me the gate
of the leafy garden. From now on, I will tell you the whole
story as best I can. First of all, I wish, without making a long
story of it, to recount what Pleasure's office was and the
company he had, and then I will tell you everything about
the garden. I cannot tell you everything at once, but I will
recount it all in order, so that no one will have any reproach
to make.

699   Sweetly, pleasantly, and diligently the birds performed their
service; the songs they sang, some high, some low, were
amorous lays and courtly airs. I am not jesting when I say
that the sweetness and melody of their song filled my heart
with a new rapture. But when I had listened to the birds for
a little, I could not restrain myself from going at once to see
Pleasure, for I longed to see how he behaved and what kind
of person he was. I set off, straight down a little path on the

right, which was full of fennel and mint; but I found Pleasure quite close by, for I came at once to where he was, in a secluded place. Pleasure was disporting himself there, and he had such handsome people with him that when I saw them I could not tell where they might have come from, for in truth they seemed to be winged angels: no man living ever saw such fair folk. These people of whom I speak had begun to dance, and a lady was singing to them, whose name was Joy. She could sing well and pleasantly, and no one could have made the refrains sound better or more agreeable. Singing suited her wonderfully, for her voice was clear and pure, and she was by no means clumsy, but knew well how to move her body when dancing, to stamp her feet and have fun. It was her habit always and everywhere to be the first to sing, for singing was her favourite occupation.

Then you might have seen the dancers move and the 741 people tread daintily, executing many fine steps and turns on the fresh grass. There you might have seen flute-players, minstrels, and *jongleurs*, one singing a *rotruenge*, another an air from Lorraine, for the airs composed in Lorraine are finer than those of any other kingdom. Around and about were many ladies performing admirably with castanets and tambourines, for they kept on throwing the tambourine up in the air and then catching it again on one finger, without ever missing. Two very charming maidens with their hair in a single braid and dressed only in their tunics were led into the dance by Pleasure, who bore himself most nobly; but I need not say how beautifully they danced: one would approach the other very elegantly, and when they were close together, their lips would touch in such a way that you might have thought they were kissing one another's faces. They knew well how to sway in the dance. I cannot describe it to you, but as long as I could have seen those people thus exerting themselves in the rounds and dances, I would never have wanted to move.

I stood watching the dance until a very mirthful lady noticed 775 me: it was Courtesy, a worthy and gracious lady whom God preserve from harm! Courtesy then called out to me and said 'Fair friend, what are you doing there? Come here if you

please and join in the dance with us.' Without delay or
hesitation I joined in the dance; I was not too embarrassed,
for I can tell you that I was very pleased when Courtesy asked
and commanded me to dance, being very eager and anxious
to dance, if only I had dared.

I then began to examine the bodies and figures and faces
of those who were dancing there, and their outward forms
and manners, and I shall tell you about them. Pleasure was
handsome, straight, and tall: never in any company would
you find a better-looking man. His face was pale, with cheeks
as rosy as an apple, and he was elegant and well dressed; his
eyes were bright, his mouth charming, and his nose very
finely formed; his hair was blond and curly, his shoulders
rather broad, and his waist slender. He was so handsome and
elegant and had such shapely limbs that he looked like a
painting. He was lively, spirited, and agile, the nimblest man
you have ever seen, and he wore no beard or moustache
except for a slight downy growth, for he was a very young
man. He was richly dressed in samite embroidered with birds
and decorated with beaten gold. His coat was very ornately
styled, elegantly slashed and cut in various places, and he was
most skilfully shod in shoes that were laced and slashed. For
love and for pleasure, his sweetheart had made him a chaplet
of roses, which suited him very well. And do you know the
name of his sweetheart? It was Joy, with her gaiety and sweet
voice, who did not hate him in the least, but had given him
her love when she was no more than seven years old. Pleasure
held her by the finger in the dance, and she him. They suited
each other well, for he was handsome and she beautiful. The
colour of her tender flesh was like a rose newly sprung, for
one might have torn it with a tiny thorn. Her brow was fair
and smooth and unwrinkled, her eyebrows brown and arched, her eyes gay and so full of joy that they always laughed
before her mouth did, as was fitting. I do not know how to
describe her nose: you could not have made a better one out
of wax. Her mouth was tiny, and ready to kiss her lover, and
her hair was blond and shining. What more should I say? She
was fair and beautifully adorned, her hair was braided with
gold thread, and she wore a new gold-embroidered chaplet.

I, who have seen twenty-nine, had never seen a chaplet so beautifully worked in silk. She was clothed and adorned in the same samite decorated with gold that her lover wore, and for that reason she was all the more proud of it.

On her other side stood the God of Love, who distributes 863 the joys of love as he chooses. He it is who rules over lovers and humbles men's pride, making lords into servants, and ladies—when he finds them too haughty—into maidservants. In appearance, the God of Love was no lackey, and he was of rare beauty. I am very much afraid that I shall find it difficult to describe his robe, for it was made not of silk but rather of tiny flowers, and fashioned by courtly loves. It was decorated all over with diamond and shield shapes, birds, lions, leopards, and other animals, and was made of flowers of various colours. There were flowers of many different kinds, most skilfully arranged. No summer flower was absent, not broom nor violet nor periwinkle, not yellow nor indigo nor white,* while intertwined in places were great, broad rose-leaves. On his head was a chaplet of roses, but the nightingales fluttering around his head knocked down the leaves, for he was entirely covered with birds, with parrots and nightingales, larks and titmice. He seemed to be an angel come straight from heaven. By his side stood a young man whom he kept by him and whose name was Pleasant Looks.

This young bachelor watched the dance and kept two 907 Turkish bows belonging to the God of Love. One of these bows was made of a wood that bears an evil-tasting fruit; it was covered above and below with knots and lumps, and it was blacker than mulberry. The other bow was rather long and elegantly fashioned from the trunk of a shrub; it was well made and polished smooth, and beautifully decorated on all sides with pictures of ladies and handsome, joyful young men. Pleasant Looks, who did not look like a minion, kept these two bows, together with ten of his master's arrows. Five he held in his right hand: the nocks and flights of these were very well made, and they were painted all in gold. The points were strong and razor-sharp and would pierce deeply, though there was no iron or steel in them, indeed everything was made of gold except for the flights and the shaft, for they were tipped with barbed golden heads.

935   The best and swiftest of these arrows, the fairest and best-flighted, was called Beauty, while the name of the one that wounded most deeply was, I think, Simplicity. Another, named Generosity of Spirit, was feathered with valour and courtesy, and the fourth, whose name was Company, bore a very heavy point; it would not travel far, but fired at close range it could cause serious injury. The fifth was named Fair Seeming, and was the least harmful of all, although it could inflict a serious wound. Anyone struck by this arrow could expect protection and to regain his health before too long, so that his pain was less.

There were five arrows of a different kind, as ugly as you like, whose points and shafts were blacker than demons from hell. The name of the first was Pride, and the next, which was no better, was called Baseness, and was steeped in the venom of wickedness. The third was named Shame and the fourth Despair, while the name of the last was most certainly Inconstancy. The five arrows were of the same kind, all alike, and one of the bows (the hideous one, all knotted and gnarled) matched them well, being made to fire such arrows. The force of these five arrows was undoubtedly opposed to that of the others, but I shall not now tell you all about their force and their power. Their true significance will be told, for I shall not forget to do so, but will tell you what they all mean before my story is ended.

985   Now I shall return to my tale, for I have to tell you about the bearing, form, and appearance of the noble dancers. The God of Love had done the right thing, for he had attached himself very closely to a most worthy lady, whose name, like one of the five arrows, was Beauty. She had every good quality, for she was not dark or brunette, but resplendent as the moon, which makes the other stars look like tiny candles. Her flesh was dewy soft and she was as simple as a bride, lily-white, with a smooth, delicate face. She stood straight and slender, wearing no paint or make-up, for she had no need of adornment or embellishment. She had long blond hair falling to her heels, and her nose, eyes, and mouth were

well formed. So help me God, my heart is filled with great sweetness when I remember the shapeliness of each limb, for there was no woman so beautiful in all the world. In short, she was young and blond, pleasant and agreeable, courteous and elegant, with rounded, slender form and charming and lively manners.

Next to Beauty stood Wealth, a lady of great dignity,   1017 worth, and rank. It would be a bold, arrogant man who dared say or do anything to injure her or her followers, for she had great power to harm or to help. The great power of the rich to help or to injure does not date from today or yesterday; all the greatest and the humblest honoured Wealth and sought to serve her, the better to earn her favour; each man called her his lady, for everyone feared her, and the whole world was in her power. There were many flatterers at her court, and many treacherous and envious men, such as take pains to blame and disparage all those who are better loved than they. In the beginning, these flatterers praise men in order to delude them, and ingratiate themselves with everyone, but their flatteries stab men in the back and touch the bone, so that through their deceitful compliments they cause many who should be intimate there to be ostracized and banished from court. May such envious flatterers come to a bad end, for no good man loves them.

Wealth wore a purple gown, and do not imagine that   1051 I am deceiving you when I say and affirm that there was none so beautiful, costly, or gay in all the world. The purple was all braided, and embroidered in gold with stories of dukes and kings. The neck of the gown was most richly edged with a band of gold inlaid with niello, and there were, make no mistake about it, a great many precious stones, which shone very brightly. Wealth had a most elegant belt: no woman ever wore one more costly. The buckle was made from a stone that had great power and virtue, for he who wore it need fear no poison, and no venom could harm him. Such a stone deserved to be prized; it would have been worth more to a rich man than all the gold in Rome. The clasp was made of another stone, which could cure the toothache and also had such virtue that the eyesight of the one who saw it before breakfast would be safe for the whole day.

1081   The studs on the gold-embroidered cloth were of pure gold, and so large and heavy that each was worth fully a bezant. On her blond hair, Wealth wore a golden circlet: I do not think that such a fine one was ever seen. The circlet was of fine, toughened gold, and only an expert in the art of description could recount and describe all the stones that were in it, for it would be impossible to estimate the worth of the stones that were set in the gold. There were rubies, sapphires, zircons, emeralds of more than two ounces, and, skilfully set at the front of the circlet, a carbuncle so clear that when night fell one could, if need be, see one's way for a league ahead. Such light came from the stones that the face and countenance of Wealth shone radiantly, as did the area round about her. Wealth held by the hand a very handsome young man who was her true lover, a man who very much liked living in rich mansions. He was well shod and well dressed, and owned valuable horses, for he would have thought the presence of a hack in his stables to be as great a reproach as murder or robbery. The reason why he so much appreciated the friendship and favour of Wealth was that he was always intent upon lavish expenditure, and she was able to achieve this and to support his spending, for she gave him coins as though she had granaries full of them.

1125   Next came Largesse, who was well trained and instructed in the art of doing honour and spending money. She was of Alexander's line, and was never happier than when she could say 'Take this.' Even wretched Avarice was not so anxious to take as Largesse was to give, and God caused her wealth to multiply, so that however much she gave away, she always had more. Largesse was greatly praised and esteemed; she had achieved so much by her generous gifts that wise and foolish alike were entirely at her mercy. If anyone happened to hate her, I believe she would make him her friend by the great service she did him, and therefore she was dearly loved by rich and poor alike. It is very foolish for a great man to be miserly; no vice is so harmful to a great man as avarice, for a miser cannot win lordship or great territory, because he does not have a large number of friends with whom he has influence. The man who wants friends should not be too attached to his possessions, but should acquire friends by giving them fine gifts, for just as the magnet subtly draws iron to itself, so the gold and silver that we give attract the hearts of men.

Largesse wore a new robe of purple from the Orient; her face was fair and well shaped, but her collar was unfastened, for a short time ago she had, there and then, given the clasp to a lady. But it rather suited her for the neck to be open and her throat disclosed, so that the soft whiteness of her skin showed through her chemise. The wise and valiant Largesse held by the hand a knight of the lineage of good King Arthur of Britain; that same Arthur bore the banner and standard of valour, and his fame is still so great that stories of him are told before kings and counts. This knight had recently come from a tournament where he had achieved many jousts and combats for the sake of his mistress; many a green helm had been uncircled,* many a bossed shield pierced, many a knight unhorsed and captured through his strength and courage.

After all these came Generosity of Spirit, who was neither 1189 dark nor swarthy, but whiter than snow. She did not have an Orleans nose, for hers was long and well shaped; she had bright, laughing eyes, arched brows, and long blond hair, and she was more innocent than a dove. Her heart was gentle and gracious, and she would not have dared to speak or act towards anyone otherwise than as she ought. If she knew a man to be tormented by his love for her, I believe she would soon take pity on him, for her heart was so compassionate, so gentle and loving, that if anyone suffered harm for her sake and she failed to help him, she would be afraid of committing a great wickedness. She wore a sorquenie* that was not made of sackcloth; there was none richer between here and Arras, and it fitted so well and closely that there was not a stitch that was not in the right place. Generosity of Spirit was very nicely dressed, for no dress suits a maiden so well as a sorquenie; a woman looks daintier and more elegant in a sorquenie than in a tunic. The sorquenie, which was white, signified that she who wore it was gentle and noble. A young

man beside her had attached himself to Generosity of Spirit
and they were side by side; I do not know his name, but he
was as handsome as if he had been a son of the Lord of
Windsor.*

1227   Next came Courtesy, who was greatly esteemed by everyone, for she was neither haughty nor foolish. It was she who
was gracious enough to call me into the dance as soon as I
arrived there. She was neither stupid nor irritable, but sensible
and prudent, not given to excess, but speaking and answering
fairly; she never contradicted anyone, nor did she bear anyone
a grudge. She was charming, fair, and comely, with shining
dark hair; I know of no more pleasing woman. She was
worthy to be queen or empress in any court. By her stood a
knight, agreeable in manner and conversation and one who
honoured others. He was fair and handsome, very skilled in
arms and beloved of his sweetheart.

Fair Idleness came next, and stayed close by me. I have
certainly described to you her appearance and figure and will
say no more of her, for she was the first to show me kindness,
by graciously opening the door of the garden for me.

Next, as far as I remember, came Youth, with her bright,
laughing face, who was not, I believe, much more than
twelve years old. She was innocent, never suspecting the
existence of any evil or trickery, and very joyful and gay, for,
as you know, young people's only care is to amuse themselves. Her lover was so intimate with her that he kissed her
as often as he liked, in full view of all the dancers. They
would not have been ashamed if people had talked about the
two of them; on the contrary, you could have seen them
kissing each other like two doves. The boy was young and
handsome, of the same age and disposition as his sweetheart.

1277   Thus they danced there, those people and others of their
household with them. They were all noble, cultivated, and
well-brought-up people. When I had observed the appearance of the dancers, I wanted to go and see the garden, to
walk around it and gaze on the handsome laurels, the pines,
hazels, and nut-trees. The dances now came to an end, for
most of the dancers went off with their sweethearts to make
love in the shade of the trees. God knows they led a pleasant

life, and one which it is foolish not to desire for oneself. A man who could have such a life would be prepared to do without a greater good, for there is no better paradise than having the sweetheart of one's choice. I then left that spot and set off alone, wandering happily from place to place in the garden, whereupon the God of Love instantly summoned Pleasant Looks. No longer did he want him to keep his golden bow, but ordered him without further ado to string it. Immediately and without hesitation Pleasant Looks strung the bow and gave it to him, together with five strong, shining arrows, ready to be shot. Bow in hand, the God of Love then began to follow me at a distance. Now may God keep me from mortal wound if he should happen to shoot at me. I, unheeding, continued to wander happily and freely through the garden while he made haste to follow me, but I did not stop in any place until I had been everywhere. The garden had been laid out in a perfect square, being as long as it was wide. Except for a few hideous ones, there was no fruit-bearing tree of which there were not two or three or perhaps more in the garden. I well remember that there were trees bearing pomegranates, excellent fruit for the sick, and abundant nut-trees, which, at the proper season, bore fruit such as nutmeg, which is neither bitter nor bland. Many almond-trees had been planted in the garden, and he who had need of them could find many fig-trees and good date-palms. There were many spices in the garden, cloves and liquorice, fresh cardamum, zedoary, anise, and cinnamon, and many delicious spices good to eat after a meal.

CHAPTER 2

THE SPRING OF NARCISSUS

1345 There were domestic varieties in the garden, bearing quinces and peaches, nuts, chestnuts, apples and pears, medlars, white and black plums, fresh, rosy cherries, service-berries, sorb-apples, and hazel-nuts. The whole garden was covered with tall laurels and pines, and there were many olives and cypresses. There were great branching elms, together with hornbeams and beeches, straight hazels, aspens and ash trees, maples, tall firs, and oaks. Why should I go on? There were so many different trees that I should be in great difficulty before I had enumerated them all. But the trees, I assure you, were spaced just as they should be, more than ten or twelve yards separating one from another, and yet the branches were long and high and so dense up above in order to protect the place from heat, that the sun could never penetrate to the earth and damage the tender grass. There were fallow deer and roe-deer in the garden and a great number of squirrels climbing among the trees. There were rabbits, continually coming out of their burrows and engaged in more than forty different games on the fresh green grass. Here and there were bright springs, free from insects and frogs and shaded by the trees, but I cannot say how many. Little streams ran in channels constructed by Pleasure, and the water made a sweet and pleasant sound. Around the streams and the banks of the bright and lively springs the fresh grass grew thickly, so that one could have lain with one's mistress as if on a feather bed, for the earth was soft and cool, and because of the springs, the grass was as abundant as could be. But the beauty of all this was greatly enhanced by the place itself, which was of such a kind that flowers were always plentiful, both in winter and in summer: there were beautiful violets, blooming, fresh, and new; there were white flowers and red, and yellow ones in great profusion. That ground was extremely pretty, for it was decorated and, as it were, painted with sweet-smelling flowers of various colours. I shall not speak at length about this pleasant and delightful place, and it is now time for me to stop, for I could not possibly recount all the beauties and charms of the garden. I wandered to right and to left until I had seen the whole garden and explored all its features. And all this time the God of Love followed me, watching like the hunter, who waits until the animal is in a good position before loosing his arrow. I reached a most delightful spot, rather out of the way, where I came across a spring beneath a pine-tree. Never since Charlemagne or Pepin* had such a handsome pine been seen, and it had grown so high that it was the tallest tree in the garden. Nature by her great skill had sent the water gushing from a marble stone beneath the pine, and had written in small letters around the upper edge of the stone that fair Narcissus* had died there. Narcissus was a young man whom Love caught in his snares, and so tormented him and made him weep and groan that he must needs die. For Echo, a noble lady, had loved him more than any living thing, and was so distressed on his account that she said that she would die if he did not give her his love. But he was so haughty, so proud of his own beauty that he would not grant her his love in spite of her requests and prayers. When she heard him refuse her, her grief and anger were so great and she held him in such contempt that she died at once. But just before she died she asked and prayed God that hardhearted Narcissus, whom she had found so unwilling a lover, should one day be tortured and tormented by just such a love as hers, for which he could expect no cure; thus he who so basely refused loyal lovers might understand and realize how much they suffered. Since that prayer was reasonable, God granted it, for one day when Narcissus was returning from hunting, he happened to seek the shade of the pine by the clear, pure spring. He had followed the hunt uphill and down, and had endured such hardship that he was thirsty, for the heat was fierce and he was breathless with weariness. When he came to the spring shaded by the branches of the pine-tree he decided to drink there, and lay face down on the ground above the spring to drink from it. And so it was that he saw in the bright, clean water his own face, his nose and his mouth, and he was at once astounded,

for his reflection had so deceived him that he imagined it to
be the face of a wonderfully handsome youth. And then Love
had his revenge for the proud, arrogant way in which Narcissus had treated him. He had his just reward then, for he
lingered so long at the spring that he fell in love with his own
reflection and finally died, and that is the end of the story.
For when he saw that he could not accomplish his desire, a
desire which had so inexorably taken possession of him that
he could in no way whatsoever be consoled, he swooned
away for grief and soon died. And so he received his reward
and his just deserts from the maiden whom he had earlier
refused.

1505   You ladies who behave badly to your lovers, learn from
this example, for if you leave them to die, God will repay
you. When I had discovered from the inscription that this
was most certainly the spring of fair Narcissus, I withdrew a
little, not daring to look into it, and began to feel afraid,
remembering how badly Narcissus had fared. But I reflected
that I could safely approach the spring without fear of ill
fortune, and that it was foolish of me to retreat. I drew near
to the spring and, on reaching it, bent down to see the
running water and the gravel, brighter than fine silver, that
seethed in its depths. All that can be said of the spring is that
there was none so beautiful in all the world. The water is
always cool and fresh, and gushes out day and night in great
waves through two channels, bright and deep. Because of the
water, the dense grass all around grows thick and strong, and
cannot die in winter, just as the water cannot dry up or cease
to flow. Down at the bottom of the spring were two crystals,
which I gazed at most attentively. And I shall tell you something that will, I think, seem marvellous to you when you
hear it. When the all-seeing sun sends down its rays into the
spring, and light descends into its depths, more than a hundred colours appear in the crystal,* which turns blue and
yellow and red in the sunlight. The crystal is so marvellous
and has such power that the whole place, with its trees and
flowers and everything adorning the garden, is revealed there
in due order. To help you understand the phenomenon I shall
give you an illustration. Just as things placed in front of a

mirror are reflected in it, and their appearance and colour are seen quite plainly, exactly so, I assure you, does the crystal truly disclose the whole of the garden to him who gazes into the water. For whichever side he is on, he can always see half of the garden, and by turning he is at once able to see the remainder. And so there is nothing so small, so secret, or so hidden that it is not displayed there, as if it were etched in the crystal.

This is the perilous mirror where proud Narcissus looked 1569 at his face and his bright eyes, and afterwards lay stretched out in death. Whoever looks at himself in this mirror can have no help or remedy against seeing something which promptly causes him to fall in love. This mirror has caused the deaths of many valiant men, for the wisest, the bravest, and the most experienced are all caught and ensnared here. Here new and violent feelings spring up in men, and their hearts are changed; here sense and moderation are of no use, and there is only the total will to love; here no one knows what to do, for Cupid, Venus' son, sowed here the seed of Love which covers the whole spring; here he set his nets and snares to trap young men and maidens, for Love wants no other birds. Because of the seed that was sown here, this spring was rightly called the Spring of Love, and many have spoken of it in many places, in books and romances. But you will never hear a better exposition of the truth of the matter, once I have explained the mystery.

I was happy then to linger, admiring the spring and the 1601 crystals which revealed to me a thousand things around me. But it was an evil hour when I looked at my reflection. Alas, how often I have since sighed about it! The mirror deceived me, and if I had known in advance what force and power it had, I would never have approached it, for at once I fell into the trap that has captured and betrayed many men.

I perceived in the mirror, among a thousand other things, 1613 rose-bushes laden with roses in a secluded place completely enclosed by a hedge. Immediately I was seized with such desire that not for Pavia or Paris would I have failed to go to the place where I saw the greatest number of them. Possessed by this madness, as many others have been, I at once approached the rose-bushes, and I assure you that when I drew near, the sweet scent of the roses penetrated my very entrails and I was all but filled with their fragrance. If I had not imagined that I would be attacked or insulted, I would have plucked at least one and held it in my hand, savouring its scent. But I was afraid that I might repent my action, since it could easily have displeased the lord of the garden.

1635   There were roses in profusion, the most beautiful in all the world. There were buds, some tiny and closed up and others slightly larger, and some much larger ones which were coming into flower and were on the point of bursting. These buds are attractive, for wide-open roses have completely faded after a day, whereas buds stay fresh for at least two or three days. The buds pleased me greatly, for none finer grew anywhere. The man who could pluck one should cherish it greatly, and if I could have made a garland of them, there is nothing I would have loved so well. From among these buds I chose one so beautiful that when I had observed it carefully, all the others seemed worthless in comparison. It shone with colour, the purest vermilion that Nature could provide, and Nature's masterly hand had arranged its four pairs of leaves, one after the other. Its stem was as straight as a reed, and the bud was set on top in such a way that it neither bent nor drooped. The area around it was filled with its perfume, and the sweet scent that rose from it pervaded the whole place. When I became aware of this scent, I had no wish to depart, but drew nearer and would have plucked it had I dared stretch out my hands. But sharp, pointed thistles forced me to draw back, while barbed, keen-edged thorns and prickly nettles and brambles prevented me from advancing, for I was afraid of hurting myself.

1679   The God of Love, whose constant endeavour had been to watch and follow me with drawn bow, had stopped beneath a fig-tree; and when he observed that I had chosen that bud, which pleased me better than any of the others, he at once took an arrow. When the string was in the nock, he drew the bow, which was wonderfully strong, back to his ear, and loosed his arrow at me in such a way and with such force that the point entered my eye and penetrated my heart. Then

I was seized with a chill which has often made me shiver since, even when wearing a warm, fur-lined cloak. When I had been thus shot, I immediately fell backwards. My heart was false and failed me and I lay for a long time in a swoon. When I recovered consciousness and came to my senses I was very weak and therefore imagined that I had lost a lot of blood. But the point that pierced me drew no blood at all, and the wound was quite dry. Then I took hold of the arrow with both hands and began to pull hard, sighing a great deal as I pulled. I pulled so hard that I drew out the flighted shaft, but the barbed point, which was named Beauty was so fixed in my heart that it could not be torn out; it remains there still, and yet the wound has never bled.

I was in great trouble and torment, unable, on account of 1719 this double danger, to do or say anything or to find a physician for my wound, for no medicine could be expected from herb or root; instead my heart drew me towards the rose-bud, and desired nothing else. If I had had it in my possession, it would have given me back my life; the mere sight and scent of it brought me considerable relief from pain.

Then, as I began to make my way towards the sweetly 1731 scented rose-bud, Love had already grasped another arrow, worked in gold. It was the second arrow, named Simplicity, and it has caused many men and women throughout the world to fall in love. When Love saw me approach, without warning he loosed the arrow, which was made without steel, so that it entered my eye and wounded my heart. No man living will ever cure me of it, for when I pulled, I drew out the shaft without much effort, but the point remains within. Now you may know for certain that if I had greatly desired the rose-bud before, my longing was now increased, and as the pain grew more intense, so also did my desire continually to approach the little rose that smelled sweeter than violets. It would have been better for me to draw back, but I could not refuse the bidding of my heart. I was always compelled to go where it longed to be. But the archer, who strove hard and mightily to wound me, would not allow me to pass that way unharmed and, the better to hurt me, loosed his third arrow, named Courtesy, at me. The wound was deep and wide, and I perforce fell swooning beneath a spreading olive-tree, where I lay for a long time without moving. When I recovered my strength, I took hold of the arrow and removed the shaft from my side, but, do what I might, I could not draw out the point.

1775   Then I sat down, very anxious and pensive. The wound caused me great distress, and urged me to approach the rose-bud that I desired. But the archer rekindled my fear, and I was right to be afraid, for the man who has been scalded should fear water. However, necessity is a powerful force, and even if I had seen it raining crossbow bolts and stones, pelting down as thick as hail, I would still have had to approach, for Love, who is greater than anything, gave me courage and daring to obey his command. I got to my feet, weak and feeble as a wounded man, and, undaunted by the archer, made a great effort to walk towards the little rose to which my heart was drawn; but there were so many thorns and thistles and brambles that I was unable to get past them and reach the rose-bud. I had to stay near the hedge of very sharp thorns which was next to the roses. I was very happy to be so close to the rose-bud that I could smell the sweet scent that issued from it, and filled with delight to be able to look upon it freely. Thus I was well rewarded and forgot my troubles in my joy and delight. I was very glad and joyful, for nothing ever pleased me so greatly as being in that place, and I would never have wished to depart. But when I had been there for some time, the God of Love, tearing apart my body, which had become his target, launched a new assault. In order to hurt me, he loosed yet another arrow and wounded me once more in my heart, beneath my breast. The arrow's name was Company, and there is none that conquers ladies or maidens more quickly. At once the great pain of my wounds was reawakened, and I swooned away three times in succession.

1829   On coming to my senses, I moaned and sighed, for my pain was growing worse and I had no hope of cure or relief. I would rather have been dead than alive, for in the end, I thought, I would become a martyr to Love, there was no other way out. Meanwhile he took another arrow, which he prized greatly and which I hold to be most wounding: it was Fair Seeming, which does not permit a lover to repent of serving Love, whatever he may feel. It is sharp and piercing and keen as a steel razor, but Love had thoroughly anointed its tip with precious ointment so that it would not hurt me too much, for Love did not want me to die, but rather to find relief through the application of the ointment, which was full of comfort. Love has made it with his own hands to comfort true lovers, and to soothe my hurts he shot this arrow at me, and made a great wound in my heart. The ointment spread through my wounds and gave me back my heart, which had failed me completely. I would have been dead and in a bad way had it not been for that sweet ointment. I quickly drew out the shaft, but the point, newly sharpened, remained within. Five arrowheads were thus embedded and it will scarcely be possible to remove them. The ointment was very good for my wounds, yet the wound hurt me so much that the pain made me change colour. It is the strange property of this arrow to be both sweet and bitter. I felt and realized that it helped me, but it also hurt me; the point was painful although the unction brought relief. On the one hand it soothed, on the other it made me smart, and thus it both helped and harmed. Straightaway Love came towards me with rapid steps, crying as he came: 'Vassal, you are captured, there is no way to escape or defend yourself. Yield, and do not resist. The more willingly you surrender, the sooner you will find mercy. It is foolish to behave arrogantly towards one whom you should flatter and beseech. You cannot struggle against me, and I wish you to learn that wickedness and pride will avail you nothing. Surrender, since I wish it, peacefully and with good grace.'

Immediately I replied: 'In God's name, I give myself up willingly, and will never defend myself against you. God forbid that I should ever think of so defending myself, for it would be neither reasonable nor right. You may do with me whatever you like, hang me or kill me, for I know that I am helpless, my life is in your hands. I cannot live until tomorrow unless it is your will. I hope for joy and health from you, for I shall never have them from anyone else, but only if your hand, which wounded me, provides a remedy; and whether you wish to make me your prisoner or prefer not to, I shall not count myself deceived, nor, I assure you, will I be angry. I have heard so much good of you that I wish to place my heart and body entirely at your service, for nothing can hurt me if I do your will. I will also, I think, receive at some time the mercy that I hope for, and under these conditions I surrender.'

1924   Thereupon I wanted to kiss his foot, but he took me by the hand and said: 'I love and esteem you for the way you have answered. Indeed, no rough, untutored man ever gave such an answer, and it has so benefited you that now, for your own good, I wish you to do me homage and to kiss my mouth, which no low-born man has ever touched. I do not allow every peasant and swineherd to touch my mouth; the man whom I thus take into my service must be courteous and noble. Serving me is always painful and burdensome, nevertheless I do you great honour, and you should be very happy to have so good a master and so renowned a lord, for Love bears the standard and the banner of Courtesy and is so kind and noble, so excellently and gently mannered that the man who strives to serve and honour him will be free from all baseness and misconduct and from every bad habit.'

1953   Thereupon I joined my hands and became his liegeman, and you may be sure that I was very proud when his mouth kissed mine: it was this that gave me the greatest joy. Then he asked me for sureties: 'My friend,' he said, 'I have received the homage of many men who have since disappointed me. These false traitors have often deceived me, and I have heard many complaints about them, but they shall know how much they have grieved me. If I can get them into my power, I will make them pay dearly. Now because I love you, I wish to be so certain of you and bind you to me so closely that you are unable to be false to your promise and agreement, or to commit any wrong act. It would be a crime for you to cheat, for you seem to me to be fair-minded.'

'Sir,' I said, 'now hear me. I do not know why you are asking me for pledges and securities. You know for certain that you have so stolen and taken my heart that, even if it wished to, it could do nothing for me unless you permitted it. My heart is yours and not my own, for it must do your will, for good or ill, and no one can take it from you. You have set a guard about it which guards it very diligently and if, in spite of all this, you fear anything, make a key for it and take it with you; it will serve instead of sureties.'

'By my head,' replied Love, 'that is not unreasonable, and I accept. He who commands the heart has sufficient power over the body, and would be unreasonable if he asked for more.' Then he took from his purse a beautifully made little key of purest gold. 'With this', he said, 'I will lock your heart, and I ask no other guarantee. My jewels are under this key, and I promise you on my soul that it is mistress of my jewel-case and thus has very great power.' Then he touched my side and locked my heart so gently that I could scarcely feel the key.

Thus he did his will perfectly, and when I had removed his doubts I said: 'Sir, I desire greatly to do your will, but I beg you by the faith you owe me to receive my service graciously. I do not say this because of cowardice, for I am not afraid to serve you, but a servant strives in vain to do valuable service if that service fails to please the lord to whom it is offered.'

Love replied: 'Do not be distressed. Since you have placed yourself in my following, I will readily accept your service, and will raise you to high rank, provided that you do not forfeit it by wickedness. However, this may not happen quickly, for we do not achieve great benefits in a short space of time, but must wait and struggle for them. Wait, and endure the torment that now hurts and wounds you, for I know the potion that will cure you. If you remain loyal, I shall give you a sweet salve that will heal you of your wound, but by my head, we shall see whether or not you serve me wholeheartedly, and how you carry out, day and night, the commandments that I give to true lovers.'

'Sir,' I said, 'by God's grace, give me your commandments before you depart from here. I am encouraged to perform them, but I would perhaps soon go astray if I did not know them. I am longing to learn them, for I have no wish to commit any kind of fault.'

Love answered: 'You have spoken well; now hear my commandments and remember them. A master wastes his time completely when his disciple does not make an effort to retain what he hears, so that he can remember it.' Then the God of Love gave me his commandments, word for word as you shall hear them now. They are well expounded in this romance, and anyone who aspires to love should pay attention, for the romance now improves. From now on it will be well worth listening to, if there is anyone to recite it, for the end of the dream is very beautiful and the matter of it is new. I can assure you that whoever hears the end of the dream will be able to learn a great deal about the games of Love, provided that he is willing to wait until I have begun to expound the significance of the dream.* The truth, which is hidden, will be completely plain when you have heard me explain the dream, for it contains no lies. 'First of all,' said Love, 'if you wish to avoid committing an offence against me, I desire and command that you abandon Baseness for ever. I curse and excommunicate all those who love Baseness. Baseness makes men base, therefore it would be morally wrong for me to love it. A base man is cruel and pitiless, and offers no service or friendship.

'Now be very careful not to repeat things about other people which should not be told. Slander is unworthy: look at Kay* the seneschal, who in former times earned himself hatred and an evil reputation by his spiteful tongue. Just as the well-trained Gawain* was esteemed for his courtesy, so Kay was blamed because he was more wicked and cruel, more insolent and evil-tongued than all other knights.

2087   'Be courteous and approachable, speaking gently and reasonably to high and low alike, and when you go along the streets, be sure to make it your habit to be the first to greet other people. And if someone should greet you first, do not remain dumb, but take care to return the greeting at once, and without delay. Next, be sure never to use rude words or coarse expressions: your mouth should never be opened to pronounce the name of anything base. I do not consider a

man to be courteous if he names filthy, ugly things.* Serve
and honour all women, toil and labour in their service, and
if you hear any slanderer speaking ill of women, reproach him
and tell him to be quiet. If you can, do things to please ladies
and maidens, so that they may hear good reports of you; in
this way your reputation will be enhanced.

'Besides all this, keep yourself from pride, for he who has
understanding and discernment knows that pride is foolish
and sinful. A man tainted with pride is incapable of subduing   2113
his heart to serve and beg. The proud man does precisely the
opposite of what the true lover should do. But he who wishes
to toil in the service of love should bear himself with elegance. It is useless for a man who lacks elegance to aspire to
love. Elegance is not pride, for the elegant man is all the more
worthy for being free from pride and foolish presumption.
Provide yourself, as far as your income will permit, with fine
clothes and shoes, for fine clothes and garments improve a
man wonderfully. Also, you should entrust your wardrobe to
an experienced tailor who can make the stitches sit properly
and the sleeves fit elegantly. Your boots and your laced shoes
should always be fresh and new, and make sure that they fit
so closely that the ignorant will argue about how you managed to put them on and which way you got into them. Deck
yourself out in gloves, a belt, and a purse of silk; if you are
not rich enough to do this, then do the best you can, but
you should live as elegantly as possible, without ruining
yourself. Anyone can have a chaplet of flowers, which does
not cost very much, or of roses at Whitsuntide; great wealth
is not required.

'Do not allow any dirt upon your person; wash your hands   2153
and clean your teeth, and if any speck of black appears in
your nails, do not let it stay there. Lace up your sleeves and
comb your hair, but do not paint your face or wear make-up:
only women do that, and those of evil reputation who have
unfortunately found an unlawful love.

'Besides this, you must always remember to be blithe.   2163
Prepare yourself for joy and pleasure, for Love cares nothing
for gloomy men. It is a very courtly sickness which makes
men laugh and be glad and enjoy themselves. So it is that

lovers are sometimes joyful and sometimes in torment, and the pains of love sometimes seem sweet to them and sometimes bitter. The pain of love is very changeable: at one moment the lover is at play, the next he laments his distress; now he weeps, now he sings. If you know how to do something entertaining that will bring pleasure to others, I order you to do it. Everyone must always do what he knows suits him best, for as a result he will be praised and esteemed and favoured.

2183 'If you know yourself to be agile and athletic, do not make difficulties about jumping, and if you are an accomplished horseman, you should gallop uphill and down dale. If you are good at breaking lances, you can win great renown, and if you are skilful in arms, the love men have for you will be increased tenfold. If your voice is clear and pure, you should never excuse yourself from singing, if you are asked, for good singing is a great enhancement. Also, a young man ought to learn how to play on the viol and the citole, and how to dance, for in this way he will win great advancement. Avoid a reputation for meanness, which could do you considerable harm. It is fitting that lovers should give more generously than the simple, foolish, common folk. No man who did not like to give ever knew how to love. Anyone who wishes to toil in the service of Love should be careful to avoid avarice, for he who has given his whole heart for a look, or a sweet, untroubled laugh should, after so rich a gift, give freely of what he has. 'Now, I would like to remind you briefly of what I have said so that you will remember it, for words are less difficult to recall when they are brief. Anyone who wishes to make Love his master must be courteous and free from pride, elegant and light-hearted and esteemed for his generosity.

2221 'Next I will give you a penance; it is that day and night, without backsliding, you should fix your thoughts on love. Think of it always and unceasingly, and remember the sweet hour whose joy remains with you. In order that you might be a true lover, it is my wish and my command that your whole heart may be set in a single place, and that it should not be divided, but whole and entire, without deceit, for I do not like sharing. Whoever divides his heart between many places leaves a poor part of it everywhere, but I have no fear for him who sets his whole heart in one place, and I therefore wish you to do so. But take care that you do not lend it, for if you had lent it, I would consider that you had behaved unworthily. By giving it freely and absolutely you will win greater merit, for when something is lent, the favour is soon returned and the debt discharged, whereas the reward for something given as a gift must be great. Therefore give it absolutely and graciously, for something given with a good grace should be greatly cherished, whereas I do not give a fig for a gift unwillingly given.

'When you have given your heart as I have exhorted you, 2253 things will befall you that are hard and painful for lovers. Often, when you remember your love, you will perforce have to leave the company of other people, lest they notice the pain that torments you. You will withdraw by yourself, apart from the rest, and then you will sigh and lament and tremble and suffer many other pains. You will endure many sorts of distress, being sometimes hot and sometimes cold, sometimes flushed and sometimes pale; no quartan or quotidian fever was ever so bad. Before you leave that place, you will have experienced fully all the pains of love. Another time it will happen that you lose yourself in your thoughts and remain for a long time like a dumb image, still and motionless, without moving foot or hand, finger or eye, and without speaking. At last you will come to your senses, quivering with agitation as you do so, like a man afraid, and you will sigh from the depths of your heart; know, then, that this is the behaviour of those who have experienced those pains which so terrify you now.

'You should then remember that your sweetheart is a long 2287 way away, and say: "Oh God, how wretched I am when I cannot go where my heart is! And why do I send my heart alone? I think constantly about this place and never see it. Since I can send my eyes after my heart to escort it, then if my eyes do not escort my heart, nothing that they see has any value for me. Should they then stay here? No, instead they should visit the object of my heart's desire. I may indeed

consider myself a laggard when I am so far from my heart:
God help me, I must be a fool! I shall go, then, and not omit
to do so, for I shall never be at peace until I have some news
of it." Then you will set off on your way to that place, but
in such circumstances that you frequently fail in your purpose,
wasting your steps: you will not see what you seek, and will
be unable to do anything but return, gloomy and pensive.

2313   'Then you will be in a sorry state, and once again you will
endure sighs and pains and fits of trembling that prick more
sharply than a hedgehog. If anyone does not know this, let
him ask those who are faithful lovers. You will not be able
to pacify your heart, and instead you will set off again to see
whether by chance you can glimpse what you desire so
greatly. And if by dint of much toil you succeed in seeing it,
you will be completely occupied in feasting and satisfying
your eyes, rejoicing greatly in your heart at the beauty you
see; and I assure you that the sight will cause your heart to
burn and sizzle and that the raging fire will be fanned continually as you gaze. The more a man gazes on what he loves,
the more he sets fire to his heart and bastes it with bacon fat;
this basting kindles and fans the fire that makes men love. It
is every lover's habit to pursue the fire that burns and inflames
him, and when he feels the fire close by, he approaches even
closer. The fire is his contemplation of his sweetheart, who
causes him to be consumed by the flames: the closer he is to
her, the more eager he is to love. Everyone knows this, both
wise men and fools: the nearer a man is to the fire, the more
he burns.

2347   'As long as you see your joy thus, you will never want to
move away, and when you have to depart, you will remember
all day what you have seen, and will consider yourself most
cruelly disappointed in one thing: that you were never bold
or courageous enough to speak to her, but instead stood by
her side without uttering a word, as if you were foolish and
embarrassed. You will certainly think that you were wrong
not to address the fair lady before she went away. You will
suffer for it, for if you had managed to elicit from her nothing
more than a fair greeting, it would have been worth a hundred marks.

'Then you will curse your fate and seek an opportunity to   2365
go again to the street where you saw her whom you dared
not address. You would be very glad to go into her house,
if you had an opportunity. It is right that all your excursions,
all your comings and goings should end up in that neighbour-
hood; but be careful to conceal this from other people, and
seek another reason for going there, for it is sensible to be
discreet. If you should happen to find the fair lady in a
situation where you should address her or greet her, you will
be constrained to blush, your blood will thrill, and speech
and reason will desert you just as you are about to begin. And
if you can progress sufficiently to dare begin your speech, you
will be so overcome with shyness in her presence that you
will not say two of the three things you should have said. No
one was ever so sensible as not to forget things at such a
moment, unless he were a deceiver. But false lovers chatter
away fearlessly, just as they like; they are flatterers indeed,
saying one thing and thinking another, the cruel, wicked
traitors.

'When you have finished your speech without saying any-   2399
thing unworthy, you will consider yourself very much mor-
tified because you have forgotten something appropriate you
should have said. Then you will be in great torment: this is
the battle, the suffering, the combat that lasts for ever. The
lover will never have what he seeks: something is always
lacking and he will never be at peace, and this war will never
end until I choose to bring about peace. When night falls,
you will suffer more than a thousand torments. You will lie
down in your bed but will have little joy, for when you think
yourself about to fall asleep, you will begin to shake and toss
and tremble with agitation; you will have to turn on your
side, then on your back, then on your front, like a man with
the toothache. Then you will remember her form and appearance, unequalled by any other woman, and I shall tell
you something strange and marvellous: sometimes it will seem
to you that you clasp the bright-faced girl quite naked in your
arms, just as if she had become entirely your sweetheart and
companion. Then you will build castles in the air and rejoice
without reason, as long as you are mad enough to entertain

this delightful thought, which is nothing but a lie and a delusion. But you will not be able to remain for long in this state, and then you will start to weep, saying: "Oh God, what have I dreamed? What is this? Where was I? Where did this thought come from? Indeed, I wish it would return ten or twenty times a day, for it nourishes me and fills me with joy and happiness, but I must die because it does not last. Oh God, shall I ever see the day when I am in the position that I imagined? I would like to be in that position, even if I had to die there and then; death would not hurt me, if I died in my sweetheart's arms. Love hurts and torments me greatly and I often weep and lament, but if Love can bring it about that I have complete joy of my beloved, then I shall have paid a fair price for my sufferings. I lie! These goods are too dear! I do not think that I was wise to make such an excessive request, for if someone asks for something foolish, it is reasonable that he be denied.

2459   ' "I do not know how I dared to say it. Many a man, worthier and more renowned than I, would be greatly honoured by a much smaller recompense. But if my fair one would only deign to gratify me with a single kiss, I would be richly rewarded for the pain I have suffered. But it is unlikely to happen; I have good reason to think myself mad, since I have set my heart on something from which I shall have neither joy nor profit. Now I am talking like a fool and a knave, for one look from her is worth more than the complete enjoyment of anyone else. God help me, but I would be very glad to see her at this moment; anyone who saw her for a little would be cured! Oh God, when will it be day? I have stayed too long in this bed, and lying here like this is worthless when I do not have what I desire. It is tiresome to lie down when one neither sleeps nor rests. Indeed, I find it very wearisome and distressing that the dawn does not break this instant, and the night is not soon over, for if it were day, I would get up. Ah sun, for God's sake make haste and do not linger and delay; banish dark night and its pain, which I have endured too long."

2491   'Thus, if ever I knew love's sickness, you will carry on all night, and get little rest, and when you can no longer endure to lie in bed awake, you will have to get ready, putting on your clothes and shoes and decking yourself out before you see day break. Then, whether it is raining or freezing, you will go secretly straight to the house of your beloved, who will be sound asleep and scarcely thinking of you. One time you will go to the back door to see if it has been left open, and there you will perch outside, all alone in the wind and rain; next you will go to the front door, and if you find an opening—a window or a lock—you will apply your ear to it and listen to see if those inside are asleep. If your fair one alone is awake, I recommend and suggest to you that she should hear you weeping and lamenting, so that she knows that you are unable to rest in your bed for love of her. Unless she is very hard-hearted, a woman will certainly have pity on a man who endures such pain for her sake. Now I shall tell you what you must do for love of that high sanctuary which gives you no comfort: kiss the door as you leave, and be careful to leave before it gets light, so that you are not seen in front of the house or in the street.

'Such comings and goings, such sleepless nights and medi- 2529
tations cause lovers to grow lean beneath their clothes: you will discover this through your own experience. It is fitting that you should lose weight, for love, you know, leaves the true lover with neither colour nor flesh. Because of this, you can tell those who betray women, for they flatter them by saying that they have no appetite for food or drink, but I see them, the cheats, fatter than abbots or priors.

'I charge and command you also to ensure that the serv- 2543
ing-maid of the house thinks you generous: give her such a garment that she sings your praises. You must honour and cherish your sweetheart and all her friends, for great good may come to you through them; when those who are intimate with her tell her that they have found you worthy and courteous and well bred, she will love you half as much again. Do not leave the country, and if some great necessity compels you to do so, be sure that your heart remains behind, and plan to return quickly. You must not delay: show that you are longing to see her who keeps your heart.

2563   'Now I have told you how and in what way a lover must
do my service: do it, then, if you wish to have joy of your
fair one.' When Love had thus commanded me I asked him:
'Sir, how and in what way may lovers endure the pains you
have recounted? I am quite terrified of them. How does a
man live and survive such pain and suffering, such grief, sighs,
and tears, such constant and unvarying worry and watchful-
ness? So help me God, I am very surprised that a man, even
one made of iron, can live for a year in such hell.'

Then the God of Love answered my question and offered
a clear explanation: 'Fair friend, by my father's soul, nothing
good was ever obtained without payment; thus the more we
pay for something, the better we appreciate the purchase, and
good things painfully acquired are the more gladly received.
It is true that no pain can equal that suffered by lovers. The
pains of love can no more be recounted in a book or a
romance than the sea can be drained dry, yet lovers must live,
for life is necessary to them. Everyone is glad to escape from
death. A man imprisoned in a dark, filthy, and verminous
dungeon, with nothing but black or oaten bread to eat, does
not die from his suffering, for Hope comforts him and he still
imagines that some fortunate occurrence will release him.
The man held captive by Love has exactly the same desire.
He hopes to be saved, and this hope gives him the strength,
the courage, and the desire to endure his martyrdom. Hope
gives him patience to endure countless sufferings, for the sake
of a joy that will be one hundred times greater. Hope
triumphs through endurance and gives life to lovers; blessed
be Hope, who thus serves the cause of lovers. For Hope is
truly courteous; she will stand by the man of courage to the
end and never, in spite of dangers and difficulties, separate
herself from him by so much as an arm's length. She even
induces the thief about to be hanged to live in hope of a
reprieve. Hope will protect you, for she will never fail to
help you in your hour of need.

2626   'I will also give you three other gifts, which bring great
comfort to those I hold in my toils. The first gift which brings
comfort to those trapped in Love's toils is Pleasant Thought,
who reminds them of Hope's promises. When the lover sighs

and complains in his grief and suffering, Pleasant Thought comes in due course to dispel his sorrow and wretchedness and, as he comes, reminds the lover of the joy that Hope promises. Then Pleasant Thought recalls to his mind a pair of laughing eyes and a well-formed nose, neither too large nor too small, and a little red mouth with such fragrant breath, and he is delighted to be reminded of the beauty of each limb. His pleasure is doubled when he remembers a smile, a friendly greeting, or a kind glance bestowed on him by his lady. In this way, Pleasant Thought calms the pain and torment of love. I would like you to accept this gift, and if you refuse the next one, which is no less sweet, you must be very hard to please.

'The next gift is Pleasant Conversation, who has come to 2657
the aid of many young men and many ladies, for everyone is delighted when people talk to them of their love. Because of this, I remember, the song of a lady very much in love contained these courteous words: "How happy I am", she says, "when people talk to me about my beloved! I swear that whoever does so brings me relief, no matter what he says to me about him." That lady was well aware of the worth of Pleasant Conversation, for she had experienced it in many ways. I therefore strongly recommend you to seek out a wise and discreet friend, to whom you can speak of your desire and reveal your inmost thoughts. He will be of great use to you, for when your suffering is intense, you will be able to go to him for comfort, and the two of you will speak together of the lady who has stolen away your heart. You will bare your soul to him and ask his advice about how best to please your beloved. If this trusty friend is himself a true lover, his company will be all the more valuable, for in his turn he will of course tell you who his lady is and what her name is, and whether or not she is a maid, and you will not be worried that he might pay attention to your beloved on his own account or try to separate you from her. Instead you will keep faith, one with another. I assure you that it is extremely agreeable to have someone with whom one is not afraid to share one's secrets and one's intimate thoughts; you will find it a pleasure, and will consider yourself well rewarded when you have tried it.

2701   'The third gift comes from looking; it is Pleasant Looks,
who often comes late to those who love from afar. But I
advise you to stay close to the object of your love, so that
the consolation of Pleasant Looks may not be long delayed,
for he brings great joy and delight to lovers. It is a happy
morning for the eyes when God shows them the precious
sanctuary that they so much desire. On the day when they
see it, nothing can trouble them, and they fear neither dust
nor wind nor any other irritation. Moreover, when the eyes
rejoice, they are so well bred and have been so well brought
up that they wish to share their happiness and want the heart
to be happy too, and so relieve its pain. For the eyes, being
excellent messengers, send the heart immediate reports of
what they have seen, and the heart is then so happy that it
must needs forget its earlier pain and gloom. Just as light
drives away darkness, so the gloom surrounding the heart that
pines away night and day for love is dispersed by Pleasant
Looks, for the heart no longer suffers when the eyes behold
the object of its desire.

2735   'Now, I think I have explained what I saw was troubling
you, for I have told you truthfully about the benefits that can
protect lovers and keep them from death. Now you know
who will comfort you, for you will at least have Hope, and
certainly Pleasant Thoughts as well, and Pleasant Conversation and Pleasant Looks. I wish each of these to protect you
until you can expect something better, for in the future you
will have other good things that will not be less but greater;
for the moment, however, I give you this much.'

CHAPTER 3

HOPE AND DESPAIR

As soon as he had told me his pleasure, he vanished before
I could speak, and I was quite amazed to see that no one was
with me. I suffered greatly from my wounds, knowing that I
could only be cured by the rose-bud which was the sole
object of my heart's desire. I had no confidence that anyone
except the God of Love could obtain it for me, and I knew
for certain that I had no chance of obtaining it unless Love
took a hand.

The roses were enclosed and surrounded by a hedge, as was
proper, but I would gladly have penetrated the enclosure for
the sake of the rose-bud that smelled sweeter than balm, if I
had not thought that I would be blamed for it; however, it
would soon have seemed that I wanted to steal the roses.

As I was deliberating whether to cross to the other side
of the hedge, I saw coming straight towards me a handsome and pleasant and quite irreproachable young man. His
name was Fair Welcome, and he was the son of generous
Courtesy. He very politely relinquished the path through
the hedge to me and said in a friendly tone: 'My dear and
fair friend, please pass through the hedge without delay to
smell the scent of the roses. I can assure you that you will
suffer no evil or discourtesy, provided that you do not behave foolishly. If I can help you in any way, you will not
need to beg, for I am ready to serve you. I tell you this in
all sincerity.'

'Sir,' I said to Fair Welcome, 'I readily accept this assurance, and give you thanks and credit for your kind words,
for they are the expression of your great nobility of spirit. If
it pleases you, I accept your offer of service.' I promptly
passed through thorns and wild roses, of which there were
many in the hedge, and made my way to the rose that smelled
sweeter than the others, escorted by Fair Welcome. And I
assure you that I was very pleased to be able to stay so close
to the rose-bud that I could have touched it.

Fair Welcome did me a great service when I saw the rose-bud from so close. But there was a lout (may his shame be great) hiding close by whose name was Rebuff* and who was the guardian and keeper of all the roses. The villain was in a place apart, all covered in grass and leaves so that he could spy on and surprise those he saw stretching out their hands to the roses. And the brute was not alone but had with him Evil Tongue, the tattle-tale, together with Shame and Fear. The most valiant of these was Shame, for you know that, to tell her ancestry and lineage correctly, she was the daughter of wise Reason and her father's name was Fiend, a man so hideous and ugly that Reason never lay with him but conceived Shame at the sight of him. When God had brought Shame to birth, Chastity, who should be mistress of roses and rose-buds, was so assailed by lecherous scoundrels that she needed help, and was beset night and day by Venus, who often stole her roses and rose-buds together. Then Chastity, assailed by Venus, asked Reason for her daughter, and since she was undefended, Reason, wishing to grant her prayer, lent her Shame, who is simple and honest, in answer to her request. Then Jealousy, the better to provide for the roses, summoned Fear, who desires ardently to obey her commands. So there are four to guard the roses, and these four would suffer a severe beating before anyone carried off a bud or a rose. Now I would have reached a safe haven had they not surprised me, for Fair Welcome, who was noble and court-eous, exerted himself to do all he could to please me. Often he exhorted me to approach the rose-bud and to touch the bush that bore it. He gave me licence to do all this because he thought it was what I wanted, and he picked a green leaf near to the rose-bud and gave it to me, because it had been born close by.

2863   I was soon very proud of the leaf, and, feeling so familiar and intimate with Fair Welcome, I was sure I had arrived. Then, taking heart, I plucked up my courage and told Fair Welcome how Love had captured and wounded me. 'Sir,' I said, 'only one thing can ever bring me joy, for deep within my heart is a most serious malady, but I do not know how to tell you about it for fear of angering you greatly. I would rather be cut up into pieces by steel knives than that you should be angered by it.'

'Tell me what it is you want,' he said, 'for nothing you might wish to say could ever cause me pain.' Then I said to him 'Know, fair sir, that Love causes me bitter torment, and do not imagine that I am lying to you. He has inflicted five wounds upon my body, and their pain will never be relieved unless you give me the rose-bud that is more beautifully shaped than the others: it is my death and my life and there is nothing that I desire more.'

Then Fair Welcome was alarmed and said: 'Brother, you 2891 aspire to something that cannot happen. What then, do you want to shame me? You would indeed have deceived me if you had removed the rose-bud from its bush, for it is not right that it should be taken from its natural place and it is unworthy of you to ask it! Let it grow and flourish, for I love it so well that I would not wish to have separated it from the bush that bore it for any man living.'

At once uncouth Rebuff jumped out from his hiding-place. He was big and black, with bristly hair and fiery red eyes, a wrinkled nose and a hideous face, and he bellowed like a madman: 'Fair Welcome, why have you brought this young man among the roses? You are doing wrong, as I hope to be saved, for he wishes you harm. Woe betide anyone, except you alone, who brought him into this garden! Anyone who serves a traitor is as bad as he is. You imagine you are doing him a kindness, but he seeks to shame and hurt you. Flee young man, flee from here, for I am close to killing you. Fair Welcome did not know you properly and took pains to serve you, whereas you are trying to deceive him. I do not care to trust you any longer, for the treason you have hatched is now well proven.'

I no longer dared remain there because of the black and 2927 hideous wretch who threatened to attack me. He made me jump over the hedge in great fear and haste and, shaking his head, told me that if I ever came back I would suffer at his hands.

Then Fair Welcome fled and I remained, shocked and overcome with shame and repenting of ever having spoken my thoughts. I remembered my foolishness, realizing that I was now given over to grief and pain and torment, and above all I was dismayed that I dared not cross the hedge. No one has suffered who has not tried Love; do not imagine that anyone who has not loved knows what acute anguish is. Love paid in full the pain of which he had told me. No heart could conceive nor mouth of man relate a quarter of what I suffered. My heart was close to breaking at the thought of the rose that I must now leave behind. I was a long time in this state, until the lady from her high vantage-point in the tower looked down and saw me thus downcast. The lady's name was Reason, and, descending from her tower, she came directly to me. She was neither young nor old, neither too tall nor too short, neither too thin nor too fat. The eyes in her head shone like two stars and she wore a crown upon her head; she looked like a person of importance. It was apparent from her form and her face that she was made in paradise, for Nature could not have fashioned anything so perfectly proportioned. Know that if the books do not lie, she was made in the firmament by God in his own image and likeness, and that he gave her such virtue that she has power and authority to keep a man from folly, provided that he be such as to trust in her. As I stood in sorrow there, behold, Reason began:

2982 'Fair friend, folly and childishness have caused you this pain and trouble. It was an unlucky day when you saw the beauty of May that so gladdened your heart, and unfortunate that you ever sought the shade of the garden where Idleness keeps the key with which she opened the door for you. It is foolish to make a friend of Idleness, for hers is dangerous company. She has betrayed and deceived you; Love would never have seen you if Idleness had not led you to the beautiful garden of Pleasure. If you have behaved foolishly, now do what is necessary to retrieve the situation and take care no longer to believe the advice that led you into folly. Happy is the man who learns from his folly, and we should not be surprised when a young man acts foolishly. Now I would like to tell you and advise you to forget that love, which I can see has greatly weakened, subdued, and tormented you. I see no other prospect of health or recovery, for cruel Rebuff is

longing to wage bitter war against you, and you ought not
to put him to the test. And Rebuff is nothing in comparison
with my daughter, Shame, who guards and defends the roses
and is certainly no fool; you should fear her greatly, for no
one is more dangerous to you.

'As well as these, there is Evil Tongue, who allows no one 3017
to touch them. Even before the deed is done he has recounted
it in three hundred places. You are dealing with some very
formidable people. Now consider which is better, to give it
up completely or to pursue the thing that is making your life
a torment, the disorder called love, which is nothing but
foolishness. Utter foolishness, so help me God! A man in love
can do nothing well, and pays no attention to worldly profit;
if he is a clerk, he wastes his learning, and if he has another
profession, he can scarcely pursue it. Moreover, he suffers
more than a hermit or a White Monk. The pain is immeasur-
able, and the joy lasts only a short time. If there is joy, it does
not last long and it depends on chance, for I see many who
strive for it and fail completely to obtain it in the end. You
never heeded my advice when you surrendered to the God
of Love. Your too-fickle heart led you into this folly, folly
that you were quick to undertake but will require much skill
to abandon. Now forget love, which makes your life value-
less, for this folly will constantly increase if you do not stop
it. Take the bit firmly between your teeth, subdue your heart
and master it. You must use your strength to protect yourself
against the thoughts of your heart, for the man who always
believes his heart cannot avoid folly.'

When I heard these rebukes, I replied angrily: 'My lady, I 3057
would ask you to refrain from rebuking me. You tell me to
subdue my heart so that Love may no longer have the mastery
over it. Do you imagine, then, that Love would allow me to
quell and subdue the heart that belongs to him absolutely?
What you say is impossible, rather has Love so subdued my
heart that it is entirely at his mercy; his power over it is so
great that he has made a key to lock it. Now leave me in
peace, for you are wasting your words to no purpose. I would
rather die than that Love should have accused me of falseness
or treachery. In the end, I wish to be praised or blamed

according as I have been a true lover, and it is vexing to be
rebuked.' At that, Reason departed, for she saw clearly that
she could not turn me from my purpose by lecturing me.

3083   I remained, angry and sorrowful, often weeping and lamenting, for I could see no way out of my difficulty; until I
remembered that Love had told me to seek out a companion
to whom I could reveal all my intimate thoughts, and that
this would deliver me from my great torment. Then I reflected that I had a companion whom I knew to be most
loyal; his name was Friend, and I never had a better one. I
went quickly to him and, just as Love had advised me, told
him of the obstacle that I felt impeded me. I also complained
to him of Rebuff, who was all but ready to devour me and
sent Fair Welcome away when he saw me talking to him
about the rose-bud that I longed for, and told me that if he
ever for any reason saw me cross over the hedge, I would
pay for it.

3107   When Friend learned the truth, he did not frighten me but
said: 'My friend, be reassured and do not be dismayed. I have
known Rebuff for a long time, and discovered long ago that
he is in the habit of insulting and attacking and threatening
those who love, at first. But if you have found him cruel, he
will be different in the end. I know him through and through,
and he can be softened by fair words and entreaties. Now I
shall tell you what you must do. I advise you to ask him to
remit his animosity in a spirit of love and conciliation, and
you should promise him faithfully that from now on you will
never do anything to displease him. He is greatly mollified
when anyone speaks to him in a flattering way.' Friend talked
and spoke so eloquently that he comforted me somewhat, for
he gave me the courage and desire to go and try to appease
Rebuff.

3135   Shamefaced, I approached Rebuff, desirous of making
peace but not crossing the hedge, since he had forbidden me
to do so. I found him standing erect, cruel and angry in
appearance, with a thorn club in his hand. With head bowed
I said to him: 'Sir, I have come here to beg for mercy. I am
very sorry if I have ever done anything to anger you, but I
am ready now to make amends in whatever way you com-

mand. I assure you that it was Love, from whom I cannot withdraw my heart, who made me do it, but I shall never aspire to anything that might cause you displeasure. I would rather endure my own suffering than do anything that might displease you. Now I beg you to have pity on me and calm your anger, which fills me with terror; and I give you my solemn word that I will so conduct myself towards you that I will not transgress in any way, provided that you are willing to grant me what you cannot withhold. Only let me love, I ask nothing else, and if you grant this, I will do everything else that you want. In any case, you cannot prevent me, I have no wish to deceive you about that, for I shall love because it becomes me to do so, no matter who is pleased or displeased. But not for my own weight in silver would I wish to love against your will.'

I found Rebuff to be very severe and unwilling to forgive   3173 me and forget his animosity, but I spoke so eloquently to him that in the end he did forgive me and said in a brief speech: 'Your request does not displease me and I have no wish to refuse it; be assured that I am not in the least angry with you. What does it matter to me if you love? I am neither chilled nor warmed by it. Love, then, as long as you always keep away from my roses. I shall have no pity on you if you ever cross the hedge.'

Thus he granted my request, and I went quickly to tell   3187 Friend, who rejoiced when he heard it, like a good comrade. 'Now,' he said, 'your affair is going well. Rebuff will yet be gracious to you, for he often lets people have their way once he has displayed his arrogance. If he were caught in a good humour he would take pity on your pain. Now you must endure and wait until you can catch him in a good mood. In my experience, the cruel are conquered and tamed by endurance.'

Friend, who desired my success as much as I did, comforted   3201 me very sweetly. Then I took my leave of him and went back to the hedge guarded by Rebuff, for I was longing at least to see the rose-bud, since I could have no other joy of it. Rebuff often took care to see if I was keeping my promise, but I was so afraid of his threats that I had no wish to do anything against him; instead I strove long and hard to do his bidding, in order to win his friendship. But I suffered greatly from the fact that his mercy was so long delayed. He often saw me weeping and sighing and lamenting because he made me languish so long beside the hedge, not daring to cross and approach the rose, and he certainly saw from my behaviour that Love governed me cruelly and that I was neither treacherous nor false. But he was so cruel that he would not deign to relent, however much he heard me sighing and lamenting.

3231   As I was in this distress, behold, God sent Generosity of Spirit, and Pity with her. Without any more delay, they both went straight to Rebuff, for both would gladly have helped me if they could, since they saw my need.

In her kindness, Lady Generosity of Spirit spoke first and said: 'Rebuff, in God's name you wrong this lover, who suffers such ill-treatment at your hands. I tell you that your behaviour is unworthy, for I am not aware that he has been guilty of any misconduct towards you. If Love compels him to love, ought you to blame him for that? His loss is greater than yours, for he has suffered much distress because of it. But Love will not allow him to repent; he could not prevent himself, were he to be skewered alive. But, fair sir, how does it benefit you to cause him pain and torment? Have you declared war on him just because he fears and honours you and is your subject? If Love holds him fast in his bonds and makes him obey you, should you hate him for that? You should rather have spared him more readily than you would a boastful rogue. Courtesy decrees that we should succour those who are beneath us, and it is a hard heart indeed that does not yield when it encounters supplication.' Pity then spoke: 'It is true that violence conquers humility, but it is wicked and cruel to maintain that violence for too long. Therefore, Rebuff, I would beg you no longer to wage war on the wretch languishing there, who never played Love false. It seems to me that you hurt him far more than you should; he has endured too hard a penance since you robbed him of the friendship of Fair Welcome, for that was the thing he most desired. He was distressed enough before, but now his torment is doubled. Now he is in desperate straits, as good as dead, for he lacks Fair Welcome. Why do you do him any harm, when Love already treats him very badly? His sufferings are such that he would need nothing worse, even to please you. So do not ill-treat him any more, for you gain nothing by it. Allow Fair Welcome to be gracious to him from now on, and let the sinner find mercy. Since Generosity of Spirit agrees, and I beg and urge you, do not deny her request. The man who will not do our bidding is most cruel and ignoble.'

At this, Rebuff grew calmer, for he could hold out no 3301 longer. 'Ladies,' he said, 'I dare not refuse you this, for it would be too base an act. Since you wish it, I will permit him the company of Fair Welcome and will set no obstacle in his way.'

Then eloquent Generosity of Spirit went to Fair Welcome and said courteously to him: 'You have kept away from this lover for too long, Fair Welcome, and not deigned to look on him. Since you stopped seeing him he has been very melancholy and sad. Now if you want to enjoy my love, take care to treat him kindly and to do as he wishes. For you should know that, between us, Pity and I have mastered Rebuff, who estranged you from him.'

'I shall do whatever you wish,' said Fair Welcome, 'for it is right, since Rebuff has permitted it.' Then Generosity of Spirit sent him to me.

First of all, Fair Welcome greeted me very tenderly and behaved more pleasantly to me than he ever had before. Then he took my hand to lead me into the enclosure that Rebuff had forbidden me. Now I had permission to go everywhere, and it seemed to me that I had been wafted from deepest hell to heaven, for Fair Welcome led me everywhere and took pains to do what pleased me.

When I approached the rose, I found that it was a little 3339 larger and saw that it had grown since the time I first saw it. The rose was a little larger on top, but I was pleased that it had not opened enough to reveal the seed but was still enclosed by the rose leaves, which stood up straight and filled the place within, so that the seed with which the rose was full could not appear. May God bless it, it was even more beautiful and redder as it opened than it had been before, and I was astounded at the wonder of it. Love bound me more and more firmly as its beauty increased, and continually tightened his knots as I experienced greater pleasure.

3361   I remained there a long time, for I found much love and companionship in Fair Welcome, and when I saw that he refused me neither comfort nor service, I made a request of him which it is right that I should mention. 'Sir,' I said, 'I tell you truly that I long desperately to have a precious kiss from that sweet-scented rose, and if it did not displease you, I would ask you for it as a gift. For God's sake, sir, tell me then if you will allow me to kiss it, for I will not do so until you allow it.'

3377   'Friend,' he said, 'so help me God, were it not that I should earn the hatred of Chastity, I should never refuse it to you, but I dare not because of Chastity, against whom I have no wish to sin. She always forbids me to give any lover who urges me permission to kiss, for if a man achieves a kiss, it is difficult for him to stop there; and you should know that whoever is granted a kiss has the best and pleasantest part of his prize, and an earnest of what remains.'

3391   When I heard him answer thus I did not want to keep on begging him for a kiss, for I was afraid of angering him. One should not badger people more than they want, or torment them excessively. You know that the oak is never cut down at the first stroke nor the wine extracted from the grapes until the press is tightened. I longed continually for permission to take the kiss that I desired; but Venus, who wages constant war on Chastity, came to my aid. She is the mother of the God of Love and has helped many lovers. In her right hand she held a burning torch whose flame has warmed many a lady.* She was so elegantly adorned that she looked like a goddess or a fairy. Her splendid finery made it clear to anyone who saw her that she did not belong to a religious order. I shall not now mention her dress and veil, the gold braid that adorned her hair, her clasp and her belt, for it would take too long. But you may be quite certain that she was extremely elegant, and yet absolutely free from pride. Venus went to Fair Welcome and began to speak to him: 'Fair sir, why are you making such difficulties about allowing this lover a de-lightful kiss? It ought not to be refused him, for you know and see clearly that he is a loyal servant and lover, and he is handsome enough to be worthy of being loved. See how elegant and good-looking he is, how charming, how gentle and open towards everyone; and what is more, he is not old but only a youth and therefore even more to be valued. There is no lady or chatelaine whom I would not judge unworthy if she were hard to please where he was concerned. He will not change; and you will be very well occupied in granting him a kiss, since his breath, I imagine, is very sweet and his mouth is not ugly but seems to be made expressly to give pleasure and delight, with rosy lips and white teeth so clean that they are free from tartar and dirt. In my opinion, it is reasonable to bestow a kiss upon him. If you take my advice, you will give it to him, for you may be sure that the longer you wait, the more time you will waste.'

Such was the power of Venus and her torch that Fair 3455 Welcome, feeling the warmth of the torch, accorded me the gift of a kiss without further delay. Wasting no more time, therefore, I immediately took from the rose a sweet and delicious kiss. Let no one ask if I had joy of it, for a perfume entered my body, casting out the pain and soothing the torments of love, which used to be so bitter. Never had I been so happy; one is truly cured by kissing so delightful and sweet-scented a flower; I shall never be so sorrowful that the remembrance of it will not fill me with joy and delight. Nevertheless, I have endured many troubles and many painful nights since kissing the rose. The sea will never be so calm that a little wind will not disturb it: Love is very changeable, sometimes soothing, sometimes hurting; Love hardly ever stays the same.

Now it is right that I should tell you of my struggle 3481 with Shame, who later hurt me grievously, and of how the wall was raised and the rich and powerful castle that Love after-wards captured through his efforts.* I wish to continue with the whole story and shall never be lazy about writing it down, for I believe that it pleases the fair one (God bless her!) who will reward me better than anyone when she wishes to.

3493   Evil Tongue, who thinks out and guesses the situation of
many lovers and recounts all the evil that he knows, observed
the kind welcome that Fair Welcome deigned to give me,
and could not keep quiet about it, since he was the son of a
spiteful old woman and his tongue was most offensive, sharp,
and bitter: he took after his mother in that respect. From then
on, Evil Tongue began to accuse me, saying that he would
wager his eye that there was an improper liaison between me
and Fair Welcome. The wretch spoke so wildly about me
and Courtesy's son that he awakened Jealousy, who arose in
great agitation when she heard the slanderer and, having
arisen, immediately ran to Fair Welcome like one distraught,
for she was greatly distressed. Then she attacked him in these
words: 'Worthless wretch, why have you lost your senses and
become friendly with a youth whom I suspect of behaving
badly? I see clearly that you are easily convinced by the
flatteries of strange young men. I will no longer trust you;
indeed, I shall have you bound or imprisoned in a tower, for
I can see no other solution. Shame has gone too far from you,
and has not taken the trouble to watch over you and restrain
you; it seems to me that she is of very little help to Chastity
when she allows an insolent scoundrel into our enclosure to
dishonour both me and her.'

3535   Fair Welcome did not know what to reply, and would have
gone away to hide had she not found him there and caught
him with me, red-handed. But when I saw the scold coming
to argue and quarrel with us, I immediately turned and fled,
for the altercation distressed me.

Then Shame, fearing that she was greatly at fault, stepped
forward. She was humble and simple and wore a veil instead
of a wimple, like a nun in a convent. Since she was quite
taken aback, she began her speech in a low voice: 'For God's
sake, my lady, do not believe the slanderous words of Evil
Tongue; he is a man who lies easily and has deceived many
worthy men. Fair Welcome is not the first he has accused,
for Evil Tongue is in the habit of telling false tales about
young men and ladies. Certainly it is not untrue that Fair
Welcome has too long a rein, and that he has been allowed
to attract people he had no business with, but I truly do not

believe that he has intended anything wicked or foolish. But it is true that Courtesy, his mother, taught him that he should take pains to make friends with people, since she never loved a stupid man. And I assure you that Fair Welcome has no other fault or defect except that he is full of gaiety and talks playfully to people. Doubtless I have been remiss in my duty of watching over him and rebuking him, and for this I ask your pardon; if I have been a little slow to do what is right, I grieve for it; I repent of my foolishness, but from now on I shall give my full attention to watching over Fair Welcome and shall never fail in this.'

'Shame, Shame,' said Jealousy, 'I am very much afraid of being betrayed, for Lechery has grown very strong and I could soon be dishonoured. It is not surprising if I am afraid, for Lust reigns everywhere; his power grows continually and Chastity is no longer safe in the abbey or in the cloister. Therefore I will have the rose-bushes and the roses enclosed within a new wall; I shall no longer leave them exposed here, for I have little trust in your guardianship, since I see clearly and know for certain that even with the best of guards one may suffer loss. Before the year was out I would be judged a fool unless I took care of this. I must take appropriate steps. I will certainly bar the way to those who come spying on my roses in order to trick me, and I shall not delay in building a fortress to enclose the roses. In the middle there will be a tower where Fair Welcome will be imprisoned, for I am afraid he may do something wrong. I intend to guard him so closely that he will be unable to get out or to spend time with the young scoundrels who speak flatteringly to him in order to dishonour him. These wretches have found him to be too foolish, too easily deceived, but if I live, he will know for certain that it was an evil day for him when he gave them a friendly greeting.' 3583

At these words Fear arrived, trembling, but she was so taken aback when she heard Jealousy that she dared not say a word to her, knowing that she was angry. She withdrew to one side, whereupon Jealousy departed, leaving Fear and Shame together, their very buttocks quivering with fright. Fear, whose head was bent, addressed her cousin, Shame: 3620

'Shame,' she said, 'I am greatly distressed that we should be reproached with something that we could not help. April and May have often come and gone without our incurring blame, but now Jealousy does not trust us, and insults and abuses us. Let us go straight to Rebuff and explain to him clearly that he has acted very wrongly in not taking greater pains to guard the enclosure properly. He has been too lenient in allowing Fair Welcome to do openly as he liked, but now he must reform; otherwise he may be quite certain that he will have to flee the country, for he could not endure the hostile fury of Jealousy, were she to conceive a hatred for him.'

3651 Abiding by this decision, they went to Rebuff and found the churl lying beneath a hawthorn. Instead of a pillow for his head, he had a large heap of grass, and was just falling asleep, when Shame woke him up, berating and abusing him:

'By what evil chance are you asleep at this hour?' she said. 'Only a fool would trust you any more than a sheep's tail to guard roses or rose-buds. You are a most faint-hearted coward, whereas you ought to be fierce and bully everyone. Madness made you allow Fair Welcome to admit into the enclosure a man who would bring blame upon us.

3671 'While you sleep, we, who can do nothing about it, hear the complaints. Were you lying down just now? Get up at once and block up all the openings in this hedge. Do not take pity on anyone, for it does not befit someone with your name to cause anything but distress; let Fair Welcome be open and gentle, you should be cruel and violent, insolent and offensive. A courtly churl talks nonsense, as I have heard said in the proverb, and there is no way you can make a sparrow-hawk out of a buzzard. All those who have found you gracious take you for a fool. Do you then want to please people, to do them kindness and service? You are getting slack, and you will have the universal reputation of being soft and weak, and of believing those who flatter you.' Then Fear spoke next:

3695 'Indeed, Rebuff, I am most surprised that you are not wide awake to guard what you should be guarding. You could soon suffer for it if Jealousy's anger increased, for she is very cruel, very pitiless and ready to quarrel. Today she has vigorously attacked Shame, and driven Fair Welcome away from this place by her threats, swearing that if he remains she will wall him up alive. All this is the result of your weakness, for you have lost all your spirit. I imagine your heart has failed you, but it will go hard with you and you will suffer pain and distress, if ever I knew Jealousy.'

Then the wretch pushed back his hood, rubbed his eyes 3713 and shook himself, wrinkled his nose and rolled his eyes, full of anger and fury when he heard himself threatened in this way: 'I could go absolutely out of my mind when you say that I am defeated. I have indeed lived too long if I cannot guard this enclosure. May I be skewered alive if ever a living man enters here. My very heart is greatly angered that anyone ever set foot here. I would rather two spears had been thrust through my body. I fully realize that I have acted like a fool, but now the two of you will help me to make amends. Never shall I be idle in defending this enclosure, and if I catch anyone there, he would be better off in Pavia. Never as long as I live will anyone judge me faint-hearted, I give you my oath and my word.'

Then Rebuff rose to his feet, wearing an angry look, and, 3737 taking a stick in his hand, set off around the enclosure to see if he could find a path or a track or an opening that ought to be blocked. And now the situation is completely changed, for Rebuff has become more cruel and disagreeable than he used to be. The one who drove him into such a rage has taken my life, for now I shall never be able to see what I desire. The heart within me is greatly chagrined because I have angered Fair Welcome, and I assure you that I tremble in every limb when I remember the rose that I used to see from close by whenever I wanted to. And when I recall the kiss that filled my body with a scent sweeter than balsam, I am near to fainting, for the sweet fragrance of the rose is still enclosed within my heart. I tell you that when I remember that I must give up all this, I would rather be dead than alive. It was the worse for me when I pressed the rose to my face, to my eyes and to my lips, if Love does not allow me to touch it at any other time, no, never again. Now that I have tasted

its savour, the desire that inflames and excites my heart is all
the keener. Now tears and sighs will return, and long, sleepless meditations, tremblings, lamentations, and complaints: I
shall endure many such torments, for I have fallen into hell.
Cursed be Evil Tongue! It is because of his false and treacherous tongue that I must swallow this bitter pill.

3779　　Now it is time for me to tell you about what Jealousy was
doing, in her deep mistrust. There was not a mason or a
workman in the land whom she did not summon to construct
ditches, first of all around the roses, ditches that cost a great
deal of silver, for they were very wide and deep. Above the
ditches, the masons made a wall of cut stone, not built on
shifting earth but founded on solid rock. The foundations
were well proportioned, going down to the bottom of the
ditches and narrowing as they rose, so that the construction
was much stronger. The wall was built in the form of a perfect
square, each of whose sides measured six hundred feet, so that
it was as long as it was wide. The turrets standing side by side
had high battlements and were made of squared stones; it
would have been hard to break down the four that stood at
the four corners. There were also four gateways, whose walls
were thick and high, one at the front, suitably capable of easy
defence, one on either side, and one behind, that feared no
catapulted stone. There were also fine portcullises to cause
distress to those outside and to catch and hold them if they
dared come too close.

3815　　In the very middle of the enclosure, those who were masters of this craft built a tower with great skill; there could be
none more beautiful, for it was great and broad and high.
The wall would not fail, whatever engine of war hurled its
missiles, for the mortar was made with quicklime slaked with
strong vinegar. The stone from which the foundations were
made was the natural rock, as hard as adamant. The tower
was completely round; there was none more splendid in all
the world nor better arranged within. On the outside it was
surrounded by a bailey* that went all around it, so that the
rose-bushes with their abundant roses were thickly planted
between the bailey and the tower. Within the castle were
catapults and engines of many kinds. You could have seen

the mangonels* above the battlements, while at the loopholes
all around were cross-bows bent by means of screw-jacks*
and that no armour could withstand. Anyone who wanted to
approach close to the walls would indeed be foolish. Beyond
the ditch was an enclosure of good strong walls with low
battlements, so that the horses could not reach the ditch
directly without first being involved in a fight.

Jealousy had garrisoned the castle that I have described to   3849
you, and I believe that Rebuff held the key to the first gate,
which opened eastwards. He had with him, to the best of my
knowledge, a total of thirty armed followers. The next gate,
which opened southwards, was guarded by Shame, who was
very wise and had, as I can tell you, a large number of
followers ready to do her will. Fear also had a great troop
and was stationed on guard at the next gate, situated on the
left, towards the north. Fear will never feel safe there unless
the gate is locked; she seldom opens it, for when she hears
the wind howling or sees two grasshoppers jump, she is
sometimes seized with panic. Evil Tongue (God curse him!)
had Norman soldiers. He guarded the gate at the back, and
I can tell you that he often went back and forth to the other
three. When he knew that he had to take the night watch,
that evening he mounted to the battlements and tuned his
pipes, trumpets, and horns; sometimes he sang songs and lays
and improvised new songs to the accompaniment of the
bagpipes, while at other times, accompanied by the flute, he
would sing that he had never found an honest woman:

'There is not a woman who does not laugh when she hears   3885
talk of loose living; one is immoral, another paints her face,
and yet another gives you come-hither looks; this one is
coarse, that one mad, and the third talks too much.' Evil
Tongue, who spares no one, finds some fault with each.

Jealousy, whom God confound, garrisoned the round   3893
tower, and you should know that she placed her closest
friends there, so that there was a great troop. And Fair Welcome was imprisoned high up in the tower, whose door was
so well barred that it was impossible for him to escape. An
old woman, may God bring shame upon her, was with him
to guard him. Her only job was simply to watch him in case

he did anything foolish. No one could trick her by sign or gesture, for there was no deception with which she was not familiar, having in her youth enjoyed her share of the joys and torments that Love metes out to his followers. Fair Welcome was silent and listened, for he feared the Old Woman and dared not move in case she perceived him to be behaving badly, for she was well acquainted with all the old tricks. As soon as Jealousy had captured Fair Welcome, she had him imprisoned, which made her feel safe. Her castle, which she saw to be so strong, gave her great comfort, and she was no longer afraid that scoundrels might rob her of her roses or rose-buds; the rose-bushes were very stoutly enclosed, and, waking or sleeping, she could feel quite secure. But I, outside the wall, was given over to grief and torment. Anyone who knew what my life was like would surely feel great pity for me. Now Love certainly knew how to exact a price for the good things he had lent me. I thought I had bought them, but now he sold them to me again and I was worse off because of the joy that I had lost than if I had never had it. What more can I say? I was like the peasant who casts his seed upon the ground and is full of joy when the blades begin to grow well and thickly; but before he can reap a single sheaf he may be harmed and distressed by an evil cloud that arises when the ears are due to sprout, causing the grain within to die and robbing the peasant of the hope that he had felt too soon.

3943   I too feared that I had lost my hope and my expectation, for Love had so favoured me that I had already begun to speak very intimately to Fair Welcome, who was ready to receive my advances, but Love is so capricious that he robbed me of everything at once, just when I thought that I had won. It is the same with Fortune, who fills men's hearts with bitterness but at other times flatters and caresses them. Her appearance changes swiftly, smiling one moment and sad the next. She has a wheel that turns, and when she wishes, she raises the lowest to the very highest place, while he who is at the top is plunged with one turn into the mud. And it is I who am thus brought down! It was the worse for me when I saw the walls and the ditch that I dare not and cannot cross. I have had no blessings or joys since Fair Welcome was put in prison, for all my joy and my salvation is in him and in the rose that is confined within the walls. He will have to come out from there if Love wants me to be cured, for I seek neither honour nor good, neither health nor joy from any other source. Ah, Fair Welcome, fair sweet friend, if you are imprisoned, at least keep your heart for me, and do not on any account allow fierce Jealousy to enslave your heart as she has your body; and if she chastens you outwardly, have a heart of adamant within to resist her admonition. If your body remains in thrall, at least take care that your heart loves me. A noble heart does not stop loving because it is beaten or mistreated. If Jealousy is harsh towards you, torments and insults you, oppose her fiercely and avenge yourself in spirit at least, since no other vengeance is possible, for her arrogant treatment of you. If you acted thus I would consider myself well rewarded. But I am very much afraid that you might not do this, for you are perhaps angry with me because you have been put in thrall on my account. And yet it is not because of any fault in my conduct towards you, for I never recounted anything that should have been kept secret, and, so help me God, I am suffering more than you as a result of this misfortune, for the penance I endure is greater than anyone can say. I almost boil with rage when I remember my loss, which is so great and so apparent, and I believe that the fear and distress I suffer will result in my death. Should I not be afraid, knowing that slanderers and envious traitors are eager to do me harm? Ah, Fair Welcome, I know for certain that they long to deceive you, and have perhaps already done so. I do not know how things are going, but I am dreadfully afraid that you might have forgotten me, and so I am in pain and distress. Nothing will ever bring me comfort if I lose your favour, for I have no confidence in anyone else.

Guillaume de Lorris's poem ends at this point, and the continuation by Jean de Meun begins.

CHAPTER 4

THE ADVICE OF REASON

4029   Perhaps I have lost it; I am on the point of despair. Despair! Alas, I shall not do so, I shall never despair, for if Hope failed me, I should be unworthy. I must take comfort from her, for Love told me, so that I would better be able to endure my pain, that she would protect me and accompany me everywhere. But what of that? What is that to me? Although she is courteous and gracious, she is certain of nothing and brings great suffering to lovers, making herself their lady and their mistress. She deceives many with her promise, for she often makes promises that she will never keep. And so, God help me, she is dangerous, for many true lovers sustain and will sustain themselves in their love by Hope, but will never achieve their goal. We do not know what to believe, since she does not know what will happen. Therefore it is foolish to approach too close to her, for when she constructs a good syllogism, we should be very much afraid that she will draw the negative conclusion;* she has often been seen to do so, with the result that many have been deceived by her. Nevertheless, she wishes him who keeps her with him to have the best of it, so it was foolish of me to dare find fault with her. But what use are her wishes to me, since she does not end my suffering? Very little, for the only remedy she can offer is her promise, and a promise without a gift is not worth much. No one can know the extent of the sufferings she allows me to endure. I am oppressed by Rebuff, Shame, and Fear, by Jealousy and by Evil Tongue, who poisons and envenoms all his victims, making martyrs of them with his tongue. These hold Fair Welcome captive; he is constantly in my thoughts, and I know that if I cannot have him, I shall not be able to live much longer. I am slain above all by the dirty, stinking, filthy old woman who must guard him so closely that he dares not look at anyone.

4083   From now on my misery will certainly increase. It is true that in his mercy the God of Love gave me three gifts, but I lose them here: Pleasant Thoughts gives me no help, Pleasant Conversation also fails to help me, and, so help me God, I have also lost the third, whose name was Pleasant Looks. They are fair gifts indeed, but they will never be worth anything to me unless Fair Welcome leaves the prison where he is most unjustly held. I think I shall die for his sake, since I do not believe he will ever come out alive. Come out? No indeed. Through whose prowess could he escape such a fortress? Certainly it will never be through my efforts. I do not believe I had even half my senses, but rather that I was raving mad when I did homage to the God of Love. Lady Idleness made me do it: shame upon her and her actions when she answered my prayer and gave me shelter in the lovely garden. For if she had known anything of good, she would never have listened to me. A foolish man does not deserve an apple's worth of credit; he should be blamed and rebuked before being allowed to commit folly. I was a fool and she heeded me: my prosperity never increased through her efforts. She carried out my wishes too well, and now I must lament and suffer. Reason explained it clearly to me, and I may count myself a madman for not taking her advice and renouncing love at once.

Reason was right to reproach me for ever becoming in- 4121 volved with love; I must suffer most painfully as a result and I believe I wish to repent. Repent! Alas, why should I do that? I would be shamed as a false traitor. The devil would have assailed me indeed, and I would have betrayed my lord! Fair Welcome would also be betrayed: should I then hate him if, because of his courteous behaviour towards me, he languishes in Jealousy's tower? Courtesy to me? Certainly, more courteous than anyone could believe, for he was willing to allow me to cross over the hedge and kiss the rose: I ought not to be ungrateful to him and I certainly never shall be. Never, please God, shall I complain about the God of Love or cry out against him, or against Hope or Idleness, who were so gracious to me, for I would be wrong to complain about their kindness.

So there is nothing left to do except to suffer and offer my 4145 body to be martyred, and wait with firm hope until Love

sends me relief. I must wait for mercy, for I remember well
that he said to me: 'I will readily accept your service and will
raise you to high rank, provided that you do not forfeit it by
wickedness. However, this may not happen quickly.'* This
was what he said, word for word; it is quite clear that he
loved me tenderly. So there is nothing to do but serve him
well, if I wish to deserve his gratitude, for any fault would
lie with me; the God of Love has no failings, for indeed, no
God was ever at fault. The fault must therefore be mine, but
I do not know where it comes from, and perhaps I shall never
know.

4165   Let things go as best they can, and let the God of Love do
as he wishes, whether I escape or face what comes. He may
let me die if he wishes. I shall never achieve my goal, yet I
shall die if I do not, or if someone does not achieve it for
me. But if Love, who inflicts such suffering upon me, wished
to achieve it for me, then no pain endured in his service could
hurt me. Let it all go exactly as he desires, and let him supply
the remedy if he wishes; I can no longer take an active part.

But whatever becomes of me, I beseech him after my death
to remember Fair Welcome, who has killed me but not hurt
me. And in any case, in order to please him before I die,
unable to bear the burden of the suffering he imposes, I make
my unrepentant confession to you, Love, as loyal lovers do,
and I wish to make my will: when I die, I leave my heart to
Fair Welcome and have no other legacy to make.

As I thus bewailed the great sufferings that I endured, and
knew not where to seek a healer for my frantic grief, I saw
the fair and charming Reason, who had come down from her
tower on hearing my lamentations, coming straight towards
me once again.

4199   'Fair friend,' said lovely Reason, 'How is this case progress-
ing? Are you now weary of loving? Have you not suffered
enough? What do you think now of the torments of love?
Are they too sweet or too bitter? Can you now choose from
among them the happy medium that will be sufficient to
support you? Was it a good lord you served who thus captured and enslaved you and torments you incessantly? It was
an unhappy day for you when you did him homage, and you

were foolish to get involved. Doubtless you did not know what lord you were dealing with, for if you had known him well you would never have become his man, or if you had done, you would not have served him for a single summer, or even for a day or an hour. On the contrary, I believe that you would without delay have renounced the homage you did him and would never have loved *par amour.** Have you any knowledge of him?'

'Yes, lady.'

'You do not.'

'Yes I do.'

'How, by your soul?'

'From the fact that he said to me: "You should be very glad that you have so good a master and so renowned a lord." '

'Have you any other knowledge of him?'

'No, except that he gave me his commandments and then fled away more swiftly than an eagle, while I remained in trouble.'

'That is poor knowledge indeed. But I want you to know 4232 him now, for you have drunk so deeply of his bitterness that you are quite warped. No unhappy, miserable wretch could bear a greater burden. It is good to know one's lord, and if you knew this one well you could easily escape from the duress in which you languish.'

'In truth, lady, since he is my lord and I his liegeman, heart and soul, my heart would be very glad to hear and learn more about him, if there were anyone to teach it.'

'By my head, I am glad to teach you, since your heart wants to hear. Now I shall soberly demonstrate to you something that is not demonstrable, and you will soon know without knowledge and understand without understanding that which cannot be known or demonstrated or understood. This is in order that any man who fixes his heart on love should know more about it, although his suffering will not be lessened as a result unless he wishes to flee from love. Then I shall have untied for you the knot that you will always find tied. Now pay close attention, for this is the description of love.

'Love is hostile peace and loving hatred, disloyal loyalty 4263 and loyal disloyalty; it is confident fear and desperate hope, demented reason and reasonable madness. It is the sweet danger of drowning and a heavy burden that is easy to handle; it is perilous Charybdis,* disagreeable and gracious at the same time; it is a most healthful sickness and a most sickly health; a hunger abundantly satisfied and a covetous affluence, a thirst that is always drunk, an intoxication drunk with thirst. It is a false delight, a joyful sorrow and an unhappy joy, a sweet torment and an unkind sweetness, a taste at once pleasant and distasteful; it is a sin touched by pardon and a pardon tainted by sin, a most joyful suffering and a merciful cruelty. It is an ever-shifting game, a state which is very firm but also very changeable, an infirm strength and a strong infirmity that sets everything in motion through its efforts, a foolish sense and a wise folly, a sad and joyful prosperity; it is laughter that sobs and weeps, repose that toils unceasingly, a hell that soothes and a heaven that tortures, a prison that offers relief to prisoners, a cold and wintry spring-time. It is a moth that refuses nothing and consumes purple and homespun alike, for lovemaking is no better in fine clothes than in homespun. No one has been found who is so highly born, so wise, of such proven strength or courage, or so virtuous in other respects that Love has not conquered him. The whole world treads that path, for he is the god who leads everyone astray except those excommunicated by Genius* because their evil ways are an offence against Nature. I am not concerned with these, however, but I do not want people to love in such a way, to be so maddened by Love that in the end they admit themselves to be unhappy and sorrowful wretches. But if you really want to avoid being hurt by Love and to be cured of this madness, you cannot drink a better draught than the thought of fleeing from him. This is the only way you can be happy: if you follow him, he will follow you, and if you flee him he will flee away.'

4329   When I had listened carefully to Reason, who had exerted herself in vain, I said: 'Lady, for my part I declare that I know no better than before how to detach myself from Love. There are so many contradictions in this lesson that I can learn nothing from it.

'Although I can recite it by heart, since my heart has forgotten none of it, and can understand it well enough to give a public lecture on the subject, to me alone it means nothing. But since you have described love to me, both praising and condemning it to such an extent, I would beg you to define it in such a way that I can better remember it, for I have never heard a definition of it.'

'Gladly, now pay attention. Love, if my judgement is correct, is a mental illness afflicting two persons of opposite sex in close proximity who are both free agents. It comes upon people through a burning desire, born of disordered perception, to embrace and to kiss and to seek carnal gratification. A lover is concerned with nothing else but is filled with this ardent delight. He attaches no importance to procreation, but strives only for pleasure. There are people of such a kind that they do not care for this love; nevertheless, they pretend to be true lovers while disdaining to love *par amour*, and they make fools of ladies, promising them their bodies and souls and swearing false and deceitful oaths to those whom they are able to deceive, until they have had their pleasure. But these are the least deceived, for it is always better, fair master, to deceive than to be deceived, especially in this war in which they cannot seek a compromise. But I know well, and this is no conjecture, that anyone who lies with a woman should wish to the best of his ability to perpetuate his divine essence and to preserve himself in a creature like himself (for all men are subject to decay), so that the succession of generations should not fail. For since fathers and mothers pass away, Nature wants their children to spring up to continue this work, so that one is replaced by another. Therefore Nature made the work pleasurable, desiring that it should be so delightful that the workmen should not take to their heels or hate it, for there are many who would never perform this task unless they were attracted by pleasure.

'Thus Nature used her ingenuity. You should know that 4391 no one can love as he ought or with the right intentions if he desires only delight. Do you know what he does, the man who seeks delight? He surrenders, a wretched and foolish slave, to the prince of all the vices, for such behaviour is the

root of all evils, as Cicero establishes in his book *On Old
Age*,* which he praises and desires more than Youth. Youth
brings men and women into contact with every bodily and
spiritual danger; it is a hard period to pass through without
dying or breaking a limb or bringing shame or harm to oneself
or to one's family. Because of Youth a man abandons himself
to every vice, gets into bad company, and associates with
those of dissolute life; he has no stability. He may enter some
monastery, being unable to preserve the freedom that Nature
had given him, and imagines that he is performing some
marvel in mewing himself up there and remaining until he is
professed. If he finds the burden too heavy, he may repent
and then leave, or perhaps he will end his days there, not
daring to come out but kept there by shame and remaining
against his will. There he lives in great distress, bewailing the
freedom he has lost and which cannot be restored to him
unless God has mercy upon him, ending his torment and
keeping him in obedience through the virtue of patience.

4433   'Youth makes men commit follies, indulge in evil debaucheries and lewd excesses; it encourages fickleness of purpose
and provokes disputes that are hard to solve afterwards. Such
are the dangers they face when Youth inclines their hearts to
Delight. Thus Delight ensnares and leads men's minds and
bodies through his chambermaid, Youth, who is accustomed
to doing wrong and attracting men to Delight, and who
would not wish for any other work.

4447   'But Old Age retrieves them. If anyone does not know this,
let him learn it now or ask old people, whom Youth once
held in her bonds, for they still remember well the great
dangers they endured and the follies they committed. Now,
however, the strength to do these things and the foolish
desires that used to tempt them have been taken from them
by Old Age, who walks with them and is a very good
companion, bringing them back to the right way and giving
them escort to the end. But her services are wasted, for no
one loves or values her, or at least not enough, as far as I
know, to want her for himself, for no one wants to grow old
or to end his life while still young. And so when they look
into their memories and recall, as they must, the follies they

committed, they are amazed and astounded that they could have done such things without suffering shame and disgrace, or if they were hurt and disgraced, that they could have escaped such dangers without suffering greater damage to their souls, their bodies, or their property.

'And do you know where Youth lives, whom so many men 4477 and women value? Delight keeps her in his house while she is in her prime; he wants her to serve him and even wants her to be his servant for nothing. She does this so willingly that she follows him everywhere he goes and freely abandons herself to him, not wishing to live without him.

'And do you know where Old Age lives? I will tell you without delay, for you will have to come to that, unless Death sends you down into his dark and gloomy cave while you are still young. Travail and Suffering give her lodging, but they bind and fetter her and so beat and torment her and make her suffer such tortures as to offer her an early death and a desire for repentance. And then, when she is at last in the presence of death and sees that she is weak and her hair all white, it comes into her mind that Youth, who has made her spend all her past life in vanity, has cruelly deceived her, and that she has wasted her life unless the future comes to her aid, maintaining her in a state of repentance for the sins she committed in her youth and bringing her back, through her virtuous conduct in the midst of this suffering, to the sovereign good from which Youth, drunk with vanities, had estranged her. For her present lasts so short a time that it cannot be counted or measured.

'However things may go, anyone, whether man or woman, 4515 lady or maiden, who desires the certain enjoyment of love must also desire its fruit, although they need not relinquish their share of delight. But I know very well that there are many women who do not want to be pregnant and who are distressed if this happens to them, and yet they do not complain or protest about it, except for those foolish silly ones over whom Shame has no authority. In a word, all those who devote themselves to this work follow Delight, except for those worthless people who basely sell themselves for money and whose foul and filthy lives are not bound by the laws.

4533   'It is certain, however, that no good woman would aban-
        don herself in return for a gift, and no man should attach
        himself to a woman who was willing to sell her flesh. Does
        he think that a woman cares for her body when she is willing
        to flay it alive? He is wretchedly abused and miserably de-
        ceived, imagining that such a woman loves him just because
        she calls him her lover, smiles at him, and makes much of
        him! Certainly no such beast ought to be called "sweetheart",
        nor is she worthy of being loved. A woman who seeks to rob
        a man should be considered worthless. I do not mean that for
        her own pleasure and happiness she should not perfectly well
        wear a jewel, if her lover has given or sent it to her, but she
        should not ask for it, for that would be an ignoble way to
        take it. She may also give him something of hers in return,
        if she can do so without shame. Thus their hearts are joined
        together, they love each other well and pledge themselves
        to one another. Do not imagine that I would separate them!
        I am glad for them to be together and to act in all things
        as courteous and gracious lovers should. But they should
        keep themselves from the intemperate passion that kindles
        and inflames men's hearts, and their love should be free
        from that covetousness that incites false hearts to greed. True
        love ought to be born of a true heart; it ought not to
        be ruled by gifts any more than by bodily pleasures. But the
        love that has ensnared you offers you carnal delight, so that
        you have no interest in anything else. That is why you want
        to have the rose, and dream of no other possession. But you
        are not two fingers' breadth away, that is what makes you
        waste away and robs you of all courage. In giving shelter to
        Love you took in a guest who would cause you great pain:
        you have an evil guest in your house. Therefore I advise
        you to throw him out, for he takes from you all the thoughts
        that ought to be profitable for you: do not let him stay any
        longer.

4585   'Hearts drunk with love are given up to great misfortune;
        you will know this in the end, when you have wasted your
        time and ruined your youth in this unhappy delight. If you
        live long enough to see yourself freed from Love, you will
        bewail the time you have wasted but will be unable to recover

it. And that is if you escape even to that extent, for I venture to say that the love which has entrapped you has cost many their sense, their time, their possessions, bodies, souls, and reputations.'

Thus Reason preached to me, but Love completely prevented me from putting any of it into practice, even though I understood all her discourse word for word. For Love drew me strongly, pursuing me through all my thoughts like the hunter who hunts everywhere, and always keeping my heart under his wing. Whenever he spied me sitting listening to the sermon, he took a spade and threw out of my head by one ear whatever Reason had put in the other, with the result that she wasted her time completely and filled me with anger and rage. Then I addressed her angrily: 'Lady, you clearly wish to betray me. Must I then hate people? Why should I hate everyone? Since love is never good, shall I never love truly but always live in hate? In that case I would be a mortal sinner, worse indeed than a thief, by God. There is nothing for it but to jump in one direction or the other: either I will love or I will hate. But even though love may well not be worth a penny, I might perhaps pay more for hate in the end. You have given me good advice in continually exhorting me to renounce love, and anyone who is unwilling to believe you is a fool.

'You have also reminded me of another, unknown love 4633 which people may have for one another, and one which I did not hear you condemn. If you would supply a definition I would consider myself a fool not to hear it gladly, and find out at least if I could learn the different natures of love, if you would attend to my instruction.'

'Indeed, fair friend, you are foolish, since you do not care a straw for my preaching, although it is for your own good; nevertheless, I am willing to preach another sermon, being ready to fulfil your worthy request to the best of my ability, but I do not know if it will be of any use to you. There are various kinds of love apart from the one that has so changed you and driven you from your senses. It was your misfortune to become acquainted with it; for God's sake take care to avoid it in future.

4655   'Friendship is the name of one kind of love, that is to say
         of mutual goodwill between people, free from strife and in
         accordance with the benevolence of God. Through charity,
         all their goods should be held in common, so that there may
         never be any intention to make an exception. The one should
         not be slow to help the other with firmness and wisdom,
         discretion and loyalty, for sense is worthless where loyalty is
         lacking. Either one should be able to tell his friend whatever
         he dares to think, as safely as if he were talking to himself,
         without fear of accusation. Such are the ways that those who
         wish to love perfectly should be and are accustomed to fol-
         low. A man cannot be truly lovable unless he is so firm and
         dependable that Fortune cannot move him, so that his friend,
         who is wholeheartedly devoted to him, finds him, rich or
         poor, always the same. And if he sees him slipping into
         poverty, he should not wait to be asked for help, for a
         kindness that has been begged for is evilly and dearly sold to
         hearts that are truly worthy.

4685   'A worthy man is most ashamed to ask for a gift; he is very
         pensive and troubled and suffers great distress before making
         his request, so ashamed is he to utter it and so fearful of a
         refusal. But when he has found a man whom he has already
         so tested that he is quite certain of his love, he will tell him
         everything he dare think of, whether it be a matter for joy
         or complaint, without feeling any shame about anything, for
         why should he be ashamed if his friend is such as I have
         described? When he has told his secret, no third person will
         ever discover it, and he need not fear a reproach, since a wise
         man watches his tongue. (This is something that no foolish
         man can ever do, for a fool can never keep silent.) He will
         do more than this, for he will help him in every way he can,
         and, truth to tell, he will have more joy in giving help than
         his friend in receiving it. Moreover, the power of love is so
         great that if he does not fulfil his friend's request he will suffer
         just as much as he who made the request. If love is properly
         shared, he will bear half of his friend's grief, and comfort him
         as much as he can while also participating in his joy.

4717   'Cicero says in one of his discourses* that by the laws of
         this friendship we ought to ask things of our friends, provided

such requests be honourable, and in our turn we should grant their requests, provided they are right and reasonable. Otherwise a request should not be granted save in two exceptional cases: if someone wanted to have them killed, we ought to try to rescue them, and if their reputation is attacked, we should make sure that they are not slandered. In these two cases he permits us to defend them without waiting for right or reason, and no man should refuse to do this in so far as love can excuse it. The love that I put forward here is not incompatible with my purpose, and I would be glad if you would practise it, shunning the other love. The first is attracted to every virtue, while the other leads men to their death.

'I would like to tell you about another love which is also opposed to true love and strongly to be condemned: it is the feigned desire to love found in hearts that are sick and diseased with a covetous desire for gain. This love is so uncertain that as soon as it loses hope of the profit that it wants to gain, it must fail and die, for no heart that does not love people for themselves can love truly; instead it dissembles and flatters them in expectation of gain. 4739

'This is the love that comes from Fortune and is eclipsed like the moon when it is darkened and shaded by the earth. When the moon falls into the earth's shadow, it loses sight of the sun and so loses much of its brightness, and when it has passed through the shadow, it returns all luminous from the rays of the sun that shines upon it from the other side. Such is the nature of this love, which is sometimes bright and sometimes dark. As soon as Poverty wraps it in her ugly black cloak and it no longer sees the glow of wealth, it must darken and take flight, and when riches shine on it once more, they bring it back in brightness, for it fails when wealth fails and appears when wealth does.

'All rich men are loved with the love I have described to you, and especially misers, who will not wash their hearts clean of the vicious and inordinate desires of covetous Avarice. A rich man who imagines himself loved has more horns than an antlered stag. For is this not great foolishness? It is certain that he loves no one, so how, without proclaiming 4773 himself a fool, could he imagine that anyone loves him? If he does, he is no wiser than a fine antlered stag. In God's name, anyone who desires true friends must be worthy of love. I can prove that he does not love, for, having wealth and seeing his friends in poverty, he holds on to his wealth and keeps it from them, intending to keep it always, until his mouth is closed and evil death destroys him, for he would allow his body to be torn limb from limb rather than endure separation from his wealth, and therefore he will not give them any of it. And so love has no part in this, for how could there be any friendship in a heart that does not know true pity? Moreover, he knows this when he acts in this way, for everyone knows his own business. Indeed, a man who neither loves nor is loved is greatly to be blamed.

4807   'Now since our discourse on love has led us to Fortune, I should like to tell you of a most wondrous thing, the like of which I do not believe you will ever have heard. I do not know if you will be able to believe it, but it is true nevertheless and found in books. It is that people benefit and profit more from Fortune when she is perverse and unfavourable than when she is gentle and gracious. And if this seems doubtful to you, it can be proved by argument, for when Fortune is gracious and gentle, she lies to people and deceives them into madness, suckling them like a mother who does not appear to be harsh. She pretends to be true to them when she gives them her jewels, which are honours and wealth, dignities and high offices, and, placing them on her wheel, she promises them stability where all is changeable, and feeds them all with vainglory in their worldly prosperity. Then they imagine themselves to be so exalted and their state to be so secure that they could never fall from it. When she has established them in this condition, she makes them believe that they have so many friends that they can neither count them all nor be free of them, for they are always coming and going around them, making lords of them and promising to serve them; indeed they are ready to lose the shirts on their backs and to spill their blood in order to protect and defend them, and they are prepared to follow and obey them all the days of their lives. Those who hear such words glory in them and believe them as they would the Gospel, but it is all flattery and deception, as they would later discover if they had lost all their goods with no prospect of recovery. Then they would see their friends in action, for if out of one hundred ostensible friends, whether companions or relatives, they were left with one, then they should praise God for it. When this Fortune whom I have described makes her home with men, she confuses their understanding and nurtures them in ignorance.

'But when she is unfavourable and perverse, topples them 4863 from their high estates and with a turn of her wheel tumbles them from the summit down into the mud; when, like a cruel stepmother, she sticks a painful plaster to their hearts, moistened not with vinegar but with thin and wretched poverty, then she shows that she is sincere and that no one should trust Fortune's favour, for it is utterly unreliable. When men have lost their wealth, she makes them know and understand the kind of love felt for them by their former friends, for friends bestowed upon them by good fortune are so dazed by misfortune that they all become enemies and not one, not even half a one, remains. They all run away and disown them as soon as they see that they are poor, nor do they stop there, but criticize and slander them everywhere they go, and call them wretched fools. Even those whom they most helped when they were men of high estate go around cheerfully swearing that they are well aware of their folly; they find not a single one to aid them. But their true friends remain to them, those whose hearts are so noble that they do not love for the sake of wealth or with any expectation of gain. These aid and defend them, for Fortune has no stake in them. A friend loves for ever. A man is not cut off from his friend's love, not even if he draws his sword upon him, except in the circumstances that I will now describe: such love is lost by pride and anger, by reproaches, by the disclosure of secrets that ought to be concealed, and by the painful wound of venomous detraction. In these circumstances a friend would take flight; nothing else could harm the friendship. But such friends are worth a great deal if but a single one is found among a thousand. And since no wealth can compare with

the value of a friend or attain such heights that the worth of
a friend would not be greater, then a friend on the road is
always worth more than money in one's belt. And when
Fortune falls unfavourably on men, this adversity makes them
all see so clearly that they discover their friends and prove by
experiment that they are worth more than any wealth the
world could offer them. Thus adversity is of more use to them
than prosperity, for from prosperity comes ignorance and
from adversity knowledge.

4931   'As for the poor man who has thus proved which friends
are true and which false and now knows them and can
distinguish between them, when he was as rich as he could
desire and everyone offered him their hearts and bodies and
everything they had for ever, what would he not then have
paid for the knowledge he has now? He would have been
less deceived if he had realized it then. Thus the misfortune
that he now receives, in turning him from a fool into a wise
man, brings him greater profit than the wealth that deceives.

'Wealth does not enrich the man who locks it up in treasure; a simple competence allows a man to live richly, for a
man not worth two loaves may be wealthier and more com-
fortable than one who has a hundred barrels of grain, and I
can tell you why. The latter may perhaps be a merchant
whose heart is so wretched that he has suffered great torments
before amassing his pile, and continues to fret about increasing and multiplying it, for he will never have enough, however much he manages to acquire. But the other, who relies
only on having enough to live on for the day, is satisfied with
what he earns and lives on his income. He imagines that he
lacks for nothing and although he has not a halfpenny, he sees
that he will earn enough to eat when the need arises, and to
buy shoes and suitable clothes. Or if he happens to fall ill and
finds his food tasteless, he reflects that in any case he will not
need to eat in order to get off this unpleasant path and out
of danger, or that a little nourishment will be sufficient come
what may, or again that he will be taken to the *hôtel-Dieu,**
where he will be well looked after. Perhaps he does not think
that he will ever get into such a state, or if he believes that
it might happen to him, he thinks that he will have saved up

enough before he falls ill to deal with the situation when it arises. If he cares nothing about saving against the time when cold or heat or hunger might cause his death, perhaps he comforts himself with the thought that the sooner he dies, the sooner he will go to heaven, for he believes that God will grant him paradise when he leaves this present exile. (Pythagoras himself tells you, if you have read that book of his that we call *Golden Verses** on account of its honoured sayings: "When you have left the body, you will mount freely into the blessedness of the upper air, leaving humanity behind and living in pure deity." He is a wretched and stupid fool who believes that this is his country: your country is not on earth, as you can learn from the clerks who explain Boethius' *Consolation* and the thoughts contained in it. If someone were to translate this book for the laity, he would do them a great service.)*

'Or again he may be such a man as can live on his income, not coveting other men's goods but believing himself to be free from poverty, for, as your masters say, no one is wretched who does not believe himself to be so, whether he be king, knight, or pauper. Many poor men are so gay at heart, carrying their sacks of charcoal on La Grève,* that their difficulties do not worry them. They work patiently and dance and skip and jump and go to Saint-Marcel* for their tripe. They do not give a fig for treasure, but spend all their earnings and savings in the tavern and then go back to carry their loads, but with joy, not lamentations. They earn their bread honestly, disdaining theft and robbery, then they go back to drink from the barrel and live as they should. All such are abundantly wealthy if they believe that they have enough: indeed, as the good God knows, they are wealthier than if they were usurers, for usurers, I can tell you, can never be rich but are so mean and covetous that they are always in poverty and penury.

'And so it is true, no matter who does not like it, that no merchant lives in comfort, for such a war rages in his heart that he burns alive to acquire more goods and will never have enough. He is afraid of losing what he has acquired and chases after what remains to be gained but which he will never possess, for his greatest desire is to acquire the property of others. He has undertaken an extraordinarily difficult task, for he aspires to drink the whole of the Seine but will never be able to do it, because there will always be some left. This is the burning anguish, the everlasting torment, the agonizing conflict that tears at his vitals and tortures him with his lack; it is that the more he gains, the more he lacks.

'Lawyers and physicians are all bound with these bonds, all hanged with this rope, if they sell their knowledge for money. They find gain so sweet and desirable and are so fired with covetousness and trickery that the one would like to have sixty patients for every one he has, and the other thirty cases, or indeed two hundred or two thousand. The same is true of theologians who walk the earth: when they preach in order to acquire honours or favours or wealth, the same anguish tears their hearts. Such men do not live honest lives, but those above all who chase after vainglory pursue also the death of their souls. Such a deceiver is himself deceived, for you should know that however much such a preacher may benefit others, he does himself no good. An evil intention may well produce a good sermon, which, although worth nothing to the preacher, may bring salvation to others who learn a good lesson from it while he is so filled with vainglory.

5089   'But let us leave aside such preachers and talk about misers. It is certain that they neither love God nor fear him, for they amass hoards of money and keep more than they need, when they can see the poor outside, trembling with cold and dying of hunger. God will know how to repay them. Three great misfortunes befall those who lead such lives: they seek most laboriously after wealth, then are so tormented by fear that they must guard it ceaselessly, and finally they grieve to leave it behind. Those who seek after great wealth live and die in such torment, and it is all because of an absence of love, which is lacking all over the world. If those who heap up riches loved and were loved, and true love reigned everywhere and was not bewitched by evil, and he who had more gave more to those he knew to be in need, or lent, not as a usurer but in pure and simple charity, provided that the recipients were well intentioned and avoided idleness, then there would be no poor men in the world, nor should there be any. But the world is so sick that love has been put up for sale: no one loves except for his own benefit, in order to obtain gifts or services, and even women are willing to sell themselves; may evil come of such sales!

'Thus Fraud has disgraced everything by causing goods that 5125 were once held in common to become men's property. People are so bound by Avarice that they have submitted their natural freedom to vile servitude, and are all the slaves of the money that they keep locked up in their storehouses. Do they keep it? Indeed, it is rather they who are kept, having fallen into such misfortune.

'These wretched earthy toads have turned their possessions 5135 into their masters. Wealth is worthless unless it is spent, that is what they cannot understand, and they would all reply instead that wealth is worthless unless it is hidden away. This is not so, nevertheless they do hide it and neither spend it nor give it away. Whatever happens, it will be spent, even though they had all been hanged; when at last they die, whoever they leave it to will spend it joyfully and they will have no profit from it. They are not even sure of keeping it until then, for someone might lay hands on it and carry it all off tomorrow.

'Wealth is seriously injured by being robbed of its true nature, which is to help men and go to their aid and not to be loaned at interest. This is why God has provided it, but now men have hidden it and locked it away. But riches avenge themselves honourably upon such hosts, for although, according to their destiny, they ought to follow in men's wake, instead it is they who lead men, dragging and pulling them ignominiously behind them and piercing their hearts with three swords. The first of these is the toil of acquisition; the second that wrings their hearts and keeps them in continual terror is the fear that someone might steal their wealth or rob them of it when they have amassed it; the third is the pain of leaving it behind. As I have said before, they are wretchedly deceived.

'It is thus that Wealth, like a noble lady and queen, avenges 5175 herself upon the slaves who keep her locked up. She takes

her ease in peace and makes the wicked lie awake and worry
and toil. She keeps them so close and subdued beneath her
feet that she enjoys the honour while they, who languish in
slavery to her, endure shame and torment and suffering.
There is no profit in such guardianship as theirs, at least not
for those who have Wealth in their keeping, but when they
die without ever having dared to attack her or make her run
and jump, she will of course remain with absolutely anyone.

'But valiant men attack her; they sit astride her and goad
her and so prick her with their spurs that they are able to
enjoy themselves and take pleasure in the liberal generosity
of their hearts. They follow the example of Daedalus, who
once made wings for Icarus;* through his art, and contrary
to established custom, the two of them made their way
together through the air. These men do just the same for
Wealth, by making her wings to fly, for they would rather
allow themselves to be injured than gain neither glory nor
prestige. They have no wish to be reproached with the
vicious and inordinate desires of covetous Avarice; instead
they use their wealth to perform deeds of great courtesy, so
that their exploits are praised and celebrated throughout the
world and they abound in virtue, and their generous and
charitable hearts are most pleasing to God. When God had
created the world, as I alone have taught you, he sustained it
with his gifts, and just as he abhors the stench of Avarice, he
delights in courteous and beneficent Largesse. God hates
misers, utter wretches that they are, and condemns them as
idolaters, as hapless, trembling, miserable, immoderate slaves.
And yet they imagine and maintain it to be true that they
only bind themselves to riches in order to be secure and to
live prosperously.

5227   'Oh sweet mortal riches, tell us, do you make men happy
when they have so confined you? For the more of you they
amass, the more they tremble with fear, and how can a man
be happy when he is not secure? Would happiness come his
way when security was lacking?

'But some who heard my words and wished to criticize and
condemn my discourse might contend that there are kings
who, in order to exalt their nobility, as the ordinary folk

think, make strenuous efforts to surround themselves with armed men, five hundred or five thousand troops, and it is generally said that this is because of their great courage. But God knows that the opposite is true, and that it is Fear who makes them act this way, by constantly torturing and tormenting them. It would be easier for a poor man from La Grève to go about alone and in safety and to dance among thieves without fear of them or of what they might do than for a king in his fur-lined robe, even if he were carrying with him a large part of the enormous treasure of gold and precious stones that he had amassed. Every thief would take his share; they would rob him of everything he carried and would perhaps want to kill him. Indeed, I believe he would be killed before he moved from that spot, for the thieves would be afraid that if they let him escape alive, he would have them seized, wherever they were, and taken away by force and hanged. By force? Rather by his men, for his own strength is not worth three apples more than that of the poor man who would wend his way so lightheartedly. By his men? By my faith, I lie, or at least I do not express it properly. In truth they are not his, although he has lordship over them. Lordship? No, rather service, for he must maintain their freedom. Instead they are their own men, for they can withdraw their help from the king whenever they want to and the king must remain alone as soon as the people wish it. For neither their kindness nor their prowess, neither their bodies, their strength, nor their wisdom belong to him, and he has no part of them. Nature has denied them to him. And however gracious Fortune is to men, she cannot give them possession of anything from which they are alienated by Nature, however they might have gained it.'

'Ah Lady, by the king of the angels, teach me nevertheless 5290 the things that can be mine and whether I can have anything of my own: I would very much like to know this.'

'Yes,' replied Reason, 'but do not expect fields or houses, robes or ornaments, earthly lands or chattels of any kind. You have something much better and more precious: all those gifts that you feel within you and understand so well in yourself, which remain with you constantly and may not

leave you so as to serve others in the same way, these gifts
are rightly yours. The other, external gifts that you have are
not worth an old strap; they are not worth a shallot to you
or any man alive, for you should know that everything you
own is enclosed within yourself. All other gifts belong to
Fortune, who scatters them and gathers them in, gives them
and takes them away as she pleases, causing fools to laugh
and weep.

'But no wise man would value anything that Fortune did,
nor would the turn of her whirling wheel make him glad or
sorrowful, for all her actions make us afraid in that they lack
stability. Therefore there is neither profit nor pleasure for a
worthy man in the love of Fortune, nor is it right that it
should be pleasing when it is so easily eclipsed. I want you
to know this so that nothing may cause you to become
attached to this love. You are not tainted by it, but it would
be a most evil act if you were so tainted in the future and
sinned against men to such an extent that you called yourself
their friend simply in order to acquire their wealth or any
profit that might come to you from them. No worthy man
would think it right. Flee from the love that I have described,
for it is vile and base, and renounce also love *par amour*. Be
wise and believe in me.

5341   'But I see that you are foolish in another way, for you have
charged me with the wickedness of ordering you to hate.
Now tell me when, where, and how I did this.'

'You have not stopped telling me all day that I should spurn
my lord on account of some strange love. If a man searched
from here to Carthage, from east to west, and lived until his
teeth dropped out through old age, if he ran continually and
tirelessly, coursing north and south until he had seen everything, he would not attain the love you have described. The
world was washed clean of it when the giants put the gods
to flight,* and Right, Chastity, and Faith fled at the same
time. That love was so dismayed that it also fled and was lost,
while Justice, weightier than the rest, was the last to flee. And
thus they all left the earth, for they could not endure the
wars, and made their home in heaven, and since that time
they have never, except by some miracle, dared come down

to earth. Fraud, who has inherited the earth through his strength and excesses, drove them all away.

'Even Cicero, who took great pains to search out the 5375 secrets contained in books, could not, however hard he thought, find more than three or four pairs of friends, in all the centuries that had passed since the world was made, who had known such perfect love. And I believe that he would have found even less of it among those of his own time who said they were his friends, nor have I read anywhere that he ever had any such friend. Am I wiser than Cicero? It would be very foolish and silly of me to wish to seek for such a love, for there is none of it left on earth. Where, then, would I seek it, since I would not find it here below? Can I fly with the cranes or leap beyond the clouds, as did the swan of Socrates?* I will be silent, for I do not want to talk about it any more. I have no such foolish hopes. The gods might imagine that I was attacking heaven as the giants once did, and might strike me down with their thunderbolts. I do not know if that is what you want, but I ought not to take that risk.'

'Fair friend,' she said, 'now listen. If you cannot attain this 5404 love, for the reason it is lacking may be as much your fault as someone else's, then I shall now tell you about a different love. Different? No indeed, but the same, to which everyone can attain provided he understand love in a rather wider sense. Let him love generally rather than in particular, and create a fellowship in which many may participate.* You can love everyone in the world both generally and loyally. Love them all as one, at least with as much love as you have for mankind in general. See to it that you behave towards everyone as you would wish them to behave towards you. Do not act towards anyone or seek to obtain anything from him except as you would have him do to you. If you were willing to love in this way, everyone would be satisfied, and you are bound to pursue this love, for no man should live without it.

'And since those who are eager to do evil abandon this love, judges are appointed on earth to serve as a defence and refuge for those whom the world has wronged, to make reparation for the crime, to punish and chastise those who, renouncing this love, murder people and injure them, rob and take and steal, or hurt by detraction or false accusation or by some misdeed, whether evident or hidden, and it is right that they be judged.'

'Ah Lady, since we are speaking of Justice, whose fame was formerly so great, and since you are taking the trouble to instruct me, for God's sake teach me if you please a little about her.'

'Tell me what you want to know.'

'Gladly. I should like you to arbitrate between Love and Justice: which seems to you to be worth more?'

'Which love are you talking about?'

'The one you desire me to embrace, for I have no wish to submit to judgement the love that is already within me.'

5457   'You have certainly convinced me of that, you foolish man. But if you are looking for a true judgement, then good love is worth more.'

'Prove it.'

'Most willingly. When you find two things that are appropriate, necessary, and useful, then the one that is more necessary is better.'

'Lady, that is true.'

'Now pay close attention and consider the nature of both. Wherever these two things are found, they are necessary and useful.'

'That is true.'

'So I have established that the more useful of the two is worth more.'

'Lady, I readily agree.'

'Then I will not say any more about that. But Love, which comes from charity, is far more necessary than Justice.'

'Prove it, lady, before you go on.'

'Gladly. I tell you truthfully that the gift that is self-sufficient is greater and more necessary and therefore much to be preferred to the one that needs help. You will not dispute that.'

'Why not? Explain yourself, so that I may know if there is anything to object to. I should like to hear an example to see whether I can agree.'

'By my faith, it becomes very burdensome when you demand examples and proofs. Nevertheless, you shall have an example, because it will help you to understand better. If a man can drag a boat without needing anyone else's help when you by yourself could not drag it, can he not pull better than you?'

'Yes, lady, at least with a rope.'

'Now take this as your analogy. If Justice were always asleep, Love would be sufficient for the leading of a good and virtuous life, and there would be no need to judge anyone. But Justice without Love would not be enough, that is why I say that Love is better.'

'Prove this to me.'

'Willingly. Now be quiet while I do so. Justice reigned formerly, in the days when Saturn held sway, Saturn, whose son Jupiter cut off his testicles as though they were sausages (a harsh and bitter son indeed) and flung them into the sea, whence sprang the goddess Venus, as the book says.* If Justice were to return to earth and were to be as highly regarded now as she was then, men would still need to love each other, however well they observed Justice, for as soon as Love fled, Justice would cause great destruction. But if men loved one another properly, they would never wrong each other, and when Crime departed, what use would Justice be?'

'Lady, I do not know.'

'I believe you, for everyone in the world would live peacefully and quietly. There would be no kings or princes, no bailiffs or provosts; people would thus live honestly and no judge would ever hear any clamour. That is why I say that Love by itself is worth more than Justice, although Justice combats Malice, mother of lordship, through whom freedom has been lost. For had it not been for the crimes and sins with which the world is stained, no king would ever have been seen nor judge known upon earth. Such men as these behave badly, for they should have begun by proving their own fitness, since men want to be able to trust them. In order to do justice to the plaintiffs, they should have been loyal and diligent, not weak and negligent, covetous, false, and deceitful. But now they sell their judgements and make nonsense of the documents in the case; they tally, count, and erase, and poor men pay for everything. They are all trying to take from others. The judge who hangs a thief ought rather to be hanged himself, were he to be judged for the crimes and depredations that he has used his power to commit.

5559   'Did Appius* not deserve to be hanged when, according to Titus Livy, who is well able to give an account of those events, he caused his servant to bring a false case supported by false witnesses against the maiden Virginia, daughter of Virginius, because he was unable to intimidate the maiden, who wanted nothing to do with him or his lustful desires? The wretch said in court: "Lord judge, give judgement in my favour, for the maiden is mine. I shall prove against any man alive that she is my slave, for wherever she was brought up, she was taken from my house at birth, by my faith, and given to Virginius. I therefore call upon you, Lord Appius, to deliver my slave to me, for it is right that she should serve me and not the man who brought her up. If Virginius denies this, I am ready to prove it all, and I can find good witnesses."

'Thus spoke the evil traitor, who was the servant of the false judge, and the case proceeded in such a way that before Virginius could speak (and he was quite ready to reply and confound his enemies), Appius gave a hasty judgement to the effect that the maiden should be given to the servant without delay. And when that fine and worthy man whom I have mentioned, that excellent and renowned knight Virginius heard it, realizing that he could not defend his daughter against Appius but would be forced to give her up and deliver her body to shame, he found a terrible way of exchanging shame for injury. For if Titus Livy does not lie, in love rather than in hate he instantly cut off the head of his beautiful daughter Virginia and then presented it to the judge before all, in open court. According to the story, the judge at once commanded that he be seized and led away to be killed or hanged, but he was neither killed nor hanged, for the people defended him, since all were moved to pity as soon as the facts were known. Appius was imprisoned for this injustice, and hastily killed himself before the day of his trial, while Claudius, the plaintiff, would have been sentenced to die like a thief had Virginius in his pity not spared him and implored the people to send him into exile. All the witnesses to Claudius' case were condemned to death.

'In a word, judges commit too many excesses. According 5629 to Lucan,* who was a very wise man, virtue and great power are never seen together. But such judges should know that unless they mend their ways and give back what they have wrongly appropriated, the powerful and eternal judge will put a rope around their necks and send them to hell with the devils. Neither kings nor prelates nor any kind of judge, temporal or ecclesiastical, will be exempt, for they do not hold their offices in order to act in this way. They ought, without payment, to bring the cases brought before them to a conclusion, and open their door to plaintiffs and hear cases, whether just or unjust, in person. They do not hold their offices for nothing and should not go around giving themselves airs, for they are all servants of the ordinary people who enrich and populate the land, and they have sworn an oath to right wrongs as long as they live. They should enable the people to live in peace, pursuing criminals and hanging thieves with their own hands if no one wished to undertake these offices personally, for they are obliged to administer justice. That is what they should be attending to, that is what they were paid for, and that is the promise made to the people by those who first assumed these offices.

'I have now done what you asked, if you have properly understood, and you have seen the reasons which seem to me appropriate to this judgement.'

'Lady, you have certainly paid me well, and I consider myself well recompensed, for which I thank you. But it seems to me that I heard you use a word so shameless and outrageous that if anyone wished to waste his time in trying to excuse you, I do not believe he would be able to find any defence.'

'I know what you are thinking about,' she said, 'and another time, whenever you wish, if you will be kind enough to remind me, you will hear my excuses.'

'I shall indeed remind you', I said with lively memory, 5680 'of the very word you spoke. My master, as I have clearly understood, has forbidden me to allow any word which is in the least indecent to fall from my lips.* But since I am not the perpetrator, I may certainly repeat the word, so I shall say it straight out. If you see someone acting foolishly, you do well to make him aware of his folly. This is what I now reproach you with, and you, who pretended to be so wise, will now perceive your offence.'

'I will gladly wait for you to do so,' she said, 'but I for my part must defend myself against the objections you have raised on the subject of hatred. I am amazed that you dare say it. Do you not know that it does not follow, if I abandon one folly, that I must adopt another, as bad as the first, or worse? The fact that I wish you to extinguish that foolish love you so desire does not mean that I order you to hate. Do you not remember Horace,* who had so much sense and grace? Horace, who was no fool, said that if, when madmen abandon vices, they turn to the opposite extremes, they are no better off. Now I have no wish to forbid anyone to occupy himself with love, but only with the love that is harmful. Though I may forbid drunkenness, I do not wish to forbid drinking; such counsel would not be worth a grain of pepper. Though I may ban extravagant generosity, men would think me mad if I ordered them to be avaricious, for both the one and the other are great vices. I do not use such arguments.'

'Indeed you do.'

'That simply is not true. I will not flatter you; you have not examined the old books* in order to defeat me, and you are not a good logician. This is not a lecture on love, but I have never said that men should hate anything. It is possible to find a middle way; it is the love that I so love and esteem and that I have taught you in order that you might put it into practice.

5733   'There is another, natural, kind of love, which Nature created in the animals and that enables them to produce their young, and to suckle and rear them. If you wish me to define for you the love of which I speak, it is a natural and properly motivated inclination to wish to preserve one's fellow creatures, either by engendering them or by seeing to their rearing. Men and beasts are equally well fitted for this love,

which, however profitable it may be, carries with it no praise
or blame or merit, and those who love thus deserve neither
blame nor praise. In truth, Nature pledges them to it by force,
and it does not involve any victory over vice, but if they did
not practise it, they would most certainly deserve blame.
When a man eats, what praise is due to him for that? Whereas
if he forswore eating he would certainly deserve to be abused.
But I know very well that you are not concerned with this
love, and therefore I do not insist upon it. You have em-
barked upon a far more foolish enterprise in the love that you
have undertaken, and you would be better off abandoning it
if you wish to seek what is good for you.

'Nevertheless, I have no wish for you to remain without a   5765
sweetheart. If it please you, fix your thoughts on me. Am I
not a beautiful and noble lady, fit to serve any worthy man,
were he emperor of Rome? I would like to become your
beloved, and if you will be true to me, do you know what
my love will be worth to you? So much that you will never
lack anything you need, whatever misfortune may befall you.
Then you will find yourself to be so great a lord that you
never heard tell of a greater. I shall do whatever you want;
no wish of yours can be too extreme, provided only that you
carry out my works, nor is it fitting that you act otherwise.
And you will have the advantage that your beloved is of such
high lineage that none can compare with her, being the
daughter of God, the lord and father who thus made and
shaped me. Gaze on this form and see yourself in my bright
face. No high-born maiden was ever so free to love as I am,
for I have my father's permission to take a lover and to be
loved, and he says that I shall not be blamed for it. You need
not fear blame either, for you will be in my father's keeping
and he will nurture both of us together. Do I say well?
Answer, how does that seem to you? Does the god who drives
you to this folly reward his people so well? Does he prepare
such good wages for the madmen who pay him homage? For
God's sake take care not to refuse me. Maidens who are not
accustomed to beg are very sad and abashed when men refuse
them, as you yourself can demonstrate through the example
of Echo, without seeking other proofs.'

5809   'Now tell me, not in Latin but in French, what you want
me to do for you.'

'Allow me to be your servant, and be yourself my loyal
friend. You shall leave the god who has brought you to this,
and not give so much as a fig for the whole of Fortune's
wheel. You shall be like Socrates, who was so firm and strong
that he was neither happy in prosperity nor sad in adversity.
He put everything in one balance, both good and evil fortune, and gave them equal weight, so that they caused him
neither joy nor sorrow, for he was never happy nor sad about
anything, whatever it was. He it was, as Solinus* says, who,
according to Apollo's answer,* was judged the wisest man in
the world; he it was whose expression, whatever befell him,
always stayed the same, and was found unchanged even by
those who killed him with hemlock because he denied that
there were many gods and trusted in one, and preached that
men should avoid swearing by many gods. Heraclitus and
Diogenes* were also of such a spirit that they were never
saddened, not even by poverty or distress. Firm in their
purpose, they endured every misfortune that befell them. This
is the only way for you to behave: serve me in no other way.
Take care not to be cast down by Fortune, whatever blows
and torments she may administer, for there is no good or
strong fighter who will not do battle with Fortune when she
strives to defeat and overcome him. We should not allow
ourselves to be taken, but should defend ourselves vigorously,
for she knows so little of fighting that anyone who fights with
her, be it in a palace or on a dunghill, can overcome her in
the first round. No man of courage will have any fear of her,
for no one who was aware of the limits of her strength and
knew himself to be without fear could be tripped up by her,
unless he threw himself voluntarily to the ground. It is also
most shameful to see a man who is perfectly well able to
defend himself allowing himself to be taken off and hanged,
and you would be wrong to want to pity him, for there is
no greater slackness. Take care, then, that you place no value
on her honours or services; leave her to turn her wheel, as
she does continually and ceaselessly, sitting in the centre like
one who is blind. Some she blinds with riches, honours, and

dignities, while to others she gives poverty, and when it
pleases her, she takes everything back. So it is very foolish to
feel sorrow or joy about anything, given that you can prevent
yourself from doing so, and you certainly can prevent yourself, provided the will is there. Moreover, it is also clear that
you are making Fortune into a goddess and raising her to the
heavens, which you ought not to do, for it is neither right
nor reasonable that she should dwell in paradise. She is not
so blessed; instead her dwelling is very perilous.

'There is a rock standing in the sea, out in the middle in   5891
very deep water; it juts up high above the sea, which mur-
murs angrily against it. The waves beat and dash against it in
continual conflict, often pounding it so hard that it is entirely
engulfed; but then, as the waves draw back, it sheds the water
that has soaked it and, rising into the air, it breathes. But it
never keeps the same shape; instead it is changed and transformed, altered and disguised. It always wears a borrowed
form, for when it appears thus in the air and Zephyrus* rides
the sea, he makes flowers appear, as bright as stars, and causes
the grass to spring up green. But when the North Wind
blows, he cuts down the flowers and grass with his chill
sword, so that the flowers lose their life as soon as they are
born.

'The rock is clothed in an ambiguous forest* of wondrous   5917
trees: one is sterile and bears nothing, another takes delight
in bearing fruit; one continually puts forth leaves, while
another is bare of them; where one remains green, many have
lost their leaves; and when one begins to blossom, the flowers
on many others are dying. One stands up tall, while its neighbours are bowed down to earth; and when buds are sprouting
on one, the others are all withered. The broom plants there
are giants, while pine and cedar remain as dwarfs: every tree
is thus deformed, and each takes the shape of another. There
the laurel bears a withered leaf when it should be green, while
the olive, which should be fertile and vigorous, is dried up.
The willows, which should be sterile, flower and bear fruit,
while the elm contends with the vine and takes from it the
form of the grape. The nightingale rarely sings there, but the
tawny owl, with its great head, prophet of misfortune and

hideous messenger of grief, utters loud cries and lamentations. Two rivers, different in taste, form, and colour, flow there in winter and summer alike; they spring from different sources, which come in turn from very different streams. One gives such sweet, such deliciously honeyed water that no one who drinks from it, even if he drinks more than he should, will ever be able to quench his thirst, so sweet and pleasant is the drink. For those who drink more of it burn more with thirst than before; no one drinks it without getting drunk, but no one satisfies his thirst thereby, for the sweetness is so deceiving that however much men swallow, they always want to swallow more. They are so deceived by the sweetness, so driven by greed that they are all hydropic.

5969   'This river flows and babbles along so delightfully that its resonant thrumming and drumming is pleasanter than drum or timbrel, and the hearts of all who go that way are gladdened. There are many who hasten to enter the stream but who stop on the bank, powerless to advance and scarcely wetting their feet. They touch the sweet waters with difficulty; although they come close to the river, they merely drink a little of it, then, when they perceive its sweetness, they would gladly go so deep into it as to be completely immersed. Others go in so far that they plunge into the current, congratulating themselves on the pleasure they enjoy as they thus swim and bathe. But then a gentle wave sweeps them back to the bank and replaces them on dry land, so that their hearts are burned and parched.

'Now I shall tell you what nature of river you will find the other to be. Its waters are sulphurous, dark and evil-tasting like a smoky fireplace, covered with stinking scum. It does not flow sweetly along but falls so hideously that as it passes it shakes the air more than any fearful thunder. I tell you truly that Zephyrus never blows over this river nor ruffles its waters, which are very ugly and deep, but the sorrowful North Wind has engaged it in battle and so torments the river that it is compelled to stir up its waves, and its depths and plains must rise up like mountains and do battle with each other. Many men dwell on the bank, sighing and weeping and with no end or limit to their lamentations, so that they are quite sunk in tears and live in constant terror of drowning in the river. Many people enter the river and do not just go in up to their waists but plunge so far into the waves that they are entirely swallowed up. There, they are pushed backwards and forwards by the fearful, hideous flood. Many are submerged and engulfed by the water, while many others are cast out by the current, and there are many who hurl themselves so far into the depths that they are swallowed up by the waves and, being unable to find their way out, are obliged to stay there, without ever returning to the surface.

'This river swirls about, winding its way through many 6035 narrow gorges until it empties itself, with all its agonizing poison, into the pleasant river, changing its nature with its stench and filth, infecting it with its evil and unlucky pestilence, and so clouding and poisoning it as to make it bitter and murky. Its excessive heat robs the other of its mildness, and the stench it emits even takes away its host's pleasant smell.

'High on top of the mountain, slanting down the slope 6049 rather than standing on the plateau, is Fortune's house, which is always threatening to fall and on the point of collapsing. It must endure every single storm or torment that the winds can offer, and is attacked and assailed by many tempests. Zephyrus, that sweet and incomparable wind, rarely comes to temper the horrible onslaught of the harsh winds with his soft and peaceful breath.

'One part of the hall slopes upwards, while the other descends, and it is visibly so askew that it seems it must fall. I do not believe that any man ever saw such an extraordinary house. On one side it is all shining, for the walls are fair with gold and silver, and the roof is of the same workmanship, aflame with bright and precious stones that have great powers; everyone praises it as a marvel. On the other side the walls are made of mud, less than one palm thick, and the roof is all thatched. On one side, the house stands proudly in its great and wondrous beauty, on the other it shakes with fear, knowing itself to be weak and split and cracked wide open in more than five hundred thousand places. If an unstable, crazy, changeable thing has any certain home, Fortune has her dwelling there. When she wants to be honoured, she betakes herself to the golden part of her house and remains there, adorning and beautifying her body, dressing herself like a queen, in a long robe that trails behind her and is variously scented and brightly coloured, as silks and woollens can be, depending on the plants and seeds and many other things used to dye the cloths worn by all rich people who are preparing to receive honours. So Fortune disguises herself, but I tell you truly that when she sees her person attired in this way, she gives not a straw for anyone in the world but is so proud and haughty that there is no pride to be compared with hers. For when she sees her great riches, honours, and dignities, she is so exceedingly foolish as to believe that there is not a man or a woman in the world to equal her, however things may go afterwards. Then, with her wheel all flying, she goes turning through the house until she comes to the part that is dirty and ramshackle, cracked and tottering. Then she stumbles and falls to the ground as if completely blind, and, seeing herself fallen there, she changes her appearance and her dress, denuding and stripping herself to such an extent that she is bereft of clothes, so lacking in goods that she seems to have nothing of worth. When she sees this misfortune, she looks for a shameful way out, and betakes herself to a brothel, where she lies, sighing and lamenting. There she sheds floods of tears over the great honours that she has lost and the delights she enjoyed when she used to wear fine clothes. And since she is so perverse as to dishonour good men and injure them and cast them into the mire, while raising the wicked on high and giving them an abundance of dignities, honours, and power which she then steals and takes away from them when it suits her, since in fact she does not seem to know what she wants, she was blindfolded by the ancients, who knew her. Even though I have already told you of Socrates, that valiant man whom I loved very much and who so loved me that he had recourse to me in all his deeds, since I want you to be particularly mindful of this point, I can find many other examples of Fortune acting in this way, degrading and destroying the good while holding the wicked in honour. It can be quickly proved through the example of Seneca and

Nero,* on whom we will not dwell, because our subject is so lengthy; it would take me too long to tell you of Nero's deeds, cruel man that he was, of how he set fire to Rome and had the senators killed. He had indeed a heart harder than stone when he had his brother killed and when he had his mother dismembered so that he could see the place where he was conceived. According to tradition, when he saw her dismembered, he judged the beauty of her limbs (Oh God! what a cruel judge she had!), nor, the story recounts, did a single tear fall from his eye, but as he judged her limbs, he commanded that wine be brought him from his chamber and he drank for his pleasure. But he had known her before, that false man of whom I speak, and he had also possessed his sister and given himself to men. He made a martyr of his good master Seneca and made him choose the death by which he wished to die. Seeing that he could not escape, since the devil was so powerful, Seneca said: "Since there is no escape, let a bath be heated and let me bleed to death there in the warm water until I give up my gay and joyful spirit to God who made it, and may he protect it from further torments." After these words, Nero had the bath prepared without delay and the good man put into it. Then, according to the text, he had him bled until he lost so much blood that he had to give up the ghost. Nero had no reason for this except that since his childhood he had been accustomed to show respect to Seneca, as a disciple does to his master. "But that should not be," he said. "Nowhere is it fitting that a man, after he has become emperor, should do reverence to another man, whether he be his master or his father." And since it irked him greatly to stand up in the presence of his master when he saw him coming, but through force of habit he could not prevent himself from showing reverence, he had the worthy man destroyed. And this false man of whom I speak ruled over the Roman empire and had in his jurisdiction the east and the south, the west and the north.

'If you can understand me correctly, you will learn by these 6221 words that neither riches nor reverence, neither dignities, honours, nor power, nor any of Fortune's favours (for I do not except a single one) have the strength to make those who possess them good or worthy to enjoy those riches, honours, and status. But if there is violence in them, or pride or any other evil, the exalted station on which they perch will show up these failings and reveal them more quickly than if they were of lowly estate, and therefore unable to do so much harm. For when they use their power, their deeds denounce their intentions, showing and signifying that they are neither good nor worthy of their riches, dignities, honours, and powers.

'There is a common saying, which is very silly, although everyone, misled by foolish reasoning, believes it to be true, that honours change manners. But these men reason falsely, for honours do not change manners, rather they offer a sign or demonstration of the manners already possessed, when they were of lowly estate, by those who have followed the paths that have brought them to honour. For if they are cruel and proud, arrogant and cunning when they have received honours, you may know that if they had had the power, they would have been the same before as you see them to be afterwards. Therefore I do not give the name of power to evil or unregulated force, for, as our text* rightly states, all power comes from good, and no one ever fails to do what is right except through some weakness or fault. The truly perceptive man sees that evil is nothing, for this is what our text says. And if you are indifferent to authority, perhaps because you are unwilling to believe that all authority is true, I am ready to find a reason. There is nothing that God cannot do, but, truth to tell, God is powerless to do evil. Now if your understanding is good and you perceive that God is all-powerful yet powerless to do evil, then you can see clearly that, if you reckon the things in existence, evil adds nothing to their number. Just as a shadow puts nothing into the darkened air except a lack of light, in the same way, evil puts nothing into the creature who lacks goodness except that very lack of goodness; it is incapable of putting in anything else. And our text, which understands the true nature of the wicked, also says, and gives powerful reasons for it, that the wicked are not men. Now I do not want to go to the trouble of proving everything I say when you can find it written down; nevertheless, if it does not bore you, I can briefly give you some of the reasons. One is that they abandon the common purpose to which everything that has being aspires and should aspire, the purpose that we call primary and that is the sovereign good. And he who understands arguments properly, fair master, will have another reason why the wicked have no being: it is that they are not part of the order in which everything that exists has placed its being, from which it can clearly be seen that the wicked have no *raison d'être*.

'See now how Fortune serves here below in this earthly 6313 desert, and how despicably she behaves, for she chose the worst of the wicked and set him above all men as lord and master of this world, thus causing Seneca to be destroyed. Her favour is certainly to be shunned, for no one, however fortunate, can be certain of it, and I therefore wish you to scorn her and to place no value on her favour. Even Claudian* used to wonder at it, and wished to reproach the gods for allowing the wicked to rise to such great honour and position, power and wealth. But as one who reasons well, he supplies the answer himself and explains the reason to us. He absolves the gods and excuses them, saying that the reason they permit this is so that, having been more seriously injured, they may more cruelly torment the wicked afterwards. Wicked men are raised on high so that afterwards they may be seen to fall from a greater height.

'If you do me the service that I here enjoin and describe, 6341 you will never find any man richer than you, and you will never be distressed, however much you may suffer in body or in the loss of friends or wealth. Instead you will desire patience, and you will have it as soon as you decide to be my friend. Why then do you remain in sadness? I often see you weeping like an alembic on an aludel.* You should be dipped into a dirty puddle like an old rag. Certainly if anyone called you a man I would think him very deceitful. For no man, provided he used his reason, was ever sad or sorrowful. The living devils, the fiends, have heated the furnace that makes your eyes run with tears, but if you had any understanding, nothing that happened to you could have dismayed you. This

is the work of the god who has brought you to this; it is
Love, your good master and your good friend, who blows
and fans the coals that he has put in your heart and makes
your eyes shed tears. He would sell you his friendship dearly,
for it is unseemly for a man renowned for sense and prowess
to weep. Certainly you damage your reputation thereby.
Leave weeping to women and children, who are weak and
inconstant creatures; you must be strong and firm when you
see Fortune coming. Do you want to hold back her wheel?
It cannot be held back, either by the great or by the lowly.
Nero himself, that great emperor whose example I have cited,
whose empire stretched so far that he was lord of all the
world, could never stop it in spite of all the honours he
gained. For if the tale does not lie, he died an evil death,
hated by all his people and fearful that they would attack him.
He summoned his close friends, but the messengers he sent
never found any of them who would open their doors, whatever they said. Then Nero came, afraid and in secret, and
knocked with his own hands, at which they did not more
but less, for the more he called each of them, the more they
shut themselves away and hid themselves, and no one was
willing to answer him a single word. Then he had to go and
hide, and he took refuge with two of his slaves in a garden,
for there were already many people rushing around looking
for him to kill him and crying "Nero! Nero! Who has seen
him? Where shall we find him?" so that, even though he
heard them clearly, he could not do anything about it. He
was so greatly astonished that he began to hate himself, and,
perceiving that he had reached a point where there was no
more hope, he begged his slaves to kill him or to help him
kill himself. And so he killed himself, but first he asked that
no one should find his head, so that it should not be recognized if his body was seen afterwards, and he begged them
to burn the body as soon as they could. And according to the
old book entitled *The Twelve Caesars*, where we find the
account of his death as Suetonius* wrote it down (he who
calls Christianity a false, new, and evil religion: so he calls it,
using the words of a faithless man!), the line of the Caesars
ended with Nero. By his deeds he achieved the obliteration

of his entire lineage. Nevertheless, during his first five years he was so much in the habit of doing right that you would never have found a prince who governed his land so well as he, so valiant and merciful did he seem, this false and cruel man. And he was not ashamed to say publicly in Rome, when in order to condemn a man he was required to write his death sentence, that he would rather not know how to write than set his hand to write it. The book tells us that he ruled the empire for around seventeen years and lived for thirty-two years. But pride and cruelty so overcame him that he fell, as you have heard me relate, from a great height to a great depth. And, as you may hear and understand, it was Fortune, who had raised him so high, who afterwards brought him so low.

'Nor could Croesus prevent Fortune's wheel from spinning 6459 him up and down. He again was king of all Lydia,* but then a bridle was put on his neck and he was given up to be burned in the fire. At that point he was saved by the rain, which put out the great fire, and no one dared remain there, but all fled because of the rain. When Croesus saw that he was alone there, he immediately took flight and was neither hindered nor pursued. Later he became lord of his land once again, started a new war, was captured again and then hanged. This was the fulfilment of the dream of two gods who appeared to him and served him, high up in a tree. It is said that Jupiter washed him, while Phoebus held the towel and dried him with care. It was unfortunate for him that he chose to rely upon that dream, for it gave him so much confidence that he became foolishly proud. His daughter Phania, who was so wise and clever that she could interpret dreams, spoke sensibly to him and answered him without flattery. "Fair father," said the girl, "this is sad news. Your pride is not worth a shell, and you should understand that Fortune is making a fool of you. You may learn from this dream that she wants to have you hanged on a gibbet, and when you are hanging there in the wind, without covering or shelter, the rain will fall upon you, fair lord and king, and the radiant sun will dry your body and face with its rays. Fortune is driving you to this destiny, she who bestows honours and takes them away, and

often brings great men low while exalting the lowly and
giving them lordship over lords. Why should I flatter you?
Fortune awaits you at the gibbet, and when she has you there
with a noose about your neck, she will take back the fair
golden crown with which she crowned your head, and another, who has escaped your notice, will be crowned with it.

6511   ' "To explain the matter more clearly, Jupiter, who gave
you the water, is the air that rains and thunders, and Phoebus,
who held the towel, is undoubtedly the sun. I interpret the
tree as the gibbet, for I cannot understand anything else by
it. You will have to cross that bridge, for it is thus that
Fortune avenges the people for your arrogant behaviour and
insane pride. And so she destroys many worthy men, for she
does not give a fig for treachery or loyalty, lowly estate or
royalty, and flings wealth, honour, and reverence about in
great confusion, like a silly, foolish girl tossing a ball about.
She bestows dignities and powers but does not care whom
she gives them to, and when she distributes her favours she
so spreads them about that she casts them over dirty pools
and meadows like so much dust. She considers nothing worth
a ball except for her daughter Nobility, who is a cousin and
close relative of Chance, for Fortune keeps her in great
uncertainty. But it is certainly true that, whatever the prospect of taking her back, Fortune will not give her to anyone
who cannot refine his heart sufficiently to become courteous,
brave, and valiant. For however fine a fighter a man may be,
any inclination towards baseness will cause Nobility to abandon him.

6549   ' "Nobility is noble, that is why I love her, for she will not
enter any base heart. Therefore, dearest father, I beg you not
to let any baseness appear in you. Do not be proud or
avaricious, but in order to set an example to the rich, let your
heart be generous, courteous, noble, and compassionate towards the poor. That is how every king should be: his heart
should be generous, courteous, gracious, and full of compassion, if he seeks the people's friendship, without which no
king can ever do more than an ordinary man."

6563   'Thus Phania admonished him, but the fool sees nothing
in his folly but sense and reason combined: this is how his

foolish heart perceives it. Croesus, who would not humble himself and was full of pride and folly, imagined that all his deeds were wise, however great the excesses he committed. "Daughter," he said, "do not give me lessons in courtesy or sense; I know more about them than you, who have so admonished me. And in thus explaining my dream in your foolish reply, you have told me a great falsehood, for you should understand that this noble dream on which you would put a false gloss ought to be understood literally, and I myself understand it in this way, as we shall see in due course. Never was so noble a vision so atrociously explained. Know that all the gods are so much my friends that they will come to me and render me the service that they have conveyed in this dream, for I have well deserved it for a long time." See how Fortune served him, for he was quite unable to prevent her from having him hanged on the gibbet. Is it not then possible to prove that her wheel is unstoppable, since no one can hold it back, however exalted the station to which he attains? And if you know anything of logic, which is a genuine science, you will know that since great lords fail to stop it, the lowly will strive in vain. And if you attach no value to proofs taken from ancient history, you have new ones from your own time in fine and recent battles (for you should know that they were as fine as battles could be). I speak of Manfred, king of Sicily,* who, through his strength and cunning, had preserved the peace of his land for a long time when war was declared upon him by Charles, the good count of Anjou and Provence, who is now, by divine providence, king of Sicily, this being the will of the true God, who has always supported him. This good King Charles took from Manfred not only his lordship but also the life of his body. When, bearing his keen-edged sword and astride his grey war-horse he assailed and vanquished him in the front rank of the army, he declared him checkmated by the move of an errant pawn in the middle of the chess-board. I have no wish to mention Manfred's nephew Conradin, an apt example, whose head King Charles cut off in spite of the German princes, while putting Henry, brother of the king of Spain and full of pride and treachery, in prison to die. These two, like foolish boys, lost rooks and bishops, pawns and knights in the game and jumped up from the chess-board, terrified of being captured in the game they had undertaken. For, truth to tell, they had no need to fear being mated; since they fought without a king they were not afraid of check or mate, and no one who played chess against them, whether on foot or on horseback, could checkmate them, because you cannot checkmate pawns, bishops, knights, queens, or rooks. If I dare tell the truth without seeking to deceive anyone, as far as checkmating is concerned, according to my memory of chess and if you know anything about it, only a king can be checkmated, when all his men are taken and he sees that he is alone in that place. He sees nothing there to cheer him, but flees instead from the enemies who have reduced him to such poverty. Everyone, generous and miserly alike, knows that no other man can be checkmated, for this was the wish of Athalus, who invented the rules of chess in his treatise on arithmetic. And you will see in the *Polycraticus** that he digressed from his subject, for he should have been writing about numbers, when he discovered this excellent and enjoyable game, which he tested by demonstration.

6669   'Therefore Henry and Conradin took flight, to avoid the distress of being captured. Why do I say to avoid capture? It was rather to avoid death, which could have hurt them more and would have been worse. For the game was going badly, at least on their side, which had forsaken God and was waging war in opposition to the faith of Holy Church. If anyone had said "check" to them, there would have been none to protect them, for the queen had been captured in the first attack of the game, when the foolish king lost rooks, knights, pawns, and bishops. She was not present there herself but, wretched and grieving, she could neither flee nor defend herself, because she had been told that Manfred lay fallen and slain, his head, feet, and hands all cold. And when this good king heard that they had taken flight, he captured them both as they fled, and then did as he wished with them and with many other prisoners, their accomplices in folly.

6697   'This valiant king of whom I speak, who was usually known as "count" (may God protect and defend and counsel him and all his heirs night and day, morning and evening, body and soul), this king subdued the pride of Marseilles and cut off the heads of the greatest men of the town before being given the kingdom of Sicily, whose crowned king he now is and vicar of the whole empire. But I do not want to say any more about him, for it would take a great book to recount all his deeds.

'These are men who held great honours, and you now 6711 know the end they came to. Fortune, then, is unsure. Is it not foolish to place one's confidence in her when she could thus anoint men's foreheads and then stab them in the back? And you, who kissed the rose and bear as a result so great a burden of suffering that you can find no relief, did you imagine that you would always be kissing, always enjoying comfort and delights? By my head, you are foolish and silly! But in order that that god should no longer have you in his power, I would like you to remember Manfred, Henry, and Conradin, whose action in starting a bitter battle against their holy mother Church was worse than that of Saracens. Remember also the deeds of the Marseillais and of the great men of antiquity such as Nero and Croesus of whom I have already told you and who, with all the great power they had, could not restrain Fortune. The free man, therefore, who values himself so highly that he takes pride in his freedom, does not know when it was that King Croesus entered into his bondage, nor, as far as I know, does he remember the stories of Hecuba,* wife of King Priam, or of Sisigambis,* mother of Darius the king of Persia, to both of whom Fortune was so unkind that although they enjoyed liberty and ruled over kingdoms, in the end they became slaves.

'Moreover, I consider it most shameful that, knowing as 6747 you do the importance of education and the necessity of study, and having studied Homer, you should not remember him; but it seems that you have forgotten him. Is this not vain and futile exertion? You study books and then forget everything through your negligence. What is the use of all your study if, entirely through your own fault, the meaning of it fails you when you need it? Indeed, you should always be mindful of Homer's opinion, as should every wise man, and it should be so fixed in their hearts as never to escape until death overtakes them. For if a man understood this opinion and always kept it in his heart and knew how to evaluate it properly, nothing that befell him could ever disturb him, and he would always stand firm, whatever happened, good or bad, mild or harsh. And indeed, to judge from Fortune's works, this opinion is of such general application that anyone possessed of a good understanding can see it every day. It is amazing that you, who have taken such trouble over it, do not understand it; but in your intemperate love you have directed your attention elsewhere. Therefore I would like to remind you of it, so that you will understand it better.

6783 'Homer tells us* that Jupiter always keeps two full casks on the threshold of his house, and that no one who receives life in this world, be he old man or boy, woman or girl, old or young, ugly or beautiful, fails to drink from those casks. It is a crowded tavern kept by Fortune, who draws cups of absinthe and spiced wine to make sops for everyone. With her own hands she gives them all to drink, but some receive more, others less. There is no one who does not drink a quart or a pint from these casks each day, or a hogshead or a pail or a mug, just as the girl pleases, or a palmful, or a few drops that Fortune drips into his mouth, for she pours out good and evil for everyone, according as she is gentle or unkind. No one will ever be so happy that, on careful reflection, he does not find something in his greatest comfort that displeases him; and no one will ever suffer such misfortune that, on careful reflection, he does not find something in his distress to comfort him, whether it be something he has done or something he has to do, that is if he considers his situation properly and does not fall into the despair that does harm to sinners, and for which no man can find a remedy, however deeply he may have read and studied. What use is it, then, to grow angry, to weep or to complain? Take courage and go forward to receive in patience whatever Fortune may give you, fair or ugly, bad or good.

6825 'I could not tell you of all the tricks of deceitful Fortune and her perilous wheel. It is the three-card trick,* and Fortune can arrange it in such a way that no one when he begins can know clearly whether he will win or lose. But now I shall say no more about her, except to return briefly to her once more because of three honest requests that I make of you, for the mouth is glad to explain the things that come near to our hearts. If you choose to refuse these requests, then nothing can excuse you from serious blame; they are that you should love me, spurn the God of Love, and attach no value to Fortune.

'If you are too weak to endure this triple burden, I am 6845 ready to lighten it, so that you may carry it more easily. Fulfil just the first request, and if you understand me properly, you will be freed from the other two. For unless you are mad or drunk, you must know, and I remind you of it, that whoever is at one with Reason will never love *par amour*, nor value Fortune. Thus Socrates was of such a kind as to be my true friend. He never feared the God of Love, nor was he moved by Fortune. I wish, therefore, that you would be like him and bring your whole heart into conformity with mine; if you have planted your heart in mine, that will be amply sufficient for me. Now you see how the matter stands: I only make one request of you. Fulfil the first request I make and I shall release you from the others. Now do not keep your mouth closed any longer. Answer me! Will you do this thing?'

'Lady,' I said, 'only one answer is possible. I must serve my 6871 master, who will make me much richer, a hundred thousand times as much, if it pleases him, for he must grant me the rose if I strive hard enough for it. If through him I may have the rose, I would not need any other possession. I would not give three chick-peas for Socrates, however rich he was, and I have no wish to hear any more about him. I must return to my master, and I wish to keep my covenant with him, because it is right and pleasing to do so. Were it to lead me to hell, I could not restrain my heart. My heart? It is no longer mine. I have not yet altered my will for the love of anyone else, nor do I desire to do so. I left my heart entirely to Fair Welcome (for I know all my legacy by heart), and then I made my impetuous and unrepentant confession.* Not for anything would I be willing to exchange that rose for you, and it is right that that should be the direction of my thoughts. Also, I do not think it was courteous of you to pronounce the word "testicles": no well-bred girl should call them by their name. I do not know how you dared name them, you who are so wise and fair, without at least glossing the word with some courteous utterance, as a virtuous woman would when speaking of them. I often see even nurses, many of whom are bawdy and ignorant, who when they hold and bathe their charges, fondling and caressing them, use other names for those parts. You know very well whether or not I am lying.'

6913   Then Reason began to smile, and said to me as she smiled: 'Fair friend, I may certainly and without harming my reputation name openly and by its proper name anything which is good. Indeed, I may safely speak in the correct terms about evil, for I am not ashamed of anything that is not sinful. But there is nothing that could make me do anything involving sin, for I never sinned in my life. And it is not sinful of me to name, in plain and unglossed language, the noble things that my heavenly father formerly made with his own hands, together with all the other instruments, the pillars and arguments by which human nature is sustained and without which it would now be empty and decayed. For it was by his own will rather than against it that God in his wonderful purpose put the generative power into the testicles and penis, in order that the race would live forever, renewed by new births. It is through a birth that is perishable and a loss that leads to rebirth that God made it live so long that it cannot suffer death. He did the same for the dumb beasts, who are thus sustained in their turn, for when animals die, their form remains in other animals.'

'Now that is worse than before,' I said, 'for I now see clearly by your bawdy talk that you are a foolish and loose woman; even though God may have made the things you have just told me about, at least he did not make the words, which are altogether vile.'

'Fair friend,' said wise Reason, 'folly is not courage; it never was and it never will be. You may say whatever you like, for you have plenty of time and space to do so, and you need not fear me, who desire your love and your favour, for I am ready to listen and endure and keep silence, however much you set yourself to abuse me, provided you do no worse. By my faith, it seems that you want me to give you a foolish answer, but I shall not do so. I, who rebuke you for your own good, am not so much like you that I would embark on anything so base as slander or quarrelling, for it is true (do not take offence) that quarrelling is evil vengeance, and you ought to know that slander is even worse. If I wanted vengeance, I would avenge myself quite differently, for if you do or say anything wrong, I can correct you in secret, by my actions or my words, in order to rebuke and teach you without blaming or slandering you. Or if you did not want to believe my words that were good and true, I could avenge myself differently by appealing at the appropriate time to the judge, who would decide in my favour, or I could take some other honourable vengeance in some reasonable way. I have no wish to quarrel with people nor by my words to harm or slander anyone, whoever it may be, bad or good. Let everyone bear his own burden, and confess it if he wishes, but not otherwise: I shall not press him to do so. I have no desire to do anything foolish if I can help it, and I shall not even say anything foolish. To remain silent is a small virtue, but to say things that should not be said is a most diabolical deed.

'The tongue should be kept in check, for we read a most 7007 excellent remark of Ptolemy's at the beginning of his *Almagest*:* that the wise man makes an effort to curb his tongue except when he is talking about God. One cannot talk too much about that, for no one can praise God too much or acknowledge him too frequently as lord, no one can fear or obey him, love or bless him, implore his mercy or thank him too much. No one can give too much attention to this, for all those who receive his favours should call on him continually. Those who remember Cato's book* will know that he himself agrees with this. There you will find it written that the prime virtue is to curb one's tongue. Subdue your own, therefore, and refrain from saying foolish and outrageous things; in this way you will be acting virtuously and wisely, for it is right to believe the pagans, since we may obtain great benefits from their remarks.

7033   'But I can say one thing to you without hatred or anger, blame or provocation (for it is foolish to provoke people). I do not wish to offend or displease you, but you have behaved very badly towards me, who love you and bring you comfort, in so losing your temper as to call me a loose and foolish woman and to insult me without justification. My father, God, king of the angels, courteous and free from baseness, source of all courtesy, brought me up and educated me and does not consider me to be badly taught. On the contrary, it was he who taught me this habit, and it is by his will that I am accustomed to call things by their names when I want to, without glossing them.

'And when in your turn you wish to raise an objection and require me to supply a gloss—raise an objection do I say?—rather you do in fact object that although God made things, at least he did not make their names—this is my reply: perhaps he did not, or at least not the names they now have (although he could certainly name them when he first created the whole world and everything in it), but he wanted me to find proper and common names for them as it pleased me, in order to increase our understanding, and he gave me speech, a most precious gift. And you may find authority for what I have told you, for Plato taught in his school that speech was given to us to make our wishes understood, to teach, and to learn. You will find this idea, here expressed in verse, in the *Timaeus* of Plato,* who was not stupid. And if you object on the other hand that the words are ugly and base, I tell you before God who hears me that if, when I gave things the names that you dare find fault with and condemn, I had called testicles relics and relics testicles, then you who thus attack and reproach me would tell me instead that relics was an ugly, base word. "Testicles" is a good name and I like it and so, in faith, are "testes" and "penis"; none more beautiful have ever been seen. I made the words and I am certain that I never made anything base, and God, who is wise and sure, considers whatever I made to be well made. By the body of Saint Omer, how could I not dare to give their proper names to my father's works? Ought I to compete with him? They had to have names, or men would not have been able to name them, and therefore we gave them names, so that they might be called by those very names. If women do not name them in France, it is only because they are not accustomed to do so, for they would have liked the proper name had it been made familiar to them, and in giving them their proper name they would certainly have committed no sin.

'Habit is very powerful, and if I am any judge, many things 7107 that offend when they are new become beautiful through habit. The women who name them call them all sorts of things: purses, harness, things, torches, pricks, as though they were thorns, but when they feel them very near they do not find them painful. Now they may call them whatever is usual if they do not want to give them their proper names; I shall not make an issue of it. But let none of them force me into anything when I want to say something openly and call things by their proper names.

'Certainly in our schools many things are expressed in 7123 figurative language which is very fair to hear, and not everything one hears should be taken literally. My words, at least when I spoke of testicles, which I wished to mention briefly, had a different meaning from the one you want to give them, and anyone who understood the text properly would find a meaning in it which would clarify the obscure discourse. The truth concealed within would be clear if it were explained; you will certainly understand it if you recall to mind the integuments on the poets.* You will find there a great number of the secrets of philosophy, in which you will gladly take delight and from which you will also be able to gain great benefit: you will profit from your enjoyment and enjoy what is profitable, for there are most profitable delights in the entertaining fables of the poets who thus covered their thoughts when they clothed the truth in fables. This is how you should approach the matter if you want to understand my words properly.

'But afterwards I gave you two words which you well 7151 understood and which must be taken literally and exactly, without any gloss.'

'Lady, I understand them well, for they are so readily intelligble that no one who knew French could fail to understand them; further clarification is unnecessary. But my aim is not to gloss the ideas, fables, and metaphors of the poets. If I can be saved, and recompensed for the service for which I expect so great a reward, I will certainly gloss them in time, at least so far as is appropriate, so that everyone will understand them clearly. And so I consider you well excused for the expression you used and for the two words you pronounced earlier, for you use them so appropriately that I do not need to delay any longer over them nor waste my time in glossing. But in God's name I beg you: do not reproach me any more for loving. If I am mad, then it is my loss, but at least, as I believe for certain, I acted wisely then in doing homage to my master. And if I am mad, do not let it concern you; whatever happens, I will love the rose to which I am vowed, and my heart will never receive another. If I promised you my love, I would certainly not keep my promise; thus I would either deceive you or, if I kept my word to you, I would rob my master. But I have often told you that I have no wish to think about anything except the rose on which my thoughts are concentrated, and when you make me think about something else with the words you utter here, words that I am quite weary of hearing, you will see me flee from here unless you are silent at once, for my heart is bestowed elsewhere.' When Reason heard me, she returned to her tower, leaving me sad and pensive.

CHAPTER 5

THE ADVICE OF FRIEND

Then I remembered Friend: now I had to call on all my 7201
strength, for I wanted to go to him, however difficult it might
prove. And there he was, sent by God, and when he saw me
in this state, my heart pierced with such grief, he said: 'What
is this, fair, sweet friend, what has brought you to this torment? As soon as I saw you so downcast I knew that some
misfortune had befallen you. But now tell me your news.'

'So help me God, it is neither good nor fair.'

'Tell me everything.'

And I told him, just as you have heard it in this tale. (I will
not repeat it for you.)

'You see,' he said, 'by God's sweet body, you have pacified
Rebuff and kissed the rose-bud: you have no reason to be
worried by the capture of Fair Welcome. Since he has gone
so far as to grant you a kiss, then prison will never hold him,
but you will certainly have to behave more discreetly if you
want to succeed. Take comfort, for you may be sure that he
will be rescued from the prison into which he has been cast
for your sake.'

'Oh! the enemy is too strong, even if Evil Tongue were
the only one. It is he who wounds me nearest the heart and
who egged the others on. I would never have been found
out if the wretch had not spread it abroad. Fear and Shame
would most gladly have hidden me, and even Rebuff had
stopped insulting me. All three were very quiet when the
devils arrived, mustered by that wretch. Anyone would have
been filled with pity at the sight of Fair Welcome trembling when Jealousy shouted at him, for that old woman had
a most evil voice. I fled without delay and then they built
the castle in which the gentle fellow is imprisoned. Therefore,
Friend, I ask your advice, for I am dead unless you can find
a remedy.'

Then Friend said, like one well taught, for he had learned 7251
much concerning love: 'My friend, do not be discouraged,

but take your pleasure in true love and serve the God of Love night and day, loyally and ceaselessly. Do not be false to him, for it would be a very grave act of treachery if he found that you had renounced his service; he would consider himself greatly deceived in having received you as his man, for no loyal heart ever deceived him. Do whatever he charged you to do and keep all his commandments, for no man who keeps them well will ever fail in his purpose, however long it takes, unless, as Fortune may decree, some adversity befall him from another quarter. Concentrate on serving the God of Love and think only of him, for such thoughts are sweet and lovely. Therefore it would be extremely foolish to abandon him, since he has not abandoned you. Nevertheless, he has you on a leash, and because of this you must submit to him, since you cannot abandon him.

7277   'Now I will tell you what you must do. You must wait a while before going to see the fortress. Although you do not want to do this, avoid playing or sitting by the walls or in front of the door, do not be heard or seen there, or at least not as often as you are accustomed to, until this storm has completely subsided. And if by chance you do go there, whatever happens, pretend that you do not care about Fair Welcome. And if you see him from afar at a crenel or a window, gaze at him piteously but do it very secretly. If, for his part, he sees you, he will be glad, and his guards will not stop him from looking, but he will not show it in his face or expression, unless perhaps by stealth. Or perhaps, when he hears you talking to people, he will close his window and spy through the crack as long as you remain there and until you turn away, unless someone prevents him from doing so.

'At any rate, take care that Evil Tongue does not see you. If he does see you, then greet him, but be careful not to change colour or to give any sign of hatred or bitterness, and if you encounter him anywhere else, do not show him any animosity. The wise man conceals his dislike, and you may be sure that those who deceive the deceivers do well, and that all lovers, at least the wise ones, should do so. I advise you to serve and honour Evil Tongue and all his kin, even though they would destroy you. Make a great pretence of offering them everything, heart and body, possessions and service. "Craft against cunning", as it is said, and I believe it to be true. It is no sin to deceive those who are tainted with deceit. Evil Tongue is a trickster; take away the tricks and you are left with a thief. He is a thief, you may be quite sure, and you can clearly see that he should have no other name, since he robs men of their good reputation and never has the power to restore it. It would be better to hang him than all those other thieves who steal piles of money. If a thief is caught in the act of stealing money, or a robe from its pole, or grain from the granary, he is liable for at least four times the amount of his theft, according to the written laws. But Evil Tongue commits a most serious crime with his filthy, mean, and spiteful tongue, for once he has spoken slander with his ill-famed mouth, he cannot undo it, nor stifle a single word that his gossip has provoked.

'It is good to appease Evil Tongue, for men are often 7347 accustomed to kiss the hand that they would like to see burned. Would that the wretch was now in Tarsus; he could gossip there as much as he wanted, provided that he took nothing from lovers. It is good to stop the mouth of Evil Tongue, so that he utters no accusations or reproaches. Evil Tongue and all his family (and may God not preserve them) should be deceived and defrauded; they should be served and complimented, praised and flattered with insincere adulation and sham pretences; they should be bowed to and greeted, for it is quite right to pet the dog until one has got past it. His gossiping would be silenced if he could at least get the impression that you have no desire to steal the bud that he has made safe from you, and in this way you might get the better of him.

'As for the Old Woman who guards Fair Welcome (may 7369 she burn in hell!), treat her in the same way. And do the same with Jealousy (may Our Lord curse her!), that fierce, tormented creature who is always enraged by the joy of others and who is so cruel and greedy that she wants to keep something all for herself, although she would not find it diminished if she let everyone take a share. It is very foolish to hoard such a thing, for it is the candle in the lantern, and if you gave its light to a thousand people, you would not find its flame smaller. Everyone whose mind is not completely untutored is familiar with this image. If these two have need of you, serve them to the best of your ability; you should show them courtesy, for courtesy is very highly prized, provided that they do not perceive that you wish to deceive them. This is how you should behave; you should take your enemy to be hanged or drowned with your arms around his neck, with blandishments and caresses, if there is no other way to succeed. But I can swear and guarantee that there is no other solution in this case, for they are so powerful that anyone who attacked them openly would fail, I believe, in his purpose.

7401   'Afterwards, when you come to the other gatekeepers, if you ever get there, you must behave as follows. In order to appease them, and if you have the means to do so without ruining yourself, give them such gifts as you now hear me describe: chaplets of flowers on wicker frames, purses or hair-ornaments, or other pretty, charming, elegant little trinkets. Then lament the evils and toil and suffering that Love, who brings you there, has caused you. And if you have nothing to give, you should make promises. Do not delay but make great promises, whether or not you can keep them; swear vigorously and pledge your word rather than go away defeated; beg them to help you. And if your eyes should shed tears in their presence, that will be very much to your advantage: it will be very sensible of you to weep. Kneel down before them in that place with your hands joined, and let your eyes fill with hot tears that run down your face, so that they can clearly see them fall: it is a most piteous sight, and tears are not scorned, especially by men of pity.

7433   'And if you cannot weep, go secretly and without delay and take some of your saliva or squeeze the juice of onions or garlic or many other juices and anoint your eyelids with it; if you do this you will weep as often as you like. Thus has many a deceiver behaved who later became a true lover and whom the ladies allowed to hang in the noose he wanted to prepare for them until they had mercy on him and removed the rope from his neck. And many have used such tricks to weep who never loved *par amour* but deceived maidens with their tears and lying words. Tears will draw the hearts of such people, provided only that they see no deceit in them. But if they knew your deceit, they would never have mercy on you; it would be of no use to cry for mercy, for they would never let you in. And if you cannot go to them, send a suitable messenger to speak to them by voice or letter or tablets, but never set down your real name, and let the man always be called a lady and the lady a man in her turn; in this way the affair will be very well hidden. Let him be a lady and her a lord, and write your messages in this way, for many a thief has deceived many a lover by reading what he has written: the lovers are accused by them and the pleasures of love banished. But never trust children, for you would be tricked: they are not good messengers, for children always want to run wild and gossip or show what they are carrying to the traitors who egg them on; or else they deliver the message stupidly because they are not sensible. Everything would immediately be made public if they were not very clever.

'It is certain that these gatekeepers have such compassionate 7481 natures that if they deign to receive your gifts they will not wish to deceive you. You may be sure that you yourself will be received after the gifts you make: once they have accepted them, the thing is done. For just as the noble hawk is trained by the lure to come to the hand night and day, in the same way the gatekeepers are influenced by gifts to show mercy and favour to true lovers; all are conquered by them.

'And should you happen to find them so proud that you 7495 are unable to soften them by gifts or prayers or tears or in any other way, and they repel you with harsh actions and insolent words and insult you cruelly, take your departure courteously and leave them in their grease: no autumn cheese ever matured better than they will. As a result of your flight they will often learn to pursue you, which could be greatly to your advantage.

'Base hearts are so harsh towards those who love them best that the more they beg, the less they are valued and the more they serve, the more they are despised. But when men abandon them, their pride is soon humbled. Now they love those

whom they despised; now they are subdued and calm, for it
is not pleasant for them when people leave them, but extremely unpleasant. Although the mariner who sails upon the
sea in search of many unexplored lands may keep his eye upon
a single star, he does not always rely on one sail, but changes
it often in order to avoid storms or wind. In the same way,
a heart that loves ceaselessly does not always succeed in a
single sprint; he who wishes to enjoy true love must sometimes chase and sometimes flee.

7529   'Moreover, it is quite clear (and I shall not supply you with
a gloss, for you may trust the text) that it is good to entreat
these three gatekeepers, for, however arrogant they may be,
no one who applies himself to prayer can lose anything, and
he may gain a lot of ground. He may safely entreat them,
because it is certain that he will either be refused entry or
admitted, so he can scarcely be deceived. Those who are
refused lose nothing except the time they have wasted, and
the gatekeepers will not be angry with those who have entreated them but will be pleased, even when they have rejected them, for there is none so cruel that he does not feel
great joy in his heart when he hears them. They think quietly
to themselves that they must be worthy and fair and agreeable
and possessed of every good quality, since such people love
them, whether they refuse the prayer or make excuses or
grant it. If the lovers' prayer is granted, then all is well, for
they have what they sought, and if they are so unfortunate
as to fail, they may depart freely and without obligation. Thus
it is scarcely possible to fail, since new delights are so
pleasant.

7561   'But they should not be in the habit of telling the gatekeepers immediately that they want to make friends with
them in order to take the flower from the rose-bush: they
should say instead that their love is loyal and true and their
thoughts pure and sincere. You may be sure that they can all
be conquered, there is no doubt about that; provided he who
entreats them does so properly, he will never be rejected, and
no one should be refused. But if you take my advice, you
will not take the trouble to plead with them unless you
achieve your goal, for perhaps if they were not vanquished

they might boast about having been entreated, but they will never boast if they are partners in the deed.

'And they are all of such a kind, however haughty their 7579 expression, that if they were not first entreated they would certainly entreat themselves and give themselves for nothing to anyone who did not treat them harshly. But those who make hasty speeches and give foolish and extravagant presents make them so very proud that they increase the price of their roses; while they expect in this way to advance their suit, they actually do serious harm, since they could have had everything for nothing if they had never made any entreaty, provided that everyone did the same and no earlier entreaty had been made. And if they wanted to sell their services, they could get a very good price, provided they all agreed that none would ever address the gatekeepers or give themselves for nothing but that instead, the better to subdue them, they would leave their roses to wither. But no man who sold his body could please me, nor should he ever please me, at least not if he did so for such a purpose. Do not delay on that account: make your entreaties and set traps to catch your prey, for you could delay so long that a dozen, or two or three or four, in fact fifty-two dozens could quickly attack within fifty-two weeks. The gatekeepers would soon have turned elsewhere if you had waited too long, and it would be difficult for you to arrive in time because of your long delay. I do not recommend that any man wait for a woman to ask for his love, for anyone who waits for a woman to ask him has too much confidence in his beauty. And anyone who wishes to begin and to advance his suit quickly should not be afraid that his lady might strike him, however proud and haughty she may be, or that his ship will not come to port, provided he behave properly. This, my friend, is how you will act when you come to the gatekeepers. But if you see that they are angry, do not make your request: spy out when they are happy, and do not entreat them when they are sad, unless their sadness is born of mad Jealousy, who might have beaten them for your sake and caused them to be assaulted by anger.

'And if you manage to take them on one side in so con- 7639 venient a place that you have no fear of intruders, and if Fair

Welcome, now captured for your sake, has escaped, then when Fair Welcome has looked as kindly on you as he can (and he knows very well how to welcome the fair), you must pluck the rose, even if you see Rebuff himself beginning to abuse you, or Shame and Fear grumbling at you. They are only pretending to be angry and putting up a weak defence, since in defending themselves they admit defeat, as it will seem to you then. Even if you see Fear tremble, Shame blush, and Rebuff shudder, or all three groan and lament, do not give a fig for that but pluck the rose by force and show that you are a man, when the place and time and season are right, for nothing could please them so well as that force, applied by one who understands it. For many people are accustomed to behave so strangely that they want to be forced to give something that they dare not give freely, and pretend that it has been stolen from them when they have allowed and wished it to be taken. And so you may be sure that they would be sad to escape by this defence; however great the joy they feigned, I am afraid that they would be so angry that they would hate you for it, however much they might have grumbled.

7677   'But if they speak clearly and you feel that they are really angry and defending themselves vigorously, you must not stretch out your hand but in all cases yield yourself captive and beg for mercy. Then wait until these three gatekeepers who so torture and torment you have gone away and Fair Welcome alone remains, who will vouchsafe you everything. This is how you should behave towards them, as a worthy, valiant, and sensible man.

'You should also pay attention to the way in which Fair Welcome looks at you: however he looks and whatever his expression, you should adapt your manner to his. If he seems venerable and mature, you also should take every care to behave in a mature way, and if he acts foolishly, act foolishly yourself. Make an effort to imitate him: wear a joyful expression if he is joyful and an angry one if he is angry; if he laughs, laugh too, and weep if he weeps. Behave in this way at all times: love what he loves, condemn what he chooses to condemn, and praise whatever he praises: his confidence in you will be far greater as a result.

'Do you imagine that a woman whose heart was worthy 7707
could love a foolish, petulant boy who mooned around at
night as if he had gone mad and sang at midnight whether
people liked it or not? She would be afraid of being censured,
despised, and slandered. Such love affairs are soon known
about, for these youths flute them in the streets, scarcely
caring who knows about them; it is a foolish woman who
gives them her heart.

'And if a wise man speaks of love to a foolish girl, he will
never turn her heart by giving her the impression that he is
wise. Do not imagine that he will achieve his aim if he
behaves sensibly. Let him make his behaviour identical with
hers, otherwise he will be shamed, for she will think that he
is a trickster, a fox, or an enchanter. The wretched girl will
soon leave him and take another, thus greatly lowering herself. She will reject the worthy man and take the worst of the
lot; there she will nurture her love and brood over it like the
she-wolf, who is so degenerate in her madness that she always
takes the worst of the wolves.

'If you can find Fair Welcome and play chess with him or 7737
dice or backgammon or other delightful games, you should
always have the worst of the game, always be the loser; in
every game you undertake, lose whatever you stake; let him
win the games and laugh and joke about your losses. Praise
all his behaviour, his dress, and his appearance and serve him
to the best of your ability. Even bring him a cushion or a
chair when he is about to sit down; your suit will prosper as
a result. If you see dirt fall on him from somewhere, remove
it at once, even if it was never there, or if his coat gets too
dirty, lift it out of the dirt for him. In short, wherever you
are, do whatever you think will please him. If you do this,
then have no fear, you will never be rejected but will achieve
your aim, just as I tell you.'

'Sweet friend, what are you saying? No man other than a 7765
false hypocrite would commit this devilry, the greatest ever
conceived. You want me to honour and serve these people
who are false and base? They are indeed base and false,
with the single exception of Fair Welcome. Is this then
your advice? It would be deadly treachery for me to serve

in order to deceive, for I can say in all truth that when I want
to spy on people, I always challenge them first. Let me at
least challenge Evil Tongue, who spies on me so much,
before I deceive him in this way; or let me ask him to calm
the storm that he has raised against me, if he wants to avoid
a beating, or to make me amends for it if he likes, unless
he wants me to exact the payment myself. At the very least
let me complain to the judge, so that he can exact retribution.'

'My friend, my friend, those who are openly at war can
seek such remedies. But Evil Tongue is too secretive; he is
not openly your enemy, for when he hates a man or woman,
he condemns and slanders them behind their backs. He is a
traitor, God shame him, and so it is right that he should be
betrayed. Fie upon the traitor I say; since he is not trust-
worthy I do not trust him. In his heart he hates people, but
smiles at them with his mouth and his teeth. I never liked
such a man; let him beware of me and me of him. It is right
that a man who practices treachery should die himself through
treachery, if there is no way of taking a different and more
honourable revenge.

7807   'And if you wish to complain about him, do you imagine
that you will thus suppress his gossip? You might not be able
to prove your case nor find competent witnesses, and if you
did have proof, he still would not keep quiet; the more you
prove, the more he will gossip, and you will lose more than
he. As a result the affair will be more widely known and your
shame increased, for a man may think that he is reducing or
avenging his shame when in fact he is increasing and intensi-
fying it. If you asked him to suppress these accusations on
pain of a beating, he would certainly not suppress them, no
by God, not if he were beaten; and so help me God it would
be no use waiting for him to make you amends. Indeed, I
would not accept reparation, even if he offered it, but would
pardon him instead. If you challenge him, I swear to you by
the saints that Fair Welcome really will be put in irons or
burned in flames or drowned in water, or else he will be
so closely imprisoned that you will perhaps never see him,
and then you will feel more grief in your heart than ever

Charlemagne did for Roland when he died at Roncevaus as
a result of Ganelon's treachery.'*

'Oh, that is not what I want! Let him go, I consign him 7837
to the devil. I would have liked to hang him for upsetting
my plans like this.'

'Do not worry about hanging him, my friend, you should
take a different revenge; that office does not belong to you
but rather to the law courts. But if you take my advice, you
will foil him with trickery.'

'My friend, I agree with your advice and will never dissent
from this agreement. Nevertheless, if you knew any skill
which might lead to the discovery of a way to capture the
castle more easily, I would be glad to learn it, if you would
teach me.'

'Yes, a fair and pleasant way, but it is of no use to poor
people.

'My friend, without my art and my teaching you could 7857
choose a much shorter way to destroy the castle and raze the
fortress to the ground at the first onslaught. Not a gate would
be held against you, but all would let themselves be taken,
for nothing could defend the fortress and no one would dare
say a word. The name of the road is Lavish Giving, and it
was established by Unrestrained Generosity, who has swallowed up many lovers there. I know that way very well, for
I emerged from it the day before yesterday and I have been
a pilgrim there for more than a winter and a summer. You
will leave Largesse on your right and turn to your left. Before
you have walked more than a bowshot's length along the
beaten track, and without wearing out your shoes in the least,
you will see the walls tremble and the towers and turrets
sway, however strong and fair they are, and all the gates will
open by themselves, better than if the people had been dead.
On that side the castle is so weak that it is harder to divide
a toasted cake into four than to knock down the walls. That
way it would soon be taken, and you would need less of an
army than Charlemagne would need to conquer Maine.

'No poor man to my knowledge can ever enter that way; 7891
no one can take a poor man there and he cannot get there
by himself. But if anyone did take him there, he would then

know the way as well as I, however well I had been taught, and you shall know it if you wish, for you will soon have learned it, provided only that you have great wealth and can spend excessive amounts. But I shall not take you there, for Poverty has forbidden me the path; she prohibited it when I left that road. I spent all that I had there and all that I received from others; I deceived all my creditors and could not repay any of them if I were to be hanged or drowned for it. "Do not ever come here," she said, "since you have nothing to spend." '

7913   'You will find it very difficult to enter there if Wealth does not take you; but all those whom she escorts there are refused her escort on the return journey. She will stay close to you on your way there but will never bring you back; and you may be sure of this: if by any chance you do enter the road, you will never leave it, morning or night, unless Poverty intervenes, who has caused distress to many. Unrestrained Generosity dwells in that road, and thinks of nothing but playing and spending excessively, for she spends her money as if she found it in granaries, without counting or reckoning, for as long as it lasts.

7931   'Poverty lives at the other end, full of shame and misery; she endures great torments in her heart, for she makes many shameful requests and receives many harsh refusals. Neither her actions nor her words are good or agreeable or pleasant, and she will never do anything well enough to prevent everyone from condemning her handiwork. Everyone treats her with scorn and contempt. But do not worry about Poverty, except to think how you can avoid her whatever happens. Nothing can hurt a man so much as the descent into poverty; debtors who have spent all they have know this well, and many have been hanged by her. Those who have become beggars against their will also know this well and say it; they have to suffer much pain before people will give them anything. And those who want to find joy in love also know it, for as Ovid* affirms, the poor man has nothing with which to feed his love.

7957   'Poverty makes a man despised and hated and his life a martyrdom; she even robs people of their sanity. For God's sake, my friend, keep away from her and strive to believe my true and tested words, for you know, everything that I am preaching to you is what I have gone through myself and discovered through my own personal experience. And therefore, fair companion, through my own suffering and shame I understand the meaning of Poverty better than you, who have not suffered it so much. You should trust me, then, for I am telling you this in order to instruct you. The man who accepts instruction from another leads a very blessed life.

'I was accustomed to be called a worthy man, beloved of 7975 all my companions, and I was happy to spend money more than generously everywhere, so much so that I was considered a rich man. But now, through the prodigality of Unrestrained Generosity, who has placed me in this wretched situation, I have become so poor that I have not, except with great difficulty, the means to eat or drink, to buy shoes or clothes; such is the extent to which Poverty, who steals away all one's friends, has subdued and mastered me. And I tell you, my friend, that as soon as Fortune had done this to me I lost all my friends except one, who, as I truly believe, was the only one who remained to me. Fortune thus stole them from me through Poverty, who came with her. Stole? No, by my faith, I lie, but rather took back her own things, for I know for certain that if they had been mine, they would not have left me for her. Therefore she did me no wrong when she took back her own friends; hers indeed, but I knew nothing of that, for I had so used up my heart and body and possessions in order to buy them, and thought I had them all, that in the end I had nothing worth a penny. And when all these friends realized that I had come to this, they all left me and mocked me, seeing me cast down on my back beneath the wheel of Fortune, who had thus struck me down through Poverty.

'But I must not complain about it, for she has done me a 8013 greater courtesy than I ever deserved from her; she anointed my eyes with a fine ointment that she made and prepared for me when Poverty came and took away more than twenty of my friends, more than four hundred and fifty indeed, and that is no lie, and I saw so clearly round about me that the eyes of a lynx, if he had used them, would not have seen what I saw. For straightaway and on the spot Fortune showed me through Poverty the true love, fully disclosed, of my good friend who came to meet me, and whom I would never have known if he had not seen my need. But when he knew it he ran to me and gave me all the help he could and offered me all he had because he knew my need. "My friend," he said, "I tell you, here is my body and here are my goods, which are as much yours as mine. Take them without asking permission."

' "But how much?"

' "If you do not know, take everything if you need it, for a friend cares not a fig for the gifts of Fortune in comparison with his friend. Since we have seen each other so much that we have come to know one another well and have joined our hearts together (thus we tested each other and found that we were good friends, for no one knows without such testing whether he can find a loyal friend), I will always reserve even my natural goods as yours by right, such is the power of love's bonds. For," he said, "if it will save you, you may put me in prison as a guarantee or a hostage and sell my goods and offer them as security." Nor did he stop there, lest he might seem to be deceiving me, but forced me to take from him, since I did not want to stretch out my hand. I was quite overwhelmed with shame, like the poor wretch whose shame has so closed his lips that he dare not speak of his pain but suffers and shuts himself away in hiding so that no one will know of his poverty, and puts up the best possible show: that is how I behaved then.

8069 'This is not, I remind you, the way those beggars behave who are able-bodied and intrude everywhere with gentle, flattering words, displaying their ugliest features to everyone who encounters them, and concealing what is fair within in order to trick those who give to them; these say that they are poor but they have ample rations and large stores of money. But I shall say no more about them, for I could say so much that things would get worse and worse for me, for hypocrites always hate the truth when it is uttered against them.

'Thus my foolish heart strove to win the friends I have 8085
mentioned, and thus, for no other cause or reason than the
loss of which I have spoken, am I betrayed by my weak mind
and scorned, slandered, and hated by everyone together, except for you alone. You have not lost your love, but remain
and always will remain attached to my heart, God willing; so
I believe, who have not ceased to love you. But though,
when the last day comes and Death claims his rights in our
bodies, you will lose me, or rather my bodily companionship
in this earthly life (for that day, I remind you, will only rob
us of our bodies and all the appurtenances of bodily substances); though I know that we shall both die, and perhaps
sooner than we wish, for Death separates all companions and
perhaps we shall not die together, nevertheless I know for
certain that if true love does not lie, I would always live in
your heart if you lived and I died. And if you died before
me, you would continue to live in my heart after your death,
through memory, just as, according to the story, Pirithous,
whom Theseus loved so much, lived on after his death. For
he lived on in Theseus' heart, and Theseus had loved him so
well while he lived on earth that after his death he sought
him and pursued him so much that he even went alive into
the underworld to look for him.* And Poverty is worse than
death, for she torments and gnaws at soul and body, not just
for an hour but as long as they dwell together, and brings
them not only to condemnation but also to larceny and
perjury and many other difficulties which hit them very hard.
Death never wants to do this, but makes them all leave these
things behind them; her coming brings to an end all their
earthly torments and hurts them only for an hour, however
painful that hour may be. Therefore, fair companion, I urge
you to remember Solomon who was king of Jerusalem, for
we have inherited many good things from him. He says, and
you should pay attention to this: "Fair son, keep yourself from
poverty all the days of your life", and he gives the reason in
his book: "for in this earthly life it is better to die than to be
poor."* When referring to cringing poverty, he talks about
the needy creature whom we call want and who does such
harm to her hosts that the indigent are the most despised

people ever seen. They are even refused as witnesses by those
who observe the proper canons, for in law they are said to
be equivalent to those who have lost their reputation.

8159   'Poverty is a very ugly thing; at any rate I dare say that if you
had amassed enough money and jewels and were willing to
give as much away as you could promise, you would be able
to pluck roses and rose-buds, however strictly enclosed they
were. But since you are neither rich nor mean nor miserly,
you should give nice, reasonable little gifts and give them
gladly, so that you do not fall into poverty and suffer harm
and loss. Many people would mock you and would not help
you if you had paid more for the goods than they were worth.

'It is very suitable to make an attractive present of fresh
fruit in a cloth or a basket, so do not neglect that. Send them
apples, pears, nuts or cherries, service-berries, plums, strawberries, wild cherries, chestnuts, quinces, figs, barberries,
peaches, large pears or sorb-apples, grafted medlars, raspberries, bullaces, damsons, horse-plums or fresh grapes, and have
some fresh mulberries. And if you have bought them, say that
they come from distant places and were given to you by a
friend of yours, even though you have bought them in the
street. Or give red roses or primroses or violets in handsome
baskets during the season: there is nothing unreasonable in
such a gift.

8197   'I tell you that gifts turn people's heads and deprive the
scandalmongers of their gossip: even if they knew any evil of
the givers, they would speak all the good in the world of
them. Fair gifts sustain many bailiffs who would otherwise
have been in difficulties; fine gifts of food and wine have
secured many prebends, and you should have no doubt that
fine gifts bear witness to a good life: gifts are highly esteemed
everywhere. Whoever gives fine gifts is a worthy man; gifts
enhance the reputation of the givers while putting those who
receive them at a disadvantage in that their natural freedom
is placed under an obligation to serve someone else. What
can I say? In short, both gods and men are won over by gifts.

8215   'My friend, pay attention to the observation and admonition that I now address to you. Know that if you are willing
to do what you have heard me tell you to do, the God of

Love will not fail to keep his promise when you attack the stronghold, for he and the goddess Venus will fight so strongly against the gatekeepers that they will destroy the fortress. Then you will be able to pluck the rose, however strong the prison in which they have enclosed it.

'But once the prize is gained, great skill must be exercised 8227 in keeping it well and wisely if you want to enjoy it for a long time, for there is no less virtue in keeping things and protecting them well, once they are acquired, than in acquiring them in whatever way. Therefore it is quite right that the young man who through his own fault loses the one he loves should call himself wretched, for it is a high and noble thing to be able to keep one's beloved and never to lose her, especially when God has granted one a lady who is wise and simple, courteous and good, who gives her love and does not sell it. Venal love was never invented by any woman except a proven harlot, and there is certainly no love in a woman who gives herself in exchange for a gift. This sham kind of love should be burned in hell and no attention should be paid to it.

'And yet in truth, nearly all women take greedily and steal 8251 and devour rapaciously, so that those who say that they are most truly theirs and love them most loyally are left with nothing. For Juvenal* relates, when telling the story of Hiberina, that she was made of such hot material that no one man could suffice her; she would rather have lost one of her eyes than remain attached to just one man; no woman was ever so ardent or so persistent in her love that she was not willing to see her lover tormented and robbed. Now see what the others would do, who give themselves to men in exchange for gifts; you could not find one who would be unwilling to behave in this way, however great her mastery over her man: they are all intent on one thing. This is the rule that Juvenal gives, but there is no infallible rule, and he meant bad women when he made this judgement. But if she is as I describe, loyal of heart and innocent of face, I shall tell you what you must do.

'A courteous and well-mannered young man desirous of taking trouble over this should be careful not to put the least

reliance on his beauty or his shape; it is right that he should
instruct his mind concerning manners, arts, and sciences. For
beauty, for those who know its origins and its ends, lasts only
a very short time; like the flowers of the field, its day is soon
over, for the substance of beauty is such that the more it lives,
the more it fades.

8293   'But if a man is willing to acquire intelligence, it will
accompany its master as long as he lives on earth and is worth
more at the end of his life than it ever was at the beginning;
it always grows and will never be diminished by time. A
young man of noble understanding must always be loved and
valued if he uses it wisely, while for her part a woman should
be very happy to have given her love to a handsome young
man who is courteous and wise and gives such evidence of
intelligence.

8307   'Nevertheless, if he asked my advice as to whether it would
be good for him to write pretty little verses, motets, stories,
and songs that he might wish to send to his sweetheart in
order to keep her and please her, alas, they would make no
difference: fine verses are not worth much in these circumstances. The verses will be praised, perhaps, but will bring
little profit in other respects.

'But if all at once she saw a great heavy purse appear, all
bulging with bezants, she would run to it straightaway with
open arms, for women nowadays are such demented creatures
that they run after nothing but purses. Things were different
once, but now everything is degenerating.

'Formerly, in the days of our first fathers and our first
mothers, according to the evidence of the literature through
which we learn of these matters, love was loyal and true, free
from covetousness and rapine, and the world was a very
simple place. Men were not so fastidious in the matter of food
and dress. Instead of bread, meat, and fish, they gathered
acorns in the woods and searched through the thickets, valleys, plains, and mountains for apples, pears, nuts, and chestnuts, rose-hips, mulberries, and sloes, raspberries, strawberries,
and haws, beans and peas, and such things as fruit, roots, and
plants. And they rubbed the grain from the ears of corn and
gathered grapes in the vineyards without putting them in

presses or vats. They sustained themselves abundantly with the honey that ran down the oak-trees and drank pure water, without asking for spiced or aromatic wine, nor did they ever drink wine that had been decanted.

'At that time the earth was not ploughed but was just as   8351
God had prepared it and bore of its own accord the things with which each man fortified himself. They did not look for salmon or pike but wore shaggy skins and made garments from wool just as it came from the animals, without dyeing it with plants or seeds. Their huts and villages were covered with broom plants, leaves, and branches, and they made ditches in the earth. When they feared the stormy air of some approaching tempest, they took refuge among the rocks or the great trunks of full-grown oaks where they had fled for safety. And when at night they wanted to sleep, they brought piles and bundles of leaves or moss or grasses into their huts instead of feather beds.

'And when the air was calm, the weather mild and fine,   8373
and the breeze soft and pleasant, as if in an eternal springtime, and every morning the birds were at pains to greet the dawn, which stirred all their hearts, in their own language, then Zephyrus, with Flora, his wife, who is goddess and lady of the flowers, would spread out their quilts of flowers for men. (These two bring the flowers to birth and the flowers know no other master, for he and she go throughout the world together, sowing flowers; they give them their shape, and colour them with the colours which the flowers use to honour maidens and favoured young men with lovely, gay chaplets. They do this for the sake of true lovers, who are very dear to them.) These flowers shone with such splendour in the pastures, meadows, and woods that you would have thought that the earth wanted to compete and contend with the sky as to which had the better stars, so proud was she in her flowers.

'On such couches as I have described, those who enjoyed   8401
the games of love embraced and kissed each other, free from greed and rapaciousness. In these woods, the green trees spread the tents and curtains of their branches over them in order to protect them from the sun. There, these simple,

secure folk would have their dances, games, and gentle
amusements, free from every care except to enjoy their loyal
and loving pleasures. No king or prince had as yet committed
the crime of robbing or stealing from others. All were accustomed to be equal and did not want to have anything of their
own. They well knew the saying, which is neither false nor
foolish, that love and lordship never bore each other company
nor dwelt together: the one which dominates always separates
them.

8425   'Thus we see that in marriages where the husband imagines
that he is wise to scold and beat his wife and fill her life with
wrangling, and tells her she is silly and foolish for spending
so much time dancing and so regularly frequenting the society
of handsome young men, true love cannot last, since they
inflict so many evils upon each other and he wants to be
master of his wife's body and possessions. "You are too
flighty", he says, "and your behaviour is too foolish. When
I go to work you immediately start dancing and capering and
making so merry that it seems positively immoral, and singing
like a siren. May God send you a bad week!

' "And when I take our merchandise to Rome or Frisia,
you immediately become so coquettish (for I know someone
who keeps me informed) that word of it spreads everywhere.
And when anyone speaks to you about why you are so
elegantly dressed everywhere you go, you answer: 'Aha! it is
for love of my husband.' For me! Alas, miserable wretch that
I am, who knows whether I forge or weave, whether I live
or die? They should flap a sheep's bladder* in my face. I am
certainly not worth a button if I do not chastise you in some
other way. You have established a fine reputation for me by
boasting of such things. Everyone knows very well that you
are lying. For me! Alas, poor wretch, for me! I put ill-fitting
gloves on my hands and deceived myself cruelly when I
accepted your vows on our wedding day. It is for me that
you indulge in these revels, for me that you conduct yourself
so proudly! Whom do you imagine you are deceiving? I am
unable to see the finery that is gazed on and admired by the
lustful, lecherous libertines, the oglers of harlots who surround you when they escort you through the streets. You

can't pull the wool over my eyes. Who could cause me greater displeasure? I am a convenient protection for you, and when I approach you, I see that you are more innocent in your coat and wimple than a dove or a turtle-dove. You do not care whether it is short or long when only I am with you. Although I am a good-natured man, I would not restrain myself from beating you in order to humble your great pride, not if I were offered four bezants to refrain for shame from doing it. And you should know that I do not like you to wear any ornaments in the dance or the ring except in my presence.

' "Moreover, I can no longer hide it, is there anything 8497 between you and young Robichonet with the green hat, who comes so quickly when you call? You cannot keep away from him, you two are always piping the same tune; I do not know what you can be taking from each other or saying to each other. Your irresponsible behaviour makes me wild with rage and anger. By our God, who never lies, if you ever speak to him, your face will lose its colour, or indeed it will be blacker than a mulberry; for so help me God, before I make you stop wasting your time, I will give you so many blows on that face of yours which idlers find so attractive that you will stay nice and quiet. You will never go out without me but will serve me at home, fastened with stout iron rings. Devils have made you so intimate with these deceitful libertines who should be strangers to you. Did I not take you to serve me? Do you imagine that you deserve my love, when you frequent these filthy womanizers because their hearts are so gay and they find you gay in return? You are a wicked harlot and I cannot trust you. The devils made me get married.

' "Ah, if I had believed Theophrastus, I would never have 8531 married. He does not think that a man is wise who takes a woman in marriage, whether she be fair or ugly, poor or rich, for he says and affirms as true in his noble book *Aureolus*,* which is a good book to study at school, that the life of a married man is very unpleasant, full of toil and pain, quarrels and disputes, because of the pride of stupid women, full of the arrogant and reproachful remarks that their mouths pronounce and utter, and full of the requests and complaints that they find many opportunities of making. He will find it very difficult to keep them straight and restrain their foolish desires. If a man wants to take a poor wife, he must undertake to feed her and buy her clothes and shoes, and if he thinks to advance himself by taking one who is very rich, then too he will suffer great torments, so proud and haughty, so arrogant, high, and mighty will he find her to be. If on the one hand she is beautiful, everyone will run after her, pursue and flatter her; they will assail her and toil and struggle and fight, exert themselves to serve her, surround and beseech her, hang around her and desire her and work so hard that in the end they will have her, for a tower that is besieged from all sides will find it difficult to avoid being taken.

8567   ' "If on the other hand she is ugly, she will want to please everyone. And how could anyone keep a creature whom everyone is fighting for or who wants all those who see her? If he makes war against the whole world, he will be unable to live on earth. No one could prevent a woman from being captured, once she had been well solicited. Even Penelope* could be taken by a man who applied himself seriously to taking her, and yet there was no better wife in Greece; so could Lucretia, by my faith, even though she killed herself because Tarquinius' son had taken her by force:* Titus Livy tells us that neither her husband nor her father nor her relatives could save her, however hard they tried, from killing herself in front of them. They entreated her vigorously to abandon her grief and gave her many good reasons; her husband especially comforted her compassionately, and gladly forgave her everything, urging her and exerting himself to find powerful arguments to prove to her that her body had not sinned, since her heart did not desire the sin, for the body cannot commit a sin if the heart does not consent to it. But she, racked with grief, had a knife hidden in her bosom so that no one would see it until she took it to strike herself, and she answered them without shame: 'Fair sirs, whoever forgives me the foul sin that weighs so heavily upon me, and whatever becomes of that forgiveness, I do not spare myself the penalty.' Then, filled with great anguish, she struck and clove her heart and fell dead to the ground before them; but first she begged them to strive to avenge her death. She wanted this to be an example that would reassure women that anyone who took them by force would have to die for it; the outcome was that the king and his sons were sent into exile and died there, and as a result of this violence, the Romans never again wanted to have a king in Rome. There is no Lucretia now, nor any Penelope in Greece, nor any worthy lady anywhere on earth if they are properly solicited; the pagans say that no woman ever defended herself against a man who made a serious effort to conquer her, and no one ever found a compromise. Many even give themselves of their own accord when suitors are lacking.

' "And those who marry follow a very dangerous practice, 8631 a custom so strange that I marvel greatly at it. I do not know where this folly comes from unless it be the result of madness and lunacy. I see that no one who buys a horse would be so foolish as to pay a penny until he had seen it completely uncovered, however well it had been covered up; he would test it and examine it all over. But one takes a woman without trying her out; win or lose, for better or worse, she will never be uncovered, simply in order to avoid putting one off before she is married. And when she sees that the deed is done, then and only then does she reveal her evil nature, only then is it apparent whether or not she has any blemishes, only then, when repentance is useless, does she make the fool aware of her disposition. Now I know for certain that, however well his wife may behave, there is no one who feels himself to be married and does not repent of it, unless he is a fool.

' "Honest woman! By Saint Denis, the honest woman, as 8657 Valerius* testifies, is rarer than the phoenix, and no one can love without being pierced with great fear and worry and other cruel misfortunes. Rarer than the phoenix? By my head, it would be a more honest comparison to say that they are rarer than white crows, however beautiful their bodies may be. Whatever I may say, however, in order that those who are alive should not say that I am overconfident in my attacks on all women, I affirm that if anyone wants to know an honest woman, whether secular or cloistered, and is willing to expend some effort in his search, he will find that such birds are thinly scattered on earth and so easily recognizable as to be like the black swan. Juvenal himself confirms this and gives it as his firm opinion that 'if you find a chaste woman, go and kneel down in the temple, bow down and worship Jupiter and make every effort to sacrifice a golden cow to your honoured lady Juno', for no more marvellous event ever befell any creature.

8687 ' "And if a man wants to love bad women, of whom Valerius, who is not ashamed to speak the truth, tells us that there are swarms on both sides of the sea greater than those of bees gathered in their hives, what does he imagine he will achieve? He will do himself harm by clinging to such a branch, and I tell you that if anyone does cling to it, he will lose his body and his soul.

8697 ' "Valerius, who was grieved because Rufinus, who was his friend, wanted to get married, spoke sternly to him: 'My friend,' he said, 'may the all-powerful God forbid that you should ever be caught in the net of an all-powerful woman who contrives to destroy everything.' Juvenal himself cried out to Postumus, who was getting married: 'Postumus, do you want to take a wife? Can you not find any rope or cord or halter for sale, or jump out of a high window from which you can see a long way, or let yourself fall from a bridge? What madness drives you to this pain and torment.?'*

' "King Phoroneus* himself, who, as we have learned, gave the Greeks their laws, addressed his brother Leontius on his deathbed and spoke to him: 'My brother,' he said, 'I tell you that I would have died very happy if I had never married.' And Leontius immediately demanded to know the reason for this opinion. 'All husbands', he said, 'discover this through testing and experience, and when you take a wife, you will understand it perfectly.'

' "Peter Abelard* admits in his turn that sister Heloise, abbess of the Paraclete, who was his beloved, would not for anything agree to his marrying her. Instead the intelligent and well-read young woman, who loved truly and was truly loved, reasoned with him and admonished him not to marry, and proved to him with texts and arguments that the conditions of marriage are too hard, however dutiful the wife. For she had seen and studied and understood the books and she understood feminine ways, for she had them all in herself. She asked him to love her but without claiming any rights over her except those that were freely and graciously given, without recourse to lordship and domination. This was so that he could study independently, freely, and without tying himself down, while she too, who was not devoid of learning, busied herself with her studies. And she often said to him that in any case, their joys were more agreeable and their pleasures heightened when they saw one another more rarely. But he, as he has told us in his writing, loved her so well that he later married her in spite of her admonition, and it turned out very badly for him; for after she had, I think, taken the habit of a nun at Argenteuil, as they had both agreed, Peter's testicles were removed as he lay in bed one night in Paris, which caused him great suffering and anguish. After this misfortune he became a monk of Saint-Denis in France, then abbot of another abbey, and then, as he tells us in his *Life*, he founded a famous abbey, which he named the Paraclete, where Heloise, who had formerly been a professed nun, was abbess. She herself was not ashamed to write in her letters to her beloved, whom she loved so well that she called him father and lord, strange words that many people would think absurd. It is written in her letters, if you examine the chapters carefully, that even after she became abbess, she sent an explicit letter to him saying 'If the emperor of Rome, to whom all men should be subject, deigned to want to marry me and make me mistress of the world, I call God to witness that I would rather', she said, 'be called your whore than be crowned empress.' But by my soul, I do not think that there has ever been such a woman since; and I believe that her erudition enabled her better to conquer and subdue her nature and its feminine ways. If Peter had believed her, he would never have married her.

' "Marriage is an evil bond; may Saint Julian, who shelters   8803
wandering pilgrims, preserve me, and Saint Leonard, who unshackles those prisoners who truly repent when he sees them lamenting. It would have been better for me to be

hanged on the day I married and bound myself to such an elegant wife. This elegant wife is the death of me.

' "But by Saint Mary's son, what use is this elegance to me, this costly and expensive dress that makes you hold your head so high and so vexes and torments me, that is so long and so trails behind you and makes you give yourself such airs that I am driven quite mad? What does it profit me? However much it may profit others, it does me nothing but harm, for when I want to take my pleasure with you, I find it such an encumbrance, so irritating and annoying, that I am unable to achieve my aim. I can never hold you properly, because you twist and turn so much, fighting and parrying with arms and legs and hips. I do not know how it is, except that I can clearly see that neither my lovemaking nor the pleasure I offer are in any way to your liking. Even in the evening, when I lie down before receiving you in my bed, as a worthy man receives his wife, you have to get undressed; you have nothing on your head or your body or your hips but a cap of white cloth, and perhaps the blue or green hair-braids covered by the cap. Then the dresses and miniver furs are put on a pole to hang all night outside. What, then, can all this be worth to me, except to sell or pawn? You will see me grow quite wild and die of an evil madness if I do not sell and pawn everything. For since they give me so much trouble by day and no pleasure by night, what profit can I expect from them unless I pawn or sell them? And you, if the truth be told, are not worth one whit more because of them, not in intelligence nor in loyalty nor even, by God, in beauty.

8859   ' "And if any man, in order to confound me, wanted to argue or reply that the virtues of good things are communicated to other people, and that fine ornaments give beauty to ladies and maidens, I would certainly say that he lied, whoever he was, for I have read in a book that the beauties of beautiful things, whether of violets or roses or silken cloths or fleurs-de-lis, are in themselves and not in ladies. All women should know that as long as they live they will never have anything but their natural beauty, and I say the same about goodness as I have about beauty. I will begin my remarks by saying that if anyone wanted to cover a dung-heap with silken cloths or brightly coloured and neatly arranged little flowers, it would undoubtedly be the same, habitually foul-smelling dung-heap that it had been before. And if any man said: 'If the dung-heap is ugly within, it appears fairer on the outside; in the same way ladies adorn themselves in order to appear more beautiful or to hide their ugliness', by my faith, I do not know how to answer except to say that such deception comes from the eyes' disordered vision, which sees their adornment; hearts are thus so misled by the pleasant impression received by the imagination that they are unable to distinguish lies from truth or, through lack of proper observation, to explicate the sophism.

'"But if men had the eyes of a lynx, and had looked 8901 carefully at them, no sable mantles, surcoats or skirts, no braids or kerchiefs, dresses or cloaks, no jewels or precious things, no false smirks or shining and seemingly artificial exterior, no garlands of fresh flowers could make them appear beautiful. For the body of Alcibiades,* which had been so well shaped by Nature as to be extremely beautiful in colour and form, would have been considered very ugly by anyone who could have looked inside it; so Boethius, that wise and most worthy man, tells us, and he calls Aristotle to witness when he says that the eyesight of the lynx is so good and sharp and clear that he sees quite plainly the exterior and the interior of everything that he is shown.

'"And so I say that Beauty and Chastity have never been 8927 at peace in any age: there is always such conflict between them that I have never heard it said or told in any story or song that anything could reconcile them, for they wage such deadly war against each other that one will never allow the other to hold a foot of land, provided she can gain the upper hand. But they are so unevenly matched that when Chastity for her part attacks or defends herself, she knows so little of fighting or parrying that she has to surrender her arms, for she is powerless to defend herself against Beauty, who is very cruel. Even Ugliness, her chambermaid, who owes her honour and service, does not love and value her enough to refrain from banishing her from her home; she rushes at her, with her mace, which is very large and heavy, at her shoulder, for it is a source of extraordinary vexation to her that her mistress remains alive for as long as a single hour. And so Chastity is in a very bad situation, for she is beset from both sides and has no help from anywhere, so that she must run away, for she sees that she is fighting alone. Even if she had sworn it by her mouth and knew enough of fighting, she would not dare resist when everyone was ranged against her, and so she could not conquer.

8963 ' "Now woe betide Ugliness, who thus attacks Chastity when she should have defended and protected her! If she could have hidden her, even between her shift and her skin, she should have put her there. And Beauty is also very much to blame, for she should have loved Chastity and, if she liked, secured peace between them; at least, she should have done her best to do so, or else submitted to Chastity, for had she been worthy, courteous, and wise, she should have paid her homage and not shamed and disgraced her. Even the text of the sixth book of Virgil* bears witness by the authority of the Sibyl* that no one who leads a chaste life will be damned.

' "Therefore I swear by God, the heavenly king, that any woman who wants to be beautiful or who strives to appear so, gazing at herself and making great efforts to adorn and beautify herself, is willing to make war on Chastity, who certainly has many enemies. All those in cloisters and abbeys have sworn hostility to her; however strictly they are enclosed, they still hate Chastity so much that they are all bent on shaming her. All pay homage to Venus, regardless of whether they will gain or lose by it; they beautify themselves and paint their faces in order to fool those who look at them, they scour the streets in order to see and be seen and to fill men with desire to lie with them. This is why they wear their finery at the dances and in churches, for no woman would do this if she did not imagine that she would be seen, and thus attract those whom she could deceive all the sooner.

9009 ' "But certainly, if the truth were told, those foolish and erring women bring great shame to God by not considering themselves well rewarded by the beauty God has given them. Each one wears a crown of gold or silk flowers on her head, and thus proudly adorns herself as she goes around the town, showing herself off; unhappy wretch, she demeans herself most wickedly when, in order to increase and perfect her beauty, she is willing to put something on her head that is lower and baser than she; thus she despises God, believing that he did not do enough and thinking in her foolish heart that God did her a great wrong in that, when he formed her beauty, he was content to do it very negligently. Thus she searches for beauty in things that God has made much baser in appearance, such as metals or flowers or other strange things.

' "The same is doubtless true of men. If, in order to be more beautiful, we make chaplets and ornaments for the beauties that God has put in us, then we do him a great wrong in not considering ourselves well rewarded by the beauties he has given to us above all living creatures. But I care nothing for such trumpery; I want just enough clothing to protect me from the cold and the heat. With God's help, my homespun lined with lamb will protect my head and body from wind and rain and storms just as well as fine blue cloth lined with squirrel. It seems to me that I am wasting my money if I buy you a robe of fine blue cloth, of camlet or wool dyed green or scarlet, and line it with squirrel or miniver. It would make you run wild, prancing and smirking through the dust and mud, and caring nothing for God or for me. Even at night, when you lie naked beside me in my bed, you cannot be held; for when I want to embrace you in order to kiss you and take my pleasure, when I am thoroughly inflamed, then you grind your teeth like a devil and will not turn your face towards me, whatever I do; instead, you pretend to be so ill, sighing and complaining and seeming so hard to please, that I become quite frightened and dare not attack you again when I wake after having slept, because I am so afraid of failing. But I marvel greatly how these gallants manage, embracing you fully clothed during the day, if you twist and turn in the same way when you disport yourself with them, and give them as much trouble as you do me, night and day. But I do not think you have any desire to do that; instead you go singing and dancing through the gardens and meadows with these disloyal libertines, who drag a married

9033

woman through the green, dewy grass, despising me and saying scornfully to each other: 'This is to spite that filthy, jealous wretch!' May the flesh that has brought me such shame be given to wolves and the bones to mad dogs! It is your fault, you hussy, with your wanton behaviour, you lewd, dissolute, filthy, vile, depraved bitch. May your body not see the end of this year, since you surrender it to such curs! It is because of you that I am shamed, because of you and your lechery that I am enrolled in the confraternity of Saint Arnold, patron of cuckolds, from whom, as far as I know, no man who has a wife is safe, however carefully he guards and watches her, and even if he has a thousand eyes. All women get themselves laid, for no guard can do anything about it; and if it should happen that the deed is wanting, the will to do it will never be wanting, and as a result, if she can, she will jump at the chance, for her wish is always to do it. But Juvenal gives you great comfort when he says of the business we call bedding that it is the least of the sins that stains the heart of woman, for their nature prompts each one of them to set her mind on doing worse. Do we not see how mothers-in-law brew poisons for their sons-in-law and cast spells and enchantments and so many other great devilries that no one could count them all, however hard he thought.

9125   ' "All of you are, will be, and have been, in deed or in intention, unchaste; for even if the deed can be prevented, no man can constrain the will. All women have the advantage of being mistress of their own wills: beatings and insults cannot change your hearts. But anyone who could change them would be master of your bodies. Now let us forget what cannot be. But fair, sweet God, fair heavenly king, what can I do with these libertines who cause me such shame and suffering? If I should threaten them, what will my threat be worth to them? If I go and fight them, they will soon be able to kill me or beat me, for they are cruel and wicked, bold enough to commit any crime, young and handsome, wild and headstrong. They will not give a straw for me, for youth inflames them, filling them with a fiery blaze and of necessity inspiring all their hearts to madness; they are so lively and agile that each one imagines himself a Roland, or indeed a

Hercules or a Samson. Men think, and I remember that it is
written, that these latter two were alike in bodily strength.
Hercules, according to the author Solinus, was seven feet tall
and no man, as he says, could ever reach a greater height.
Hercules had many adventures: he overcame twelve horrible
monsters, and when he had overcome the twelfth, he could
not escape the thirteenth, his sweetheart Deïaneira, who lacer-
ated and inflamed his flesh with poison, by means of the
poisoned shirt. For his heart had already been maddened by
love for Iole. Thus Hercules, who had so many virtues, was
subdued by a woman. In the same way, Samson, who would
not have feared ten men any more than ten apples if he had
had his hair, was deceived by Delilah. It is foolish of me to
say this, for I know that when you leave me you will repeat
all my words one after the other; you will complain to those
libertines and, if you can reach them, you might have them
smash my head or break my thighs or slash my shoulders. But
if I hear talk of this before it happens to me, and my arms
are not held nor my club taken from me, I shall break your
ribs. No friend, neighbour, relative, nor even your lecherous
lover will be able to protect you. Alas, why did we ever set
eyes on each other? Alas, in what hour was I born that you
so despise me as to allow these lecherous, stinking curs who
fawn on you and flatter you to be your lords and masters? I
alone should be your lord, by whom you are supported,
clothed, shod, and fed, but you make me share with these
filthy, debauched scoundrels who bring you nothing but
shame. They have robbed you of your good name, for you
care nothing for that when you hold them in your arms. They
tell you to your face that they love you, but behind your
back they call you a whore, and when they all get together
again, they say the worst they can think of about how each
of them has served you, for I know very well how they talk.
It is quite true, without a doubt: when you abandon yourself
to them, they are very good at getting you where they want
you, for you have no resistance once you are in the crowd
where everyone is pulling you and pushing you. I am sometimes very envious of their pleasures and their life. But you
should know, and I remind you of it, that it is not because

of your body or the pleasure of making love with you, but simply because it is they who enjoy the jewels, the golden clasps and buttons, the dresses and cloaks that I let you have, foolish simpleton that I am. For when you go to dances or to your wild gatherings while I stay behind as if I were a drunken fool, you wear a hundred pounds' worth of gold and silver on your head and demand to be dressed in camlet,* squirrel, and miniver.* I am so tormented with anxiety about it that I am growing quite gaunt with anger and worry.

9241   ' "What use to me are these headbands, these caps striped with gold, these decorated braids and ivory mirrors, these carefully crafted golden circlets with their precious enamelling, these coronets of purest gold which never cease to enrage me, being so fair and finely polished, studded with such beautiful stones, with sapphires, rubies, and emeralds, and which make you look so joyous. These clasps of gold and precious stones at your throat and on your bosom, these fabrics and these girdles whose fittings are worth as much as gold or seed-pearls, what are such baubles worth to me? And you wear such close-fitting shoes that you often lift your skirts to show your feet to those philanderers. So help me Saint Thibaut, I shall sell everything in three days and keep you crushed beneath my feet. By God's body, you will have nothing from me but a homespun dress and surcoat and a hempen kerchief which will not be fine but coarse and badly woven, torn and darned, whoever moans and complains about it. And you will be well girded, by my head, but I will tell you with what kind of girdle: it will be of plain leather without a buckle. And from my old boots you will have loose-fitting shoes with laces, ample enough to stuff with great rags. I will take from you all the trumperies that give you the opportunity to commit fornication, and you will no longer go showing yourself off in order to get yourself seduced by the philanderers.

9283   ' "Now tell me without fabrication, that other fine new dress in which you arrayed yourself the other day when you went dancing—I know very well and I am right to think that I never gave it to you—where, for love's sake, did you get it? You swore to me by Saint Denis, Saint Philibert, and Saint

Peter that it came to you from your mother, who sent you the cloth because, as you give me to understand, her love for me is so great that she is happy to spend her money so that I can keep mine. May she be skewered alive, the filthy, shameless old whore, the pimping witch, and you too, for you will have deserved it, if it is not just as you say. I would ask her indeed, but the effort would be in vain, not worth a button; like mother, like daughter. I know very well that you have spoken together, and it is apparent that your two hearts beat as one. I know which foot you limp with. The filthy, painted old whore is in agreement with you; she used to twist the same rope herself and has travelled along so many different roads that she has been bitten by many curs. But her face is now so ravaged that she can do nothing herself, and so now she sells you, as I know very well. She comes here and takes you away three or four times a week, pretending to make new pilgrimages, just as she used to, for I am familiar with all that business. She constantly parades you about as if you were a horse for sale, taking and teaching you to take. Do you imagine that I do not know you? Who will stop me from breaking your bones like a chicken in a pie with this pestle or this spit?"

'Then perhaps, boiling with rage, he takes her there and 9331 then by the hair and pulls her and tugs her, tearing and rending her locks in his jealousy, setting upon her (a lion attacking a bear is nothing in comparison), dragging her all through the house in his anger and fury and insulting her cruelly. Whatever she swears, he bears her such ill will that he will accept no excuses; instead he strikes her and beats her, flogs her and thrashes her, while she cries and shouts and shrieks and the wind carries her voice through windows and across roofs, and she hurls at him whatever reproaches she can think of, just as they come to her lips, in front of the neighbours who arrive and think they are both mad, and separate him from her with great difficulty when he is exhausted.

'And when the lady experiences this torment and this 9353 dispute, and sees what a charming viol her jongleur plays for her, do you think she will love him more as a result? She

wishes him in Meaux or indeed in Greece.* I will go further.
I do not think she will ever be willing to love him. Perhaps
she will pretend to, but even if he could fly as high as the
clouds or raise his vantage point so high that he could see,
without falling, all men's deeds, and contemplate them all at
his leisure, he would still fail to perceive the danger into
which he had fallen, unless he had seen all the deceits that
women can think of to protect and defend themselves. If he
then sleeps with her, he seriously imperils his life; indeed,
whether sleeping or waking, he should go in great fear lest
she take her revenge by having him poisoned or cut to pieces,
or make him adopt the desperate ruse of living as an invalid,
or decide to run away, if there is no other way in which she
can achieve her ends. Women care nothing for honour or
shame when they get an idea into their heads, for it is true
without a doubt that women know nothing. Valerius even
calls them bold and cunning towards those they hate and
those they love, and very intent on doing harm.

9391   'My friend, this mad, jealous wretch, whose flesh should
be given to the wolves, is full of jealousy, as I have illustrated
here, and makes himself his wife's lord; however, she ought
not to be his lady but his equal and his companion, as the
law joins them together, and he for his part should be her
companion, without making himself her lord and master.
When he prepares such torments for her and does not consider her his equal but makes her live in great suffering, do
you imagine that he does not displease her and that love
between them does not fail, whatever she may say? There is
no doubt that no man who wants to be called lord will be
loved by his wife, for love must die when lovers assume
authority. Love cannot last or survive except in hearts that
are free and at liberty.

9413   'In the same way we see that when all those who were
formerly accustomed to love each other *par amour* want to
marry, it may perhaps be difficult for their love to survive,
for when a man loved *par amour*, he called himself the servant
of her who was accustomed to be his mistress, but now he
calls himself lord and master over her whom he had called
his lady when she was loved *par amour*. Loved?—Indeed.—

But how?—In such a way that if, without entreaty, she ordered him: "My friend, jump!" or "Give me that thing", he would give it to her immediately and without fail, and jump if she commanded him to jump. Indeed, whatever she said, he would jump so that she might see him, for all his desire was to do all her pleasure. But as I have told you, when they are married, then the situation is reversed, so that he who used to serve her now commands her to serve him as if she were his slave. He keeps her on a short rein and orders her to give an account of her doings. And he used to call her his lady! Everyone knows this by the time he dies. Then she considers herself very hardly used, when she sees that the best, the most tried and tested man she has found in all the world attacks and opposes her in this way. She no longer knows whom she can trust, when she sees her master, with whom she had never been on her guard, now at her throat. Things have changed for the worse; now that he has turned the tables, the game is going so badly for her, so cruelly and unfavourably, that she cannot and dare not play. How can she be counselled? If she does not obey, he grows angry and insults her, and she resents it: behold them full of anger and, through their anger, immediately enemies.

'For this reason, my friend, the ancients bore one another 9463 company without binding themselves in servitude, peacefully and without baseness; not for all the gold of Arabia or Phrygia would they have given up their freedom, for it would be wrong to sell it, even in exchange for all that gold.

'At that time there were no pilgrimages and no one left his own shore in search of a foreign country; Jason had not crossed the sea, who first crossed it when he built ships to go in search of the Golden Fleece. When Neptune saw them sail, he imagined that they were making war against him, while for his part Triton* grew wild with rage, as did Doris and all her daughters.* At the coming of these wondrous creatures, they all imagined themselves betrayed, so astounded were they by the ships that flew over the sea at the will of the sailors.

'But the first men, whom I am telling you about, did not 9487 know what sailing was. Whatever seemed to them to be worth seeking, they found all of it in their own land; all were equally rich, and loved one another loyally. And therefore those simple, decent people lived in peace, for they loved one another with a natural love. At that time there was no simony in love, men did not demand things from each other, but then Fraud came, with his lance in rest, and Sin and Misfortune too, who care nothing for Contentment. Pride, who scorns his equals, came in great state, together with Covetousness and Avarice, Envy and all the other vices, and these made Poverty spring from hell, where she had been for so long that no one knew anything about her, for she had never been on earth. It was unfortunate that she came so soon, for her coming was a disaster!

9511   'Drear Poverty brought her son, Larceny, who runs to the gibbet to help his mother and sometimes gets himself hanged there, for his mother cannot help him, nor can Faint Heart, his father, who is wretched with grief as a result. Even Lady Laverna, goddess of thieves, who guides them and governs them, shrouding their sins in thick darkness and their knavery in clouds so that they do not in fact appear in the open until they are discovered and caught at last in the act, even she is not so merciful as to be willing to protect him when they put the rope around his neck, however much he repents.

9531   'Straightaway these dreadful devils, fired with rage and grief, anger and envy at the sight of men living such a life, rushed through all the lands, sowing discord, strife, and wars, slander, malice, and hate in their anger and fury. And since they loved gold, they flayed the earth, drawing from its bowels its ancient hidden treasures of metals and precious stones, which men began to desire, for Avarice and Covetousness have set in men's hearts a burning desire to acquire possessions. One acquires them; the other, miserable wretch, locks them away, and will never spend them as long as she lives; instead, she will leave them in the guardianship of her heirs or her executors, unless some setback occurs in the meantime. And if she goes to perdition, I do not imagine that any of them will pity her, but if she has done well, they will take her goods.

9557   'As soon as men had been corrupted and seduced by this tribe, they abandoned their former life and never afterwards ceased from doing evil, for they became false and treacherous. They established private property, dividing up the very earth and setting boundaries to the divisions. And when they set these boundaries, they often fought with one another and robbed one another of whatever they could, and the strongest obtained the largest share. And when they chased off in search of more, the lazy ones who remained behind would enter their caves and steal what they had amassed. And so they had to choose someone to guard their dwellings, catch the malefactors, give justice to the plaintiffs, someone whom no one would dare contradict. Thus they assembled to make their choice.

'They chose from among themselves a great lout, the big-   9579
gest, brawniest, bulkiest of them all, and made him their prince and their lord. He swore to give them justice and protect their dwellings if each for his part gave him goods to enable him to live. Thus they agreed to what he said and suggested, and he held that office for a long time. Full of malice, the thieves got together when they saw that he was alone, and often beat him when they came to steal. Then the people had to assemble once again, and each one for his own part had to tax himself in order to provide the prince with soldiers. Then they taxed themselves collectively and paid him tribute and revenues and gave him great lands: this, according to the testimony of the ancients, was the origin of kings and earthly princes. It is through their writings, now in our possession, that we know about the deeds of the ancients, and we should give them grateful thanks and praise for it.

'Then they heaped up treasure of silver, precious stones,   9607
and gold. Because gold and silver were malleable and valuable, they used them to forge vessels and coins, clasps, rings, buttons, and belts; their arms were made of hard iron: knives, swords, halberds, spears, and coats of mail to wage war on their neighbours. Then they made towers and entrenchments and walls of ashlar; those who had heaped up treasure built walled castles and cities and great decorated palaces, for they all trembled with fear lest the wealth they had amassed be stolen from them or somehow taken by force. Unfortunate wretches, their sorrows were greatly increased, and they never felt secure once they had bound themselves to wealth

and in their covetousness appropriated things that had formerly been as free for all as the sun and the wind, so that one man has more than twenty others: this did not spring from good nature.

9635 'To be sure, I care not a button for the wretched scoundrels; although they lack a good heart, that fault does not concern me: let them love or hate one another or sell their love to each other. But it is a great sorrow and a grievous loss when those bright-faced, gay, vivacious ladies by whom true love should be valued and protected are so basely sold. It is a very ugly thing to hear that a noble body is capable of selling itself.

9649 'However that may be, the young man should take care not to neglect his study of the arts and sciences by which, if necessary, he can protect and defend himself and his sweetheart, so that she will never abandon him. Such study can greatly advance a young man, and certainly will not do him any harm.

'For his part, he should remember and be mindful of my advice: if he has a sweetheart, whether she be young or old, and he thinks and knows that she wants to seek another lover, or has already sought one, he should not blame her or rebuke her for seeking or acquiring a lover, but correct her kindly, without rebukes or insults. Or again, in order to minimize estrangement, if he finds her in the very act, he should take care to close his eyes in that direction. He should pretend to be blind or simpler than an ox, so that she thinks for certain that he cannot see anything.

9673 'And if anyone sends her a letter, he ought not to make it his business to read or examine it or to try to find out their secrets. His heart should not desire to oppose her wishes: she should be welcome when she comes in from any street, and she should be free to go wherever she likes, and follow her own wishes and inclinations, for she does not like to be restrained. I should like what I want to say to you to become well known: it ought to be in a book for people to read. Anyone who wants to enjoy a woman's favour should always give her freedom and never keep her to a rule but allow her to come and go as she wishes. If a man tries to restrain her from coming and going, whether she be his wife or his mistress, he will soon have lost her love.

'He should not believe anything against her, however re-   9695 liable the source. Instead he should say to those men or women who bring him the news that their words were foolish and that they never saw a more virtuous woman, that she has never ceased to do good and that therefore no man should suspect her.

'He should never reproach her for her vices, nor should he beat or touch her, for the man who beats his wife the better to worm his way into her affections when he tries to make his peace with her afterwards is like the man who tames his cat by beating it and then calling it back to fasten on its lead. If the cat can jump away, he might well fail to catch it.

'But if the woman beats him or insults him, he should take   9713 care that his heart does not change. If he sees himself beaten or insulted, even if she were to tear his living flesh with her nails, he should take no revenge, but rather thank her and say that he would be happy to spend his whole life in such torment provided he knew that his service was pleasing to her, or even indeed that he would freely die there and then rather than live without her.

'And if he should happen to strike her because she seems too aggressive or has angered him too much with the violence of her complaints, or perhaps because she wants to threaten him, he should immediately make sure, in order to secure his peace, that he makes love to her before she leaves. This is especially true for a poor man, for she might soon leave a poor man with very little excuse if she did not see him submit to her. The poor man must love wisely and suffer humbly, without showing anger or irritation, whatever he may see her do or say; in particular he should be more like this than the rich man, who would perhaps not give two chick-peas, in his arrogance and pride, and might revile her.

'And if he is the kind of man who has no desire to be loyal   9745 to his sweetheart, he still would not want to lose her but simply to attach himself to someone else, and if he wants to give his new sweetheart a kerchief or headscarf, a chaplet, ring, clasp, or girdle, or any kind of jewel, he should take care that the other is not familiar with them, for her heart would be full of anguish when she saw her successor wearing them, and nothing would comfort her. He should also take care not to have his new sweetheart come to the place where his first sweetheart used to meet him, and where she is accustomed to go, for if she goes there and happens to find her, then no one will be able to put things right. For no bristly old boar is so fierce when goaded by the dogs, no lioness so grim and cruel when the huntsman who is attacking her intensifies his assault at the moment when she is suckling her cubs, no serpent so venomous when his tail is trampled underfoot (for he does not like being trampled upon) as is a woman when she finds her lover with his new sweetheart. She breathes fire and flames in all directions and is prepared to lose both her body and her soul.

9777   'And if she has not caught them red-handed in their nest, but is sunk in jealousy because she knows or imagines herself to be deceived, then however things may be, whether she knows it or merely believes it, he should take care never to stop denying absolutely what she knows for certain, and he should not hesitate to swear it. There and then, he should make her submit to his lovemaking: then he will be free of her complaints.

9789   'And if she attacks and torments him so much that he has to confess, being perhaps unable to defend himself, then he must try, if possible, to force her to understand that he did it under protest, for the woman had him on so tight a rein and used him so ill that he could not escape without making love to her, and that it had only happened on that one occasion. Then he must swear and vow and promise that it will never happen again; he will conduct himself so faithfully that if she ever hears talk of that kind of thing, he will be glad for her to kill him or beat him, for he would rather the other treacherous renegade be drowned than that he should ever get into a position where she has so tight a hold on him. If she happens to summon him, he will no longer obey her summons, and if he can prevent her, he will not allow her to come to any place where she might embrace him. Then he must clasp his former sweetheart tightly and kiss her and please her with loving words and beg for mercy for his crime since it will never be committed again and he is truly sorry and ready to perform any penance that she can impose upon him, now that she has pardoned him. Then, if he wants her to forgive him, let him do love's work.

'And he should take care not to boast about her, since this 9823 might grieve her. Many men have boasted about many ladies with false and deceitful words, wickedly blackening the reputations of those whose bodies they could not possess. But such men lack courage; they are neither courteous nor brave. Boasting is a most base vice and the man who boasts of such things behaves very foolishly, for even if he had done them, he ought in any case to conceal the fact. Love likes to hide his treasures from all but his faithful friends who are willing to be silent and keep them secret; in such cases they may be revealed.

'And if she falls sick, he should try, if he can, to be very 9839 helpful to her, so that afterwards he will be better received. Let him see to it that no problem keeps him away from her sick-bed; he should stay by her side, kissing her and weeping, and if he is wise, he will vow to undertake many distant pilgrimages, provided she hears his vows. He should not forbid her to eat meat nor offer her anything that tastes unpleasant but only things that are sweet and tender.

'Then he should invent new dreams full of pleasant deceits, 9853 such as that when he lies down on his couch in the evening, all alone in his room, it seems to him when he sleeps (for he sleeps little and lies awake a great deal) that he has held her naked in his arms all night in pleasant lovemaking and that she was quite well and quite cured, and that he has done the same by day in delightful places; such stories, or ones like them, he should tell her.

'So far I have told you in verse how a man should serve women in sickness and in health if he wants to deserve their favour and their continued love, for their love can easily change if a man is not willing to take the greatest care to do whatever gives them pleasure. No woman will ever be so knowledgeable, so firm of heart, so loyal or mature that a man can be sure of holding her, however much trouble he takes, any more than if in the Seine he held an eel by the tail; however securely he caught it, he would not be able to stop it from struggling so much that it would soon escape. The creature is not properly tamed, being always ready to flee; it changes so much that no one can have confidence in it.

9887   'I am not speaking of good women, whose limits are set by virtue, but I have not found any such, however well I have tested them. Even Solomon could not find them, however well he tested them, and he himself declares that he never found a constant woman. If you take the trouble to look for one and find her, then take her, for you will have a most excellent sweetheart and one who will be wholly yours. If she is unable to hunt about and provide for herself elsewhere, and if she finds no one to ask for her favours, a woman may give herself up to Chastity. But there is one more little thing I would like to say before I leave this subject.

9905   'Briefly, whatever the maidens are like, whether ugly or beautiful, the man who wishes to keep their love must observe this commandment of mine and remember it always and count it very precious: he must give all of them to understand that he has no defence against them, so astounded and amazed is he by their beauty and merit. For there is no woman, however good, whether old or young, worldly or cloistered, nor any religious lady, however chaste in body or spirit, who is not delighted to hear her beauty praised. Even though she may be called ugly, he should swear that she is more beautiful than a fairy; he may do so confidently, for she will believe him easily, for I know that every woman, even though she may be manifestly ugly, believes that she has sufficient beauty to be worthy of being loved.

9929   'Thus all handsome, worthy, noble young men should take care to keep their sweethearts, without reproaching them for their foolishness.

9933   'Women do not like to be corrected; instead, their minds are fashioned in such a way that they do not think that they need to be taught their business and no man, if he does not want to displease them, will advise against anything they wish to do.

'Just as the cat knows instinctively how to catch mice and cannot be prevented from doing it, since all cats are born with this sense and never had to be taught it, so every woman, however foolish, knows through her own natural judgement that in absolutely everything she does, good or bad, wrong or right, everything you like, she is always acting as she ought, and so she hates anyone who corrects her. She has not acquired this faculty from a teacher but has had it since birth and so cannot be prevented from exercising it; all women are born with this faculty, so that no man who tried to correct them would ever enjoy their love.

'And so my friend, as for your rose, which is such a precious 9957 thing that if you could have it you would not exchange it for anything, be sure that when, as you hope, you come into possession of it and your joy is complete, you keep it as one ought to keep such a little flower. Then you will enjoy a love to which no other can be compared and whose equal you would perhaps not find in fourteen cities.' 'It is indeed true,' I said, 'nowhere in the world, I am sure of it, for its virtue was and is so great.' Thus Friend comforted me and I was greatly heartened by his advice, and it seems to me that, in this case at least, he knows more than Reason does. But before he had finished his discourse, which gave me such pleasure, Pleasant Thought and Pleasant Conversation returned and stayed close to me from then on and scarcely ever left me again, but they did not bring Pleasant Looks with them. I did not blame them for leaving him behind, for I knew very well that they could not bring him.

CHAPTER 6

THE ARMY OF LOVE

I took my leave and departed forthwith, wandering happily all alone across the meadow bright with grass and flowers and listening to the sweet birds singing their new songs. It did my heart good to hear their sweet strains that gave me such pleasure. But Friend has given me one cause for sorrow, since he has commanded me to avoid the castle and turn away from it and not to disport myself around it. I do not know if I will be able to restrain myself, for I shall always want to go there.

9999   After my departure, then, I shunned the right-hand side and made my way to the left, looking for the shortest path. I would have been glad to seek that path and, had I found it, to strike out along it at full speed, taking no denial unless someone stronger had forbidden me, in order to rescue the gentle, open, gracious Fair Welcome from prison. Once I had seen the castle, weaker than a crumbly cake, with its gates open and no one defending it against me, the devil would certainly have had my guts unless I had captured and entered it. Then Fair Welcome would have been free, and I tell you truly that it would have been worth more than a hundred thousand pounds to me to get on to that road. Nevertheless I walked away from the castle, but not very far.

10021   I was beside a bright spring in a fair and most delightful spot, thinking about the new rose, when I saw, in the shade of an elm-tree, an exalted and honourable lady, noble and beautiful in figure and in form, and her lover by her side. I do not know his name, but the lady's name was Wealth and she was of great nobility. She was guarding the entrance to a little path but she had not entered it herself. When I saw them, I bowed and greeted them with bent head, and they soon returned my greeting, which did me little good. Nevertheless, I asked them which was the right way to Lavish Giving. Wealth, who spoke first, said rather proudly: 'Here is the road, and I am guarding it.'

'Ah, lady, may God protect you! Then I beg you, if you do not mind, to allow me to go this way to the newly built castle that Jealousy has established.'

'Young man, this cannot be, for I do not yet know you. 10047 You are not welcome here, since you are not one of my close friends. It may be that I will not set you upon this way until ten years have passed. No one enters here, whether he comes from Paris or Amiens, unless he is a friend of mine. I allow my friends to go that way, to dance and prance and caper and enjoy a little pleasant living that no wise man envies them. There they have their fill of rejoicing, of dances and frolics, of drums and viols and new *rotruenges*, of games of dice, of chess, and of backgammon, and of exotic and delicious food. Young men and maidens who have been brought together by old procuresses go there, exploring the meadows and gardens and woods, gayer than parrots; then with chaplets of flowers on their heads they return together to the baths and bathe together in tubs that are all prepared in the rooms of the house of Unrestrained Generosity. She injures and impoverishes them so much, and sells her services and her hospitality at so high a price, that it is hard for them to recover afterwards, for she exacts such a cruel toll that they have to sell their land before they can pay it all. I escort them there, full of joy, but bare, cold, trembling Poverty brings them back. I keep the entrance and she the exit. After that I will have nothing more to do with them, however wise or educated they may be: they can go to the devil, since they are down to their last penny.

'I do not mean that if they contrived to make their peace 10089 with me (though that would be hard to do) I would be too tired to take them back there as often as they liked. But you must know that in the end, it is those who have spent most time on this road who regret it most, and dare not look at me for shame. Such is their rage and fury that they are ready to kill themselves, and so I abandon them because they abandon me. I promise you most truly that if you ever set foot here, you will regret it in the end. No bear, however much he is baited, is so weak and wretched as you will be if you go there. If Poverty can get you into her power, she will make you linger so long on a little straw or hay that she will let you die of Hunger. Hunger used to be her chambermaid and served her so well that, in exchange for her eager and zealous service, Poverty taught her every kind of malice and made her the governess and nurse of that ugly young fellow Theft. She suckled him with her milk, having no other pap to feed him with. And if you want to know about her land, which is neither easy to cultivate nor rich, Hunger lives in a stony field where no corn grows nor any bush or scrub; this field is at the farthest tip of Scotland and is almost as cold as marble. Hunger, who sees neither corn nor trees there, pulls up the very grass with her sharp nails and tough teeth, but finds it very sparse because of the thickly scattered stones. And if I wanted to describe her I could soon do it.

10133   'She is long and thin, weak and feeble, and in great want of oaten bread; her hair is all unkempt, her eyes hollow and deeply sunken, her face pale, with dry lips and cheeks smeared with filth. Anyone who wanted to could see her entrails beneath her hard skin. From her flanks, devoid of every humour, her bones protrude, and she seems to have no stomach but only the place where it should be, so deeply hollowed out that the girl's breasts hang from her backbone. She is so thin that her fingers seem elongated and her knees have lost their roundness, so crushed in the grip of thinness that her heels are high and sharp and prominent, and seem to have no flesh on them. Ceres, goddess of plenty, who causes the corn to grow, does not know the way there, nor does Triptolemus, who guides her dragons.* The Fates keep them far away, for they do not want the Goddess of Plenty and weary, suffering Hunger to join together. But if you want to go there where you can be idle as is your habit, Poverty will soon take you, once she has you in her grip, for the road that I am guarding here is not the only one that leads to Poverty; one can come to Poverty through an idle and lazy life. If, in order to attack the fortress, you wished to take the road of which I have just spoken to you, towards weary, contemptible Poverty, you might well fail to capture it. But I think it certain that Hunger will be your near neighbour, for Poverty knows that way better by heart than by any parchment map. And you should know that wretched Hunger is still so attentive and courteous towards her mistress (she does not love or esteem her, but is nurtured by her, even though she is weary and naked herself) that she comes to see her and sit with her all day, and takes her by the chin and kisses her, which is uncomfortable and unpleasant. Then, when she sees Theft asleep, she takes him by the ear and wakes him, leaning towards him in her distress and advising and teaching him how to obtain things, whatever he has to endure in order to get them. And Faint Heart agrees with them, although he dreams about the rope, which makes his every hair stand on end in case he should see his trembling son Theft hanged if he is caught stealing. But you may not enter here and must seek your way elsewhere, for you have not served me enough to deserve my love.'

'By God, my lady, were it possible, I would be glad to have 10205 your favour. As soon as I entered upon the path, I would release Fair Welcome from the prison where he is held captive. If it pleases you, grant me this.'

'I have understood you well', she said, 'and I know that you have not sold all your timber, large and small; you have retained one beech-tree, for no man, as long as he wants to follow Love, can live without some folly.* Men think themselves very wise while they live in such madness. Live? Indeed they do not, but rather die as long as they remain in such torment, for this raving madness ought not to be called life. Reason explained it to you well, but could not cure you of your stupidity. You should know that in failing to believe her you deceived yourself cruelly; indeed before Reason came, there was nothing to hold you back, nor did you care anything for me after you began to love *par amour*. Lovers do not respect me; instead they strive to belittle the goods that I allot to them, and fling them away. Where the devil could one find all that lovers want to spend? Get away from here and let me be.'

Since I could gain nothing here, I departed without delay. The fair lady stayed with her lover, who was also well dressed and adorned. Deep in thought, I wandered through the lovely garden, which was as fine and beautiful as you have heard before. But I had very little joy of it, for all my thoughts were elsewhere. Everywhere I went, I thought continually about how I could best perform my service without deceit, for I would have been very glad to do it, provided I could avoid committing any fault; my reputation would not have been in the least enhanced if I had committed the slightest fault.

10255 My heart held vigilantly to the advice Friend had given me. Wherever I found Evil Tongue, I always treated him with respect, and I was very careful to honour all my other enemies and serve them as best I could. I do not know whether I deserved their favour, but I considered myself a captive and therefore did not dare approach the enclosure as I had been used to do, for I always wanted to go there. Thus I performed my penance with such a conscience as God knows, for I did one thing and thought another. And so I played a double game, although I had never been guilty of such duplicity before. I had to follow a treacherous course in order to gain my ends, although I had never been a traitor before and no one has yet accused me of it.

10277 When Love had tested me thoroughly and saw that he had found me loyal, as loyal, at any rate, as I ought to be towards him, he appeared, smiling at my misfortune, and, placing his hand upon my head, he asked if I had done all his bidding, and how things were with me and what I thought of the rose who had stolen away my heart. And yet he knew everything I had done, for God knows all that men do. 'Are all those orders carried out', he said, 'that I give to true lovers, for I will not give them to anyone else, and lovers ought never to disregard them.'

10293 'I do not know, my lord, but I have carried them out as loyally as I could.'

'Indeed, but you are too changeable. Your heart is not secure but wretchedly full of doubt; I know the truth of it. You wanted to leave me the other day and almost withdrew your homage from me. You complained bitterly about Idleness and me, while as for Hope, you said she had no certain knowledge. You even thought yourself mad for entering my service and you agreed with Reason. Were you not a wicked man?'

'Have mercy, my lord. I have confessed, and you know   10309
that I did not flee. And I well remember that I made my will*
in a way befitting those who pay you homage. When Reason
came to me, she certainly did not think me wise but reproached me bitterly and exhorted me at length, imagining
that by preaching to me she could prevent me from serving
you. But in spite of all her efforts I did not believe her.
Certainly I would be lying if I said she did not make me
doubt, but no more than that. With God's help, whatever
may befall me, Reason will never persuade me to do anything
against you or anyone else who is in the least worthy, as long
as my heart remains attached to you, and it will so remain, I
assure you, as long as it is not torn from my body. I am even
angry with myself for ever thinking such things and for
listening to her. I beg pardon for it and desire to amend my
life as you have commanded, by dying and living in your
service, without ever following Reason. Nothing can erase
this from my heart. And whatever I do, may Atropos* deign
not to take my life except when I am engaged in your work;
instead, may she take me in the very act that Venus performs most willingly, for I have no doubt that no one has
such delight as he does in this. As for those who should
mourn me when they see that I am dead, may they be able
to say: "Fair sweet friend, who now find yourself in this
situation, it is no tale but the plain truth that your death was
appropriate to the life you led when you held body and soul
together." '

'By my head, you speak wisely. I see now that you have   10355
used my service well. You are not one of those false renegades, those scoundrels who renounce my service when they
have done what they sought to do. Your heart is very loyal;
since you navigate so well, your ship will come safe to port,
and I forgive you in response to your prayers rather than to
your gifts, for I want neither silver nor gold. But before you
are reconciled with me, instead of a *confiteor** I would like
you to recite all my commandments, for your romance will
contain ten of them, including both prohibitions and commandments. If you have retained them well, then you have
not thrown a double ace.* Say them.'

10373　'Gladly. I must avoid baseness and slanderous gossip and be prompt in offering and returning greetings. I should refrain from using coarse language, and always do my utmost to honour all women. I ought to avoid pride, keep myself elegant, and become gay and agreeable; and I should abandon myself to generous impulses and give my heart entire and undivided.'

'By my faith, you know your lesson well, I doubt you no longer. How are you?'

'In great pain, my heart is almost dead from it.'

'Have you not my three comforts?'

'No. Pleasant Looks is not here, whose sweet scent used to take the poison from my pain. All three of them fled, but two of them came back to me.'

'Do you not have Hope?'

'Yes, my lord, and therefore I am not cast down, for Hope is maintained for a long time after one has put one's trust in her.'

'What has become of Fair Welcome?'

'That open, gentle fellow, whom I loved so well, is held in prison.'

'Do not worry or be dismayed about that, for, by my eyes, you will have him again, even more ready to do your will than you were wont to expect. Since you serve me so loyally, I will summon my people at once to besiege the fortress. The barons are strong and agile, and before we leave the siege, Fair Welcome will be free again.'

10409　The God of Love, with no limit of time or place in the terms of his letter, summoned all his barons; some were asked and others ordered to come to his parliament. They all came, making no excuses and ready to do whatever he wanted to the best of their ability. I shall name them quickly and in no particular order, so as to make them rhyme more easily.

Lady Idleness, the garden-keeper, came with the largest banner, then Nobility of Heart, Wealth, Generosity of Spirit, Pity, and Largesse; Boldness, Honour, Courtesy, Delight, Simplicity, and Company; Security, Delight, and Joy; Gaiety, Beauty, Youth, Humility, and Patience; Discretion, and Constrained Abstinence, who brought False Seeming with her, for she could scarcely have come without him. These were there with all their followers, and each of them had a most noble heart, except for Constrained Abstinence and False Seeming with his deceitful face. Whatever their outward appearance, these two embrace Fraud in their hearts.

Fraud engendered False Seeming, who steals men's hearts; his mother, the shameful thief, was called Hypocrisy. It was she who suckled and reared him, the filthy hypocrite with the rotten heart who has betrayed many a region with his religious habit.

When the God of Love saw him, his heart was greatly shocked. 'What is this?' he said, 'Have I dreamed it? Tell me, False Seeming, by whose permission you have come into my presence.' At once, Constrained Abstinence jumped up and took False Seeming by the hand: 'My lord,' she said, 'I brought him with me, and I hope you do not mind. He has done me many honours and kindnesses; he supports and comforts me. Had it not been for him, I would have died of hunger, and so you should not blame me so much. Although he has no wish to love people, I still need him to be loved, and to be known as a worthy and a saintly man. He is my friend and I his, and so he comes to bear me company.'

'So be it,' said he, and then he briefly addressed them all:

'I have summoned you here', he said, 'to conquer Jealousy, 10465 who torments our lovers, and desires to hold against me this fortress that she has built, and that has grievously wounded my heart. She has fortified it so strongly that we will have to fight hard before we can conquer it, and I am therefore very grieved and worried about Fair Welcome, whom she has placed there, and who used to advance the causes of our friends so much. If he does not escape, I will be wretched, for Tibullus* is gone, who understood my nature so well, and at whose death I broke my arrows, snapped my bows, and let my torn quivers trail on the ground. So great was my anguish that I dragged my poor wings to his tomb all torn because I had beaten them so much in my grief, and my mother wept so much at his death that she almost died. No one who saw us weeping for him could have failed to pity us, for our grief was unrestrained and unbridled. Gallus, Catullus, and Ovid, who were skilled in writing about love, would have been very useful to us then, but each of them is dead and decayed. Here is Guillaume de Lorris, whose enemy, Jealousy, causes him such grief and torment that he is in danger of dying if I do not see about saving him. He would gladly have advised me as one who belongs entirely to me, and that would have been right, for it was for him that we took the trouble to assemble all our barons in order to rescue Fair Welcome and carry him off, but he says he is not very wise. Nevertheless, it would be a great pity if I were to lose so loyal a servant when I could and should help him, for he has served me so faithfully that he has deserved that I should sally forth and prepare to breach the walls and the tower and besiege the fortress with all my might. And he must serve me still further, for in order to deserve my favour, he must begin the romance that will contain all my commandments, and he will continue it to the point where he will say to Fair Welcome, now languishing unjustly and sorrowfully in prison: "I am dreadfully afraid lest you have forgotten me and so I am in pain and distress. Nothing will ever bring me comfort if I lose your favour, for I have no confidence in anyone else." Here Guillaume will rest. May his tomb be filled with balm and incense, myrrh and aloes, for he has served and praised me well.

10535   'Then will come Jean Chopinel, gay in heart and alert in body, who will be born in Meung-sur-Loire and will serve me, feasting and fasting, his whole life long, without avarice or envy. He will be so wise that he will care nothing for Reason, who hates and condemns my ointments, which smell sweeter than balm. And if, however things go, he should happen to fail in some respect (for there is no one who does not sin, everyone has some fault), his heart will be so true to me that when he feels himself at fault he will always, at least in the end, repent of his misdeed, having no wish to betray me. This romance will be so dear to him that he will want to complete it, if he has sufficient time and opportunity, for where Guillaume stops, Jean will continue, more than forty years after his death, and that is no lie. Full of fear and despair lest, as a result of the misfortune I have described, he should have lost the goodwill of Fair Welcome that he had had before, he will say: "And perhaps I have lost it; I am on the brink of despair" and all the other words, whatever they are, wise or foolish, until he has plucked the fair red rose from the green and leafy branch, and it is daylight and he awakes. Then he will explain the story in such a way that nothing remains hidden. If these two could have found a remedy, they would have counselled me at once, but the first cannot do so now, nor can he who is yet to be born, for he is not present here. And yet the thing remains so serious that unless, when he is born, I take my wings and fly to read him your thoughts the moment he emerges from childhood, I dare swear and pledge that he could never finish it.*

'And since something could perhaps happen to hamper this 10587 Jean who is yet to be born, which would be a sad shame and a great loss for lovers, for he will do them a great deal of good, I pray Lucina, goddess of childbirth, to grant that he be born without difficulty or mishap and that he have a long life. Afterwards, when the moment comes for him to be taken alive by Jupiter and to drink, even before he is weaned, from the casks of which there are always two,* one clear and one murky, one sweet and one more bitter than soot or gall, and then to be placed in his cradle, I will cover him with my wings, because he will be my dear friend. Then I will sing him such songs that when he has left childhood behind and has acquired all my learning, he will proclaim our words in the language of France at crossroads and in schools, publicly throughout the kingdom, and those who hear them will never die from the sweet pains of love, provided only that they believe him. For he will read so well that all those who are yet to live should call this book the *Mirror of Lovers*,* since they will see great benefits in it for them, provided they do not believe Reason, the miserable wretch. Therefore I would like to take counsel with you, since you are all my counsellors, and beg with joined hands for mercy for poor, sorrowful Guillaume, who has behaved so well towards me; may he be helped and comforted. If I did not pray to you on his behalf, I certainly ought to pray you at least to relieve Jean and make it easier for him to write; you confer this benefit upon him (for he will be born, I prophesy it) for the sake of those who

will come after, who will dedicate themselves to the task of
following my commandments, which they will find written
in this book, so as to overcome the wrath and envy of
Jealousy and destroy all the castles that she ever dares to build.
Advise me! What should we do? How should we deploy our
host? Where will we best be able to hurt them, the sooner
to destroy their castle?' Thus Love addressed them and his
speech was well received.

10651   When he had finished his address, the barons took counsel.
Their opinions were divided; different ones said different
things, but, after various conflicts, they reached agreement
and reported their agreement to the God of Love.

'Sire,' they said, 'all of our men have reached agreement
except for Wealth alone, who has sworn on oath never to
besiege this castle nor, she says, to strike a blow with dart,
lance, axe, or any other arm, whatever anyone may say. She
so scorns this young man that she has also scorned our enterprise and left our host, at least as far as this operation is
concerned. The reason why she scorns and condemns him
and looks at him askance is, she says, that he never loved her.
Therefore she hates him and will continue to hate him from
now on, because he has no wish to amass treasure; he has
never committed any other crime against her. This is the sum
total of his crime: she says without a doubt that the other day
he asked her permission to enter the path called Lavish Giving, and flattered her besides, but he was poor when he asked
her and therefore she denied him entry. Since then, according
to what Wealth has told us, he has not managed to obtain a
single penny of his own. When she had explained this to us,
we reached our agreement without her.

10689   'We find in our agreement that False Seeming and Abstinence and all who fight under their banners will attack the
rear gate, which is guarded by Evil Tongue and his Normans
(may they burn in hell!). Courtesy and Largesse will go with
them and display their prowess against the Old Woman who
holds Fair Welcome in harsh subjection.

'Next, Delight and Discretion will go to murder Shame;
they will assemble their host to attack him and will lay siege
to that gate.

'They have set Boldness and Security against Fear; those two will be there with all their followers, who have never known what it was to flee.

'Generosity of Spirit and Pity will volunteer to attack Rebuff, and thus the host will be well deployed. These will destroy the castle if everyone does the best he can and provided that Venus, your mother, is there, for she is very wise and experienced in this kind of operation. It will never be achieved without her, not by word or by deed, and therefore she should be summoned, for the task would then be easier.'

'My lords, the goddess my mother, who is my lady and my mistress, is not entirely at my beck and call to do whatever I desire. If she wished to do so, she could very well come herself to help me achieve my tasks. But I have no wish to trouble her now; she is my mother and I have feared her since my childhood. I hold her in great reverence, for the child who does not fear his father and mother will certainly pay for it. Nevertheless, we will certainly be able to summon her when we need her. Were she close at hand, she would soon come, for I do not think that anything could restrain her. 10719

'My mother has great prowess and has, in my absence, captured many a fortress that cost more than a thousand bezants. I was given the credit for it nevertheless, although I would never have entered there, nor would I have condoned the capture of fortresses in my absence, for it seems to me, whatever anyone says, that it is nothing but a mercenary transaction. If someone buys a horse for a hundred pounds, let him pay the money and so his debt is discharged; he owes nothing more to the merchant and the merchant owes nothing to him. I do not call a sale a gift: no recompense is necessary for a sale and no favour or merit is involved; both parties are free from obligation when they separate. 10735

'And yet this situation is not like a sale, for when a man has put his horse in the stable, he can sell it again and recover his capital or make a profit; at the very least he cannot lose everything. If he cared about the hide, he would still have that at least and he could get something for it, or if he was so fond of the horse that he kept it to ride, he would still be the horse's master. But the trade with which Venus is concerned is far worse, for however much anyone invests, he will lose all his capital, as well as everything he has bought. The seller has both the goods and the price of them, while the buyer loses everything, for however much he invests, he will never be master of the goods. Whatever he gives and however much he preaches, his resentment will not prevent a stranger, be he Breton, English, or Roman, who comes and gives the same amount, or more, or less, from receiving as much as he. Perhaps indeed the stranger will have such a way with words that he receives all for nothing. Are then such merchants wise? No, they are foolish, miserable wretches when they buy something knowing that, whatever their outlay, they will lose it all, and that, however hard they try, it will not be theirs to keep. Nevertheless, I will not deny that my mother is not in the habit of paying for it. She is not so silly or so foolish as to get involved in that kind of vice. But you should know that some men do pay for it and regret the transaction later, when, even though they may have been followers of Wealth, they are tormented by Poverty. When her wishes coincide with mine, Wealth is vigilant on my behalf.

'But I swear by holy Venus, my mother, and by her old father, Saturn, who begat her when she was already a young girl, though not on his espoused wife;* and to make things even more certain I will swear to you by the faith I owe all my brothers, whose fathers, all of whom my mother bound to herself, are so many and various that no one can name them; furthermore, I will swear by and call to witness the infernal swamp (and if this is a lie I shall drink no nectar for a year, for you know the custom of the gods, that anyone who breaks this oath shall not drink nectar until a year has passed). Now I have sworn enough and it will go hard with me if I break my oath, but you will never see me do so: since Wealth fails me now, I intend to make her pay dearly for this defection. She shall pay for it if she does not arm herself with sword or halberd at least. And since she did not behave like a friend today, knowing that I was to overthrow the fortress and the tower, then it was unfortunate for her that she ever saw the dawning of this day. If I can get a rich man into my power, you will see me tax him so heavily that, however many marks or pounds he has, he will soon be relieved of them. I will cause all his pennies to fly away, if he does not have barnfuls of them in a constant stream; our young women will so pluck him that he will need new feathers, and they will make him sell his land, unless he is very good at protecting himself.

'Poor men have taken me as their master, and even though   10835 they have nothing to feed me with, I do not scorn them: no worthy man does. Wealth is very greedy and gluttonous; she insults them, harries and hustles and kicks them. They love better than the rich do, or the grasping, tight-fisted misers, and by the faith I owe my grandfather, they are more obliging and more loyal. Therefore their good hearts and their willingness are amply sufficient for me. They think only of me, and I must therefore think of them; their cries fill me with such pity that I would soon raise them to great heights if I were god of wealth as well as of love. Moreover, I must help the man who strives so hard to serve me, for if he died from the pains of love, it would seem that there was no love in me.'

'Sire,' they said, 'everything you say is true. The oath that   10857 you have taken concerning rich men must certainly be kept, for it is a good and true and fitting one. It will be kept, we are certain of it: if rich men pay you homage, they will not be acting wisely, for you will never break your oath, never suffer the pain of abstaining from nectar. Ladies will make things so hot for them if they ever fall into their toils that they will certainly suffer for it. In their courtesy ladies will settle your account with them; you need seek no other agents, for, have no fear, they will tell them such highly coloured tales that you will consider yourself paid. Do not interfere: they will spin such yarns and make such requests, while falsely flattering them, and so beset them with kisses and embraces that if the men believe them, it is certain that all their lands will go the same way as the chattels they have already lost. Now command whatever you like, we will do it, whether it be wrong or right.

'But False Seeming does not dare to involve himself in this   10889 affair on your behalf, for he says that you hate him, and does not know whether you desire to shame him. And so, fair lord,

we all beg you to forgive him and remit your anger; may he
be one of your barons, together with Abstinence, his friend:
this is what we have agreed and sanctioned.'

'By my faith,' said Love, 'I will grant it. From now on I
am willing for him to be at my court. There, let him come
forward!' And he ran forward.

'False Seeming, you are now mine, on the understanding
that you help all our friends, never harming them but always
thinking how you can improve their position. But you shall
be charged and empowered to harm our enemies. You shall be
my Lord of Low Life, since our chapter wants it so. You are
without doubt an evil traitor and an utter scoundrel and
have broken your word countless times; nevertheless, to relieve our people of their anxiety, I command you in a loud
voice to tell them, or at least give a general indication of
where they could most easily find you if they needed to do
so, and of how you can be recognized, since sharp wits are
needed to recognize you. Tell us which places you frequent.'

10922 'My lord, I have various dwellings that I have no wish to
tell you about, if you will be kind enough to spare me, for
if I tell you the truth about them, I might suffer hurt and
shame. If my companions knew I had done so, they would
certainly hate me and make trouble for me, or I never knew
them to be cruel. They want to suppress the truth everywhere, for it is their enemy and they never wish to hear it.
I might be very harshly treated if I said anything about them
that was not agreeable and friendly, for a stinging word would
never please them in the slightest, not even if it were the
Gospel reproaching them for their treachery, such is their evil
cruelty. And so I know for certain that if I say anything to
you about them, they will know of it sooner or later, however secure your court may be. I am not worried about
worthy men, who will not, when they hear me, take anything
I say as applying to themselves; but the man who does apply
my words to himself will incur the suspicion that he wishes
to live the life of Fraud and Hypocrisy, who gave me life and
brought me up.'

'A very fine job they made of it', said Love, 'and a very
profitable one, for they gave life to the devil himself.

'Nevertheless,' said Love, 'whatever happens, you must 10957 certainly say here and now, in the hearing of all our men, what your dwellings are, and tell us about your life. It is not right for you to conceal it any longer; now that you have thrown in your lot with us, you must reveal everything about what you do and how you go about it; and if you are beaten for telling the truth, although you are not used to it, you will not be the first.'

'Lord, since it pleases you, I will do what you want, even though I die for it, for I have a great desire to do your will.'

Without further delay, False Seeming immediately began his speech and said to them all in a loud voice: 'Barons, hear what I have to say. If a man wishes to know False Seeming, he should seek him in the world or in the cloister; I dwell in no other place except these two, but more in one and less in the other. Briefly, I take my lodging where I think I can best be hidden, and the safest hiding-place is beneath the most humble garments. Religious are well covered up, whereas seculars are more exposed. I have no wish to criticize religion or slander it; in whatever habit it may be found, I shall refrain as far as I can from reproaching the religious life that is lived humbly and loyally. Nevertheless I shall never love it.

'I am talking about those false religious, wicked scoundrels 10993 who wish to don the habit of religion but will not subdue their hearts. Religious are all merciful and you will never see one who is arrogant; they do not care to pursue pride but all wish to live humbly. I will never dwell with such people, and if I do dwell there, I will dissemble. I can indeed wear their habit, but I would rather be hanged than turn aside from my purpose, whatever expression I may assume.

I dwell among the proud, the artful, and the wily, who covet worldly honours and accomplish great works, who hunt for the largest portions and seek the acquaintance of powerful men, to become their followers. They call themselves poor but they are fed with fine, delicious morsels and drink precious wines; they preach poverty to you while fishing for great wealth with their seines and trammel-nets. By my head, evil will come of it! They are neither religious nor pure; they offer to the world a syllogism that has a shameful conclusion:* a man wears a religious habit, therefore he is religious. This argument is entirely specious, not worth a privet-knife: the habit does not make the monk. And yet no one can answer it, no matter how high he tonsures his head or shaves it with the razor of Elenchis,* which divides fraud into thirteen branches; no one is so good at making distinctions that he dare utter a single word about it. But wherever I go and however I conduct myself, I pursue nothing but fraud; just as Sir Tibert the cat* is only interested in mice and rats, I am only interested in fraud. You will certainly not be able to tell by my habit which people I am living with, and I will not reveal it to you by my words, however simple and mild they are. You must look at my actions, if your eyes have not been put out, for if people do not act as they speak, they are certainly deluding you, whatever clothes they are wearing and whatever estate they belong to, whether cleric or layman, man or woman, lord or servant, maidservant or lady.'

11053   As False Seeming was speaking thus, Love addressed him once again, interrupting his speech as if it had been false or foolish: 'What is this, you devil, are you being impertinent? What people have you just told us about? Can religion be found in a secular dwelling?'

'Yes, lord. It does not follow that people lead a wicked life and therefore lose their souls because they are attached to worldly clothes; that would be a great sorrow. Holy religion can indeed thrive in coloured clothes. We have seen the death of many saintly men and many glorious saints, devout and religious women who always wore ordinary clothes and were none the less canonized, and I could tell you the names of many. Almost all the holy women to whom we pray in church, chaste virgins and married women who bore many fine children, wore worldly clothes and died in them, and they are saints, and were and will be. Even the eleven thousand virgins* who hold their candles before God and whose feast is celebrated in the churches were taken in their worldly clothes when they received martyrdom, and they are none the worse for that. A good heart makes good thoughts, and clothes take nothing away nor add anything to that, and good thoughts make the works that reveal religion. Religion consists in having a right intention.

'If you were to clothe Sir Isengrin the wolf in Dam Belin's* 11093 fleece instead of a sable cloak, so that he would resemble a sheep and dwell with the ewes, do you not think he would devour them? He would be no less likely to drink their blood, but all the swifter to deceive them, for since they would not know who he was, they would follow him, even if he chose to flee.

'If there are any young wolves like that among your new apostles,* O Church, then you are in a bad way. If your citadel is attacked by the knights of your own table, then your rule is very weak. If those to whom you entrust its defence strive to capture it, who can protect it from them? It will be taken without receiving a single blow from mangonel or catapult, without unfurling a single banner to the wind; and if you are not willing to rescue it from them, then you allow them to overrun it. Allow them, do I say? Why, even if you command them, there is nothing for it but to yield, or become their tributary by making peace and holding it feudally from them, unless a greater misfortune befall you and they become lords of all. They are good at mocking you now: by day they run around fortifying the walls and by night they ceaselessly undermine them. Think about planting somewhere else the trees from which you wish to gather fruit; you should not delay in doing so. But for the time being, peace: I shall turn my back on this subject and do not want to say any more about it at the moment, if I may leave it at that, for I might weary you too much.

'However, I will gladly agree to promote the interests of 11133 all your friends, provided they desire my company; they are dead if they do not welcome me. And they must also serve my beloved, or by God they will never prosper. I am certainly a traitor and God has judged me a thief. I am a perjurer, but when I carry something through, it is hard for people to know about it before it is over; many have died because of me without ever noticing my deceit; many die and will die without ever noticing it. If anyone does notice it, he will protect himself if he is wise, or it will be very much the worse for him. But the deception is so complete that it is very difficult to recognize; Proteus,* who used to change himself into anything he liked, was never so well versed in fraud and trickery as I am, for I have never been recognized in any town I have entered, however much I may have been heard and seen there.

11157   'I am very good at changing my clothes, at donning one outfit and discarding another. At one moment I am a knight, at another a monk, now a prelate, now a canon, now a clerk, now a priest, now disciple, now master, now lord of the manor, now forester; in short, I am of every calling. Again, I am prince one moment, page the next, and I know all languages by heart. At another time I am old and hoary, then I become young once more. Sometimes I am Robert, sometimes Robin, sometimes a Franciscan, sometimes a Dominican, and in order to follow my companion, Lady Constrained Abstinence, who comforts me and bears me company, I assume many other disguises, just as it pleases her, so as to carry out her wishes. Sometimes I don women's clothes: I may be a maiden or a lady; sometimes I am a religious, sister or prioress, nun or abbess, novice or professed nun. I go to every region and investigate all the religious orders, and from these orders I invariably take the chaff, leaving the wheat alone. I dwell there in order to deceive people, and I seek only the habit, nothing more. What can I say? I assume whatever disguise I like. I am not at all what I seem, and my deeds are very different from my words.'

With that, False Seeming was about to fall silent, but Love did not seem to be displeased by what he had heard him say; instead, in order to delight the company, he said to him: 'Tell us more particularly how you engage in treachery, and do not be ashamed to tell us, for, according to your clothes, you seem to be a holy hermit.'

'That is true, but I am a hypocrite.'

'You preach abstinence.'

'True indeed, but I fill my belly with rich food and wine, as a theologian should.'

'You preach poverty.'

'Indeed, though I am abundantly wealthy. But however much I pretend to be poor, I have no regard for poor men. By Our Lady, I would infinitely rather have the acquaintance of the king of France than of a poor man, even though his soul were just as good! When I see those poor creatures naked on their stinking dung-heaps, shivering with cold, crying and moaning with hunger, I do not get involved. If they are taken to the *hôtel-Dieu*, they will get no comfort from me, for, having nothing worth a cuttlefish, they could not feed my maw with a single gift. What can the man give who licks his knife? But it is pleasant and enjoyable to visit the rich money-lender when he is sick; I go to comfort him because I expect to carry money away with me, and if grim death should put paid to him, I will escort him to the very grave. And if anyone rebukes me for avoiding the poor man, do you know how I get out of it? I suggest by the cloak I wear that the rich man is more stained with sin than the poor, and so has greater need of counsel, and that is why I go to him and counsel him.

'Nevertheless, the soul can be just as thoroughly ruined by 11239 excessive poverty as by excessive wealth; both wound with equal severity, for wealth and beggary are two extremes. The mean is called sufficiency, and that is where abundant virtues lie, for Solomon has written, without reservation, in the thirtieth chapter, in fact, of a book of his entitled *Proverbs*: "By your power, O God, preserve me from wealth and beggary, for when a rich man takes to thinking too much about his wealth, he so sets his heart upon madness that he forgets his creator. And how can I save a man from his sin when he is assailed by beggary? It would be hard for him not to be a thief and a perjurer,"* or else God is a liar, if it was in his name that Solomon spoke those words that I have just read to you. I can swear forthwith that it is not written in any law, or at least not in ours, that when Jesus Christ and his apostles were on this earth they were ever seen seeking for bread, for they did not wish to beg* (this is what the masters of divinity were formerly accustomed to preach in the city of Paris). They could have demanded, in the full-ness of their power, without needing to beg, for they were shepherds in God's name and had the cure of souls. And immediately after their master's death, they even began again to work with their hands, supporting themselves by their work, no more, no less, and living in patience. If they had anything left over, they gave it to other poor people, and they did not found palaces or halls but laid their heads in dirty houses.

11287 'I remind you that an able-bodied man, if he does not have the means to live, should seek his living through the labour of his own hands and body, no matter how religious or anxious to serve God he may be. This is how he should behave, except in certain cases that I remember, and that I will be able to tell you about when I have time. Furthermore, Scripture has told me that if a man were perfect in goodness, he should sell everything and work for his living, for the idler who haunts another's table is a lying story-teller.

'And you know it is not right to use praying as an excuse, for in any case we have to interrupt the service of God for other necessary things, for one way or another we have to eat, it is true, and sleep and do other things, and then our prayers are hushed; we should also withdraw from prayer in order to do our work, for Scripture, which reveals the truth to us, is in agreement with this.

11315 'And thus Justinian,* who wrote our ancient books, forbids any able-bodied man to beg for bread in any way, provided he can find a way to earn it. It would be better to cripple him or make a public example of him than to support him in such wickedness. Those who receive such alms do not behave as they ought, unless perhaps they have a licence that exempts them from punishment; but I do not think that such a licence can be had except by deceiving the prince, nor do I believe that they have a right to possess one. I am not setting limits upon the prince or his power, nor do I wish my remarks to cover the question of whether his power extends to such a case; I ought not to involve myself with that. But I believe that, according to the text, alms are due to the weak and poor and naked, the old and feeble and crippled, who will never be able to earn their bread because they have no power to do so, and that anyone who harms them by consuming those alms consumes his own damnation, if he who made Adam does not lie.

'Know too that when God commands the good man to sell all he has and give it to the poor and follow him, he does not therefore want him to live to serve him in beggary, that was never his thought. He means rather that he should work with his hands and follow him with good works, for Saint Paul commanded the apostles to work in order to procure the necessities of life, forbidding them to beg and saying: "Work with your hands and do not take from others."* He did not want them to ask for anything from any of the people to whom they preached, nor to sell the Gospel; rather he feared that if they were to ask, their request might amount to extortion, for there are many almsgivers on earth who, to tell the truth, give only because they are ashamed to refuse, or because the one who asks is importunate, and they give so that he will go away. And do you know what good that does them? They lose both the gift and the merit. When the good people who heard St Paul's preaching begged him in God's name to take some of their goods, he would never stretch out his hand to them but earned what he needed to live by the labour of his hands.'

'Tell me then, when a man who is strong in body wishes 11377
to follow God, how can he live when he has sold all he has and given it to the poor and wants only to pray, without ever working with his hands? Can he do it?'

'Yes.'

'How?'

'He can if, as Scripture enjoins, he enters an abbey that has its own means, as have nowadays those of the White Monks and Black Monks, the canons regular,* the Hospitallers and Templars (for I can cite them as valid examples), and finds his livelihood there, for there is no begging in such places. Nevertheless, many monks work and afterwards run to do God's service.

'And since I remember a time when there was great discord 11395
concerning the mendicant state, I will now tell you briefly how a man who has nothing with which to feed himself may

be a beggar. You will hear the cases one by one, so that there will be nothing to object to in spite of malicious gossip, for the truth cares nothing for concealment. In this way, I will be able to atone for the fact that I ever dared plough such a field.

'The special cases are as follows: if a man is so like a beast as to know nothing of any craft, but does not want to remain ignorant, then he may resort to mendicancy until he can learn some skill that will enable him to earn an honest living, without begging. Or if he cannot work because of illness, old age, or extreme youth, he may resort to begging. Or if perhaps his upbringing has accustomed him to soft living, then respectable people should take pity on him and permit him in charity to ask and beg for bread, rather than allow him to die of hunger.

11427   'Or if he has the knowledge, the will, and the strength to work and is ready to work hard but cannot immediately find anyone who is willing to employ him, whatever he may be equal or accustomed to doing, then he may certainly provide for his wants by begging. Or if he works for money but his wages are not adequate for him to live on this earth, then he may start to beg for bread, going from door to door and searching everywhere to make up the deficit.

'Or if, in order to defend the faith, he wishes to undertake some chivalrous activity, whether in arms or scholarship or some other suitable occupation, and if he is weighed down by poverty, he may certainly beg, as I have said before, until he can work to obtain what he needs, provided he work with hands of this sort:*

Manus corporalis

not with spiritual hands:

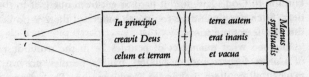

In principio creavit Deus celum et terram + terra autem erat inanis et vacua — Manus spiritualis

but with his actual bodily hands, no double meaning being implied. In all these and similar cases, if you find any others that are reasonable besides those that I have given you here, the man who wants to beg for his living may do so; in those cases but not otherwise, unless he of Saint-Amour* who used to debate and teach and preach on this subject with the Paris theologians is a liar. May bread and wine fail me if the truth of what he said was not supported both by the University and by the people who heard his preaching. No worthy man who denies it will find forgiveness with God. If anyone wants to grumble or get angry about it, let him, for I would not keep silent, even if I were to lose my life for it or be unlawfully imprisoned, like Saint Paul, in a dark dungeon, or wrongfully banished from the kingdom, like master Guillaume de Saint-Amour, whose exile was brought about by Hypocrisy in her great envy.

'My mother by plotting drove that valiant man into exile 11479 because he defended the truth. He offended my mother greatly by producing a new book in which he wrote an account of her entire life and expressed a wish that I should forswear mendicancy and go to work if I had nothing to live on. He must have thought I was drunk, for I cannot like work. I have nothing to do with work; working costs too much effort. I prefer to pray where people can see me, and hide my duplicity beneath a cloak of religious hypocrisy.'

'What is this, you devil? What are these words? What have 11495 you said?'

'What?'

'Great and flagrant treachery! Do you not fear God, then?'

'Certainly not, for it is hard for a godfearing man to achieve anything great in this world. The good, who avoid evil and live honestly on what they have, supporting themselves according to God's law, find it hard to get from one loaf to the next. Such people endure too much suffering; there is no life that displeases me more.

11507 'But see what quantities of pennies lie in the storehouses of usurers, forgers, money-lenders, bailiffs, beadles, provosts, mayors: all of them practically live by rapine. The common people bow before them and they devour them like wolves; they all assail the poor and there is none who will not fleece them and clothe himself with the spoils; they suck them dry and pluck them alive without scalding them first; the strongest takes from the weakest. But I, wearing my simple robe, dupe both dupers and duped; rob both robbers and robbed.

11523 'Through my trickery I accumulate and amass great piles and heaps of treasure that nothing can undermine; for if I use it to build palaces and obtain all the delights that company and bed and tables loaded with delicacies can supply (for I no longer want any other kind of life), then in the meantime my silver and gold increase, for before my treasure is empty, I acquire money in abundance. Do I not make my bears dance well? I concentrate all my effort on gain, and this quest is worth more than my revenues. Were I to be killed or beaten for it, I would still penetrate every place, and never seek to resign my post as confessor of emperors, kings, dukes, barons, or counts. But it is shameful to be the confessor of poor people, nor do I like such confessions. Unless there is some other reason for it, I care nothing for the poor; their estate is neither fair nor noble.

11547 'But as for empresses and duchesses, queens and countesses, noble wives of Palatines, abbesses, beguines, wives of bailiffs and knights, proud and elegant burgesses, nuns and maidens, whether naked or well dressed, provided they are rich or beautiful, they will not go away without receiving good advice.

11557 'For the salvation of their souls, I make enquiries about the property and the lives of the lords and ladies and all their household, and I instil in them the belief that their parish priests are animals in comparison with me and my companions, many of whom are evil curs, to whom I am in the habit

of revealing men's secrets without concealing anything, while
they also reveal everything to me, for there is nothing in the
world that they hide from me.

'So that you may recognize the scoundrels who continually   11570
deceive people, I will quote some words that we read in Saint
Matthew, that is to say the evangelist, in the twenty-third
chapter:* "Upon the chair of Moses" (the gloss explains that
this is the Old Testament) "the scribes and pharisees have
sat." (These are the false and treacherous people whom the
text calls hypocrites.) "Do as they say but not as they do.
They are never slow to speak good things but have no desire
to do them. Upon the shoulders of the gullible they bind
grievous, unbearable burdens that they themselves dare not
move with their fingers." '

'Why not?'

'By my faith, because they do not want to. The shoulders
of those who bear the burdens often give them pain, that is
why they have no desire to bear them. If they do good works,
it is in order to be seen doing them. They make their phyl-
acteries broad and their fringes long, and they love the
highest and most honourable places at table and the best seats
in the synagogue, for they are proud and haughty and overbearing. They like to be greeted as they go about in the streets
and to be addressed as master, but they should not be so
addressed, because this runs counter to the Gospel record,
which demonstrates their wickedness.

'We have another custom where those whom we know to   11607
be our enemies are concerned: we are all ready to hate them
violently and to make a concerted attack upon them. If one
of us hates a man, the others hate him, and each one strives
to destroy him. If we see that he might, through the agency
of certain people, succeed in obtaining worldly honour, prebends, or possessions, we try to discover by what ladder he
might ascend; then, the better to capture and subdue him,
we slander him treacherously to his patrons, for we do not
love him. In this way, we cut the rungs from the ladder and
rob him of his friends, but he will never hear a word about
their defection. If we hurt him openly, we might perhaps be
blamed for it and would thus miss our aim, for if he knew

our evil intention, he would defend himself and we would
be rebuked for it.

11631   'If one of us has done something very good, we consider
it done by us all. Even if he has feigned it, by God, or merely
condescended to boast that he has advanced the cause of
certain men, we all make ourselves partners in the deed and
say, as you must know, that we have promoted such and such
a man. And in order to win people's praise, we flatter rich
men into giving us letters testifying to our goodness, so that
the world should believe us to be abundant in every virtue.
We always pretend to be poor but, however much we may
complain, you may take it from me that we have everything
without having anything.

11649   'I am also involved in brokerage, I effect reconciliations
and arrange marriages, I undertake the duties of executor and
procurator. I deliver messages and make investigations which
are not honourable, and I am most pleasantly occupied when
busy with someone else's affairs. If you have any business
with those whom I frequent, tell me, and it will be done as
soon as you have explained it to me; you have deserved my
service if you have served me well. But anyone who tried to
rebuke me would immediately lose my favour; if a man
reproaches me with anything, I neither love nor esteem him.
I am happy to rebuke everyone else, but I have no wish to
hear their rebukes, for I who reprove others do not need their
reproofs.

11671   'Nor have I any interest in hermitages; I have given up the
deserts and woods and abandoned the desert huts and dwellings to Saint John the Baptist. I was too far away there; I
build my halls and palaces in towns, within castle walls, and
in cities, where men can rush to them with all speed. I say
that I am out of the world, but I plunge deep into it and
bathe, taking my ease and swimming better than any finny
fish.

11683   'I am one of the young men who serve Antichrist, one of
those thieves of whom it is written that they wear the habit
of sanctity but their lives are a pretence. Outwardly we seem
to be tender lambs, but within we are ravening wolves; we
overrun sea and land and have declared war on the whole

world, for we wish to lay down every detail of the life that men should lead. If heretics are reported in any castle or city, even if they come from Milan, for the Milanese also are tainted with this heresy; if anyone is so anxious for gain that he makes unreasonable terms when selling on credit or lending at interest; if anyone, even a provost or official, is also a lecher, a thief or a simonist, a jolly-living prelate, a priest who keeps a mistress, an old whore who has a house, a pimp or a brothelkeeper, or charged with some other vice for which he should be brought before the courts, then, by all the saints we pray to, unless he defend himself with lamprey, pike, salmon, or eel (if they can be found in the town), with tarts, flans, cheeses in their trays (for this is a gem of a dish when served with a *caillou* pear*), with fat geese or capons to tickle our palates; unless he quickly send for kids or rabbits roasted on the spit, or at least a loin of pork, he will be tethered with a rope and led off to be burned and his screams will be heard for a good league in all directions, or else he will be captured and imprisoned in a tower and confined there for ever, since he has not provided properly for us, or else, perhaps, he will be punished more severely for his crime than he deserves.

'But if he had sufficient wit to build a great tower, it would 11731 not matter what stone he used nor even if he built it without square or compass, or out of earth or wood or anything else whatever. Provided that he had amassed there enough of this world's goods, and surmounted the tower with a catapult to launch at us dense hails of those pebbles you have heard me mention, forwards and backwards and to both sides as well, and all in order to gain a good reputation; provided he used great mangonels to hurl wine in barrels and casks and huge sacks containing a hundred pounds, he would soon find himself free. But if he cannot find such pittances, then let him lay aside commonplaces and sophisms if he does not think that they will win our favour, and seek instead for equivalences;* otherwise we will bear such witness against him that we will have him burned alive, or else we will impose a penance on him that will be more costly than the pittances.

11757 'You will never recognize these false and deceitful traitors by the clothes they wear; you must examine their deeds if you want to protect yourself from them.

'Had it not been for the vigilance of the University, which keeps the key of Christendom, everything would have been thrown into turmoil when, with evil intent, in the year of Our Lord 1255 (and no man living will contradict me) there was released as a model for imitation, and this is true, a book written by the devil, the *Eternal Gospel*,* which, according to the title, was transmitted by the Holy Spirit, for so it is called;* it deserves to be burned. There was not a man nor a woman in Paris, in the square in front of Notre-Dame, who could not have had it to copy if he had wanted. He would have found there many outrageous comparisons such as this: just as the sun in the great excellence of its light and heat surpasses the moon, which is much dimmer and darker, just as the kernel surpasses the nutshell, I tell you truly upon my soul—and do not imagine that I am making fun of you—that in the same way this gospel surpasses those written by the four evangelists of Jesus Christ under their own names. A great many such comparisons would have been found there, which I forbear to mention.

11795 'The University, which was asleep at the time, raised its head; it awoke at the uproar that the book provoked and scarcely slept afterwards but, when it saw the horrible monster, took up arms against it, fully prepared to do battle with it and to hand over the book to the judges. But those who had issued the book leapt up and withdrew it and made haste to hide it, for they had no explanation nor gloss with which to answer the objections raised to the accursed things written in it. Now I do not know what will come of this, or how it will turn out, but the authors of the book must continue to wait until they can defend it better.

11815 'And so we will await Antichrist, and all together remain faithful to him. Those who refuse to join him will surely lose their lives. We will hatch tricks to stir up the people against them and have them slain or otherwise put to death, since they are unwilling to follow us, for thus it is written in the book whose words convey the following meaning: as long as

Peter is lord, John cannot show his power. I have given you the shell of the meaning which hides the real intention; now I will explain the kernel to you. Peter signifies the Pope and includes the secular clergy, who will keep the law of Christ, guarding and defending it against all who would obstruct it; John stands for the friars, who will say that the only tenable law is the *Eternal Gospel*, sent by the Holy Spirit to set men on the right path. By the power of John is meant the grace by which he boasts that he wants to convert sinners and make them turn back to God. Many other devilries are ordained and set down in this book of which I speak, against the law of Rome and on the side of Antichrist, as I find written in the book. Next they will order all those of Peter's party to be killed, but I can guarantee that, however many they kill or beat, they will never have the power to overthrow the law of Peter; there will always be enough people left alive who will continue to uphold it so well that in the end everyone will accept it, and the law signified by John will be vanquished. Now I do not want to say any more about this, for it would be too long a story. But if this book had been passed, my standing would have been far higher; as it is, I have some very distinguished friends who have already raised me to a position of importance.

'Fraud, my lord and father, is emperor of all the world; my 11867 mother is its empress. Our powerful lineage reigns, in spite of the Holy Spirit. We reign now in every kingdom and it is quite right that we should, for we bewitch the whole world and deceive people so cleverly that no one notices; or if anyone does notice, he does not dare to reveal the truth. But such a man incurs the wrath of God for fearing my brothers more than God. A man is not a good champion of the faith if he fears such tricks or is unwilling to accept the pain that may result from denouncing them. Such a man does not want to hear the truth or have God before his eyes, and God will certainly punish him for it. But I do not care what happens, since we have honour among men. We are thought to be so good that we have the advantage of reproving others without ourselves incurring any reproof. And who then should be honoured apart from us, who pray continually and openly in men's sight, although we may do otherwise behind their backs?

11897   'Is there a greater madness than to encourage chivalry and to love those who are noble and elegant and whose clothes are fine and well made? If they are as they appear to be, as faultless as the clothes they wear, and if their actions match their words, is that not a shame and a crime? May they be cursed if they will not be hypocrites! We will certainly never love such people; instead we love religious hypocrites, with their wide hats, their pale, smooth faces, their voluminous grey robes all trimmed with filth, their wrinkled hose and great boots like quail-hunters' pouches. Princes should hand themselves and their lands over to such folk to be governed, whether in peace or in war; princes should attach themselves to them if they want to achieve honour. But if the noble people are other than they seem, and thus steal the world's favour, then I am glad to introduce and establish myself among them in order to practise tricks and deceptions.

11923   'I do not mean, however, that one should despise humble garments, provided pride does not dwell beneath them. No one should hate a poor man because of the clothes he wears, but God does not give a straw for him if he says he has left the world but is full of worldly pride and wants to enjoy the good things of life. Who can excuse such sanctimoniousness? When such a hypocrite enters the religious life and then pursues worldly delights, saying that he has abandoned them all but later wanting to grow fat on them, he is like the dog who greedily returns to his vomit. I dare not lie to you, but if I could have felt that you would not have noticed it, I would have served you with a lie: I would certainly have tricked you and would not have refrained, even though it was a sin. I could still desert you if you were to treat me badly.'

The god smiled at this remarkable speech, and everyone laughed in amazement and said: 'Here is a fine servant and one who can be trusted!'

11951   'Tell me, False Seeming,' said Love, 'since I have brought you so near to me and you have such power in my court that you will be my Lord of Low Life, will you keep your agreement with me?'

'Yes, I swear it upon oath, neither your father nor your grandfather ever had a more loyal servant.'

'How is this? It is against your nature.'

'Take the risk, for if you require sureties, you will not be any more secure as a result, no indeed, not if I gave you hostages or letters, witnesses or pledges. I call you to witness: you cannot separate a wolf from his hide until he is flayed, however much you thrash and beat him. Do you imagine that I have abandoned trickery and duplicity just because I am wearing these simple clothes, under whose cover I have performed many great evils? By God, my heart will never change. If my face is demure and gentle, do you think I have ceased to do evil? My beloved Constrained Abstinence needs my help; she would long ago have been dead and in an evil plight if she had not had me in her power. Let us, her and me, do what is necessary.'

'Very well, I believe you without pledges.'   11980

And there and then, the thief, with his treacherous face, white on the outside and blackened within, knelt down and thanked him.

And so they had only to get ready. 'Let us attack now,   11985 without delay,' cried Love in a loud voice. So all together armed themselves suitably. They took up their arms, and once they had done so, they eagerly sallied forth. They reached the fortress, and determined never to leave it until all were slain or it was taken. They divided their battalions into four and split up into four parties, just as they had divided their men, in order to attack the four gates, whose guards were not dead or ill or lazy, but strong and vigorous.

Now I shall tell you how False Seeming and Abstinence   12003 behaved, who launched an attack on Evil Tongue. They conferred together about how they should act, whether to make themselves known or to go in disguise. They agreed to go disguised as good, pious, holy people, as if they were on a pilgrimage. At once, Constrained Abstinence donned a robe of cameline* and dressed as a beguine,* covering her head with a large kerchief and a white cloth. She did not forget her psalter, and she had beads hanging on a lace of white thread, which had not been sold to her but given by a friar

whom she called her father and whom she very frequently
visited, more than anyone else in the convent; he also visited
her and preached many fine sermons to her. In spite of False
Seeming, he never failed to hear her confession often, and
their confessions were so devout that, as it seemed to me,
their two heads were together in a single hat.

12035   I would describe her as having a fine figure, but her face
was a little pale. Wanton bitch, she was like the horse of the
Apocalypse that signifies the wicked people, pale and stained
with hypocrisy, for that horse has no colour but a deathly
pallor, and Abstinence was coloured with that same sickly
hue. Her face suggested that she repented of her state. Fraud
had given her a pilgrim's staff of theft, darkened with sombre
smoke, and her scrip was full of cares. When she was ready,
she went on her way.

12052   False Seeming, who was equipping himself well in his turn,
had donned, as though to try them out, the robes of brother
Saier.* His face was very simple and pious and his expression
far from proud, but gentle and placid. He wore a Bible
around his neck. Then he set off, without a squire, but with
a crutch of treason to support his limbs, as though they were
weak, and with a fine, sharp, steel razor, forged in a forge
known as Cut-throat, slipped into his sleeve.

12067   They each set off and approached so close that they came
to Evil Tongue, who was sitting at his gate. He saw everyone
who passed, and observed the pilgrims, who approached in
so humble a manner. They bowed to him very humbly;
Abstinence greeted him first and went up to him, then False
Seeming greeted him and he them, but he did not move, for
he neither suspected nor feared them. For when he had seen
their faces, it seemed to him that he knew them well, for he
knew Abstinence well, although he knew nothing of any
constraint about her. He did not know that her life of
thievery and pretence was the result of constraint, but imagined that it was undertaken willingly; in fact it came from
an entirely different direction, and even though it might have
begun willingly, that will had faded between then and now.

12089   He had also seen a great deal of Seeming, but had not
known that he was false. He was false indeed, but he would

never have been accused of falseness, for the seeming worked so powerfully that it covered up the falseness. Even if you had known him before seeing him in those robes, you would have sworn by the king of heaven that the man who used to be the handsome Robin of the dance had now become a Dominican. But truly, the Dominicans are all honest men, and that is that—they would be serving the order badly if they were putting on an act—and so are the Carmelites and Franciscans, even though they are large and fat, and the Friars of the Penance of Christ and all the rest: there is not one who does not seem to be honest. But in any argument, if deficiency cancels existence, you will not find that mere appearance can produce a good consequence; if you have the subtlety to see through the deception, you will always find that the consequence is undermined by a sophism.*

When the pilgrims had duly come to Evil Tongue, they 12117 put down all their equipment close beside them. They sat down by Evil Tongue, who had said to them: 'Come here now and give me your news, and tell me what reason brings you to this house.'

'Sir,' said Constrained Abstinence, 'we have come here as pilgrims in order to do penance with a true and pure and sincere heart. We are almost always on foot and our heels are all dusty. Thus we have both been sent into this errant world to set an example and to preach in order to fish for sinners, for we want no other catch. We have come for the love of God, to ask you for shelter, as our custom is; and in order to amend your life, if it should not displease you, we would like briefly to preach you a good sermon.'

At once Evil Tongue spoke: 'Take the shelter that you see,' he said, 'it will never be refused you, and say whatever you like: I shall listen to whatever it is.'

'Hearty thanks, sir.' Then Lady Abstinence began first:

'Sir, the first and greatest and most sovereign virtue that 12149 any mortal man can have, whether acquired through learning or through possessions, is the ability to curb his tongue: everyone should strive for this, for it is always better to keep silent than to say a wrong word, and anyone who is willing to listen to such a word is neither honest nor godfearing.

You, sir, are tainted with this sin more than any other. A long time ago you told a lie, which was a most wicked crime, concerning the young man who used to come here. You said that he only wanted to deceive Fair Welcome: but perhaps this was a lie and not the truth, and now he no longer comes and goes here and you may never see him here again. Because of this, Fair Welcome remains in prison. On most days of the week he used to play here with you the most delightful games he could, without ever thinking a base thought, but he dare not enjoy himself any more. You have driven away the young man who used to come and take his pleasure here. What prompted you to hurt him so much, apart from your own evil mind, which has dreamed up many lies? You have caused this with your wild gossip, by shouting and bawling and yelling and arguing, hurling reproaches at people, hurting them and humiliating them for something which cannot be proved except by appearances or inventions. I dare say openly to you that appearances can be deceptive, and moreover that it is a sin to invent something that will bring blame upon someone. You know this very well yourself, and therefore your sin is greater. Nevertheless, the young man attaches no importance to it; he cares not a jot about it, come what may. You know that he was not contemplating anything wrong, for he would have come and gone and no excuse would have detained him. But now he no longer comes, nor has any wish to, unless he passes this way by chance, which he does less often than the others. Yet you keep ceaseless watch over this gate, with your lance in rest: the fool wastes his time all day. You watch there night and day, and all your trouble is for nothing. Jealousy, who is counting on you, will not do as much for you. And there is also the injury to Fair Welcome, held as security for a loan he has not had, imprisoned though he has committed no crime, and languishing in tearful captivity. If you had committed no other crime but this in all the world, you should—please do not take it amiss—be stripped of your office and thrown into a dungeon or clapped in irons. You will go to the pit of hell if you do not repent.'

12220   'Indeed you lie!' he said. 'You are not welcome here! Was it for this that I took you in, to hear such shameful insults?

Most unfortunately for you, you must have taken me for a fool! Now go elsewhere for your lodging, since you call me a liar. You are a pair of tricksters, coming here to reproach and insult me because I speak the truth. Is that what you are trying to do? I shall hand myself over to all the devils, or may you, good God, confound me if I was not told, not more than ten days before this fortress was built, and I repeat it now, that the young man kissed the rose; I do not know whether he enjoyed more of her favours. Why would I have been told this if it were not true? By God, I shall say and say again (and I do not think it will be a lie), I shall trumpet it to all my neighbours, men and women, how he came and went.' Then False Seeming spoke:

'Sir, everything that is said around the town is not gospel. 12247 Now if you do not close your ears, I will prove to you that these rumours are false. You know for certain that no one, however ignorant he may be, can love sincerely a man who speaks ill of him, if he is aware of the fact, and it is also true, as I have often read, that all lovers like to visit the places where their sweethearts live. This young man honours and loves you and calls you his very dear friend; he shows you a friendly, cheerful face whenever he meets you, and never fails to greet you; and yet he is not too importunate, nor does he weary you too much; the others come here more often than he. You should know that if his heart tormented him on account of the rose, he would approach it and you would often see him here; why, you would have caught him red-handed, for he could not have stayed away, not even at the risk of being skewered alive, and he would not be in his present condition. Know, then, that he has no thought of it. Nor, in truth, has Fair Welcome, although he has been poorly rewarded for it. By God, if the two of them had really wanted to, they would have plucked the rose in spite of you. When you spoke ill of this young man, who loves you, as you know very well, you may be sure, make no mistake, that had this been his intention, he would never have loved you, never have called you friend; instead, if this had been the case, he would have devoted his thoughts and his waking hours to breaking down and destroying the castle, for he would have known about it, someone

would have told him. He could have discovered it for himself,
for he would not have had the access that he had before and
he would soon have realized. But his behaviour is quite
different. And therefore you have most certainly deserved the
torments of hell for oppressing such people.'

12297   Thus False Seeming proved it to him; he was unable to
reply to the proof, and yet what he saw was sophistry. He
was on the point of repenting and said to them: 'By God, it
may be so. Seeming, I consider you a good teacher, and
Abstinence very wise. You seem to be of one mind: what do
you recommend I do?'

'You must make your confession here, and tell your sin
without more ado, and you must repent of it, for I am from
an order and am a priest, the greatest master of the art of
confession throughout the world. I have charge of all the
world, which no parish priest, however devoted to his church,
ever had. And by Our Lady, I have one hundred times more
pity for your soul than your parish priest, however good a
friend he may be. I have also one very great advantage:
prelates are not nearly so wise nor so well instructed as I. I
have a degree in theology; indeed, by God, I have taught it
for a long time. The best men we know have chosen me as
their confessor on account of my intelligence and learning. If
you are willing to make your confession here and abandon
your sin without further ado and without ever referring to it
again, you will have my absolution.'

12331   Evil Tongue at once got down and knelt and made his
confession, for he was truly repentant, but False Seeming
seized him by the throat and, holding fast with his two fists,
strangled him and robbed him of the power to gossip by
cutting out his tongue with his razor. Thus they dealt with
their host, thus and not otherwise they killed him and tum-
bled him into a ditch. They broke down the undefended gate,
and when it was broken, they went through to the other side,
where they found all the Norman soldiers asleep. They had
been vying with one another in the drinking of wine that I
had not poured: they had poured it themselves in such quantities
that they were all flat on their backs. They were strangled as
they lay in their drunken sleep, and will never gossip again.

CHAPTER 7

THE ADVICE OF THE OLD WOMAN

And now Courtesy and Largesse went briskly through the
gate, so that all four were together there, furtively and in
secret. All four saw the Old Woman; she had been guarding
Fair Welcome for a long time and was not paying attention.
She had come down from the tower and was taking her ease
in the enclosure. Above her wimple, her head was covered
with a cap instead of a veil. At once, all four of them ran up
quickly and attacked her. She had no wish to be beaten and
said, when she saw all four of them gathered together: 'By
my faith, you seem to be very worthy, valiant, and courteous
people. Now tell me, without too much noise, what you are
seeking in this enclosure, for I do not suppose you have
captured me'

'Capture you, sweet, gentle mother! We have not come to
capture you, merely to see you and, if it pleases and suits you,
to make you an unconditional offering of ourselves and whatever we have of value to do your gentle bidding, without
ever failing you. Also, sweet mother who have never been
bitter, we have come without any evil intent to ask you if
you would please allow Fair Welcome to cease his languishing in there and come out and play with us for a while: he
will scarcely soil his shoes. Or at least allow him to say one
word to this young man, so that they may comfort one
another; this will be a great consolation to them and will be
quite easy for you. Then this young man will be your liegeman, even your servant, and you will be able to do whatever
you like with him, sell him, hang him, or maim him. It is
good to win a friend, and here are some of his jewels: he
gives you this clasp and these buttons, and indeed, he will
soon give you a fine ornament. He has a most noble, courteous, and generous heart, and so he will not be a burden to
you. He loves you very much, and you will never be reproached, for he is very wise and discreet. We beg you to
hide him, or to allow him to go there without any suspicion

of misconduct; in this way you will restore him to life. And now, if you please, take this chaplet of fresh flowers from him to Fair Welcome; comfort Fair Welcome on his behalf and greet him fairly; this will be worth a hundred marks to him.'

12415   'So help me God,' said the Old Woman, 'were it not that Jealousy would know of it and I would hear myself blamed, I would gladly do it. But Evil Tongue is such a gossiping scandalmonger. Jealousy has made him her sentinel and he spies on all of us, shouting and yelling without restraint whatever he knows, and indeed whatever he thinks. He even invents things when he has no gossip to spread. He could not be prevented from doing it were he to be hanged for it. If that thief were to tell Jealousy about it, I would be brought to shame.'

12431   'You need have no fear of that,' they said, 'there is no way in which he will be able to hear or see anything about it: he is lying dead outside with his mouth wide open, and that ditch serves him for a bier. You may be sure that he will never, unless by magic means, gossip about those two, for he will never come to life. Never, unless devils work miracles with poisons and antidotes, will he be able to accuse them.'

12442   'Then I will not refuse your request,' said the Old Woman, 'but tell him to hurry. I shall find a way in for him, but he must not say anything shocking or delay too long, and he must come very discreetly when I tell him. He must take care, on pain of losing his life and his possessions, that no one sees him, and he must do nothing he ought not to do, although he may say whatever he likes.'

'Lady,' they said, 'it will certainly be so,' and they both thanked her; thus they carried out their task.

12457   False Seeming, whose thoughts were running along different lines, said softly to himself: 'If he on whose behalf we undertook this task would trust me at all, and provided he did not renounce his love, I do not think that it would be in your interest, in the long run, to deny his request, for he would enter secretly, given the time and the opportunity. We do not always see the wolf who takes the lambs from the stable when they have been well guarded in the fields. You might go to church one day: you stayed there for a long time yesterday. Or perhaps Jealousy, who plays such tricks on the wolf, might have to leave town to go somewhere or other. Then he would come in secret or by night, from the garden, alone, without candle or torch, unless perhaps Friend had been warned of it and was there to watch for him. In that case he would be encouraged and led quickly to the place, unless the moon was shining, for the moon's bright rays often harm lovers. Or else he might come in through the windows (for he is familiar with every corner of the house), and let himself down on a rope: in this way he could come and go. Fair Welcome might perhaps come down to the garden where the young man was waiting, or he might flee outside the enclosure where you have held him prisoner for many days, and come and talk to the young man, if the young man could not go to him. Or, when he knew you were asleep, if he could find the time and the opportunity, he might leave the doors slightly open. In this way, the true lover might approach the rose-bud which so occupies his thoughts and pluck it without hindrance, if there were any way in which he could overcome the other gatekeepers.' And I, who was not far off, thought to myself that I would do just as he said. If the Old Woman was willing to conduct me, that would do me no harm at all; if she was not willing, I would enter where I saw my best chance, just as False Seeming had thought; in everything I would abide by what he thought.

The Old Woman did not linger there but trotted back to 12511 Fair Welcome, who remained in the tower against his will, for he would gladly have done without this imprisonment. She continued until she came to the entrance to the tower and went quickly in. Gaily she climbed the stairs, as swiftly as she could, trembling in every limb. She went from room to room looking for Fair Welcome, and found him leaning over the battlements, pensive, sad, and gloomy, and most unhappy with his captivity. She set herself to comfort him: 'Fair son,' she said, 'it troubles me greatly to find you in such distress. Tell me about these thoughts, for if I can counsel you in any way, you will never find me reluctant to do so.' Fair Welcome dared not make his complaint nor tell her all the whys and wherefores, for he did not know whether she spoke the truth or lied. He denied all his thoughts because he did not feel safe and did not trust her in the slightest. Even his fearful, trembling heart mistrusted her, but he dared not show it, because he had always been so frightened of the senile old whore. He wanted to avoid misconduct because he feared betrayal, and so he did not disclose his unhappiness but feigned an inner calm and assumed a cheerful expression. 'Truly, my dear lady,' he said, 'in spite of what you say, I am not in the least distressed, except on account of your delay. I am unwilling to remain here without you, for I love you very much. Where have you been for so long?'

12553   'Where? By my head, you will soon know, and the knowledge will bring you great joy, if you have any courage or wisdom. It is no strange messenger but the most courteous young man in the world, full of every grace, who sends you more than a thousand greetings—I saw him just now in the street as he was passing on his way, and he gave me this chaplet for you. He says he would like to see you and that, so help him God and Saint Faith, he no longer wants to live nor to enjoy a single day's health unless it is by your wish. He says he would like to be able to speak to you just once, at leisure, provided you were willing. For your sake alone, he loves his life; he would be glad to be naked in Pavia if in this way he could do something to please you; he would not care what became of him, provided he could keep you near him.'

12577   However, before he would accept the present, Fair Welcome asked who it was who sent it to him, for he suspected that it might come from such a source that he would not wish to keep it. And without beating about the bush, the old woman told him the whole truth: 'It is the young man whom you know and of whom you have heard so much, and on whose account the late departed Evil Tongue once caused you such pain by bringing blame upon you. May his soul never go to paradise! He has brought down many a worthy man and now the devils have carried him off, for he is dead and we have escaped him! I no longer give a fig for his gossip; we are quit of him for ever, and if he could come back to life, he could not hurt us, however much blame he brought upon you, for I know more than he ever did. Now trust me and take this chaplet and wear it, give the young man so much comfort at least, for have no doubt, his love for you is true and free from baseness. If he has any other intention, he did not disclose it to me. But we can certainly trust him: for your part you will be able to deny his request if he asks for anything he should not have: if he does anything foolish, he must take the consequences. However, he is not foolish but wise; he has never done anything shocking and therefore I esteem and love him all the more. He will never be so base as to ask you for something that should not be asked for. He is more loyal than any man alive. Those who bear him company have always testified to this, and so do I. He is very decorous in his habits, and no man born of woman ever heard any ill of him, except what was said by Evil Tongue, and that has already been forgotten. I have almost forgotten it myself and I do not even remember the words, except that they were false and foolish and invented by that thief, for he never behaved well. I know for certain that the young man would have killed him if he had known anything of it, for he is unfailingly valiant and brave. His heart is so noble that there is no one in the land to equal him, and his largesse would exceed that of King Arthur, or indeed of Alexander, if he had as much gold and silver to spend as they; however much they gave, he would have given one hundred times as much: his heart is so good that he would have astounded all the world with his gifts if he had had such possessions; no one can teach him about largesse. Now I recommend that you take this chaplet, whose flowers are sweeter than balm.'

'By my faith, I would be afraid of incurring blame,' said 12648 Fair Welcome, shaking and trembling, shuddering and groaning, blushing and turning pale, quite out of countenance. And the Old Woman thrust it into his hands and wanted to force him to take it, for he dared not stretch out his hand for it but said, the better to excuse himself, that it was more seemly for him to refuse it. And yet he would have liked to keep it, come what might. 'The chaplet is very fair,' he said, 'but I would be better off with my clothes all burned to ash than if I dared accept it from him. But supposing I take it, what then could we say to that quarrelsome creature Jealousy? I know very well that she will be wild with anger and will tear it from my head in pieces and then kill me if she knows it comes from there. Either I will be captured and held in worse conditions than I ever have been in my life or, if I escape her and take flight, where will I be able to flee to? You will see me buried alive if I am captured after my flight; and yet I think that I would be pursued and captured as I fled, for everyone would raise the hue and cry. I will not take it.'

'O yes you will, and without incurring any blame or loss as a result.'

'And if she asks me where it has come from?'

'You will have more than twenty answers.'

'Nevertheless, if she asks me, how can I answer her demand? If I am blamed or rebuked for it, where shall I say I got it? For I shall have to hide it or tell some lie. I assure you that if she knew, I would be better dead than alive.'

12691　　'What can you say? If you do not know, and have no better answer, say that I gave it to you. As you know, my reputation is such that you will never be reproached or shamed for taking anything that I may give you.'

Without another word, Fair Welcome took the chaplet and, placing it on his blond hair, felt more secure. The Old Woman laughed at him and swore by her soul and body, skin and bones, that no chaplet ever suited him so well. Fair Welcome admired it repeatedly, gazing at himself in the mirror to see if it became him well. When the Old Woman saw that the two of them were alone there, she sat down amicably beside him and began her sermon: 'Ah, Fair Welcome, I am extremely fond of you, for you are so handsome and worthy. My time for joy has all departed but yours is yet to come. I can scarcely stand upright any longer except with a stick or a crutch. You are still a child and do not know what you will do, but I know very well that sooner or later, whenever it may be, you will pass through the flame that burns everything, and plunge into the bath in which Venus makes women bathe. I know it well, you will feel the burning brand, and I advise you to listen to my instructions and prepare yourself before bathing there, for the young man who has no one to instruct him bathes there at his peril. But if you follow my advice you will come safe into port.

'I tell you, if, when I was your age, I had been as wise as I am now concerning the games of love—for I was very beautiful then, but now I must sigh and weep when I gaze at my ravaged face, with its inevitable wrinkles, and remember how my beauty made the young men skip. I made them thresh about to such an extent that it was nothing less than a marvel. I had a great name in those days and the fame of my celebrated beauty spread everywhere. My house was so full of people that no one ever saw the like; many hammered on my door at night, for I treated them very harshly and broke my word to them, and this often happened, for I had other company. Many foolish things were done which angered me: my door was often broken and there were frequent fights which were not settled until limbs and lives had been lost in hatred and envy. There were so many quarrels that even if Master Algus,* the great calculator, had taken the trouble to come with his ten numerals, with which he certifies and numbers everything, he could not, however good he was at sums, have certified the number of them. In those days my body was strong and active—but if, as I say, I had been as wise then as I am now, I would now have a thousand pounds in silver sterlings more than I have. But I behaved very foolishly.

'I was young and beautiful, silly and irresponsible, and I have never been to the school of Love, where they teach the theory, but I know it all through practice. Experience, which I have pursued throughout my life, has made me wise in love's ways, and since I now know all about it, it is not right that I should fail to teach you what I know, the fruits of my own experience. It is good to advise the young. It is certainly not to be wondered at that you do not know the first thing about it, for you are young and green.

'But the fact remains that I persevered until in the end I obtained the knowledge, and I could even give a public lecture on it. Not everything that is very old is to be fled from or despised: sense and experience are to be found there. We have often encountered people who were left, in the end

12731

12771

12785

at least, with a fund of sense and experience, however dearly they had bought it. And when, not without great pain, I had obtained sense and experience, I deceived many a valiant man who had fallen captive into my toils; but I was deceived by many before I realized it. It was too late, miserable wretch that I was! I had already left youth behind; my door, which once opened so often, night and day, now clung to the lintel: "No one is coming today, no one came yesterday," I thought in my grief and misery. "I must live in sorrow." My woeful heart almost broke; I wanted to leave the country when I saw my door so quiet, and I hid myself, unable to endure the shame of it. How could I have endured it, when those gay young men came who once held me so dear that they could never weary of me, and I saw them pass by and give me a sideways glance, those who had once been my dear guests? They skipped past and did not give twopence for me. Even those who had loved most in the old days called me a wrinkled crone, and each of them said much worse things before they had passed me by.

12827   'Moreover, my sweet child, no one, unless he were very studious or had experienced great grief, could know or imagine the pain in my heart when I recalled to mind the fair speeches, sweet pleasures, sweet delights, sweet kisses, and most sweet embraces that had flown away so soon. Flown? Certainly, never to return! It would have been better for me to be imprisoned for ever in a tower than to be born so early. My God, how I fretted over the fair gifts that no longer came. What torments I suffered over what remained of them! Alas, why was I born so soon? To whom can I complain, to whom but you, my son, whom I love so dearly? The only way I can avenge myself is by teaching my doctrine. Therefore, fair son, I will instruct you, so that when you are instructed, you will avenge me upon that riff-raff, for, God willing, when the time comes, you will remember my words. I assure you that your age gives you a great advantage when it comes to retaining and remembering things, for Plato says:* "It is true that the memory retains best the things that are learned in childhood, whatever kind of knowledge it may be."

'Certainly, dear son, tender youth, if my youth were of the 12863
present as yours is now, I could not adequately convey in
writing the vengeance I would take. Everywhere I went I
would do such extraordinary things to those scoundrels who
esteem me so little, insulting and despising me and passing
me by so basely, that you would never have heard the like.
Both they and others would pay for their arrogance and scorn;
they would get neither pity nor consideration. With the aid
of the intelligence God has given me, as I have told you, do
you know to what pass I would bring them? I would so pluck
them and rob them, right and left, that I would make them
dine on worms and lie stark naked on dung-hills, first and
foremost those who loved me with most loyal hearts and
exerted themselves most willingly to serve and honour me.
If I could, I would leave them with nothing worth a bean; I
would have everything in my purse. I would reduce them all
to poverty and make them all run after me, dancing with
rage. But it is pointless to regret it: what's done is done. I
shall never be able to hold a single one of them, for my face
is so wrinkled that they care nothing for my threats. They
told me so long ago, those scoundrels who despised me, and
it was then that I began to weep. And yet, by God, the
memory of my heyday still gives me pleasure, and when I
think back to the gay life that my heart so desires, my
thoughts are filled with delight and my limbs with new
vigour. The thought and the recollection of it rejuvenates my
whole body; it does me all the good in the world to remember everything that happened, for I have at least had my fun,
however I may have been deceived. A young woman leading
a life of wantonness is not idle, especially not when she takes
care to make enough to cover her expenses.

'Then I came to this country, where I met your lady, who 12919
took me into her service in order to guard you in her enclosure. God the lord and guardian of all grant that I guard you
well! And so I shall, certainly, thanks to your good behaviour.
But the wondrous beauty with which Nature has endowed
you would have made this a perilous charge, had she not
taught you such virtue and wisdom, valour and grace. And
now, since time and place have fallen so well for us and there

is nothing to prevent our saying what we want to say a little better than usual, I ought to give you some advice, and you must not be surprised if I break off now and then. I will tell you in advance that I have no wish to encourage you to love, but if you want to get involved, I will gladly show you the ways and paths I should have trodden before my beauty vanished.'

12947   Then the Old Woman sighed and fell silent in order to hear what he would say, but she did not wait long, for when she saw that he had every intention of listening and keeping quiet, she took up her theme again, thinking: 'Silence certainly indicates consent; if he is willing to listen to everything, I can say everything without fear.'

12957   Then she resumed her speech, the false and servile crone, imagining that through her teaching she could make me lick honey from thorns, for according to Fair Welcome, who remembered everything she said and recounted it to me afterwards, she wanted him to call me his lover without loving me *par amour.* If he had been the kind of person to believe her, he would certainly have betrayed me, but he pledged me his word, and this was the only assurance he gave me, that nothing she said could have made him commit such treason.

12971   'Fair, gentle son, with your sweet, tender flesh, I would like to teach you the games of love, so that when you have learned them, you will not be deceived. Shape yourself according to my art, for no one who is not well informed will be able to get through without some loss. Now make sure you listen and pay attention and commit everything to memory, for I know all about it.

12982   'Fair son, if anyone wants to enjoy the bitter-sweet pains of love, he should know Love's commandments but beware lest Love draw him to himself. I would tell you all of these commandments now, if I could not see with certainty that you have by nature more than enough of each. All told, there are ten commandments that you should know, but it is extremely foolish to burden oneself with the last two, which are not worth a brass farthing. I will allow you the first eight, but anyone who observes the other two is wasting his effort and driving himself mad: they ought not to be taught in school.

To require lovers to have a generous heart and to fix it in one place is to impose too heavy a burden upon them. It is a false text, falsely written; Love, the son of Venus, lies and no one should believe him in this. Anyone who does believe him will pay dearly for it, as will be apparent in the end.

'Never be generous, fair son; bestow your heart in several 13007 places, never just in one, and neither give it nor lend it but sell it very dearly and always to the highest bidder. Make sure that no one who buys it gets a bargain; no matter how much he gives, he must get nothing, for it would be better if he were to burn or hang or drown himself. Above all, observe these points: your hands should be closed to give and open to receive. Indeed, it is folly to give, unless the gift is a small one intended to serve as bait and we imagine it to be to our advantage, or we expect such a return that we could not have sold it more profitably. I allow you such giving; giving is good when the giver makes his gifts pay handsomely. If a man is certain of his profit, he cannot repent of the gift; I certainly agree to such a gift.

'Next, concerning the bow with the five arrows that are 13031 so full of good qualities and strike so subtly, you know so well how to shoot it that Love, that excellent archer, never loosed the arrows from that dear bow better than you, fair son, who have so often loosed them. But you have not always known where the blows have fallen, for when we shoot at random, the shot may strike someone to whom the archer has given no thought. But to judge by your manner, you draw and shoot with such skill that I can teach you nothing, and you will therefore be able to wound someone from whom, God willing, you will derive great profit.

'Nor is it necessary for me to bother teaching you about 13049 the fine clothes and trimmings with which you will adorn yourself in order to seem more admirable in men's eyes; it cannot matter to you, for you know the song by heart, having heard me sing it so often as we went out to play, the song about Pygmalion's image.* Take this as your model for personal adornment; you will then know more about it than an ox does of ploughing. There is no need whatever to teach you these skills. And if this is not sufficient, you will hear me say something presently, if you will listen, from which you might be able to learn something. But I can tell you this: if you wish to choose a lover, I advise you to give your love to the handsome young man who values you so highly, but let it not be too firmly fixed. Love others with discretion and I shall find you enough of them for you to amass great possessions. It is good to frequent rich men if their hearts are not mean and miserly and if you are skilled at fleecing them. Fair Welcome may attract as many of them as he likes, provided he gives each to understand that he would not take any other lover for a thousand marks in fine powdered gold, and provided he swears that, had he been willing to allow his rose, which is most sought after, to be taken by another, he would have been loaded with gold and jewels, but that his heart is so true and faithful that no one will stretch out his hand for the rose except him alone who is extending his hand at that moment.

13089   'If there are a thousand of them, he must say to each: "You alone will have the rose, fair sir, and no one else will ever have a share. May God fail me if I divide it!" He must swear it and give them his word. Let him not be concerned about perjuring himself; God laughs at such oaths and will gladly pardon him. 'Jupiter and the gods used to laugh when lovers perjured themselves, and the gods who loved *par amour* were often forsworn. Jupiter, when reassuring Juno, his wife, would swear a mighty oath on the river Styx and was falsely perjured. Thus true lovers should be reassured that they too may swear falsely by all the saints, convents, and churches, since the gods give them such examples. But God protect me, anyone who believes the oaths of lovers is a great fool, for their hearts are too fickle. The young are not reliable, nor, very often, are the old; instead they break their promises and their oaths.

13115   'It is true, I assure you, that the lord of the fair must collect his toll from everyone, and if you fail at one mill, hey up to the next as fast as you can! The mouse who has only one hole to retreat to has a very poor refuge and is in great danger when he goes foraging. It is just the same for a woman, for she is mistress of all the bargaining in which men engage in order to have her: she ought to take from everyone, since on mature reflection she would see that it was a very foolish idea to have only one lover. By Saint Lifard of Meung,* if anyone bestows his love in just one place, then his heart is neither free nor at liberty but basely enslaved. A woman who concentrates her efforts on loving just one man deserves to have trouble and suffering. If she has no comfort from him, then she has no one to comfort her, and it is those who bestow their hearts in just one place who are worst off. The men will all desert them in the end, when they are tired and weary of them.

'This is no way for a woman to succeed. Dido, queen of   13143
Carthage, could not hold Aeneas,* in spite of all she had done for him; for she had received him, a poor and weary fugitive from the fair country of Troy, his birthplace, and had re-clothed and fed him. She showed great honour to his com-panions because of her great love for him. In order to be of service to him and to please him, she had all his ships refitted, and she gave him her city, herself, and her possessions in exchange for his love. He gave her such strong assurances of it that he promised and swore that he was and always would be hers and would never desert her. But she had little joy of him, for the traitor fled; taking no leave, he sailed away across the sea, which cost the fair Dido her life, for before the day was out, she killed herself by her own hand in her chamber, with the sword that he had given her. Remembering her lover and seeing that she had lost his love, she took the naked sword and raised it point upwards, then, placing the point beneath her two breasts, she fell upon the blade. This must have been most pitiful to see for any who beheld the deed; it would have been a hard man who felt no pity when he saw fair Dido impaled upon the blade. She drove it through her body, such was her grief at the way he had deceived her.

'Phyllis also waited so long for Demophoön* that she   13181
hanged herself when he overstayed his leave and thus broke his promise and his word.

'How did Paris behave towards Oenone, who had given him her heart and her body and to whom he in his turn had given his love? He at once took back his gift, and yet he had carved tiny letters with his knife on a tree on the river bank instead of on paper: they were not worth a button. These letters were carved in the bark of a poplar tree and they said that Xanthus* would flow backwards if he ever deserted her. Now let Xanthus return to its source, for he left her afterwards for Helen.*

13199   'And what of Jason's conduct towards Medea* who was so basely deceived in her turn? The traitor broke his word to her, for she had saved him from death when she used her spells to deliver him without burn or injury from the bulls that breathed fire from their mouths and that would have burned him or torn him in pieces. She also drugged the dragon for him and sent it into so deep a sleep that it could not wake. As for those wild and warlike soldiers born of the earth who would have killed Jason, she made them attack and kill one another when he threw the stone among them, and she gained the fleece for him through her skill and potions. Then, the better to bind Jason to herself, she restored the youth of Aeson. She never wanted any more from him than that he should love her as he used to and, recognizing her merits, keep faith with her all the better. Then he abandoned her, the evil traitor, the false, disloyal thief, and when she knew it, in her grief and rage she strangled her children, because they were Jason's. This was not well done, for in forgetting maternal pity she behaved worse than a cruel stepmother. I could give you a thousand examples, but the tale would be too long.

13235   'In short, they are all deceitful traitors, ready to indulge their lusts with everyone, and we should deceive them in our turn and not set our hearts upon just one of them. It is a foolish woman who gives her heart in this way: she ought to have several lovers and arrange, if she can, to be so pleasing that she brings great suffering upon all of them. If she has no graces, let her acquire them and always behave more cruelly towards those who will strive all the harder to serve her in order to win her love, while exerting herself to welcome those who do not care about it. She should be familiar with games and songs, but avoid quarrels and strife. If she is not beautiful, she should enhance her appearance; the ugliest should be the most elegantly attired.*

'And if she sees that her beautiful blond hair is falling out 13253
(a most mournful sight), or if it has to be cropped as a result
of a serious illness and her beauty thus spoiled too soon, or
if some angry roisterer should happen to tear it out so that
there is no way in which she can regain her thick tresses, she
should have the hair of some dead woman brought to her,
or pads of light-coloured silk, and stuff it all into false hair-
pieces. She should wear such horns above her ears that no
stag or goat or unicorn could surpass them, not though his
head were to burst with the effort, and if they need colour
she should dye them with many different plant-extracts, for
fruit, wood, leaves, bark, and roots have powerful medicinal
properties. If her complexion loses its colour and her heart is
tormented as a result, she should arrange always to have
aqueous ointments hidden in boxes in her chamber, for the
purpose of painting her face. But she must take care that none
of her guests can smell or see them: otherwise she could be
in great trouble.

'If her neck and throat are fair and white, let her see to it 13283
that her dressmaker cuts the neck so low that half a foot of
fine white flesh is visible front and back; in this way she will
deceive men more easily. And if her shoulders are too large
to be pleasing at dances and balls, she must wear a dress of
fine cloth and thus appear less ungainly.

'If her hands are not fair and unblemished but marred by 13293
spots and pimples, she ought not to leave these alone but use a
needle to remove them; or else she should hide her hands in
her gloves so that the spots and scabs are not visible. And if
her breasts are too full, let her take a kerchief or scarf and
wrap it round her ribs to bind her bosom, and then fasten it
with a stitch or a knot; she will then be able to disport herself.

'Next she must be a good girl and keep her chamber of 13305
Venus clean. If she is virtuous and well brought up, she will
leave no spiders' webs around but will burn or destroy them,
pull them down or sweep them away so that no dirt can
collect.

'If her feet are ugly, they should always be covered; stout
legs should wear fine stockings. In short, if she is aware of
any fault, she must cover it, unless she is a fool.

'If she knows her breath is bad, it should not be too much trouble for her to take care never to fast nor ever to speak before she has eaten. And if possible, she should take care not to put her mouth close to people's noses. If she feels like laughing, she should do so with discretion and decorum, so as to reveal two dimples on either side of her lips, and she should neither puff out her cheeks nor constrain them in an affected simper. When she laughs, she must never open her mouth but hide her teeth and conceal them. A woman should laugh with her mouth closed, for a mouth wide open in laughter is not a pretty sight: it looks like a great gash. And if her teeth are not well spaced but ugly and uneven, she might be less admired if she exposed them when she laughed.

13337   'There is also a proper way to weep, but every woman has the skill to weep properly wherever she may be. Even when no one has caused them any trouble or shame or annoyance, they still have tears at the ready: they all weep in whatever way they like, and make a habit of it. But no man should be moved by it, not if he sees the tears flowing as fast as rain, for a woman only sheds such tears and suffers such sorrow and affliction in order to make a fool of him. A woman's tears are nothing but a trap, and her grief is all affectation, but she must take care not to reveal what she thinks by word or by deed.

13355   'She ought also to behave properly at table. But before sitting down, she ought to show herself around the house and let everyone know how hard she is working. Let her come and go, back and forth, and be the last to sit down: she should make people wait a little before she is ready to sit down, and, once seated at the table, she should, if possible, serve everyone else. She should carve for the others and distribute the bread to those around her, and in order to win favour, she should serve her companion, who will eat from the same bowl, before herself. Let her set before him a leg or a wing, or carve the beef or pork for him, depending on what food there is, whether fish or flesh. She should never be chary of serving others if they will allow her to do it. She must be very careful not to dip her fingers in the sauce up to the knuckles, nor to smear her lips with soup or garlic or fat meat, nor to take too many pieces or too large a piece and put them into her mouth. She must hold the morsel with the tips of her fingers and dip it into the sauce, whether it be thick, thin, or clear, then convey the mouthful with care, so that no drop of soup or sauce or pepper falls on to her chest. When drinking, she should exercise such care that not a drop is spilled upon her, for anyone who saw that happen might think her very rude and coarse. And she must be sure never to touch her goblet when there is anything in her mouth. Let her wipe her mouth so clean that no grease is allowed to remain upon it, at least not upon her upper lip, for when grease is left on the upper lip, globules appear in the wine, which is neither pretty nor nice. And however great her appetite, she should drink in little sips, never draining the full goblet or cup in a single breath but taking frequent sips. In this way, she will not cause others to accuse her of guzzling it or gulping it down: it should trickle down delicately. She ought not to stuff the rim of the goblet into her mouth, as many nurses do who are so greedy and stupid that they pour the wine straight down their throats, as if into casks, swigging it in such gulps that they become quite fuddled and dazed. She should also take care not to get drunk, for no drunken man or woman can keep anything secret, and when a woman is drunk she has no defences, but blurts out whatever she thinks; she is at everyone's mercy when she allows such a misfortune to overtake her.

'Let her avoid falling asleep at table, for she would then be far less agreeable; many unpleasant things happen to those who fall asleep in this way, and it is not sensible to doze in places where you are supposed to stay awake. Many have been deceived as a result and have often fallen, forwards or backwards or to one side, fracturing their arm or their skull or their rib: she must beware of taking such naps. She should remember Palinurus,* who steered Aeneas' ship: while he was awake he steered her well, but when sleep overcame him he fell from the helm into the sea and drowned, close to his companions, who afterwards mourned him greatly.

'A woman ought also to make sure that she does not delay 13445 too long before taking her pleasure: she could wait so long that no one would be willing to extend a hand to her. She must seek the delights of love while youth still attends her, for once she is assailed by old age, a woman loses both love's joy and its onslaught. If a woman is wise, she will pluck love's fruit while she is in her prime, for the wretched creature wastes the time she spends without enjoying love. And if she will not accept this advice of mine, which I proffer for the common good, she may be sure that she will repent of it when old age has withered her. But I know very well that they will believe me, at least those who are wise, and that they will keep our rules and say many *paternosters* for my soul when I, who now teach and comfort them, am dead. I know that these words will be taught in many schools. Fair and most sweet son, if you live—for I can see that you are happy to write in full all my instructions in the book of your heart and that when you leave me you will, God willing, continue to teach and be a master like me—I grant you a licence to teach in spite of all the chancellors, in chambers and cellars, in meadows, gardens, and woods, beneath tents and behind hangings, and to instruct your scholars in wardrobes and attics, pantries and stables if you have no pleasanter place, all this provided that you teach my doctrine when you have learned it thoroughly.

13487   'A woman must be careful not to lead too cloistered a life, for the more she stays at home, the less she is seen by everyone and the less her beauty is known, desired, and sought after. She ought often to go to the principal church and attend weddings, processions, games, festivals, and dances, for it is in such places that the God and Goddess of Love hold their classes and sing Mass to their disciples.

13499   'But first she should inspect her reflection carefully to see if she is properly attired. When she feels she is ready and goes out into the streets, she must carry herself well, neither too loosely nor too stiffly, neither too upright nor too bent, but most agreeably in any crowd. The motion of her shoulders and sides should be so noble that it would be impossible to find anyone who moved better, and she must walk daintily in her pretty little shoes, which she will have had made to fit her feet so exactly that they will not wrinkle.

13515   'If her dress trails or hangs down to the pavement, let her lift the side or the front of it as if to feel the air a little or because it is her habit, as if she were tucking up her dress in order to walk more freely. Then she must ensure that her foot is exposed, so that everyone who passes that way sees her shapely foot. And if she wears a mantle, she must wear it in such a way that it does not hinder people too much from seeing the lovely body it covers. The better to display her body and the fabric that adorns it, neither too loosely woven nor too fine spun, and decorated with silver and tiny pearls; the better to display the purse at any rate, for it is quite right for that to be seen, she must take hold of her coat with both hands and stretch her arms out wide, whether the path is good or muddy. She should have in mind the way a peacock makes his tail into a wheel and do the same thing with her mantle, so that the lining, whether it be squirrel or miniver or whatever she has used, is exhibited together with her whole body to those whom she sees hanging around her.

'If her face is not beautiful, she will, if she is wise, turn 13545 towards them her rich tresses of fair blond hair and the nape of her neck, if she knows that her hair is well arranged; a beautiful head of hair is most attractive. A woman should always strive to be like the wolf who is about to steal a sheep: to avoid failure she will attack a thousand for the sake of one, not knowing which she will take until she has captured it. A woman too should spread her nets everywhere to ensnare all men, for since she cannot know whose favour she may win, she should sink her hook into all of them in order to attract at least one to herself. If she does this, it will never happen that among so many thousands of fools she fails to win a single one to rub her flanks: she may perhaps win several, for art is a great aid to nature.

'If she hooks several who want her on their spit, she must 13571 make sure, whatever happens, that she does not assign the same time to two of them, for they would consider themselves deceived if several of them came together, and might well abandon her. This could bring her very low, for at the very least she would lose whatever each one would have brought her. She should not leave them anything to grow fat on, but plunge them into such poverty that they die wretched and in debt while she is left rich, for the rest is lost to her.

13587   'She should not trouble herself to love a poor man, for a poor man is good for nothing: were he Ovid or Homer, he would still be worth less than a couple of drinks. Nor should she take the trouble to love a visitor, for just as his body is lodged and sheltered in various hostelries, so also is his fickle heart. I do not advise her to love a visitor; nevertheless, if, while passing through, he happens to offer her money or jewels, she should take them all and stow them in her coffer, and allow him to take his pleasure, whether in haste or at leisure.

13601   'She must also be very careful not to love or esteem any man who is too elegant or prides himself on his beauty. It is pride that thus tempts him, and you may be sure that any man who thinks well of himself incurs God's wrath; Ptolemy* says so, and he held knowledge dear. The heart of a man like that is so evil and rancorous that he is incapable of true love; what he says to one woman he will say to them all, and with many he will use flattery in order to steal and take what they have. I have seen many complaints from young women who have been deceived in this way.

13617   'If a man, whether an honest man or a scoundrel, pledges his word and wishes to beg for her love and bind her to himself with a promise, she should promise him in return but take care on no account to place herself under his protection unless she has the money first. If he sends her a written message, she must see whether he is a hypocrite or whether his intentions are good and his heart true and free from deceit. Then she may write back to him betimes, but not without some delay: waiting makes lovers more eager, provided it does not last too long.

13633   'When she hears her lover's request, she must take care not to give him all her love too hastily, nor should she altogether refuse it. Instead she should keep him in suspense between fear and hope, and as he continues to beg and she to refuse her love, which has him so closely bound, the lady must take care to use her wit and her strength in order to reinforce hope. Fear, meanwhile, should gradually fade, until it disappears and there is peace and concord between them. Then, when she has made her peace with him, knowing as she does all kinds of deceitful tricks, she must swear by God and his saints that she has never before given herself to any man, however well he may have pleaded. She must say to him: "By the faith I owe to the Holy Father in Rome, my lord, it amounts to this, that I give myself to you out of pure love and not for any gift of yours. I would not have done this for any other man, however great his gift. I have refused many worthy men, for many have courted me. I think you must have bewitched me with the wicked song you sang." Then she must clasp him tightly and kiss him, so as to drive him still further out of his senses.

'But if she takes my advice, she will be interested only in 13665 what she can get. Any woman who does not fleece her lover of everything he has is mad. The woman who can best fleece him will have the best of him, and will be held more dear because she was more dearly bought. We have nothing but scorn for the things we get for nothing; we care not a jot for them, and if we lose them, we are not worried, at least not so much nor so markedly as if we had bought them at a high price. But the fleecing must be properly done. The servant and the chambermaid, the sister, the nurse, the mother too if she is not a simpleton, must all make sure that in return for their help in the affair the lover gives them coats, jackets, gloves or mittens. Like kites, they should plunder whatever they can lay their hands on, so that it is impossible for him to escape without giving them gold and jewels, until, like a gambler, he has staked his last coin. The prey is finished off far sooner when there are many hands to help.

'On occasion they might say to him: "Look here sir, since 13695 you ought to be told, my lady needs a dress. How can you let her go without one? By Saint Giles, if she were willing to yield to a certain man in this very town, she could dress like a queen and ride in great state. My lady, why do you wait so long to ask him for it? You are too shy with him when he leaves you destitute like this." And however pleased she is, she must order them to be quiet, since she has perhaps already taken so much from him as to have done him serious harm.

'If she sees that he is aware of giving her more than he 13711 should and that he imagines himself to have been straitened by the great gifts which he is in the habit of providing, if she then feels that she no longer dare exhort him to give her things, she should beg him to make her a loan, and swear that she is ready to repay it on any day that he will name. But I strictly forbid her ever to repay any of it.

'If her other friend comes back (she may have many other friends without ever having given her heart to any one of them but still calling them all her friends), she will do well to complain that her best dress is one of the securities for a loan on which the interest is mounting up and that as a result she is suffering such distress and heartache that she will do nothing to please him unless he redeems her pledges. If the young man is not very wise, and provided he has a supply of money, he will at once put his hand in his purse or contrive some way of redeeming the pledges, pledges that have no need to be redeemed, since she may have locked them all away on his account in some iron-bound chest, perhaps so that she need not worry about him searching her coffer and clothes-pole and may better keep his confidence until she gets the money.

13747   'A third friend should be served a similar trick: I advise her to ask him for a silver girdle or a dress or wimple, and also for money to spend. And if he has nothing to bring her, but, in order to comfort her, swears and promises by hand and foot that he will bring her something next day, let her turn a deaf ear to his words and believe none of them, for they are false. Men are all expert liars, lechers who have in the past broken more oaths and promises to me than there are saints in paradise. Since he cannot pay, let him at least get credit from the wine-merchant for two or three or four pence, or else look elsewhere for his amusement.

13765   'And so a woman, if she is not a simpleton, should pretend to be alarmed, to tremble with fear and be tormented with worry whenever she is about to receive her lover. She should give him to understand that it is truly very dangerous for her to receive him, since for his sake she is deceiving her husband or guardians or parents, and that if the deeds she is willing to do in secret were to come to light, she would be dead, without a doubt. She must swear that he cannot stay, for he would cause her instant death; then, once she has thoroughly bewitched him, he will remain at her pleasure.

'She ought also to remember, when her lover is to come to 13781
her, to let him in through the window, even if she can see that no one has spied him and it would be easier through the door. She must swear that she would be dead and done for and that there would be nothing left of him if anyone knew that he was there. Sharp weapons could not save him; no helm or halberd, stake or club, no coffer, recess, or chamber could prevent his being torn to pieces, limb from limb.

'Then the lady should sigh and pretend to be angry; she should attack him and rush at him, saying that he has not delayed so long without good reason, that he has another woman of some kind in his house, whose charms give him greater pleasure, and that she is now utterly betrayed, since he has conceived a hatred for her because of someone else. She deserves to be called wretched when she loves without being loved. When he hears these words, the bird-witted fellow will imagine, quite wrongly, that she truly loves him, and that she is more jealous of him than ever Vulcan was of his wife Venus when he caught her in the act with Mars.* The fool had watched them so closely that he caught them both in nets that he had forged of bronze, held with stout bonds as they were joined and linked in the game of love.

'As soon as Vulcan knew that he had caught them red- 13817
handed in the nets that he had put around the bed (it was very foolish of him to dare to do it, for any man who imagines that he can keep his wife all to himself does not know very much), he hastily summoned the gods, who laughed heartily and made merry when they saw them like that. All the gods were moved by the beauty of Venus, bemoaning and lamenting her shame and grief at being caught and bound in this way; never had there been such disgrace. And yet there was nothing very surprising in Venus' attachment to Mars, for Vulcan was so ugly, his hands and face and throat so sooty from his forge, that Venus could not possibly have loved him, however much she might call him husband. No, by God, not if it had been blond-haired Absalon* or Paris, son of the king

of Troy, would she have pitied him, for she knew very well, the charming creature, what all women know how to do.

13845   'Moreover, women are born free; the law has bound them by taking away from them the freedoms Nature had given them. For Nature, if we apply our minds to the question, is not so stupid as to create Marote simply for Robichon, nor Robichon for Mariete or for Agnes or for Perrete; on the contrary, fair son, you may be sure that she has made all women for all men and all men for all women, every woman common to every man and every man to every woman. Thus when, in order to prevent dissolute conduct, quarrelling, and killing, and to facilitate the rearing of children, which is their joint responsibility, these ladies and maidens are affianced, taken, and married by law, they still try in every way they can, and whether they be ugly or fair, to regain their freedom. They keep their freedom as best they can, and many evils come and will come of this, and have come to many in the past. I could name you ten, so many indeed (but I will pass over them) that I would be tired out and you would be weary of listening before I had reckoned them all. For in the past, when a man saw the woman who pleased him best, he would willingly carry her off at once if someone stronger did not take her from him, and leave her, if he liked, when he had had his way with her. Thus men would kill one another and neglect the bringing-up of children until, on the advice of wise men, they began to marry. If you will believe Horace, his words on the subject are sound and true, for he was a very good teacher and writer. I would like to quote him for you now, for a wise woman is not ashamed to cite a good authority.

13893   'In the times before Helen, the lust for women was the cause of battles in which those who fought perished in great suffering (but the names of the dead are not known, since we do not read of them in written accounts).* For Helen was not the first, nor will she be the last, for whose sake there were and will be wars between those whose hearts were and will be enamoured of women, and as a result of which many have lost and will lose body and soul, as long as this world endures. But look closely at Nature, for, so that you may see more clearly what wonderful power she has, I can give you many examples which are interesting to read about.

'When a bird from the green woodland is taken and put in 13911 a cage, where he is most carefully and delicately cared for, and sings for the rest of his life with a joyful heart, or so you think, he still longs for the leafy wood which it was his nature to love, and would like to be in the trees, however well fed he may be. It is his constant thought and endeavour to recover his freedom; he tramples his food underfoot in the eagerness which fills his heart, and goes up and down his cage, hunting and searching in great distress for a window or opening through which he might fly away to the wood. In the same way, I assure you, all women, whether maidens or ladies and whatever their origin, are naturally disposed to search willingly for ways and paths by which they might achieve freedom, for they would always like to have it.

'It is the same, I tell you, for the man who enters religion; 13937 later on he repents and almost hangs himself for grief. He complains and laments until he is inwardly full of torment, so great is the desire that wells up in him to do something to recover his lost freedom. For his will does not change, whatever habit he may assume and wherever he enters the religious life.

'It is foolish of the fish to go through the mouth of the 13949 net,* for when he wants to come out again, he has to stay a prisoner there for ever, in spite of himself, because there is no way to get out. The others who remain outside rush up when they see him, imagining that he is having a good time and enjoying himself delightfully. They see him turning about and apparently having fun, and above all they see clearly that there is plenty of food there, which is what they all want. And so they want to get in, and they swim and turn around the net, bumping and searching until they find the hole, through which they dart. But once they have got there and are caught and held for ever, they cannot help wanting to get out again, but that is impossible, since they are more securely caught than in a hoop-net. They must dwell there in great sorrow until death releases them.

13977   'This is just the kind of life that a young man is looking
for when he enters religion; he will never have large enough
shoes nor learn to make a cowl or hat big enough to hide
Nature in his heart. Having lost his freedom, he is wretched
and as good as dead, unless, in great humility, he makes a
virtue of necessity. But Nature, who makes him feel his
freedom, cannot lie. Even Horace, who knows very well how
important this is, tells us that if anyone took up a fork to
defend himself against Nature and cast her out from himself,
she would come back,* and I know this to be true. Nature
will always rush back, nor will she stay away because of
a habit.

13997   'Why labour the point? Every creature wants to return to
its nature, and will not fail to do so, however violent the
pressure of force or convention. This should excuse Venus
for wishing to make use of her freedom, and all those ladies
who take their pleasure although they are bound in marriage,
for it is Nature, drawing them towards their freedom, who
makes them do this. Nature is very strong, stronger even than
nurture.

14009   'Fair son, take a cat which has never seen a male or female
rat and is then fed for a long time with attentive care on
delicious food, without ever seeing a rat or a mouse. If it
suddenly saw a mouse coming and it were allowed to escape,
nothing could prevent it from catching it at once. However
famished it was, it would leave all its food for it; no effort
could succeed in making peace between them.

14023   'If a colt could be reared without seeing a mare until he
was a great charger, fit to endure the saddle and the stirrup,
and then saw a mare coming, you would hear him whinny
at once, and he would want to run towards her if there was
no one to rescue her. A black horse would not be attracted
only to a black mare but also to a sorrel or grey or dapple, if
not held back by bit or bridle, for he has looked no further
than to see if they are untethered or if he can mount them:
he would like to attack them all. And if a black mare were
not held back, she would come running to a black horse, or
indeed to a sorrel or grey, just as her desire prompted her.
The first one she found would be her husband, for she in her

turn would have looked no further than to see if she found them untethered.

'My remarks about the black mare, the sorrel horse and mare, and the grey and black horse are also true of the cow and the bull and the ewes and the rams. We have no doubt that every male desires every female, nor should you doubt, fair son, that in the same way, every female desires every male and receives him gladly. And where natural appetites are concerned, fair son, upon my soul it is just the same for every man and every woman, though law does restrain them a little. A little? Too much, in my view, for when law has joined a young man and maiden together, it will not allow that young man to have any other maiden, at least during her lifetime, nor will it allow the maiden to have any other young man. Nevertheless, they are all tempted to use their free will, for I know how important this is. Some are restrained by shame, others by fear of punishment, but Nature drives them all, just as she does the beasts that we have been talking about. I know this through my own experience, for I have always striven to have all men love me, and, but for the fear of shame which restrains and subdues many hearts, I might, as I walked along the streets (for I always liked to walk along them covered in jewels: a doll's costume was nothing in comparison), when the young men whom I found so attractive gave me loving glances (Sweet God, how my heart melted towards them when they gave me those looks!), I might, as I say, have received all or many of them, had they been willing and I able. I would have wanted them all, one after another, if I could have satisfied them all. And it seemed to me that they would all have received me gladly, had they been able (I do not except monk or priest, knight, burgher or canon, clerk or layman, fool or wise man, provided he were in the prime of life); they would have left their orders, had they not thought that they might fail when they asked for my love. But if they had really understood my thoughts and the character of women in general, they would not have felt such doubts. I believe that many, had they dared, would have broken their marriages for me. None would have remembered to be faithful, once he was alone with me; none would

14047

have stuck to his condition, his faith, his vows, or his order, unless it were some madman besotted by love who loved his sweetheart loyally: he, perhaps, might have cried quits and thought of his beloved, whom he would not have given up at any price. But by God and Saint Amand, I am quite certain that there are very few such lovers. If a man had spent a long time talking to me, whether he spoke true or falsely, I would have aroused him throughly. Whoever he was, secular or religious, girded with red leather or with cord, and whatever head-dress he wore, I believe that he would have taken his pleasure with me, had he thought that I desired it, or even simply that I would put up with it. This is Nature's way of governing us, by inciting our hearts to pleasure, and therefore Venus is the less to be blamed for loving Mars.

14131 'Thus when Mars and Venus, who loved each other, were in this situation, there were many of the gods who would have been glad to be in the same situation and to be laughed at by the others, just as Mars was. And Lord Vulcan would rather have lost two thousand marks than have this deed known. For once the two who suffered such shame saw that everyone knew about it, they did openly what they had been doing in secret and were no longer ashamed to be the subject of gossip by the gods, who spread the tale far and wide, so that it was famous throughout the heavens. Now Vulcan grew even more angry as the situation worsened and he was unable to do anything about it. According to the text, it would have been better for him to endure it than to put the nets around the bed. He ought not to have become agitated but should have pretended not to know anything about it, if he wanted Venus, whom he loved so well, to smile upon him.

14157 'And so a man should take care if he keeps watch on his wife or sweetheart and is so stupidly vigilant as to catch her in the act. He should know that she will do even worse once she is caught and that he who burns with a cruel sickness and has caught her by his skill will never again have possession of her, nor will she ever look kindly on him or serve him. Jealousy, which burns and torments the one afflicted by it, is a most senseless sickness, but the woman pretends to be jealous and makes a false complaint to befool the fool: the more she deceives him, the more he burns.

'And if he will not deign to make excuses but says, in order to provoke her, that he really has another sweetheart, he might find that she is not angry in the least. Although she may pretend to be so, if he is running after another sweetheart, she should not really care a button for his philandering, fool that he is. But she should see to it that he in his turn, since he has not ceased to love her, should believe that she would like to set her cap at another lover, but simply in order to get rid of him, since she would like to be free of him and she would be right to separate herself. She should say: "You have wronged me too much, and I must have my revenge for this injury. Since you have deceived me, I will serve you the same dish." Then, if he has any love for her, his situation will be worse than ever and he will have no way out of it, for none can feel the fierce heat of love in his breast unless he is afraid of being cuckolded.

'At this point the chambermaid in her turn should burst in with a terrified face and say "Alas, we are dead! My lord (or some other man) has entered the courtyard." Then the lady should run and interrupt whatever she is doing, but first she should hide the young man under the roof or in a stable or a chest, until she comes back again to call him out. The young man longs for her return, and, in his fear and despair' would perhaps be glad to be somewhere else.

'Now if it should prove to be another lover, with whom the lady has very unwisely made an assignation, so that his time may not be entirely wasted and although she has not forgotten the first one, she may take the second into one of the rooms. Then he may have his way with her, but he will not be able to stay and will be very unhappy and angry about it, for the lady will be able to say to him: "It is impossible for you to stay, for my lord is here with four of my cousins. So help me God and Saint Germain, some other time when you can come I will do whatever you like, but for the moment you must put up with it. Now I must go back, for they are waiting for me." But first she must show him out, so that she may have nothing further to fear from him.

14173

14197

14211

14231 'Then the lady should go back and not keep the other one waiting too long in his distress; she ought not to upset him nor he suffer too much. Then she should make him happy again and he should leave his prison and lie with her in her arms in her bed. But let her make sure that he does not lie there without fear. She must give him to understand that she is behaving foolishly and recklessly, and should swear by her father's soul that she pays too dearly for his love when she puts herself at such risk. Although she is safer than those who dance at will through fields and vineyards, delights enjoyed in security are not so gratifying or so precious.

14251 'When they are to be together, however permanent their relationship, let her take care that he does not lie with her while she can see daylight, unless she first half closes the windows. This is to make the place so dark that, if she has some mark or blemish on her body, he will never know it. She should beware lest he find anything dirty there, for if he did, he would be on his way at once, and take to flight with his tail in the air, which would be shameful and distressing for her.

14263 'And when they go to work, they should both exert themselves so conscientiously and to such good effect that both together experience pleasure before the work is finished; they should wait for each other so that they may come to a climax together. One should not abandon the other, nor should either cease his voyage until they reach port together; then they will have delight in all its fullness.

14275 'If she feels no pleasure, she should pretend to enjoy the experience and simulate all the signs that she knows are appropriate to pleasure; in this way, he will imagine that she is glad of it, when in fact she cares not a fig.

'And if, for safety's sake, he can persuade the lady to come to his home, it should be the lady's intention on the day when she is to undertake the journey to take her time, so that his desire is greatly aroused before he takes his pleasure with her. The more we delay the game of love, the more agreeable it is; those who enjoy it at will find it less desirable.

14293 'When she arrives at the house where she will be so well loved, she must swear to him and assure him that she is trembling with terror because of the jealous husband who is being kept waiting, and that she is very much afraid that he will rail at her or beat her when she goes back home. But however much she may lament, and whether her words be true or false, he must surely be made afraid and fearful for his security, and they must take all their pleasure in private.

'If she is not free to go and speak to him at his home and 14307 dare not receive him in hers because her jealous husband keeps her locked up, she should get her husband drunk if she can, unless she can think of a better way to be rid of him. And if she cannot get him drunk with wine, she could obtain about a pound of herbs which she could safely give him to eat or drink: he will then fall into a deep sleep, and as he sleeps allow her to do whatever she likes, for he will be unable to prevent her.

'If she has servants, she should send them hither and thither, 14321 or else trick them with little gifts into helping her receive her lover; or she could get them all drunk as well, if she does not want to let them into the secret. She could say to her jealous husband if she likes: "My lord, some sickness or fever, gout or abscess is burning and scorching my body and I must go to the public baths; we have two tubs here, but a bath without steam would be no good, and so I must take a steam bath."

'When the wretch has thought about it, he will perhaps 14335 give his permission, though with a bad grace, but she should take with her her chambermaid or some neighbour who knows all about the situation and who may also have a lover about whom the lady is well informed. Then she will go off to the baths, but she will perhaps not look for a bath or tub, but will lie with her lover, unless they think it a good idea to take a bath together. For he could wait there for her if he knew she would be coming that way.

'No man can set a guard over a woman who does not set 14351 a guard over herself. Were she to be guarded by Argus, who would spy on her with his hundred eyes, half of which watched while the other half slept, his vigilance would be useless. (Jupiter had Argus' head cut off to avenge Io, whom he had changed into a heifer and stripped of her human form; it was Mercury who cut it off, and thus Io had her revenge upon Juno.)* It is foolish to set a guard upon such a creature.

14365   'But whatever clerks or laymen may tell her, she should be sure not to be so stupid as to believe in anything to do with enchantment or sorcery or witchcraft. Neither Balenus* with all his science, nor any magic arts or necromancy will enable her so to move a man that he is compelled to love her or to hate another. Medea could not hold Jason, for all the spells she cast, nor could all her enchantments help Circe to prevent the flight of Ulysses.*

14379   And so a woman should be careful not to give valuable gifts to any lover, however much she may call him her sweetheart. She may certainly give him a pillow or a towel, a kerchief or a purse, provided it is not too costly. Or she might give him a needle-case or some laces or a belt with a cheap buckle, or else a pretty little knife or a ball of thread, as nuns often do, but it is silly to consort with nuns. It is better to love women of the world: less blame will result from it, and such women have more freedom to follow their own inclinations, being good at fooling husbands and relatives with words. Although both kinds of women will inevitably cost a great deal, still, nuns are much more expensive.

14399   'A really wise man would be suspicious of any gift that came from a woman, for, truth to tell, women's gifts are merely traps designed to deceive; any trace of generosity is a sin against woman's nature. We should leave generosity to men, for when we women are generous, it is a disaster and a grave error. Such stupidity is the work of devils. But this does not matter to me, for there are very few women who are in the habit of giving.

14411   'Provided your intention is to deceive, fair son, you can make good use of the kinds of gifts I have been talking about, the better to distract simpletons; and keep whatever you are given. You should be mindful of that end to which everyone's youth is leading, if he lives long enough—old age, which draws relentlessly nearer to us every day. When you reach that point, do not be thought foolish, but be so well endowed with goods that no one will jeer at you, for acquisitions are not worth a mustard seed unless they are kept.

'Alas, I did not do so, and now I am poor through my own 14427
wretched actions. The great gifts I received from those who
abandoned themselves wholly to me I relinquished to those
I loved better. Men gave things to me and I gave them away,
and so I have not kept anything. My giving has reduced me
to short rations. I never thought of my old age, which has
now cast me into such distress; I did not keep myself from
poverty but allowed the time to slip away as it came, without
taking care to control my expenditure.

'Upon my soul, if I had been wise, I could have been a 14441
very rich woman, for great men courted me when I was
pretty and charming, and I had some of them firmly in my
toils. But by the faith I owe God and Saint Thibaut, when I
had taken from them, I gave away everything to a scoundrel
who put me to great shame but whom I loved the best. I
addressed all the others as lovers, but he was the only one I
loved, although I assure you that he cared not a fig for me,
and said so. He was a bad man—I never saw a worse one—
and he had nothing but contempt for me, calling me a
common whore; scoundrel that he was, he never loved me.
Women have very poor judgement, and I was a true woman.
I never loved a man who loved me, but if this wretch had
hurt my shoulder or cracked my skull, I tell you I would have
thanked him for it. However much he beat me, I would still
have had him fall upon me, for he was so good at making
peace, whatever hurt he might have done me. However badly
he treated me, beating me and dragging me about, hurting
my face and bruising it, he would always beg my forgiveness
before he left. However humiliating his language to me, he
would always sue for peace and then take me to bed, and so
there was peace and harmony between us once more. And
so he had me on the end of a rope, the false, thieving traitor,
because he was so good in bed. I could not have lived without
him and I would willingly have followed him everywhere. If
he had run away, I would have gone in search of him as far
as London in England, such was my love and affection for
him. He put me to shame and I him, for he used the fine
gifts I gave him to lead a riotous life; he never saved anything,
but spent it all dicing in the taverns. He never learned another

trade, nor did he need to, since I gave him so much to spend and money was mine for the taking. Everyone paid me, and he was happy to spend it, and always on debaucheries, for depraved desires inflamed him. His mouth was so tender* that he would not try to do anything worthwhile, and had no fondness for any kind of life except one of pleasure and idleness. In the end, as I saw, he got into a very bad way, for he became poor and had to beg for bread, while I had not money enough for two carding-combs, nor had I married a lord. And so, as I told you, I was reduced to want and came here through these thickets. Fair son, let my condition be an example to you, and remember it. Behave sensibly, so that you will be the better for my knowledge, for when your rose is withered and white hairs assail you, then you will surely feel the lack of gifts.'

CHAPTER 8

THE ASSAULT ON THE CASTLE

This was the Old Woman's teaching. Fair Welcome, who 14517
had not uttered a word, listened very willingly to everything.
He was less afraid of the Old Woman than he ever had
been before, and he was coming to realize that, were it not
for Jealousy and her gatekeepers, in whom she had such
confidence—at least the three who remained to her and who
ran continually like madmen through the castle to defend
it—the castle would be easy to take. But because of their
great efforts, he thought, it never would be taken. Not one
of them mourned Evil Tongue, who was now dead, for no
one there had loved him. He had always slandered and betrayed them all to Jealousy, with the result that he was so
deeply hated that no one who remained there would have
given the price of a garlic-clove to save him, no one, that is,
except perhaps Jealousy herself, for Jealousy was very fond
of his gossip and listened to him gladly. And yet she was
terribly sad when the scoundrel came to her with his tales,
for he hid nothing from her that he could remember, so long
as evil would come of it. Moreover, he was very wrong to
say more than he knew, and always to pad out and embellish
what he had heard. He always exaggerated news that was
neither good nor pleasant, while playing down the good
news, and was thus able, as one who had spent all his life in
envious gossip, to excite Jealousy. So happy were they to
see him dead that they had no Mass sung for him. It seemed
to them that they had lost nothing, for they imagined that
once they had joined forces, they would be so well able to
guard the enclosure that there would be no likelihood of its
being captured, even if five hundred thousand men were
to come.

'We must indeed be weak,' they said, 'if we cannot guard 14564
all we have without that thief. False and foul traitor that he
is, may his soul go to the stinking fires of hell, to be burned
and destroyed! He never did anything but harm here.' So said

the three gatekeepers, but whatever they said, they were greatly weakened by his death.

14574   After the Old Woman's long discourse, Fair Welcome resumed. He began after a short delay and spoke little, but as one who was well informed. 'Madam,' he said, 'I thank you heartily for teaching me your art so graciously. But the love of which you spoke, that sweet sickness in which there is so much bitterness, is quite unfamiliar to me. I know nothing about it except through hearsay, and I have no desire to know any more. And then you talked about possessions, and told me to amass great quantities, but what I have is quite enough for me. I would like to concentrate on acquiring a pleasant and courteous manner. As for magic and the devilish art, I do not believe any of it, whether it be true or false.

14593   'Concerning this young man who, you say, has so many good qualities that all the graces meet in him, if he has graces, let him keep them; I have no wish that they should be mine, but leave them to him. Nevertheless, I certainly do not hate him, nor, even though I accepted his chaplet, do I love him well enough to call him my friend, except in the ordinary sense of the word, as men and women say to one another "You are welcome, my friend", or "Friend, God bless you!"

'I neither love nor honour him in any way that is not right and honest. But since he gave me the gift and I received it, I ought to be pleased and gratified if he can come to me and wishes to do so; he will never find me indifferent or unwilling to receive him, provided it happens when Jealousy is out of town, for Jealousy hates and reviles him dreadfully. And yet I am afraid that, whatever happens, even if she is away, she will appear, for when she has packed all her luggage to go away and we have permission to stay behind, ideas occur to her on her way and she often turns back when she is half-way there and wrecks and upsets everything for us. If he happens to come and she finds him here, she is so cruel and harsh to me that, even if she can prove nothing further, she may, if you remember her cruelty, dismember me alive.'

14633   The Old Woman reassured him vigorously. 'Let me worry about that,' she said. 'Even if Jealousy were here, there would be no chance of her finding him, for I know so many hiding-places and could hide him so well that, by God and Saint Remi, she would sooner find an ant's egg in a pile of straw than him, once I had hidden him away.'

'Then I am very willing for him to come,' he said, 'but he must behave properly and refrain from all excesses.'

'By God incarnate, you speak like a wise, honourable, and prudent youth of great principle and judgement.' There their talk ceased and they departed. Fair Welcome went to his room and the Old Woman also got up to busy herself about the houses. When the place, time, and season were right and the old woman could see that Fair Welcome was alone, so that one might talk to him at leisure, she descended the stairs and came out of the tower and trotted all the way to my dwelling. She arrived there, panting with weariness, to tell me about the affair. 'Am I in time for the gloves,' she said, 'if I bring you good news, all fresh and recent?'

'For the gloves! Madam, I tell you in all sincerity that you will have a cloak and a dress, a hood lined with miniver, and whatever boots you like if you have anything worthwhile to tell me.' Then the Old Woman told me to go up to the castle, where I was expected. She had no wish to leave at once, and instead told me how to get in:

'You should enter by the back door,' she said, 'and I shall open it for you for greater concealment. The passage is very well hidden, for you know, the door has been closed for the last two and a half months.'

'Madam,' I said, 'by Saint Remi, whether it costs ten or 14682 twenty pounds an ell (for I well remembered that Friend had told me to make promises, even when I could not keep them), you shall have good cloth, blue or green, if I find the door open.'

At that, the Old Woman left me; I for my part went the other way, to the back door, as she had told me, and prayed to God to guide me to the right place. I came to the door without saying a word; the Old Woman had unlocked it for me and still had it half closed. Once inside, I closed it, so that we were more secure. I felt especially safe since I knew that Evil Tongue was dead; never did I rejoice more over anyone's death. I saw that his gate was broken, and I had no sooner passed through it than I found Love and all his host within, who gave me comfort. By God, what help those vassals gave me when they broke down that gate! May God and Saint Benedict bless them! There was False Seeming, treacherous son of Fraud, false minister of Lady Hypocrisy, his mother, who is so bitter towards all virtue. And there was Lady Constrained Abstinence, who, according to what I find written in a book, is pregnant by False Seeming and ready to give birth to Antichrist. It was certainly they who broke down the gate, and so I will pray for them, come what may.

14719   My lords, if any of you wants to be a traitor, let him take False Seeming for his master and make Constrained Abstinence his own: let him feign simplicity while playing a double game.

14723   When I saw the gate of which I have spoken thus captured and brought down, and found the armed host there, ready to attack before my very eyes, no one need ask if I was glad. Then I pondered deeply how to find Pleasant Looks. And lo! there he was, God keep him, for Love sent him for my comfort. He had been lost for a long time, and the sight of him gave me such joy that I almost fainted. For his part, Pleasant Looks was very glad when he saw me coming. He pointed me out straight away to Fair Welcome, who leapt to his feet and came to meet me, being a courteous and well-bred youth, thanks to his mother's teaching. At once I bowed and greeted him, and he greeted me in return and thanked me for his chaplet. 'Sir,' I said, 'please do not trouble yourself. You ought not to thank me, but it is I who should thank you a hundred thousand times for doing me the great honour of accepting it. I assure you that I have nothing that would not be yours if you wanted it, to do with as you liked, no matter who was glad or sorry about it. I wish to be completely subject to you, to honour you and serve you. If you care to order me to to do anything, or instruct me without ordering, or if I find out about it in some other way, no conscientious scruple shall prevent my placing my body and my goods, indeed my very soul, in the balance. I beg you to put me to the test, so that you may be more certain of this; may I never

again find enjoyment in anything or any bodily pleasure if I
let you down.'

'Thank you, fair sir,' he said. 'For my part, I would like to   14765
say that if there is anything of mine that you care for, I would
be glad for you to enjoy it. Draw upon it freely, rightly, and
honourably, as if you were I.'

'Thank you, sir,' I said, 'a hundred thousand times. Since   14771
I may thus take your things, I have no mind to delay any
longer. You have something ready to hand which will bring
more joy to my heart than all the gold of Alexander.'

Then I stepped forward to stretch out my hands for the
rose that I so longed for, and so to have all my desire. I
thought indeed that it had been very easily achieved, for our
words were sweet and gentle, our exchanges pleasant, and
our demeanour affectionate, but things turned out very differently for me. Much that a fool plans remains undone, and I
encountered a most cruel obstacle, for as I went towards the
rose, my way was barred by Rebuff—may he be throttled by
an evil wolf, lout that he is! He had hidden in a corner behind
us to spy on us, and was writing down everything we said,
word for word. Without further ado, he began shouting at
me.

'Be off with you,' he said, 'be off with you, young man,
and get away from here; you are causing me a great deal of
trouble. You have been brought back here by accursed,
raging devils who have their part to play in your fine service;
may they take everything* with them before they leave here
and may no saint, whether man or woman, intervene! Young
man, young man, as I hope to be saved, for two pins I would
strike you dead!'

Then Fear arose and Shame rushed up when they heard   14806
the peasant telling me: 'Fly, fly, fly!' Nor was he silent even
then, but talked of the devil and made no mention of the
saints. By God, what an evil host he had! In their rage and
fury they all three with one accord seized me and forced my
hands back and said: 'You will never have any more or less
than you have already had. You failed to understand what
Fair Welcome was offering you when he allowed you to talk
to him. He was glad to offer you what he had, provided it

was honestly done. But you cared nothing for honesty, and took his simple offer in a way that was not intended. For when a worthy man offers his service, it goes without saying that it is in a respectable way, and that this is the intention of the one who makes the offer. Now tell us, sir trickster, when you heard his words, why did you not take them in the proper spirit? Either your uncouth understanding made you put so base a construction on them, or else you have learned to play the part of the wise fool. He would never offer you the rose, for it would not be honourable for you to ask it or to have it without asking. And when you offered him your things, in what sense did you make the offer? Was it your intention to deceive him, in order to rob him of his rose? You certainly do betray him and trick him, for you want to serve him simply in order to be his enemy in secret. Nothing so harmful or so damaging has ever been written about in books. Were you to burst with grief, we would not believe it, and you must leave this enclosure. Devils have brought you back here, for you should have remembered that you were chased away once before. Now get out! Find what you need somewhere else! I can tell you that the woman who sought passage for such an idiot was far from wise, but she did not know what you were thinking, or the treason you intended; she would never have sought it for you had she known of your disloyalty. And Fair Welcome for his part was certainly much deceived when he was so imprudent as to welcome you into his enclosure. He imagined that he was being of service to you, whereas your intention was to do him harm. By my faith, it is just the same for the man who carries a dog in a boat: the dog still barks at him when they reach the shore. Now look somewhere else for your prey and get out of this enclosure. Go down the steps politely and with good grace, or you will never be able to count them, for someone might soon be here who will make you miscount them if once he gets his hands on you and happens to lay you low.

14879 'Sir madman, sir presumptuous, devoid of all loyalty, what harm has Fair Welcome done you? For what sin, what crime have you so quickly learned to hate him that you wish to betray him, when just now you were offering him all you had? Was it because the young man received you, deceiving himself and us for your sake and straight away offering you his dogs and birds? He should know that his behaviour was foolish, and because of what he has done here, now and at other times, so help us God and Saint Faith, he will be put in a stronger prison than any captive ever entered. Because of the way in which he has disturbed and misled us, he will be chained to such rings that you will never, as long as you live, see him walk free. Woe was the day when you saw so much of him. He has deceived us all.'

Then they seized him and beat him and threw him into 14903 the tower as he ran before them. There, after much abuse, they confined him with three pairs of locks and three pairs of keys, without recourse to other irons or to a dungeon. They did him no further injury at that time, but that was because they were in a hurry; they promised to do worse things when they came back.

They did not keep their promise, but all three of them 14913 came back to me. I had stayed outside, weeping and over-whelmed with grief and sorrow, and they set upon me once again and tormented me. God grant that they yet repent of the great injury they did me! My heart almost broke with grief. I would have been glad to yield to them, but they would not take me alive, although I strove hard to make peace with them and would willingly have been thrown into prison with Fair Welcome.

'Fair, gentle Rebuff,' I said, 'noble of heart and valiant of 14926 body and more merciful than I can say, and you, Shame and Fear, you lovely, wise, excellent, and noble maidens, well governed in words and deeds and born of Reason's line, allow me to become your servant, and let us agree that I shall stay here in prison with Fair Welcome and never be ransomed. Then, if you will put me in prison, I will gladly give you my loyal promise to serve you perfectly in any way you like. By my faith, had I been a thief or a traitor or a pilferer, or accused of some murder, and if I had then wanted and asked to be put in prison, I do not think that I would have failed. No indeed, by God, I would be put there without asking in any country, provided I could be caught, and once they had caught me they would not allow me to escape, not even if they had to cut me in pieces. In God's name, I beg you to imprison me with him for ever, and if I am ever found, either without proof or caught in the act, to have failed to serve you well, let me leave that prison for ever. There is no man who does not err, but if I should fall short, have me pack my bags and promptly release me from your fetters; if ever I anger you, I want to be punished for doing so. You yourselves be the judges of it, but let no one judge me but you; I will submit myself to your judgement, provided there are only three of you and that Fair Welcome is with you, for I will accept him as the fourth. We can tell him all about it, and if you cannot agree to endure me, let him bring you to an agreement; and you must keep to this agreement, for I would not wish to swerve from it, were I to be beaten or killed for it.'

14977 Then Rebuff cried out in his turn: 'By God, what sort of a request is this? Putting you in prison with him, you with your playful heart and he with his gracious one, would be tantamount to putting Reynard* with the hens in the cause of true love. However you may serve us, we know very well that your only aim is to shame and abuse us; we want nothing to do with such service. And you for your part must be completely devoid of sense to think of making him a judge. A judge! By the fair king of heaven, how can anyone be a judge or take it upon himself to arbitrate when he has himself already been arrested and judged? Fair Welcome has been arrested and judged, and you judge him worthy to be an arbiter or a judge! There will be a second Flood before he leaves our tower, and when we get back, we will kill him; he has deserved that, if only because he was so submissive as to offer you what he had. All the roses are lost because of him; every dolt wants to pluck them when he sees that he is fairly welcomed. But if we had him well caged up, no one would ever do them any harm and no man living would carry them off, no more than the wind does, unless he were the kind of man who misbehaves to the extent of basely using force, and if he did misbehave to this extent, he would be banished or hanged for it.'

'Indeed,' I said, 'it is very wrong to kill a man who has 15015
committed no crime and to imprison him without reason.
When you keep such a man as Fair Welcome in captivity,
one who is so worthy and so noble that he shows hospitality
to all, and accuse him of nothing more than looking kindly
upon me and enjoying my company, then you do him a
serious injury. By rights he should be out of prison, if you
would allow it, and I therefore beg you to let him go and
have done with the matter. You have already wronged him
too much, now see to it that he no longer remains in captivity.'

'By my faith,' they said, 'this madman is trying to trick us. 15031
He is indeed feeding us with lies, for he wants to get Fair
Welcome out of prison and betray us with his speeches. He
is asking for the impossible: Fair Welcome will never so much
as put his head out of a door or window. Then they set upon
me once again, and each of them tried to kick me out; they
could not have hurt me any more if they had tried to crucify
me. I began to cry for mercy, not too loudly, and in a low
voice summoned to the attack those who were to come to
my aid, until I was noticed by the sentinels who mounted
guard upon the host. When they heard me being so roughly
handled, they cried out:

'Up barons, up! Unless we appear at once in arms to help
this true lover, he is lost, by God's love. The gatekeepers will
kill him or bind him, thrash him, beat him, or crucify him.
He is before them now, calling out in a faint voice and
begging so quietly for mercy that we can hardly hear his cry;
his shouts and cries are so weak that if you heard them you
would either think that he was hoarse with shouting or that
they had gripped him by the throat to strangle or kill him.
Already they have so shut off his voice that he cannot or dare
not cry aloud. We do not know what they intend, but they
are inflicting great harm upon him and he will die unless he
is promptly rescued. Fair Welcome, who used to comfort
him, has run away, and so, until he can find him again, he
needs help from another source. The time for wielding weapons has come.' And they would certainly have killed me,
had the men of the host not come.

15075   The barons leapt to arms when they heard and saw and
knew that I had lost all joy and consolation. I, caught in the
snare in which others are entangled by Love, remained on
the spot and watched the fierce fighting which then began.
For as soon as the gatekeepers knew that they had so great a
host against them, they all three made an alliance, in which
they swore and pledged to help one another to the best of
their ability, and never in any circumstances to abandon one
another, as long as they lived. And I, who never stopped
watching their faces and expressions, was very much grieved
by this alliance.

15093   When the men of the host saw for their part that those
three had made such an alliance, they assembled and gathered
together; henceforth they had no wish to separate, but swore
so to acquit themselves that they would either lie dead on
that spot or suffer defeat and capture, or else they would carry
off the prize in the encounter, so avid were they to fight and
humble the pride of the gatekeepers. And now we come to
the battle, and you shall hear how each one fought.

15105   Now pay attention, true lovers, may the God of Love love
you and grant you enjoyment of your love! In this wood you
may hear, if you understand me correctly, the hounds baying
after the very rabbit* you are after yourself, and the ferret,
which will certainly send it leaping into the net. Take note
of what I now say, and you will have art of love enough. If
you have any difficulty, I will explain whatever is troubling
you when you hear me interpret the dream. Then, when you
hear me gloss the text, you will be able to reply on behalf of
love if anyone raises objections; what I write then will enable
you to understand what I have already written, as well as what
I intend to write. But before you hear me say any more about
it, I would like briefly to turn my attention elsewhere and
defend myself against evil people, not in order to waste your
time, but to vindicate myself against them.

15129   I beg you, sir lovers, by the delectable games of Love, that
if you find any words that seem to be too bold or shameless,
such as will make the scandalmongers leap to their feet and
criticize the things we have said or are about to say, you will
courteously contradict them. And when you have rebuked

them for what they say, or stopped or contradicted them, if my words are such that I should ask pardon for them, I beg you to pardon me and to reply on my behalf that they were called for by my subject, whose intrinsic properties drew me to such language; that is why I use these words. And this is quite right, and in accordance with the authority of Sallust,* who gives it as his true opinion that 'although glory is not equally divided between the man who does something and the writer who tries to find an appropriate way of putting the deed into a book, so as to describe it as accurately as possible, nevertheless it is not easy, but on the contrary extremely difficult, to give a good written account of deeds. Whoever does the writing, if he is not to deprive us of the truth, his words must echo the deed, for when words rub shoulders with things, they should be cousins of the deeds.' And so I must speak in this way if I want to proceed correctly.

I beg all you worthy women, whether maidens or ladies, 15165 in love or without a lover, if you find any words that seem to you to be a harsh and savage attack on feminine behaviour, please do not censure me or speak ill of my writing, which is intended only to instruct. It is certain that I neither say nor wish to say anything in drunkenness or anger, hate or envy, against any woman alive. No one scorns a woman unless he has the worst of all hearts. The reason why we put these things in writing was so that we and you might know about you, for it is good to know everything. Moreover, honourable ladies, if it seems to you that I am making things up, do not call me a liar, but blame those authors who have written in their books what I have said, and those in whose company I will speak. I shall tell no lie, unless the worthy men who wrote the ancient books also lied. They all concurred with my view when they wrote about feminine behaviour, and they were neither mad nor drunk when they set it down in their books. They were well acquainted with feminine behaviour, for they had all encountered it and found it to be so in the experiences they had had with women at different times. Therefore there is all the more reason for you to excuse me: I merely repeat, except for making a few additions on my own account which cost you little. Poets do this among themselves, each one dealing with the subject that he wants to work on, for, as the text tells us,* their intention is solely to edify and to please.

15213　　　If people grumble at me and are upset and angry because they feel that I am attacking them in the chapter in which I report the words of False Seeming, and if they get together to rebuke and punish me because they have been hurt by what I said, then I protest that it was never my intention to speak against any man living who follows holy religion or spends his life in good works, whatever robe he wears.* Instead, sinner though I am, I took my bow and drew it and loosed my arrow in order to inflict a general wound. A general wound? In fact, to recognize those accursed, faithless people, whether secular or cloistered, whom Jesus called hypocrites, many of whom, in order to appear righteous, always refrain from eating meat in the name of penance and practise the same abstinence that we do in Lent, while with poisonous intent devouring men alive with the teeth of detraction. I never aimed at any other target; it was there that I wanted, and still want, my arrows to go, and so I fire upon them at random. And if it should happen that a man willingly places himself in the path of the arrow, in order to receive the blow, if in his pride he deceives himself to the extent of getting himself shot and then complains that I have injured him, it is not, nor will it be, my fault, not even if he dies. It is not possible for me to hit anyone who chooses to protect himself from the shot, provided he is careful about how he lives. Even if a man is wounded by the arrow that I point at him, he will be free of the wound if he renounces hypocrisy. Whoever complains about it and however worthy he pretends to be, it is nevertheless the case, however he may oppose it, that I have never to my knowledge said anything that was not found in writing and proved by experience, or that was not at least susceptible of proof by reason, whomsoever it might offend. And if I have said anything that Holy Church judges foolish, I am ready to make any amends she may wish, provided I am capable of doing so.

15273　　　The first to come forward was Generosity of Spirit, very humbly, to encounter Rebuff, who was very fierce and violent, cruel and wild in appearance. He held a mace in his hand, which he brandished fiercely and with which he laid about him so fearfully that none but the most marvellous shield could withstand the blow without being split; anyone who took the field against him would be bound, when once squarely struck by that mace, to yield himself up, or else, if he were not very experienced in arms, he would be crushed and overwhelmed. The ugly lout, whom I challenge, had taken his club from the wood of Refusal, while his shield was made of brutality and bordered with insolence.

Generosity of Spirit also was well armed; it would be 15291 difficult to hurt her, because she knew well how to protect herself. In an attempt to open the gate, she charged against Rebuff, holding in her hand a stout lance, fair and polished, that she had brought from the forest of Cajolery (none such grow in Biere*), and whose tip was made of gentle prayers. Being very devout, she also had a shield (and she was never without it), made of every supplication, bordered with hand-clasps, promises, agreements, oaths, and pledges, and very beautifully coloured. You would certainly have said that Largesse had given it to her and painted and engraved it, so much did it seem to be her handiwork. And Generosity of Spirit, well covered by her shield, brandished the haft of her lance and hurled it at the lout, who had no coward's heart but seemed like Renouart of the Staff* come back to life. His shield would have been broken in two, but it was so extraordinarily strong that it feared no arms, and he fended off the blows so well that his belly was not cut open. The tip of the lance broke, so that he heeded the blow less. For his part, the cruel, furious churl was well supplied with arms; he took the lance and broke it, piece by piece, with his club, then he aimed a fierce and powerful blow.

'Why should I not strike you,' he said, 'you filthy, shame- 15330 less slut? How can you have had the temerity to attack a man of worth?' He struck her unerringly upon her shield, that valiant, fair, and courteous lady, so that she jumped a good six feet in her agony and fell to her knees. He beat and insulted her, and I believe that blow would have killed her, had her shield been made of wood.

'I trusted you once before,' he said, 'you filthy madam, you cowering slut, and no good ever came of it. Your flatteries deceived me; it was because of you that I allowed that kiss to please that good-for-nothing. He certainly found me idiotically gracious; devils made me do it. By God incarnate, you should rue the day when you came to attack our castle! Here you must lose your life.'

15352   The fair creature begged him in God's name to show mercy and not to destroy her, now that she could go no further. But the lout shook his brutish head in his rage, and swore by the saints that he would kill her without compassion. Thus he earned the scorn of Pity, who made haste to advance upon the churl in order to rescue her companion.

15361   Pity, who is in sympathy with all good things, carried instead of a sword a misericord* that continually wept and dripped tears. If the author does not lie, this weapon was so sharply pointed that, provided it were well driven in, it could pierce a rock of adamant. Her shield was made of solace, bordered with groans and full of sighs and lamentations. Pity, who wept many tears, stabbed the villain on all sides, while he defended himself like a leopard. But when she had soaked the filthy, booted lout with her tears, he was compelled to weaken. It seemed to him that he was dazed and drowning in a river. No words or deeds had ever assailed him so grievously; his hardened frame failed him completely. Weak and powerless, he staggered and stumbled and tried to flee, but Shame called out to him: 'Rebuff, Rebuff, you are a proven villain. If you abandon the fight now and allow Fair Welcome to escape, you will get us all caught, for he will immediately hand over the rose that we have imprisoned here. And I can tell you for certain that if he does hand over the rose to those wretches, it will soon, you know, be faded or pale or limp or withered. And I can also declare that a wind would blow here, if it found the entrance open, which would inflict harm and loss upon us: either it would disturb the seed too much or else it would shower another seed here which would burden the rose. God grant that no such seed fall here! That would be a great misfortune for us, for there would be no help for it; before the seed fell from the rose, the flower would quickly perish. If the flower escaped death, the wind might strike such blows as to mingle the seeds, which would then overwhelm the rose with their burden. As it fell, this burden might cause one or other of the leaves to split and (God forbid!) the split in the leaf might disclose the green bud beneath. Then everyone would say that scoundrels had possessed it. This would earn us the hatred of Jealousy, who would find out about it and be so grieved by what she had learned that we would be put to death for it. Devils must have made you drunk.'

Rebuff cried out: 'Help, help!' and at once Shame ran up   15423
and threatened Pity, who greatly feared her threats. 'You have lived too long,' she said, 'I shall break that shield of yours, and today you will bite the dust. It was an unhappy day for you when you took up this war!'

Shame bore a great sword, fair and well-fashioned and finely tempered, forged in fear from the dread of discovery. She had a strong shield called Fear of Ill Fame, for this was the wood from which she had made it. Many tongues were painted round its border. She struck Pity so hard that she drove her right back and almost forced her to admit defeat, but then Delight came up, a handsome, strong, and comely young man, and made an attack on Shame. His sword was made of pleasant life and his shield of ease (I had none of that), bordered with pleasure and joy. He struck at Shame, but she defended herself so judiciously with her shield that the blow did not hurt her. Then Shame in her turn went after Delight and struck him so agonizing a blow that she broke his shield over his head and brought him sprawling to the ground. She would have split open his head down to his teeth, but then God sent a young man called Discretion.

Discretion was a doughty warrior, a wise and cunning   15457
landed lord. In his hand was a sword, silent as though its tongue had been cut out, which he brandished without making any noise that could be heard six feet away, for, however hard it was brandished, it never echoed nor resounded. His shield was made of secret place (no hen ever laid in such a spot), and bordered with discreet expeditions and secret homecomings. Raising his sword, he struck Shame such a

blow that he almost killed her, so that she was completely dazed.

15472   'Shame,' he said, 'that sad and miserable creature Jealousy will never know of it as long as she lives: I could assure you of that and would give you my hand upon it and swear you a hundred oaths. Is that not an excellent assurance? Now that Evil Tongue is dead, you are taken; do not stir.'

Shame did not know what to reply. Fear, usually a great coward, leapt up, full of anger. Gazing at her cousin Shame, and seeing her in such a predicament, she put her hand to her wickedly sharp sword. Its name was Suspicion of Ostentation, for that was what it was made of, and when she had drawn it from its scabbard, it shone more brightly than any beryl. Fear also had a shield, made of fear of danger, bordered with labour and suffering, and she strove with all her might to cut Discretion into pieces. To avenge her cousin, she struck him such a blow on his shield that he could not endure it. Stunned and staggering, he summoned Boldness, who leapt up, for it would have been an evil piece of work if Fear had struck a second blow: Discretion would have been dead for sure had she hit him again. Boldness was brave and bold, skilful in deeds and words. His good, well-polished sword was made from the steel of fury. His celebrated shield was called Contempt for Death and was bordered with complete disregard for danger. He advanced on Fear wildly and aimed a great and deadly blow at her. He dealt the blow and she warded it off, for she knew all about the business of fencing. She successfully parried the stroke, and then struck him so mighty a blow that his shield could not protect him and he was felled to the ground. When Boldness knew that he was down, he joined his hands, begging and praying her by God's mercy to spare his life, and she agreed to do so.

15526   Then Security said: 'What is this? By God, Fear, do your worst, but you will die here. You used to tremble and were a hundred times more cowardly than a hare, but now you have lost your cowardice! Devils must have given you the audacity to attack Boldness, who is so fond of fighting and knows so much about it, if he bothers to think about it, that no one ever knew more than he. Since first you walked upon the earth, you have never fought, except on this occasion. At other times you are ignorant of the techniques of combat, and in all other fights you either flee or yield, whereas now you are defending yourself. You fled with Cacus* when you saw Hercules rushing up with his club around his neck. You were quite disconcerted then, and put such wings on Cacus' feet as he had never had before, because he had stolen Hercules' cattle and herded them together in his own distant refuge, dragging them backwards by their tails so that their trail would not be discovered. Then was your valour tested, then did you demonstrate beyond a doubt that you had no aptitude for fighting, and since you have kept away from battles, you know little or nothing about them. Therefore you should not now defend yourself, but flee or surrender your arms, or else you will pay dearly for daring to measure yourself against him.'

Security had a strong sword made of flight from every care, 15563 and a shield of peace, good beyond a doubt, edged all round with concord. She struck at Fear, thinking to kill her, but Fear took care to defend herself and swung her shield in the way, which took the blow safely, so that she was not hurt in the least. The blow glanced off, and Fear in her turn smote her so hard upon the shield that she was quite stunned, and close to being badly hurt. Fear struck her with such force that her sword and shield flew from her hands. Do you know what Security did then? To give an example to the others, she seized Fear by the temples, and Fear did the same to her, and so they gripped one another. All the others intervened, grappling with one another in pairs: I never saw such duels in any battle. The conflict raged more fiercely, and the fighting was so intense that no combat ever produced such an exchange of blows. Turning this way and that, each one summoned his followers, who all rushed up, pell-mell. I never saw snow or hail fall more thickly than did the blows. They all tore and battered one another. Never was such fighting seen between so many people thus locked in combat.

But I shall not lie to you: the host besieging the castle 15597 always had the worst of it. The God of Love was very much afraid that his people would all be killed. He sent Generosity of Spirit and Pleasant Looks to tell his mother to come and to let no excuse detain her; meanwhile he arranged a truce for between ten and twelve whole days, or thereabouts, I cannot tell you for certain. Indeed, it could have been arranged for ever if he had asked for it, even if it were later to be broken or violated. But if he had thought that he had the upper hand, he would never have made a truce, and if the gatekeepers had not imagined that the others would not break it once it had been agreed, they would perhaps not have granted it willingly but would have been resentful, whatever face they put on it. And he would never have made a truce, had Venus taken a hand. But he certainly had to do it: whenever we fight someone whom we cannot overcome, we have to withdraw a little, either in flight or by making a truce, until we are better able to subdue him.

15629   The messengers left the host and journeyed like sensible men until they came to Cythera,* where they were held in great honour. Cythera is a mountain in a wooded plain, so high that no cross-bow, however strong or ready to fire, could reach it with a bolt or arrow. Venus, the inspiration of ladies, had her main dwelling and liked to spend most of her time there. But a full description of the place would perhaps be boring for you and tiring for me; therefore I prefer to be brief. Venus had gone down into the wood to go hunting in a valley. With her was the fair Adonis,* her gentle, light-hearted friend: he was still to some extent a child, and hunting in the woods was his main preoccupation. He was a boy, young and full of promise and very handsome and comely. It was after midday and everyone was weary of hunting; they were on the grass by a fish-pond, enjoying the shade of a poplar. Their hounds, tired and panting from the chase, drank from the channel of the pond. Bows, arrows, and quivers were propped up close by. Gaily they disported themselves and listened to the birds in the branches all around. After their games, Venus held him clasped in her lap and, kissing him, taught him how to hunt in the woods in the way to which she was accustomed.

15669   'My friend, when your pack is ready and you go in search of your quarry, if you find that an animal flees from you, hunt it: as soon as it turns to fly, run boldly after it; but never sound your horn against those that fiercely stand at bay. Be cowardly and hold back when you encounter bold creatures, for boldness is not safe against those in whom a bold heart is firmly fixed. When a brave man fights another brave man, the battle is dangerous. I am very happy for you to hunt harts and hinds, he-goats and she-goats, reindeer and fallow deer, rabbits and hares; you can enjoy this kind of hunting. But bears, wolves, lions, and tusked boars I forbid you to hunt. Such beasts will defend themselves, killing and ripping open the hounds and often causing the hunters themselves to miss their aim; they have killed and injured many. I will be sorely grieved and have no joy of you if you do otherwise than I have said.'

In this way Venus warned him and, as she did so, begged him fervently to keep her words in mind, wherever he hunted. Adonis, who little heeded what his sweetheart told him, always agreed to everything, whether he meant it or not, in order to be left in peace, for he did not like being lectured. Whatever she did was useless; let her lecture him as much as she please, if she leaves him she will never see him again. He did not believe her, and died as a result, for Venus never came to his aid, because she was not there. Afterwards she wept bitterly for him in her grief: he had hunted a boar, imagining that he would be able to catch and strangle it, but he neither caught it nor cut it to pieces, for the boar, being a fierce and proud beast, defended itself. It tossed its head at Adonis and sank its tusks into his groin, then, pulling out its snout with a twist, it brought him, dead, to the ground.

Fair lords, whatever may befall you, bear his example in 15721 mind. You should know that you are very foolish not to believe your sweethearts. You ought always to believe them, for what they say is as true as history. If they swear: 'We belong entirely to you', believe them as you would a *paternoster*, and never abandon that belief. If Reason comes, do not believe her. Even if she brings a crucifix, do not believe her any more than I did. If Adonis had believed his sweetheart, he would have lived much longer.

Venus and Adonis disported themselves and took their 15735 pleasure together, then, when they were ready after their dalliance, they returned to Cythera. Before Venus could change her clothes, the messengers, who had not delayed, gave her a full and complete account of the news they had to communicate. 'By my faith,' said Venus, 'it was an evil day for Jealousy when she held a castle or cottage against my son! If I do not set fire to the gatekeepers and all their equipment—unless they surrender the keys and the tower—I will not think myself or my bow or my torch worth so much as a lump of wood.' Then she summoned her household and ordered her chariot to be harnessed, since she did not want to walk through the mud. The four-wheeled chariot was very fair, studded with gold and pearls. Between the shafts were harnessed, instead of horses, six beautiful doves, taken from her dovecot.

Everything was made ready, and then Venus, who makes war on Chastity, mounted her chariot. None of the birds was disorderly; they beat their wings and set off. Cleaving and parting the air before them, they came to the army. As soon as she arrived, Venus stepped down from her chariot, and the host swept up to her with great rejoicing. Her son was first: in his haste he had already broken the truce before it expired, for he never kept an agreement in such matters, whether sworn or pledged.

15771   They were intent on fighting fiercely, and attacked while the others defended. They set up mangonels against the castle and sent over great stones of weighty prayers to breach the walls. The gatekeepers fortified the walls with strong hurdles made of refusals interwoven with flexible wands torn by main force from Rebuff's hedge. The sooner to have their reward, the army loosed barbed arrows upon them, feathered with fervent promises of services or gifts (for no shaft could penetrate there unless it was made entirely of promises), and firmly tipped with points made of pledges and oaths. The others took shelter and were not slow to defend themselves, for they had strong, hard shields, neither too heavy nor too light, made from the same wood as the hurdles that Rebuff took from his hedges; there was no use hurling any missile against them.

15796   When matters had reached this point, Love went to his mother and explained his situation to her and begged her to help him. 'May I die an evil death,' she said, 'and that soon, if I ever allow Chastity to dwell in a living woman, in spite of Jealousy's struggles! We are very often in great difficulties on her account. Fair son, swear that all men will also hasten along our paths.'

'Certainly, my lady, I will gladly do so. From now on, not 15808 one will be spared; it is true at least that none will be called worthy unless he loves or has loved. It is a great sorrow that men should live who shun the delights of Love while still capable of enjoying them. May they come to a bad end! I hate them so much that if I could, I would destroy them all. I complain about them and always shall, nor shall my complaints grow less, for I should like to harm them in every way I could until I had my revenge and their pride was crushed and they were all condemned. In an evil hour were they born of Adam, those who think to cause me such distress! May their hearts burst within them when they seek to ruin my delights! Indeed, a man could do no worse if he were to beat me or strike me down dead with four picks. I am not mortal, but this causes me such anger that if I could be mortal, I would die from the grief of it. For if my games should fail, then I have lost all that I have of worth, except for my body and my clothes, my chaplet and my armour. If they have not the power to play Love's games, they should at least be unhappy about it, and their hearts should be heavy with grief when they have to abandon them. Where can you find a better life than in the arms of your sweetheart?'

Then they took their oath before the army and, so that it 15847 might be firmly adhered to, took out, instead of relics, their quivers and arrows, bows, darts, and torches, saying: 'We ask no better relics for this purpose, nor are there any that we like so well. Were we to prove false to these pledges, we would never be believed again.' They would swear by nothing else, and the barons believed them as if they had sworn by the Trinity, because their oath was true.

CHAPTER 9

NATURE AND GENIUS

15861 When they had taken their oath in the hearing of all, Nature,* whose thoughts were on the things enclosed beneath the sky, had entered her forge, where she was concentrating all her efforts upon the forging of individual creatures to continue the species. For individuals give such life to species that, however much Death pursues them, she can never catch up with them. Nature follows her so closely that when Death takes her club to kill those individuals she considers to be her due (for there are some corruptible creatures that have no fear of Death and yet perish, worn out and consumed by time, and that serve to nourish others), when she thinks to exterminate them all, she is unable to chain them all up at the same time. No sooner has she caught one here than another over there escapes; when she has killed the father, there remains the son, daughter, or mother, who flee from Death when they see their father already dead. But however well they run, they will have to die in their turn and no medicines or vows will avail them. Then nephews and nieces appear, and flee in search of pleasure as fast as their legs will carry them, one to the dancing, one to a monastery, another to school, some to their businesses, others to the skills they have learned, and still others to the pleasures of wine, food, and bed. Others try to speed their flight and avoid being buried by Death by mounting great chargers with gilded spurs; another entrusts his life to a wooden vessel and flees across the sea in his ship, guiding his boat with its sails and oars by the stars; yet another, who has taken a vow of humility, wears a cloak of hypocrisy, with which he conceals his thoughts as he flees, until his actions reveal his true exterior.

15913 Thus all the living flee, eager to avoid Death. Death has stained her face black and runs in pursuit until she catches them, and the chase is cruel indeed. The living flee and Death hunts them for ten years or twenty, thirty or forty, fifty, sixty, seventy, or even eighty, ninety, or a hundred. She destroys all those she catches, and if they manage to get away, she is tireless in her pursuit, until, in spite of all the physicians, she has them in thrall. As for the physicians themselves, we have not seen a single one escape, not even Hippocrates or Galen, however skilled they were. Rhases, Constantine, and Avicenna* have left her their skins, while, as for those who are not so good at running, nothing can save them from Death. Thus insatiable Death greedily swallows up individuals, pursuing them by land and sea, until in the end she buries them all. But individuals are so good at running away that she is unable to catch them all at once, and so she can never manage to destroy the entire species. For even if only one individual remained, the form common to all would survive; this is quite apparent from the example of the phoenix, for there cannot be two phoenixes at the same time.

There is always just one phoenix, which lives for five 15947 hundred years before it dies, and builds at last an immense fire, scented with spices, on to which it leaps and is burned. In this way it destroys its own body. But since its form is preserved, however thoroughly it may have been burned, another phoenix emerges from its ashes, or perhaps it is the same one, revived by Nature, who gains so much from this species that she would lose her very being were she not to cause the phoenix to be reborn. In this way, when Death devours the phoenix, the phoenix yet remains alive. If she had devoured a thousand of them, a phoenix would still survive. It is the form common to all phoenixes, and which Nature reshapes in each individual, which would be lost completely were the next phoenix not to be allowed to live. Everything beneath the circle of the moon exists in the very same way: as long as one survives, the species lives in it in such a way that Death will never catch up with it.

But gentle, compassionate Nature, seeing that jealous Death 15975 and Corruption are together destroying everything they can find, is continually in her forge, hammering and forging and renewing individuals through new generations. When she has no other solution, she stamps them out bearing the impress of particular letters, for she gives them true forms in coins of different currencies. Art took these for her models, but her

forms are not so true. With most attentive care she kneels
before Nature, like a poor beggar who lacks both knowledge
and strength but who strives hard to follow her. She begs and
prays and implores Nature to teach her how to use her skill
so that her figures may properly encompass every creature,
and she watches how Nature works, for she would very much
like to do the same work herself. Like an ape, she mimics
Nature, but her understanding is so weak and bare that she
cannot make living things, however natural they seem.

16005   Now Art may struggle and take great trouble and great
pains to make things of various kinds and forms. She may
employ the techniques of painting or dyeing, forging or
sculpture, to fashion knights in their battle armour mounted
on fine chargers covered with blue, yellow, or green armour,
or variegated with other colours, if you like them variegated,
lovely birds in verdant groves, fish from every water, all the
wild beasts grazing in their wooded pastures, all the grasses
and flowers that young boys and girls go gathering in the
woods in springtime, when they see them bursting into
flower and leaf, tame birds and domestic animals, balls and
dances where beautiful and elegantly attired ladies tread the
measure, well portrayed and represented in metal, wood,
wax, or some other material, in pictures or on walls, with
good-looking young men in tow, who are also well represented and portrayed. And yet, for all their shapes and features, Art will never make them walk of their own accord,
nor live, move, feel, or speak.

16035   She may learn enough alchemy to be able to colour every
metal, but she would kill herself before she could transmute
the species, unless she first reduced them to their elemental
matter;* if she worked all her life, she would never catch up
with Nature. If she were willing to toil until she could so
reduce them, when it came to making her elixir, she would
perhaps still lack the necessary knowledge to achieve the right
compound to produce form, which separates the substances
on the basis of specific differences, as is apparent in their
definitions, when these are correct.

16053   It is worthy of note, nevertheless, that alchemy is a true art,
and that anyone who worked at it seriously would discover

great marvels. Whatever may be true of species, individuals at least, when subjected to the operations of the intellect, can be changed into so many different forms, and their complexions so altered by various transformations, that this change can rob them of their original species and put them into a different one. Have we not seen how those who are expert in glass-making can, through a simple process of purification, use ferns to produce both ash and glass? Yet glass is not fern, nor fern glass. And when we have thunder and lightning, we often see stones fall from the clouds, although they did not rise as stones. Experts may know what causes matter to be changed into different species. And thus species are transformed, or rather their individuals are alienated from them in substance and appearance, by Art in the case of glass and by Nature in the case of the stones.

The same could be done with metals, if one could manage 16083 to do it, by removing impurities from the impure metals and refining them into a pure state; they are of similar complexion and have great affinities with one another, for they are all of one substance, no matter how Nature may modify it. Books tell us that they were all born in different ways, in mines down in the earth, from sulphur and quicksilver. And so, if anyone had the skill to prepare spirits in such a way that they had the power to enter bodies* but were unable to fly away once they had entered, provided they found the bodies to be well purified, and provided the sulphur, whether white or red, did not burn, a man with such knowledge might do what he liked with metals. The masters of alchemy produce pure gold from pure silver, using things that cost almost nothing to add weight and colour to them; with pure gold they make precious stones, bright and desirable, and they strip other metals of their forms, using potions that are white and penetrating and pure to transform them into pure silver. But such things will never be achieved by those who indulge in trickery: even if they labour all their lives, they will never catch up with Nature.

Now skilful Nature, intent as she was upon the works she 16119 loved so well, declared that she was wretched with sorrow and wept so bitterly that no heart that beheld her and knew

anything of love or pity could refrain from weeping. Her
heart was in such distress because of something of which she
repented that she wanted to forsake her work and give up all
her thought, provided only she had permission from her
master. And so, in her great suffering and heaviness of heart,
she was anxious to go to him and make her request.

16135   I would gladly have described her to you, but my wit is
not equal to the task.* My wit, do I say? Not only mine! No
man's wit could depict her, whether in speech or writing,
were he Plato or Aristotle, Algus, Euclid,* or Ptolemy, who
now enjoy the reputation of having been good writers: their
powers would be too weak, and if they dared undertake the
task, they would not be equal to it. Pygmalion could not
carve her, Parrhasius would strive in vain, and even Apelles,
whom I call a very good painter, could never describe her
beauties, however long he lived. Nor would Miro or Poly-
cletus ever be successful.

16155   Even the fine painter Zeuxis* could not achieve such a
form. In order to represent Nature's image in the temple, he
took five maidens for his models, the most beautiful to be
found anywhere on earth. They stood before him, entirely
naked, so that he could use each as a model if he found any
defect on the body or limbs of any one of them. (Cicero tells
us this in his *Rhetoric*,* which is a very reliable source of
knowledge.) But Nature's beauty is so great that Zeuxis could
never have succeeded, for all his skill in executing and col-
ouring his portrait. Zeuxis? No, nor all the masters that
Nature ever bore. For even if they had grasped the extent of
her beauty and wanted to waste their time trying to portray
it, their hands would have worn out before they had managed
to depict such very great loveliness. Only God could do it.

Since, if I could, I would gladly have at least made the
attempt, and would indeed have written it down for you, had
I the skill and the wit to do it, I have myself wasted so much
time on it that I have worn out my brain, fool that I am, and
a hundred times more arrogant than you can imagine. It was
far too presumptuous of me ever to set my sights on achieving
so lofty a feat. I found such nobility and such great worth in
that beauty that I prize so highly, that however hard I had

worked, my heart would have burst within me before I had grasped it in my thoughts, or dared, for all my thinking, to utter a single word. So I have given up thinking; and now I keep silent about it for my reflections have taught me that Nature is lovely beyond my comprehension.

When God, whose beauty is beyond measure, gave Nature 16203 her beauty, he made of it an ever-full and ever-flowing stream, the source of all beauty, whose banks and depths none has fathomed. Therefore it would not be right for me to give an account of her body or of her face, which is so fair and lovely that no new May lily, no rose on its branch or snow on a bough is so red or so white. I should have to pay for it if I dared compare her to anything, for no man can comprehend her beauty or her worth.

When Nature heard the oath, the great grief she felt was 16219 very much lightened. She thought that she had been deceived and said: 'What have I done, wretch that I am? I have never repented of anything that befell me since this fair world began, except for one thing in which I was grievously at fault and for which I consider myself a fool. When I contemplate my folly, I know I am right to repent. Wretched fool! Miserable wretch! Wretched, a hundred thousand times wretched, where now is faith to be found? Have I used my energies well? Am I completely out of my mind, I who have always imagined that I was serving my friends in order to deserve their gratitude, and have in fact put all my effort into advancing my enemies! My good nature has been my undoing!' Then she addressed her priest, who was celebrating Mass in her chapel. This was not a new Mass, for he had always done this service since he became a priest of the Church.

In place of another Mass, the priest, who was in full agree- 16247 ment, recited loudly and distinctly in the presence of the goddess Nature the representative shapes of all corruptible things that were written in his book, just as Nature gave them to him. 'Genius, my fair priest,' she said, 'you are god and master of the organs of reproduction, setting all to work according to their particular properties and completing the task as is appropriate to each. I am tormented by repentance for a folly that I did not refrain from committing, and would like to make my confession to you.'

'My lady, queen of the world, before whom all earthly things bow down, if anything troubles you so much that you now repent of it, or simply want to talk about it, whether it concerns something joyful or sorrowful, you may certainly confess everything to me at your leisure. And I', said Genius, 'am entirely at your disposal and will gladly supply whatever remedy I can, and I shall keep the matter secret if it is something that should not be talked about. And if you need absolution, I will not deprive you of it. But dry your tears.'

16283   'Indeed, fair Genius,' she said, 'it is no wonder that I weep.'

'Nevertheless, my lady, I advise you to cease your weeping if you want to make a good confession, and give your mind to the subject that you have undertaken to tell me about. I am sure it is a serious offence, for I know that noble hearts are not disturbed by little things. He is a great fool who dares to trouble you. But it is doubtless true that women are easily moved to anger. Virgil himself, who knew a great deal about them, testifies that no woman was ever so steadfast as not to be fickle and inconstant.* And she is also a most irritable creature: Solomon says that no head was ever more cruel than that of the serpent, nor any creature more irritable or malicious than woman.* In short, woman has such vices that no one could relate her depraved behaviour in rhyme or verse. Furthermore, Titus Livy, who was very familiar with the habits and ways of women, tells us that they are so stupid and easily deceived, and have such pliable natures, that flattery has more power to influence their behaviour than any prayers.* And Scripture also tells us elsewhere that the root of all feminine vice is avarice.

16317   'If a man reveals his secrets to his wife, he becomes subordinate to her. No man born of woman, if he is not drunk or demented, should tell a woman anything that ought to be kept secret, unless he wants to hear it from someone else. He would be better off fleeing the country than telling a woman—however loyal and good-natured—anything that ought not to be talked about. Nor should he do anything secret if he sees a woman nearby, for I can tell you that even if there is bodily danger, she will talk about it sooner or later; even if no one asks her about it, she will give a full account, without encouragement from anyone else: nothing could make her keep quiet. She imagines she would die if it did not burst from her lips, even if danger and blame are involved. And now that she knows it, if the man who revealed it to her dares to strike or beat her just once, not three or four times, the moment he touches her, she will reproach him with it, and she will do it in public. Anyone who trusts a woman loses her. Do you know what he is bringing upon himself by trusting her, wretch that he is? He is tying his own hands and cutting his own throat, for if he has deserved death for something he has done and he dares, just once, to scold or reproach or upbraid her, his life will be in great danger, for she will have him hanged by the neck if the judges can catch him, or killed by friends, such is the evil pass to which he has come.

'But when the fool goes to bed at night and lies down in 16359 bed next to his wife, and cannot or dare not rest, perhaps because he has done something, or possibly because he intends to commit some murder or crime which he fears will mean his death if he is found out, then he tosses about and moans and sighs. And then his wife draws him to her, for she sees that he is distressed, and caresses him and kisses and embraces him, and he rests between her breasts.

' "Sir," she says, "what news? What is it that makes you sigh like this and shudder and toss about? We are quite private here, just the two of us, the two people, you the first and I the second, who in all this world should best love one another with hearts that are loyal and true and free from bitterness. I distinctly remember closing the door of our bedroom with my own hand, and I appreciate the walls all the more for being three feet thick. The rafters also are so high that we ought to be quite safe here, and the fact that we are a long way from the windows makes the place even safer for revealing secrets; and no man would have any more chance than the wind of opening those windows, unless he took them to pieces. In short, there are no ears here and your voice can be heard only by me alone, and so with tender love I beg you to trust me enough to tell me what it is."

16399 ' "Lady," he says, "as God is my witness, I would not reveal
it for anything, for it is not something that ought to be told."

' "Aha!" she says, "fair sweet lord, do you then suspect me,
who am your loyal wife? When we came together in marriage, Jesus Christ, whom we have not found to be grudging
or sparing of his grace, made the two of us to be of one flesh,
and since by right of common law we have but one flesh, and
one flesh can only have one heart on the left, our hearts are
therefore one: you have mine and I yours. There can therefore be nothing in yours that mine ought not to know, and
so I beg you to tell me, as the reward that I have deserved,
for I shall never have joy in my heart until I know about it.
If you will not tell me, I shall see that you are deceiving me,
and I shall know with what kind of heart you love me when
you call me gentle sweetheart, gentle sister, gentle friend.
Whom are you trying to deceive? It is certainly quite clear
that you are betraying me unless you admit everything to me,
for since our marriage I have trusted you so completely that
I have told you everything that was hidden in my heart. It is
also clear that I left my father and mother, uncle, nephew,
sister, brother, and all my friends and relatives for you. I made
a very poor exchange indeed, now that I find you are so
distant with me, you whom I love more than anyone alive,
not that that is worth a fig to me. You imagine that I would
behave so badly to you as to reveal your secrets, but such a
thing would be impossible. By Jesus Christ the king of heaven,
who should protect you better than I? If you know anything
about loyalty, please consider at least the fact that my body
is pledged to you. Is this security not enough for you? Do
you want a better hostage? Then I am worse than all the
others if you dare not tell me your secrets. I see all those
other women who are sufficiently mistresses of their house-
holds for their husbands to trust them and tell them all their
secrets. They all take counsel with their wives when they lie
awake together in bed; they confess to them in private,
omitting nothing, and, truth to tell, they do so more often
than they do even to the priest. I know this from the women
themselves, for I have often heard them and they have told
me everything they have seen and heard, and even everything

they think. This is their way of unburdening themselves and obtaining relief. But I am not like them, and none of them can be compared with me, for I am no wanton, scolding gossip: as far as my body is concerned, I am a good woman, however my soul may stand with God. You have never heard it said of me that I have committed adultery, unless it was a malicious tale invented by idiots. Have you not put me to the test? In what way have you found me false? And then, fair sir, consider how you keep faith with me. Indeed, you were very wrong to put a ring on my finger and pledge your faith to me. I do not know how you dared. If you dare not trust me, who made you marry me? Therefore I beg you to keep faith with me at least this once, and I assure you faithfully, and promise and pledge and swear to you by the blessed Saint Peter, that I will be as silent as the grave. I would be foolish indeed if I allowed a word to fall from my lips that might shame or hurt you. I would be bringing shame upon my own family, of which I have never spoken ill, and above all upon myself. There is a saying, and it is certainly true, that whoever is foolish enough to cut off his nose brings everlasting disgrace upon his face. So help you God, tell me what it is that troubles your heart, otherwise you will be the death of me." Then she uncovers his chest and his head and kisses him over and over again, shedding many tears over him between the feigned kisses.

'Then the unfortunate man tells her all his pain and shame, 16511 and with his words he hangs himself. When he has told her, he regrets it, but a word once spoken may not be recalled. He begs her not to reveal it, for he is in greater distress than he ever was before, when his wife knew nothing of it. And she for her part tells him that she will certainly keep quiet, come what may. But what does the wretch think he is doing? He cannot silence his own tongue: is he then to try to restrain someone else's? What does he hope to achieve?

'Now the woman sees that she has got the upper hand and 16527 knows that her husband will in no circumstances dare to scold her or complain to her about anything. She has everything she needs to keep him dumb and quiet. She may perhaps keep her word to him until there is a quarrel between them, if she can wait that long! But she will be unlikely to wait long enough for him not to suffer acutely, for his heart will be racked with uncertainty. Anyone who loved men would preach them this sermon; it ought to be spoken everywhere, so that every man could see himself in it and be drawn back from his great danger. Evil-tongued women will perhaps be offended by it, but truth does not hide in corners.

16547 'Fair lords, be on your guard against women, if you have any love for your bodies or your souls. At least do not do anything so wrong as to disclose to them the secrets locked in your hearts. Fly, fly, fly, fly, fly, my children, I advise and admonish you frankly and without deceit to fly from such a creature. Take note of these lines of Virgil,* and make your hearts so familiar with them that they cannot be erased: O children who gather flowers and fresh, clean strawberries, the cold serpent lies in the grass. Fly children, for he drugs and poisons with venom every man who comes near him. O children who search for flowers and young strawberries on the ground, the cold, evil serpent is hiding here, the malignant snake who hides and conceals his poison, secreting it beneath the tender grass until such time as he can pour it out to deceive and injure you; children, be careful to shun him. Do not let yourselves be caught if you want to escape death, for he is such a venomous beast in his body, tail, and head that you will all be poisoned if you come near him; he treacherously stings and bites whomsoever he touches, without hope of a cure, and no remedy can heal the burning of that poison. No herb or root is of any use against it; the only medicine is flight.

16587 'I am not saying, however, nor was it ever my intention to say, that you should not hold women dear, nor flee so far that you cannot lie with them. On the contrary, I enjoin you to value them highly and promote their well-being, within reason. See to it that they are well clothed and shod, and make constant efforts to serve and honour them, so that the species may continue and never be destroyed by death. But never confide in them to the extent of telling them things that ought not to be mentioned. Give them leave to come and go, to run the house and the household if they know how to take care of it; or, if they happen by chance to be good at buying or selling, let them work at that. If they are familiar with any kind of trade, let them pursue it if they feel the need, and let them know those things that are public and do not need to be hidden. But if you abandon yourself so far as to give them too much power, you will repent too late when you feel their malice. Scripture* itself cries out to us that when a woman wields power, she opposes her husband in whatever he wants to say or do. Take care nevertheless that the household does not go to ruin, for we can lose things even when we are most vigilant: a wise man keeps what is his.

'As for you who have sweethearts, be their good compan- 16623 ions. It is quite right that they should all know enough about matters that are of joint concern; but if you are wise and sensible, when you hold them in your arms and embrace them and kiss them, you will keep quiet, quiet, quiet, quiet! Be sure to hold your tongues, for nothing will succeed if they share your secrets, so proud and overbearing are they, with such biting, poisonous, hurtful tongues. But when foolish men reach the point where they are held in their arms while they hug and kiss them in the intervals between those games that give them such pleasure, then nothing can be hidden, and secrets are revealed. Then it is that husbands bare their souls; they will later suffer grief and sorrow because of it. In this situation all men reveal their thoughts, except those who are prudent and wise.

'Malicious Delilah used her poisonous flattery upon Sam- 16647 son, who was so brave and valiant, so strong and warlike. Holding him close and softly as he lay sleeping in her lap, she cut off his hair with her scissors. Thus shorn of his hair, he lost all his strength, and Delilah revealed all the secrets that the foolish man, unable to hide anything from her, had told her. But I will not give you any more examples; one will suffice for all. Even Solomon mentions it, and since I love you, I shall now tell you what he says: "Guard the gates of your mouth against her who sleeps in your bosom",* in order to avoid danger and blame. Those who love men should preach them this sermon, to keep them on their guard against women, so that they never confide in them. But I have not said this on your account, for it is undeniable that you have always been loyal and steadfast. Scripture itself affirms that God has given you such a good brain that you are infinitely wise.'

16677   Thus Genius comforted her and exhorted her with all his might to abandon her grief altogether, for, he said, no one can overcome anything in sorrow and sadness. Sorrow, he said, is a thing that does a great deal of harm and profits nothing. When he had said all he wanted, he made no further prayer but sat down in a chair that was placed next to his altar. Nature at once fell on her knees before the priest, but it is undoubtedly true that she could not forget her grief, nor, for his part, would Genius ask her again, for he would be completely wasting his time. Instead he was silent and listened to the lady, who wept as she made her devout confession. I report it to you now in writing, word for word, just as she pronounced it.

CHAPTER 10
NATURE'S CONFESSION

'When God, who abounds in beauty, created the beauty of
this fair world, before ever it had external existence he held
the loveliness of its form preordained in his thought for all
eternity; it was there that he found his model and all that he
needed, for even if he had wished to look elsewhere, he
would have found neither heaven nor earth nor anything that
could have helped him. Nothing outside his thought existed,
for he in whom there is no lack caused everything to spring
from nothing, nor did anything prompt him to do so except
his gracious will, which is generous, courteous, and free from
envy, the fountain-head of all life. In the beginning, he
created a single mass, which was all confusion, without order
or distinction, then he divided it into parts, which were not
afterwards split up. He made a tally of all things by number,
and he knows the sum of them. He completed all their shapes
in rational proportions and made them round, so that they
might move better and contain more, depending on how
movable and capacious they were supposed to be. Then he
put them in appropriate places, as he saw fit to place them:
things that were light flew aloft, while the heavy went to the
centre, and those of medium weight between the two. In this
way places were ordained, in the right proportion and vol-
ume. When he had settled his other creatures according to
his plan, this same God in his grace showed me such honour
and love that he made me chamberlain of all; he allows and
will allow me to serve him there as long as it is his will. I
claim no other right there, but thank him, great lord that he
is, for loving and valuing me enough to take so poor a maiden
as chamberlain in so grand and fair a house. As chamberlain?
Truly, as constable indeed, and vicar, titles of which I could
never have been worthy except through his benign will.

'God has done me the honour of placing in my keeping 16755
the fair golden chain that links the four elements, all of which
bow before my face. He also entrusted to me all the things

enclosed within the chain, and ordered me to guard them and maintain their forms. He wanted all things to obey me and learn my rules so well that they would never forget them, but would observe and keep them throughout all eternity. And so in truth they do, one and all; they all take great care to do so, except for one single creature.

'I have no complaint to make of heaven,* which turns continually without slackening its pace, carrying with it in its polished circle all the stars, which are brighter and have greater powers than any precious stones. It bears the world with it as it goes on its way, beginning its course in the east and ending it in the west, nor does it ever stop turning backwards, sweeping along with it all the wheels that offer resistance and retard its movement. These cannot prevent its movement to the extent of making it go so slowly that it will not in thirty-six thousand years have made a complete circle and come back to the very point at which God first created it. Its path will have followed the circumference of the great circle of the Zodiac, which turns upon itself like a wheel.* The movement of heaven is so accurate that there is no error in its course: therefore those who found it free from error called it *aplanos*, for *aplanos* in Greek means "thing without error" in French. This other heaven of which I speak cannot be seen by men, but reason, for those who accept its demonstrations, provides the proof.

16803　'Nor do I complain of the seven planets, each of which shines bright and clear throughout the whole of its course. People think that the moon is not quite clean and pure, because it looks dark in places, but it is because of its double nature that it sometimes looks dense and murky: one part of it shines but not the other, because it is both clear and opaque. Its light is extinguished because the clear part of its substance cannot reflect the rays of the sun that shine upon it; instead they pass straight through it. But the opaque part is luminous, because it is resistant to the rays and thus takes its light from them. In order to explain this, we could give a brief example instead of a gloss, the better to clarify our text.

16825　'Transparent glass allows the rays to pass through it, having nothing dense inside or behind it which might reflect them.

It cannot show shapes, because the rays of the eyes* do not encounter anything to stop them and send the image back to the eyes. But if someone were to back it with lead or some opaque substance impermeable to the rays, the image would be reflected at once; it would be reflected, I know, from any polished object which was able to reflect light because of its own opacity or that of another material. In the same way, the transparent part of the moon, which resembles its sphere, cannot intercept the rays that would illuminate it, and instead they pass through it; it is the opaque part, which does not allow them to pass through but reflects them strongly, that gives light to the moon. This is why it appears luminous in some parts and dark in others.

'Now the dark part of the moon represents the figure of a   16851 most marvellous beast: it is that of a serpent whose head is always bent towards the west, while its tail points to the east. On its back it bears a standing tree, which spreads its branches towards the east but inverts them as it does so. On the underside of the branches is a man, leaning on his arms, who has pointed both his feet and his thighs towards the west: this is what their appearance suggests.*

'These planets do excellent work; they each do their job   16865 so well that not one of the seven ever delays. They move through their twelve houses* and pass through all their degrees, remaining at each point just as long as they ought to. In order to perform their task properly, they revolve backwards and retrace each day the sections of heaven they need in order to complete their circles. Then they begin again, endlessly, holding back heaven in its course so as to be of service to the elements, for if heaven could move freely, nothing could live beneath it.

'The fair sun, which gives us the light of day, for it is the   16881 source of all light, dwells in the centre, like a king, all fiery and radiant. He has his house in the middle of the planets, and it was not without reason that God, the fair, the strong, and the wise, wanted his abode to be there. If his course had been lower, there is nothing that would not have died of heat, and if it had been higher, everything would have been doomed by the cold. There he dispenses his light in common between the stars and the moon, making them look so beautiful that Night uses them for candles when she lays her table in the evening, in order to appear less dreadful before her husband, Acheron,* whose heart is greatly saddened, for he would prefer there to be no light when he was with black Night, just as before, when they first knew each other and came together, and in their wild abandon Night conceived the three Furies, those cruel, fierce creatures who are judges in the Underworld. Nevertheless, when Night is in her pantry, her storeroom, or her cellar and gazes at her reflection, she thinks to herself that she would be too pallid and hideous, and her face too dark, without the joyful light of the resplendent heavenly bodies shining in the darkened air as they turn in their spheres, just as God the Father ordained. There among themselves they create harmonies* which are the source of the melodies and different tones that we arrange in chords in every kind of song: nothing sings except through them.

16925 'Through their influence they change the accidents and substance of things beneath the moon; through their reciprocal diversity they cause clear elements to grow dense, and dense ones to become clear. They cause cold and heat, dryness and dampness to enter every body as though it were a container, in order to hold the different parts together: however hostile these qualities may be to one another, the heavenly bodies bind them together. Thus they make peace among the four enemies when they amalgamate them like this into a reasonable and justly proportioned combination, so as to mould everything that I fashion into the best possible form. If things happen not to be good, it is because of defects in their materials.

16945 'But if you look closely, you will see that, however good the peace, it will not prevent the heat from sucking up the fluid, endlessly destroying and eating it up from day to day until death comes, death, which is their due, as I myself have justly laid down. That is, unless death comes in another way, hastened for some other reason, before the fluid has been destroyed, for although no one could find a medicine or ointment to prolong the life of the body, I know very well that it is easy for anyone to shorten it.

'Many shorten their lives before the fluid has failed: they 16961 get themselves drowned or hanged, or undertake some dangerous enterprise which leads to their being burned or buried before they can escape, or they conduct their affairs so foolishly that some misfortune destroys them. Or else their personal enemies, whose hearts are false and cruel, put many who are blameless to death by the sword or by poison. They may fall ill through bad management of their lives, through too much sleeping or staying awake, too much resting or working, through growing too fat or too thin (for one can sin in all these ways), through too much fasting, amassing too many pleasures, or desiring too much suffering, through too much rejoicing or grieving, too much drinking or eating, or through changing their physical condition too much, particularly when they suddenly make themselves too hot or too cold: it is too late then to repent. Or it might be through a change in habits, which can also kill many people when it is done suddenly; many are hurt or killed by it, for sudden changes are very harmful to nature. In this way, they thwart my efforts to bring them to a natural death. Although they are behaving very badly in pursuing such deaths in spite of me, it saddens me greatly nevertheless when the wretches stop on their journey and give up the fight, beaten by a most unfortunate death and one that they could well have avoided, had they been willing to refrain from committing the wild excesses that have shortened their lives before they have attained and achieved the limit that I have set them.

'Empedocles* took poor care of himself. He looked in his 17009 books for so long and loved philosophy so well, full, perhaps, of melancholy, that he never feared death but cast himself alive into the flames and leaped bodily into Etna. He threw himself in of his own accord to show that those who fear death are cowards indeed. He would not have taken honey or sugar in exchange, but chose his own sepulchre, there in the boiling sulphur. Origen* also, who cut off his testicles, thought little of me when he sliced them off with his own hands so that he would be able to serve religious ladies with devotion, free from any suspicion that he might lie with them.

17029   'Men say that the fates have destined them for a particular
death and determined their fate from the moment of their
conception, that their birth took place under particular con-
stellations, so that, by strict necessity, without any other
possibility and without their being able to escape, however
much it might hurt them, they must accept that death. But
I know it to be true that, however hard heaven, working
through obedient matter which influences men's hearts, may
strive to endow men with such natural characteristics as will
predispose them to do the things that will bring them to this
end, nevertheless through learning and pure, wholesome
education, through companions who are good and sensible
and virtuous, through certain medicines, provided they are
good and pure, and through soundness of intellect, men can
cause things to happen differently, provided they have been
wise enough to restrain their natural tendencies.

17057   'For when a man or woman follows his or her own nature
and wishes to turn against what is good and right, reason can
divert him from this path, provided only he believe in her.
Then things will go quite differently, for they can be different
in spite of the heavenly bodies. If they do not oppose reason,
the heavenly bodies undoubtedly have great power, but they
have no power against reason, for every wise man knows that
they are not her masters and did not give her birth.

17071   'Now it is difficult to provide lay people with a solution
to the question of how predestination and the divine prescience, which knows all things in advance, can coexist with
free will.* Anyone willing to try would find it very hard to
make it understood, even if the arguments urged against it
had been dealt with. But it is true, however things may look
to them, that the two are compatible; otherwise, if the truth
were that everything happened by necessity, then those who
acted well would deserve no reward, while those whose
efforts were directed towards sin would deserve no punishment. For the man who wished to do good would be incapable of any other desire, while the one who wanted to do
evil would be unable to restrain himself: he would do it
whether he wanted to or not, because such was his destiny.
Now it might be said, for the sake of argument, that God is

never deceived concerning deeds that he has known in advance: they will undoubtedly take place just as he knows they will, and he knows when and how they will occur and what the result of them will be. If it were otherwise, and God had no foreknowledge, then he would not be all-powerful, all-good, and all-knowing; he would not be the sovereign lord, fair, mild, and above all others. He would not know what we do, but would have to rely on belief, as men do, whose belief is doubtful and who have no certain knowledge. But it would be the work of the devil to attribute such an error to God, and no one who wished to be reasonable would listen to it. Therefore, when a man's will strives towards something, then he is constrained by force to do whatever it is that he does. Whatever he thinks, says, desires, or pursues is his destiny and cannot be averted. It must follow from this, apparently, that nothing has free will.

'Now if destiny controls all that happens, as this argument 17125 appears to prove, why should God be pleased with the man whose actions are good, or punish the one whose actions are evil, when neither can do otherwise? Even if they had sworn to do the opposite, they could not have done anything else. It would therefore be unjust of God to reward virtue and punish vice. For how could he do it? A close examination would reveal that neither virtue nor vice existed; there would be no use in offering the sacrifice of the chalice nor in praying to God, if there were neither virtue nor vice. Or if God sat in judgement in the absence of virtue and vice, he would not be just but would acquit usurers, thieves, and murderers; the good man and the hypocrite would have equal weight in his scales. They would thus be shamed indeed, those who strive to love God, if in the end they failed to obtain his love. And they would be bound to fail because it would come to this, that no one could obtain God's favour through good works.

'But he is certainly just, and shining with all goodness: 17157 otherwise there would be a defect in him who is perfect. Therefore he renders gain or loss to each according to his deserts; therefore all our deeds are rewarded and destiny abolished, at least as it is understood by lay people, who consider that all things, good and bad, false and true, are necessary occurrences, to be laid at destiny's door. Thus free will exists, in spite of the poor treatment it receives from such folk.

17171 'However, someone might wish to raise an objection in support of destiny and to do away with free will (for many have been so tempted); concerning some possible occurrence, however doubtful, he might say, at least when it had happened: "If someone had foreseen this and said: 'Such a thing will be and nothing will prevent it', would he not have spoken the truth? The occurrence must therefore be necessary, for it follows from the interchangeability of truth and necessity that if something is true, it is also necessary. It is thus bound to take place, since necessity is involved." What escape would there be for anyone who wanted to reply?

17191 'What he said would undoubtedly be true, but not necessary for all that, for although he may have foreseen it, the event did not take place as a necessary occurrence but only as a possible one. Close examination reveals that this is conditional rather than simple necessity, and therefore the argument that "if a future event is true, then it is also necessary" is not worth a button, for this kind of possible truth cannot be interchanged with simple necessity in the same way as simple truth. It cannot be claimed that such reasoning does away with free will.

17209 'Moreover, if one views the matter carefully, it is clear that people would never need to ask for advice about anything nor to perform any action here on earth. Why should they seek advice or do any work, if everything is predestined and predetermined? No advice or handiwork could make anything greater or less, better or worse, whether it were something already existing or not yet existing, something already done or yet to be done, something to be spoken of or left unexpressed. No one would need to learn anything: even without studying, a man would know as much about any art as if he had studied and worked hard all his life. But this is inadmissible, and therefore we must deny outright that the works of mankind come about through necessity. On the contrary, people are free to do good or evil simply according to their own will, and, truth to tell, there is nothing outside themselves that could make them choose a particular will, nothing that they could not take or leave alone if they were willing to use their reason.

'But it would be hard to give an answer now that would 17237 confute all the counter-arguments that might be adduced. Many have been willing to exert themselves in this direction, and have expressed the subtle opinion that the divine prescience imposes no necessity upon the works of mankind. They see clearly that it is not God's foreknowledge that forces things to happen or to turn out in a particular way; instead, they say, it is because things will happen and turn out or come about in a particular way that God knows them in advance. However, these people fail to unravel the question; anyone who understood the point of their argument and approached it rationally would see that, if their idea is correct, then it is future events that are the cause of God's foreknowledge and that make it necessary. But it is great folly to believe that God's understanding is so weak as to depend upon the deeds of others, and those who subscribe to such a view perversely strive against God, for they would undermine his prescience with their tales. Reason cannot accept that it is possible to teach God anything, and God certainly could not be all-wise if the defects in his knowledge were so great that this case could be proved against him. Therefore this reply, which hides God's prescience and shrouds his great foresight in the darkness of ignorance, is worthless. What is certain is that God's foresight can learn nothing through the works of mankind; if it could, this would certainly be the result of a lack of power. It would be painful to express such an idea, and sinful even to think it.

'Others have held a different opinion and have answered 17283 according to their understanding: they have agreed without a doubt that whatever happens, when things come about through free will and are the result of choice, God knows what will happen and how they will turn out, merely adding a point of detail, namely the way in which they will happen. In this way they would maintain that there is no necessity and that things take place through possibility, so that God knows what their end will be and whether they will take place or not. He knows that everything will go one of two ways: one negatively, another positively, but not so inevitably that they might not perhaps happen differently. For things can certainly happen differently if free will takes a hand.

17307   'But how did anyone dare say this? How did anyone dare despise God to such an extent as to credit him with the kind of prescience that knows nothing with certainty, and cannot see the truth with precision? For when he knows how an event will turn out, he nevertheless does not really know, if it can in fact happen differently. If he sees that it turns out differently from the way he knew it would, then his prescience is frustrated; it is uncertain and resembles fallible opinion, as I have already shown.

'Still others have gone a different way, and many yet hold this view, saying of events that happen through possibility here below that they all happen through necessity as far as God is concerned, but not otherwise. For whatever the effect of free will, God knows all things finally, eternally, and infallibly before they have taken place and however they may turn out, and he knows them through necessary knowledge. What they say is certainly true to the extent that all would agree and declare it to be true that God has necessary knowledge and that, free from ignorance, he knows from all eternity how things will happen. But he imposes no constraints upon himself or upon men; his knowledge of things in their entirety and of the details of every possibility derives from his great power and the goodness of his knowledge, from which nothing can hide. It would be incorrect to reply that he imposes necessity upon events; I maintain that it is not because he knows them in advance that they happen, and it is not because they happen subsequently that he knows them in advance. It is because he is all-powerful, all-good, and all-knowing that he knows the truth about everything and nothing can deceive him; nothing can exist that he does not see. This is not easy to understand, and for anyone willing to undertake the task of explaining it to illiterate lay people, the most direct way would be to give them a plain example; such people want something simple, without subtle glosses.

'The case might be as follows: suppose a man did some-   17368
thing, whatever it might be, of his own free will, or refrained
from doing it because he would be ashamed and embarrassed
if anyone saw him; suppose also that another man knew
nothing about it before the first man had done it, or not done
it if he preferred to refrain, then the man who knew it
afterwards would not therefore have imposed necessity or
constraint upon the deed. Even if he had known it in advance, provided that he did not pester the first man about it
but simply knew it, this would not have prevented the first
man from having done or from doing what pleased or suited
him, or from not doing it if his will allowed it, for his will
is so free and unfettered that he can either shun the deed or
perform it.

'In the same way, but more nobly and with absolute certainty, God knows the things that will happen and what their
ends will be, even though the event may come about through
the will of its master, who holds the power of choice and
inclines to a particular side because of his wisdom or his folly.
He also knows the things that have happened and how they
were done and achieved, while, as for those who abstained
from doing things, he knows whether they refrained from
shame or from some other cause, reasonable or unreasonable,
according to the prompting of their wills. For I am quite
certain that very many people are tempted to do evil but yet
refrain; some, whose principles are fine, do so in order to live
virtuously and for the love of God alone, but these are very
thin on the ground; others, who plan to commit sin if they
see no obstacle in their way, nevertheless curb their desires
for fear of punishment or shame. God sees all this clearly; all
the conditions and intentions of our deeds are present before
his eyes. Nothing can be kept from him, no matter how long
it is delayed, for, however distant the event, God keeps it
before him as if it were the present. Let ten years go by, or
twenty or thirty, or indeed five hundred or a hundred thousand, whether the deed be done in the country or in the
town, whether it be honest or otherwise, God sees it now as
though it had already taken place. He has seen it from all
eternity, truly represented in his everlasting mirror, which he

alone can polish, and this without in any way detracting from free will. This mirror is himself, from whom we took our being. In this beautiful polished mirror, which he keeps and always has kept with him, and in which he sees all that will happen and keeps it eternally present, he sees the destination of those souls who serve him loyally, and also of those who care nothing for loyalty or justice, and in his thought he promises them salvation or damnation according to their works. This is predestination, this the divine prescience that knows all and guesses nothing, that extends its grace to men when it sees them striving to do good, but has not therefore supplanted the power of free will. All men act of their own free will, whether for joy or sorrow. This is God's present vision, for when we unravel the definition of eternity, we find that it means the possession of life that cannot be ended, an entire and undivided whole.

17469   'But we must bring to a conclusion our account of the ordering of the world, graciously established and regulated by God in his great providence. As for the universal causes, these will necessarily remain what they must always be. The heavenly bodies will always operate their transmutations according to their separate revolutions, and use their powers through the necessary influences they exert upon individual substances contained in the elements, when their rays fall upon them, as they must. For creatures capable of reproduction will always produce similar creatures, or will come together according to their natural inclinations and the affinities between them. He who must die will die, and will live as long as he can, and natural desire will incline the hearts of certain people to idleness and pleasure, some tending to vice and others to virtue.

'But events may not always take place as the heavenly bodies direct, for creatures may resist them, although they would always obey them unless they had deliberately or accidentally been distracted away from obedience. Creatures will always be tempted to follow the inclinations of their hearts, which never cease to tend in a particular direction as though towards a predestined goal. I therefore grant that destiny may be that disposition, subject to predestination, which is superimposed on changeable things according as they are capable of being inclined in one direction or another.*

'A man may thus be blessed from birth in being bold and successful in business, wise, generous, and gracious, richly endowed with friends and wealth, and renowned for his fine qualities, or he may have nothing but bad fortune. But he should be careful how he lives, for destiny can be obstructed by virtue or by vice. If he knows that he is mean and avaricious (for some men may not be rich), he should resist these habits and keep just enough to live on for himself. Then he should pluck up courage and give away money, clothes, and food, but not to the extent that he acquires a reputation for foolish prodigality. In this way, he will have no need to fear avarice, which prompts men to hoard their money and so blights their lives that nothing can suffice them, for when men take to avarice, they are so blinded and oppressed that it prevents them from doing anything good and deprives them of all their virtuous inclinations. In the same way, anyone who is not an utter fool can resist all the other vices, or turn away from virtue, if he wishes to follow an evil path, for the power of his free will is so great, if he truly knows himself, that he can always protect himself when he feels within his heart that sin wishes to master him, in spite of the celestial influences.

'For if we could predict what heaven had in store for us, we could do something about it; if men knew in advance that heaven was about to dry up the air, so that everyone died of heat, they could build new homes in humid places or close to rivers, or hollow out great caverns and hide underground so that they would not have to fear the heat. If, on the other hand, we were eventually to suffer a flood, those who knew where safe places were to be found could leave the plains before it happened and flee to the mountains, or build ships strong enough to save their lives when the great flood came, just as Deucalion and Pyrrha* once did, when they escaped in their boat from the clutches of the waves. When these two had escaped and reached a safe haven, they saw, when the waters had subsided, that the valleys throughout the world were filled with marshes, and that there was not a single man or woman left on earth except Deucalion and his wife. They then decided to go and make their confession in the temple of the goddess Themis,* who rules over the destinies of all destined things, and, throwing themselves on their knees, they begged her to advise them how they should go about restoring their race to life. When she had heard their excellent and worthy request, Themis instructed them to go immediately and throw the bones of their great mother over their shoulders. Pyrrha was so horrified by this answer that she refused, excusing herself from her fate by saying that she ought not to break up and mutilate her mother's bones, until at last Deucalion explained. "There is no need to seek another meaning," he said. "Our great mother is the earth, and the stones, if I dare name them, must be her bones. So we must throw the stones over our shoulders in order to bring our race back to life." They did as he said, and at once men sprang up from the stones that Deucalion threw in good faith, while women, body and soul, sprang from Pyrrha's stones; they sought no other father, just as Themis had prompted them, and the resultant hardness will always be apparent throughout the human race. They acted wisely in thus using a ship to escape the flood; in the same way, anyone who was forewarned of such a flood could escape it.

'If famine were to occur, which would cause the crops to fail and people to die of hunger for lack of corn, they could keep back sufficient grain two or three or four years before it happened, so that when the famine came, everyone, great and small, would have enough to eat, and, as Joseph did in Egypt through his good sense and his merits, they could lay up such a store that they could survive the famine without hunger or hardship. Or if they could know in advance that the winter would be extraordinarily and excessively cold, men could prepare for it by providing themselves with warm clothes and great waggonloads of wood for the fire and hearth, and when the cold weather came they could cover the floors of their houses with clean white straw from their barns and make their homes more secure by closing all the doors and windows. Or they might build warm bath-houses where they could make merry and dance quite naked when they saw the air grow wild, hurling hail and tempests to kill the beasts in the fields and freezing the great rivers solid. However much such weather threatened them with storms and snow, they would only laugh at the threats and dance in their houses, since they would be quite free from danger. Indeed, they could make such good provision that they could mock at the weather. But without some miraculous vision or oracle sent by God, I am sure that no one unfamiliar with astronomy and the strange natures and different positions of the heavenly bodies, and ignorant of the particular zones subject to their influence, could possibly know all this in advance, however rich or wise he was.

'Now since the body has the power to flee the tumult of 17673 the heavens and hamper their efforts by protecting itself so well against them, and since, as I firmly maintain, the force of the soul is more powerful than that of the body (for the soul moves and carries the body, and without it the body would be dead), then free will, through the use of sound understanding, is better and more easily able to avoid anything that might cause it pain. It need not fear any distress, provided it does not consent to it, and it should know this maxim by heart, that it is the cause of its own distress. External trials are no more than the occasions of distress, and if free will considers its birth and is aware of its condition, it need have no fear of destiny. What price this preaching? However much our fates may be governed by destiny, free will is above them.

'I would say more about destiny, fixing the limits of fortune 17697 and chance, and would gladly explain everything, raising and refuting more objections and giving many examples, but it would take too long before I had said it all. It is clearly established elsewhere. Anyone who does not know about it should ask a clerk who has studied and understands it.

'Indeed, I would certainly not have mentioned destiny 17707 had it not been necessary, but it concerns my subject. For when my enemy heard me complain about him in this way, he might say, in order to cover up his disloyalty and blame his creator, that I was slandering him unjustly. For he himself is accustomed to say frequently that he has no power of choice, since God through his foresight has so subjugated him as to control all men's deeds and thoughts through destiny. The result is that if he is inclined to virtue, it is God who compels him, while if he strives to do evil, he is again compelled by God. God grasps him more firmly than if he held him by the finger, and so he does whatever he must: he sins, gives alms, speaks well or evilly, praises or criticizes, steals, kills, makes peace or marriage, whether it be right or wrong.

17733 ' "This is how it had to be," he says. "God caused this woman to be born for this man and he could have no other, whatever his intellect or his possessions. She was destined for him." And afterwards, if the match is a bad one, whether because of his folly or hers, when anyone speaks against it and curses those who allowed and effected the marriage, the senseless fellow will reply: "Lay the blame on God, whose will it is that things should happen in this way. It was certainly he who brought all this about." Then he confirms on oath that it could not be otherwise.

17749 'No, no! This reply is false, The true God, who cannot lie, does not treat people so badly as to make them consent to do wrong. It is from them that the foolish thought comes which gives birth to the wrongful yielding and prompts them to do things from which they should have refrained. For they could have refrained if they had only known themselves. They would then have called upon their creator, who would have loved them if they had loved him; for he alone loves wisely who knows himself thoroughly.

17763 'It is certain that all dumb beasts, bare and void of understanding, are unable by nature to know themselves. For if they had speech and reason, so that they could understand and instruct one another, it would go hard with men. The handsome chargers with their manes would never let themselves be tamed nor allow knights to mount them. No ox would place his horned head beneath the yoke of the plough; no ass or mule or camel would ever carry a load for man or care about him in the slightest; the elephant, who blows and trumpets through his nose and uses it to feed himself night and morning, as a man does his hand, would never bear a castle high up on his back. Cats and dogs would not serve man, for they would manage very well without him; bears, wolves, lions, leopards, and boars would all be glad to strangle him, and even the rats would strangle him when he was small and in his cradle. No bird would risk its skin in answer to any call; instead it might do man great harm by putting out his eyes as he slept. And if man chose to reply that he thought he could get the better of all of them because of his ability to make armour, helmets, hauberks, strong swords, bows, and crossbows, then the other animals could do the same. Will they not for their part have monkeys and marmosets to make them fine coats and doublets of leather and iron? Hands would not be a problem, for the monkeys could work with their hands, and so they would in no way be inferior to man; they could even be writers. They would never be so feeble as not to put their heads together to find ways of resisting these arms, and they would construct machines of their own with which they would inflict great harm on men. Even fleas and earwigs might do prodigious harm if they twisted their way into men's ears as they slept. The very lice, mites, and nits wage such frequent war upon them and torment them to such an extent that they abandon their work and turn aside, ducking and dodging, turning, jumping, and leaping about, scratching and throwing themselves this way and that, and taking off their clothes and shoes. Even flies often cause them great difficulties at the table and by flying in their faces; they make no distinction between kings and pages. Ants and other small vermin could annoy men intensely if they knew their powers. It is true that their own natures are responsible for this ignorance, but, as for rational creatures, whether mortal men or divine angels, all of whom ought to praise God, if such a creature is so foolish as not to know himself, this failing is the result of his wickedness, which dulls and fuddles his senses, for he is perfectly capable of being guided by reason and of using his own free will, and nothing can excuse him from doing so.

'I have spoken to you at great length on this subject and 1784advanced all these arguments so as to put an end to their evil talk, for which there can be no justification.

17845 'But I will say no more about it now, so as to continue with my task, of which I would like to be free, since the suffering I set down afflicts me in spirit and in body. I shall return to the heavens, which do all that they must to creatures, which in their turn receive the celestial influences according to their different substances.

17854 'The heavens cause the winds to be contrary and set fire to the air, which cries and shrieks and is shattered into many pieces by the thunder and lightning, whose blaring, booming tattoo raises such vapours that the clouds burst open. In their frightful struggles, the heat and agitation tear the bellies of the clouds, which, shaken by the storm's force, hurl thunderbolts and raise clouds of dust on earth and bring down towers and steeples. Many an old tree is so buffeted as to be torn from the ground, for, however firmly they are attached, their roots are of no avail and they must needs fall to the ground or have at least some, if not all, of their branches broken.

17875 'It is said that demons bring this about with hooks and catapults, claws and talons, but this saying is not worth two farthings; it is wrong to suspect the demons, for all the harm is done by the storms and winds; nothing else. These are the things that assail and harm the trees, that flatten the corn and shrivel the vines and dash the flowers and fruit from the trees; these last are so tossed and blown about that they do not stay on the branch long enough to grow ripe.

17889 'At certain times, indeed, the heavens cause the air to shed great tears, and the clouds feel such pity for them that they strip themselves quite naked. They care not a straw for the black cloak they have donned, for they are preparing such mourning that they tear it all to pieces. They help the sky to weep, as if they were about to be slain, and their copious tears fall so thick and fast that they cause the rivers to burst their banks and the raging flood to do battle with the fields and nearby forests. The corn is often ruined as a result, and the cost of living increases, so that poor men who till the ground bewail their ruined prospects. And when the rivers overflow their banks, the fish that follow the streams, as is right and reasonable, since these are their homes, roam like

lords and masters over the fields and meadows and vineyards
to find food. They swim everywhere, dashing at oaks and
pines and ash-trees and robbing the wild beasts of their dwellings and their heritage. Bacchus, Ceres, Pan, and Cybele* are
wild with rage when shoals of finny fish wend their way
through their delightful pastures. The thoughts of the satyrs
and fairies are very sorrowful when they lose their pleasant
groves because of these floods. The nymphs bewail and lament the loss of their springs, finding them filled to over-
flowing and covered by the rivers. The sprites and dryads*
are so sick at heart with grief that they think themselves quite
lost when they see their woods invaded in this way. They
complain about the river-gods, who commit new and wholly
unjustified crimes against them, when they have done them
no harm. The fish are also guests in nearby low-lying towns,
which they find wretched and mean. They install themselves
everywhere; no barn or cellar escapes, nor any place, however
valuable and costly. They enter temples and churches to rob
the gods of their service, and drive the household gods and
their images from the darkened rooms.

'And when, after a certain time, the good weather puts an 17951
end to the bad, and the heavens grow vexed and displeased
with all the storms and rain, they clear the air of all its wrath
and make it laugh with new joy. When, for their part, the
clouds perceive that the air they welcome is so jubilant, then
they rejoice in their turn. So as to be pleasing and beautiful
after their grief, they make dresses of every lovely colour, and
put their fleeces to dry in the fair sun's agreeable warmth.
Then, in the bright, shining weather, they tease out the wool
through the air and spin it and, when they have spun, flourish
great needlefuls of white thread, as though they were going
to sew up their sleeves.*

'When they desire once again to go on distant pilgrimages, 17971
they harness their horses, climb upwards, and go chasing
madly over hills and valleys. For when Aeolus, the god of the
winds (that is the name of this god), has harnessed the horses
well (for they have no other charioteer capable of managing
their horses), he puts wings on their feet the like of which
no bird ever had.

17983 'Then the air takes the blue mantle that it gladly wears in India and, putting it on, prepares to dress up in festal garb and await the return of the clouds in fine array. In order to give pleasure to the world, as well as to go hunting, the clouds are wont to carry a bow in their hands, or two or three, if they like. These bows are called rainbows, and no one knows, unless he is a good enough master to be able to teach optics, how the sun produces their different colours, or how many colours there are, or which ones, or why so many, or why these, or what determines their shape. Such a man should take the trouble to become a disciple of Aristotle, who made better observations of nature than any man since the time of Cain. For his part, Alhazen,* the nephew of Huchain, was neither a fool nor a simpleton: he wrote the book of *Optics*, and anyone who wants to know about rainbows should study this book. Any student of natural sciences or optics ought to know it, and he should also be familiar with geometry, mastery of which is necessary in order to test the accuracy of the book of *Optics*. Then he will be able to discover the principles and properties of mirrors: they have such marvellous powers that all tiny things, thin letters far from the eyes and minute grains of sand, are perceived as so large and brought so close to the observer (for everyone can see them in the mirror) that they can be read and counted, and this from so far away that no man who had not seen it or was ignorant of the underlying principle would believe the reports of anyone who had seen it. And then it would not be a matter of belief, since he would know about it.

18031 'If Mars and Venus, who were captured together as they lay in bed, had looked at themselves in such mirrors before climbing on to the bed, and if they had held their mirrors so as to be able to see the bed in them, they would never have been caught and bound in the fine thin net that Vulcan had put there, and of which they were both unaware. Even if he had fashioned it more finely than a spider's web, they would have seen it, and Vulcan would have been foiled, for they would not have ventured into the trap. Every cord would have seemed to them to be thicker and longer than a great beam, and wicked Vulcan, burning with anger and jealousy,

would never have proved their adultery. Nor would the gods
have known anything about it, if the pair had had such
mirrors, for, at the sight of the net stretched out for them,
they would have fled from the place and run away to find
somewhere else to lie, where their desire might be better
hidden. Or else they would have found some way of avoiding
this misfortune without suffering shame or distress. Now by
the faith you owe me, have I not spoken the truth in all you
have heard me say?'

'Yes indeed,' said the priest, 'it is quite true that these   18062
mirrors would have been invaluable, for, once they knew
their danger, they could have met elsewhere. Or perhaps
Mars, the god of battle, could have avenged himself upon the
jealous husband by cutting his net to pieces with his keen-
edged sword. Then he could have had his woman in comfort,
safe in bed, without looking for any other place, or even on
the ground beside the bed. And if, by some cruel and harsh
misfortune, Lord Vulcan had appeared, even if Mars had been
holding her in his arms at the time, Venus, who is a most
discreet lady (for women are great deceivers), would, if she
had been able to cover up her loins in time when she heard
him open the door, have used her sophistry to find excuses
and would have invented some other reason for Mars' coming
to the house. She would have sworn anything you liked, and
in the end she would have swept aside all his proofs and
forced him to believe that it had never happened. Even if he
had actually seen it, she would have told him that his sight
was dim and disturbed; she would have twisted her tongue
into many different contortions in order to find excuses, for
no one swears or lies more boldly than a woman, and Mars
would have escaped scot-free.'

'Certainly, lord priest, your words are those of a worthy,   18100
courteous, and wise man. Women's hearts are only too full
of trickery and malice, and anyone who does not know this
is silly and foolish. We have no excuses for women. They
certainly swear and lie more boldly than any man, particularly
when they feel themselves to be guilty of some misdeed; in
those circumstances, they are especially unlikely to be caught.
Thus I can honestly say that no one who sees a woman's heart

should ever put his trust in it. It is certain that no one would do so, since evil might befall him if he did.' And so it seemed to me that Nature and Genius reached agreement. Nevertheless, since I am being truthful, Solomon says that a man would be blessed if he found a good woman.*

18123   'Now mirrors', said Nature, 'have many other great and striking properties. When large, bulky objects are placed very close to them, all such objects, even the highest mountain between France and Sardinia, appear to be so far away and are perceived as so small, so tiny, that it would be hard to make them out, however much leisure one had for looking.

18133   'Other mirrors, if you look carefully, truly show the actual sizes of the objects you see in them. And there are others that burn the objects at which they are directed, provided they are correctly adjusted to gather the rays of the blazing sun as it shines on their surface.

18143   'Others may be used in various positions, to produce various images in different guises—upright, elongated, or upside down. Those who are expert in the use of mirrors can produce several images from just one; if they have set up the image properly, they can put four eyes in one head. They also cause phantoms to appear to those who look in; these even appear to come to life outside the mirror, whether in water or in the air, and they can be seen to play between the eye and the mirror. This is achieved by using different angles, and depends on whether the medium is composite or simple, of one nature or many. The responsive medium reverses the image and multiplies it many times, for the way in which the image appears to the eyes depends upon the rays that are reflected back to them, and these are so variously absorbed by the medium that the observer is deceived.

18167   'We have the testimony of Aristotle himself,* who, being a lover of all knowledge, was fully conversant with these matters. A man, he tells us, was sick, and his sickness had seriously impaired his sight. The air was dark and murky, and for these two reasons, according to Aristotle, he saw his own face in the air in front of him, going from place to place. Mirrors, in short, if nothing impedes them, can produce many miraculous appearances.

'Even without mirrors, different distances can be very de-   18179
ceptive: things that are far apart can seem to be close together,
and one thing can look like two, or three like six, or four
like eight, depending on how far away they are. If a man likes
to amuse himself with such sights, he can see more objects
or fewer, or he can so adjust his eyes as to make several things
seem like one, by grouping them all together. A man may be
so tiny that everyone calls him a dwarf, but mirrors may make
watching eyes perceive him as larger than ten giants; he seems
to stride over the woods, without bending or breaking a
branch, so that everyone trembles with fear. Conversely, giants
may look like dwarfs, because the eyes, perceiving them in
such different ways, distort them.

'And when the observers are thus deceived, having seen   18201
such things through the images revealed to them in mirrors
or by distance, they go straight to the people, with the false,
lying boast that they have seen devils, such are the optical
illusions that they experience.

'Eyes that are weak and dim can also make single things   18209
seem double, causing a double moon to appear in the sky and
one candle to look like two. No one can safeguard himself
against frequent failures of sight, and, as a result, many things
have been judged to be quite different from what they are.

'But I do not now wish to apply myself to explaining   18217
mirror-images, nor shall I say how the rays are reflected, nor
describe their angles (all this is written down elsewhere in a
book). Nor shall I comment on why the images of objects
reflected are reversed in the eyes of those who see themselves
when they turn towards the mirror, or on the location of
their appearances or the causes of the illusions. Nor, fair
priest, do I wish to say where such images have their being,
whether inside or outside the mirror, and I will not now give
any account of other marvellous sights, pleasant or painful,
that are suddenly seen to occur, or of whether, to my knowledge, they have external existence or are simply the product
of fantasy. I will not give a detailed explanation of this, nor
is it the proper time to do so; instead I will pass over them
in silence, together with the phenomena I have already mentioned and which I shall not describe. The subject would be

too long; it would be hard to explain and very difficult
to understand, even if anyone were capable of teaching it,
particularly to lay folk, without confining himself to gener-
alities. Such folk would be unable to believe the truth of all
this, especially where the diverse workings of mirrors are
concerned, unless they saw it with the aid of instruments
willingly given to them by students familiar through demonstration with this marvellous science.

18257   'Nor, whoever expounded them, could they accept the
marvellously strange kinds of visions, or the illusions produced, waking or sleeping, by such visions, by which many
have been amazed. Therefore I will pass over them, for I do
not want to weary myself with speaking, nor you with listening: prolixity is best avoided.

18269   'Women are very troublesome and annoying in their speech;
nevertheless, I beg you not to be angry with me for not being
entirely silent on this subject, provided I stick to the truth.
At any rate, I would simply like to say that many people are
so deceived by visions that they have got out of bed and even
put on their clothes and shoes and prepared all their gear
while their common sense slept and their particular senses
were all awake. Taking staffs and scrips or stakes, sickles or
bill-hooks, they journey great distances and know not where.
They even go on horseback and in this way cross mountains
and valleys, by dry or muddy tracks, until they reach foreign
lands. When their common sense awakes and they are in their
right mind once more, they are lost in wonder and amazement; then, when they are with other people, they maintain
that devils took them from their homes and brought them
there, insisting that this is no story, although they made their
own way there.

18297   'Moreover, when people are in the grip of some grave
sickness that manifests itself as a frenzy, and either do not
have enough people to watch them or are lying at home
alone, it has often happened that they have leapt up and set
off on a journey, not stopping until they reached some wild
place, some meadow, vineyard, or woodland, where they
have collapsed. If you come there afterwards, even much
later, you will see them, dead from cold and suffering because

they had no one to look after them, except perhaps people who were foolish and incompetent. Even when people are in good health, we see plenty of them who, when melancholy or irrationally fearful, are naturally inclined to indulge in intense and unregulated thought. They conjure up many different images inside themselves, quite different from those we spoke of in the discussion of mirrors that we concluded so quickly, and it seems to them that all these images exist truly and externally.

'Or there are those in whom devout and profound con-   18327
templation causes the objects of their meditations to appear in their thoughts, and who truly believe that they see them clearly and objectively. But these are merely lies and deceits, just as in the case of the man who dreams and believes that the spiritual substances he sees are really present, as Scipio once did.* He sees hell and heaven, the sky and the air, the sea and the land, and all that you might find there. He sees stars appearing, birds flying through the air, fish swimming in the sea, and beasts disporting themselves in the woods and performing fine and elegant feats. He sees many different people, some taking their pleasure indoors, others hunting over the woods, mountains, and rivers, over meadows, vine-yards, and unploughed land. He dreams of lawsuits and judg-ments, wars and tournaments, balls and dances; he hears viols and citoles, smells fragrant spices, tastes delicious food, and feels his sweetheart in his arms although she is not there. Or else he sees Jealousy coming with a pestle round her neck to catch them in the act, thanks to Evil Tongue, who invents things before they have happened, and because of whom lovers are always alarmed by day. Those who claim to be true lovers love one another with burning devotion and endure great toil and trouble as a result, then when they fall asleep at night in their beds, where they have spent a long time in thought (for I know what they are like), they dream of their beloved, whom they have so often longed for by day, or else they dream of their enemies, who cause them trouble and vexation.

'If they are in a state of mortal hatred, then they dream, by   18375
an association of opposite or similar ideas, of anger and fury

and quarrels with the enemies who are responsible for their hatred, and of the consequences of war.

18380   'Or, if they are imprisoned because of some serious crime, they either dream of freedom, if they are hopeful of obtaining it, or else, if this is what their heart suggests to them by day, they dream of the gibbet and the noose or other unpleasant things which are not outside them but inside. Yet they for their part truly believe that these things exist outside themselves, and make of them all an occasion for grief or joy; in fact they carry them all inside their own heads, which, by thus admitting phantoms, deceive the five senses.

18395   'Because of this, many people are so foolish as to imagine that they become sorcerers at night and go roaming with Lady Abundance.* They say that throughout the world, every third child born is of this kind, and sets off three times each week to go where destiny leads him. They also say that these folk get into every home; that, undeterred by keys and bars, they enter through cracks, cat-doors, and crevices, and that their souls leave their bodies to accompany the witches to strange places and houses. In proof of this, they argue that the different things they have seen have not come to them in their beds; rather it is their souls that go toiling and chasing around the world. And they give people to understand that if their bodies were to be turned over while they were on this journey, their souls would never be able to get back into them. But this is horrible madness; it is an impossibility, since the human body is a dead thing once it has no soul within it. It is certain, therefore, that those who go on this kind of journey three times each week must die and come back to life three times in a single week. If things are as we have said, the disciples of that convent must often rise from the dead. But it is an established fact, and I dare state it without further explanation, that those who are bound for death have only one death to die and will not rise again until the day of judgement, unless God in heaven performs some special miracle such as we read of in the case of Saint Lazarus, for this we do not deny.

18441   'Moreover, when they say that the soul, having departed from the body and left it bereft, is unable to re-enter the body if it finds it turned over, who can sustain these fictions? For I firmly maintain it to be true that the soul is wiser and cleverer and more intelligent when it is apart from the body than when it is joined to it, since it is influenced by the temperament of the body, which disturbs its purpose. Therefore it is better able to find the entrance than the exit, and it would find it sooner, regardless of whether the body had been turned over.

'Furthermore, if one third of the world goes roaming in 18457 this way with Lady Abundance, as foolish old women will prove on the basis of the visions that they have, then it must undoubtedly be the case that the whole world does this. For there is no one who does not see many visions in his dreams, whether true or false, and not three times a week but fifteen times a fortnight, or more or less, perhaps, depending on the strength of his imagination.

'Now for my part I do not wish to discuss the truth or 18469 falsehood of dreams, nor whether they should all be accepted or all rejected, nor why some are horrible and others fair and tranquil, according to the different temperaments in which they appear and according to the various desires of those of different ages and character. Nor shall I say whether God sends revelations through such visions or whether evil spirits do so, in order to lead men into danger. I shall not become involved in any of this, but shall return to my subject.

'I tell you, therefore, that when the clouds are weary and 18485 tired of shooting their arrows through the air, arrows that are more often wet than dry, for they have watered them with rain and dew (unless the heat has dried some of them so that they have something dry to shoot), then, when they have shot for as long as they like, they all unstring their bows together. But the bows with which these archers shoot behave very strangely, for when they are unstrung and put away in their cases, all their colours disappear. Never again will the clouds shoot with those we have seen; if they want to shoot again, they have to make new bows, and the sun will paint them with many colours, for they must not be polished in any other way.

18505 'The influence of the heavens extends still further, for they have great power in the sea, on land, and in the air. They cause the appearance of comets, which are not fixed in the heavens but ablaze in the air and only last for a short time after they have been made, and of which many tales are told. Those who continually foretell the future can use them to predict the death of princes, but comets do not keep a closer watch nor focus their influence and their rays to a greater extent upon poor men than upon kings, nor upon kings than upon poor men. Instead we are certain that their effect upon the regions of the world depends upon the disposition of the zones, men, and animals that are subject to the influences of the stars and planets, whose power over them is greater. Thus they have the significance of heavenly influences and they can disturb the temperament of things according as they find them submissive.

18531 'I neither say nor maintain that kings should be called rich any more than the common folk who go through the streets on foot, for sufficiency equals wealth, and covetousness equals poverty. Be he a king or a man without two halfpennies to rub together, the more he covets, the less rich he is. If we are to believe what is written, kings are like paintings. The author of the *Almagest** gives an example of this, and anyone who looks at pictures should pay attention: they please us when we do not come too close to them, but the pleasure disappears at close quarters; from a distance they seem quite delightful, but from close by they are entirely without appeal. The same is true of our powerful friends: for those who do not know them, the lack of experience lends charm to their service and their acquaintance, but anyone who truly put them to the test would find their favour so unpalatable and so much to be feared that he would be extremely apprehensive of involving himself. This is what Horace tells us* of the love and favour of the powerful.

18559 'Princes are no more worthy than any other man that the heavenly bodies should give a sign of their death. Their bodies are not worth a scrap more than those of a ploughman, clerk, or squire, for I make them all alike, as is apparent at their birth. Through me they are born alike in their naked-

ness, strong and weak, high and low. I make them all equal
as far as their humanity is concerned; Fortune does the rest,
but she is never permanent and bestows her gifts at will,
careless of whom she gives them to and taking them all away
as often as she likes.

'And if anyone, piquing himself on his nobility, dares con- 18577
tradict me and say that noblemen, as the people call them,
are superior in condition, by virtue of their noble birth, to
those who till the ground or work for their living, then I will
reply that no one is noble whose mind is not set on virtue,
nor is anyone base except on account of his vices, which
make him seem shocking and stupid.*

'Nobility comes from a virtuous heart, for nobility of family 18589
is worthless when the heart lacks virtue. Therefore the nobleman must display the prowess of his forebears, who achieved
nobility by dint of considerable effort and who, on leaving
the world, took all their virtues with them, leaving their
possessions to their heirs, who received nothing else from
them. They have the possessions but nothing else of theirs,
neither nobility nor worth, unless they earn nobility by their
deeds, through their own sense or virtue.

'Now clerks have better opportunities to become noble, 18605
courteous, and wise (and I will explain why) than do princes
or kings who have no scholarship. For, associated in his books
with those sciences that are capable of rational proofs and
demonstrations, the clerk finds all the evils we should avoid
and all the good we can do. He finds worldly events recorded
there, just as they occurred in word and deed; in the lives of
the ancients he finds all the baseness of the base and all the
deeds of courteous men, the whole of courtesy. In short, he
finds everything that we should avoid or cultivate written in
a book, as a result of which all clerks, whether masters or
disciples, are noble, or should be so. Those who are not
should realize that it is because their hearts are evil, for they
have far more advantages than those who hunt the wild stag.*

'Clerks whose hearts are neither noble nor gentle are worth 18629
less than anyone when they avoid what they know to be
virtuous in favour of the vices they have seen. And those
clerks who abandon themselves to vice should be more

severely punished before the emperor of heaven than the simple, foolish lay folk, who do not have virtues written down for them and who are base and contemptible in the eyes of clerks. Even if princes are literate, they cannot undertake to read and learn so much, for they have too many other calls on their attention. Therefore you may be sure that clerks have better and greater opportunities than landed lords to achieve nobility.

18647   'In order to achieve nobility, which is a most honourable thing to do here on earth, all those who wish to obtain it should know the following rule.

18651   'Anyone who aspires to nobility must avoid pride and laziness, take up arms or study, and rid himself of baseness. He should bear himself humbly, gently, and courteously in all places and towards all people, with the single exception of his enemies, when there is no possibility of coming to terms. He should honour ladies and maidens but not put excessive trust in them, for he might well suffer as a result, since no excess is good to see. Such a man should be praised and esteemed rather than blamed and reproached; he and no other deserves to be called noble.

18667   'The knight who is bold in arms, valiant in deeds, and courteous in speech as was Sir Gawain, who had nothing in common with the weak, and the good count Robert of Artois,* who from the moment he left his cradle practised largesse, honour, and chivalry all the days of his life, and disliked spending his days in idleness and instead became a man before his time, such a knight, valiant and worthy, generous, courteous, and bold in battle, ought everywhere to be welcomed, praised, loved, and held in high regard.

18681   'We ought also to honour the clerk who willingly undertakes mental exertions and concentrates upon pursuing the virtues that he finds written in his book. People certainly did so formerly, and I could name you ten of them, or indeed so many that if I enumerated them it would be wearisome to hear all the number.

18689   'In former times, the worthy gentlemen, as they are called in books, the emperors, dukes, counts, and kings of whom I shall say no more here, used to honour philosophers. Even to poets they gave towns, gardens, places of honour, and many delightful things. Virgil received Naples, a more delightful town than Paris or Lavardin, while Ennius had beautiful gardens in Calabria,* given to him by the ancients who knew him. Why should I find more examples? I could base my proof upon several cases of men whose birth was low but whose hearts were nobler than those of many a king's or count's son whose stories I shall not tell here, and who were considered noble.

'But now it has come to this, that there are good men who 18710 work at philosophy all their lives, and journey to foreign lands in order to obtain wisdom and worth, who endure great poverty as beggars or debtors and who perhaps go barefoot and naked, and who are neither loved nor held in affection. Princes do not care a fig for them, and yet—God preserve me from fevers—they are nobler men than those who hunt hares and those who are accustomed to remain on the family middens.

'What of the man who desires to take the praise and 18725 renown of another man's nobility without having his worth or prowess, is he noble? I say that he is not, and that instead he should be called base and considered vile, and loved less than if he were the son of a beggar. I shall not flatter any of them, not though he were the son of Alexander, who was so daring in arms and so persistent in war that he was lord of every land. When those who fought him had obeyed him and those who had not defended themselves had surrendered, he said, so tormented was he by pride, that this world was so narrow that he could scarcely turn round in it and no longer wished to remain there. Instead he intended to seek another world, in order to begin a new war, and he set off to conquer the underworld, so that he might be universally esteemed. At this, all the gods of the underworld quaked with fear, for when I told them of it, they imagined that this was the man who, by the power of the wooden stick,* and for the sake of souls dead through sin, was to break down the gates of hell, crushing their great pride and delivering his friends from hell.

'But let us suppose, although this is quite impossible, that 18757 I cause a number of noble people to be born, and care nothing for the others, whom they call riff-raff: what good is there in nobility? Certainly no one who applies his mind to a proper understanding of the truth will be able to see any good in nobility except that noblemen must apparently imitate the prowess of their ancestors. Anyone who wishes to resemble a nobleman must live continually under this burden, unless he wants his claim to nobility to be denied and his praise undeserved. For I assure everyone that nobility confers no other good on men than that burden, and they may be quite certain that no one should have praise through the merits of someone else, nor is it right that anyone should incur the blame that is due to another. Men should be praised when they deserve it, but as for the man who does no good, in whom we discover base wickedness, violence, and boastful pride, or who may be deceitful and treacherous, swollen with insolent pride, devoid of charity, and careless of almsgiving, or negligent and lazy (for we find too many like this), even though such a man may be born of parents in whom every virtue shone, I make bold to say that it would not be right for him to have the praise due to his parents, and that he ought instead to be considered more base than if he had come from a line of paupers.

18797   'All men capable of understanding should know that from the point of view of doing as one wishes with what one has, there is an immense difference between acquiring wisdom, nobility, and renown through one's own prowess, and acquiring extensive lands and quantities of money and jewels. For if a man chooses to work hard in order to acquire money, jewels, or land, even if he amasses as much as one hundred thousand marks in gold, he can leave everything to his friends. But the man whose efforts have been directed towards the other things we have mentioned, and who has earned them, cannot leave any of them to his friends, however much love may constrain him. Can he leave his knowledge? No, nor his nobility nor his reputation. But he can teach these things to those who are willing to follow his example. He can do nothing else with his goods, nor can his friends extract any more from them.

18821   'For their part they do not care much about that; there are many for whom nothing is worth a nutshell except the obtaining of possessions and property. And yet they call themselves noble because they are reputed to be so and because their excellent ancestors were noble and were just what they ought to be. Also, they have dogs and birds and therefore look like young noblemen, and they go hunting along rivers and through woods, fields, and heathlands, and indulge in leisurely diversions. But these, who boast of a nobility that belongs to others, are base and evil vassals. They do not speak the truth; instead they lie, and steal the name of nobility, since they do not resemble their good ancestors. For I cause men to be born equal, and the nobility I give them is most fair, and is called natural liberty. I confer it equally upon everyone, together with the reason that God gives them, which is so wise and good that it would make them like God and his angels, were it not for death, which sets men apart and makes them different, and thus separates them from God. If, then, they desire some other nobility, and they are sufficiently worthy, let them acquire new nobility, for no one else can make them noble if they do not become so by themselves. I make no exception for kings or counts. Moreover, it is more shameful for a king's son to be foolish and wild and vicious than for the son of a carter, a swineherd, or a cobbler.

'Certainly, if valiant Gawain were the son of a coward who   18861
sat by the fire all covered with ash, he would have more honour than if he were a coward, even if Renouart were his father.

'But it is undoubtedly a fact that the death of a prince is   18867
more noteworthy than that of the peasant who is found lying dead, and there is far more discussion of it. That is why, when foolish people see comets, they imagine that they were made for princes. But if there were neither kings nor princes throughout our kingdoms and provinces, and if everyone in the world were equal, whether in peace or in war, the heavenly bodies would still bring comets into being at the proper time, when the conjunction of their influences was right for such works, provided there was sufficient material in the atmosphere to make it possible.

'They also cause dragons and sparks to fly through the air   18885
and look like stars falling from the heavens, as foolish people think. But reason cannot accept that anything should fall from

the heavens, for they contain nothing that is corruptible. Everything there is firm, strong, and stable; no impression is left on them by any external force, nothing can break them, and nothing, however slender or piercing, can pass through them, unless, perhaps, it is spiritual. It is true that their rays pass through, but they do not hurt or break them.

18901   'Through their various influences they cause the hot summers and cold winters. According to their oppositions, whether they are moving apart or approaching one another or are in conjunction, they cause the snow and the hail, sometimes heavy, sometimes light, and all the other phenomena we perceive. Because of this, many men are often dismayed at the sight of eclipses in the heavens; they imagine themselves to be unfortunate because they have suddenly lost sight of the planets they saw before, and have been deprived of their influences. But if they understood the causes of this, they would not be in the least dismayed.

18917   'When the winds do battle, lifting up the waves of the sea, the heavens cause the waters and the clouds to embrace and then calm the sea once more, for she dare not grumble or whip up her waves; there is only the constant ebb and flow of the tide, a necessary movement caused by the moon, and which nothing can hold back. Anyone who wished to inquire more deeply into the miracles performed on earth by the heavenly bodies and the stars would find them to be so numerous and fair that he could not write them all down if he wanted to. In this way, the heavens discharge their obligations to me, for in their beneficence, they do such good that I can clearly see they are doing their duty well.

18937   Nor do I complain of the elements. They keep my commandments well, blending together to form combinations which later disintegrate, for I know that everything beneath the moon is corruptible. However well nourished it is, everything must rot away. All the elements are so constituted by Nature's own design as to incorporate this infallible and reliable rule: everything moves towards its beginning. This rule is so general that it cannot fail in the case of the elements.

18951   'I have no complaint to make of the plants, which are not slow to obey. They are attentive to my laws and produce their roots and little leaves, trunks, branches, fruits, and flowers throughout their lives. Every year they all, grasses, trees, and bushes, bear as much as they can, until they die. Nor do I complain of the birds and fish, which are lovely to look at. They are very good at keeping my rules and are such excellent scholars that they all accept my yoke. All produce young in their own way and are a credit to their lineage; it is delightful to see that they do not allow their families to die out.

'I do not complain of the other animals, whose heads I have 18969 bent downwards to look at the earth. None of them has ever waged war against me; all do my service as their fathers did. The male goes with the female to form a fair and pleasing couple, and they come together to beget young whenever it seems good to them. When they consent together, they do not haggle over it; instead they are pleased to perform this gracious courtesy for one another, and all consider themselves repaid by the good things that come to them through me. So do my lovely vermin: ants, moths, flies, and worms born of corruption never fail to keep my commandments, while my snakes and serpents do my work diligently.

'Only man, to whom I had given all the good things in my 18991 power; only man, who by my decree lifts his face high and turns it towards heaven; only man, whom I form and bring to birth in the true shape of his master; only man, for whom I toil and labour, who is the culmination of my work and who, except for what I give him, has nothing in his body, trunk, or limbs that would buy him so much as a pomander, nor indeed in his soul, except for one thing; only man, who has received three physical and spiritual forces from me, his mistress (for I can truthfully say that it is I who give him existence, life, and feeling); only wretched man, who has so many advantages, if he would only be wise and worthy, for he has an abundance of all the good things that God has put into the world; he is companion to all the things enclosed in the whole world and shares their bounty, having existence in common with the stones, life with the thick grass, and feeling with the dumb beasts, and he is capable of still more in that he has understanding in common with the angels; only man— what more can I say of him?—who has everything one can think of, who is a new world in miniature; only man, I say, causes me more distress than any wolf-cub.

19025   'Undoubtedly, as I know very well, it was not I, in truth, who gave him his understanding. That is outside my province, and I had neither the wisdom nor the power to make anything so intelligent. I have never made anything eternal, and whatever I make is corruptible. Plato himself bears witness to that when he speaks of my work and of the gods, who have no need to fear death. It is their creator, he says, whose will alone protects and maintains them throughout eternity, and if that will did not sustain them, they would perforce all die. All my works are perishable, he says, for my power is poor and obscure before the great power of the God who perceives the three aspects of time as present to him in a moment of eternity.

19047   'This God is the king and emperor who says to the gods that he is their father. Students of Plato know this, for the following words are to be found in his works (at least, this is their meaning in French).

' "Gods of gods, whose maker, father, and creator I am, you are my creatures, the result of my handiwork. By nature you are corruptible, by my will you are eternal, for despite all her care, Nature will never make anything that does not eventually fail. But God is unequalled in strength, goodness, and wisdom, and when, in his excellent reason, he wishes to join things together and combine them, he has never wished nor will he ever wish them to be split apart. Corruption will be powerless against them. I therefore draw the following conclusion: since you began your existence through the will of your master who made you and gave you life, that same will through which I sustain you now and in the future, you are not so entirely immune from mortality and corruption that you would not all perish before my eyes if I did not sustain you. By nature you could die, but through my will you shall never die, for my will is sovereign over the bonds that hold together the combinations of your life, the source of your immortality."* This is the meaning of the text that Plato desired to include in his book, where he dared speak better of God and give him more praise and glory than any worldly philosopher of antiquity. And yet he could not say enough, being incapable of understanding perfectly that which only a virgin's womb could comprehend. It is undoubtedly true that she whose womb was swollen with God understood more of him than Plato. From the moment she conceived him, she knew, and this fortified her in her pregnancy, that he was the wondrous sphere that knows no bounds, that has its centre everywhere and whose circumference is not in any place.* She knew that he was the marvellous triangle in which the whole is the three angles, while the three angles together make but a single whole. It was the triangular circle, the circular triangle that dwelt within the virgin. Plato did not understand as much as that; he did not see the triple unity in that single trinity, nor the sovereign deity clothed in human flesh. It was God, who is called the creator. He it was who fashioned man's understanding and, as he did so, gave it to man. And, truth to tell, man repaid him badly, for he later imagined he could deceive God but in fact deceived himself. For this my Lord suffered death, when, without my help, he took human flesh in order to save the wretch from punishment. Without my help, since I do not know how it was done, except that all things are possible at his bidding. But I was utterly astounded that he took flesh from the Virgin Mary for the sake of that wretch, and was later hanged in the flesh, for nothing can be born of a virgin through my agency. But in former times, this incarnation was foretold by many prophets, both Jewish and pagan, that we might better calm our hearts and strive to believe that the prophecy was true. In Virgil's *Eclogues* we read of the voice of the Sibyl, taught by the Holy Spirit: "Already a new line is sent down to us from high heaven to guide those who have gone astray. With this line the age of iron will perish and the age of gold will arise in the world."* Even Albumazar,* however he may have known about it, testifies that a worthy maiden would be born within the sign of the Virgin and that she would be a virgin and a mother, who would give suck to her father and whose husband would lie with her without ever touching her. Anyone who likes to have a copy of Albumazar can acquaint himself with this idea, since it is readily to be found in his book. Therefore every year in September, Christians celebrate the memory of this nativity.

19161   But Our Lord Jesus knows that all the things I have mentioned, I did for man. My work has been on behalf of that wretch who is the culmination of all my endeavours and who alone defies my laws. No payment will suffice him, disloyal renegade that he is, and nothing will satisfy him. What is the use? What more is there to say? The honours I have heaped upon him could not be told, and in return he inflicts uncountable and innumerable shames upon me.

19175   'Fair, sweet priest, fair chaplain, is it then right for me to continue to love and revere him when I find him behaving in this way? By the crucified God, I greatly regret that I ever made man. But by the death he suffered whom Judas kissed and Longinus struck with his lance, I will settle my score with man before God, who entrusted him to me when he formed him in his own image, for he has caused me great trouble. I am a woman, therefore I cannot keep silent; I wish to reveal everything straight away, for women are incapable of concealing anything, and he will be pilloried as never before. It was an evil day for him when he separated himself from me: I shall relate all his vices and give a true account of everything.

19195   'Man is a proud, murderous thief, a cruel, covetous, miserly traitor, a desperate, scandalmongering rascal, full of hatred and contempt, suspicion and envy. He is a deceitful, perjured liar, a foolish boaster, an unpredictable madman, an ungrateful idolater, a false and treacherous hypocrite, an idle sodomite. In short, he is such a wretched fool that he is the slave of every vice, and harbours them all within himself. See the irons with which the miserable creature fetters himself. Is he not seeking his own death when he gives himself up to such wickedness? And, since everything must return whence it took its origin, when man comes before his master, whom he should have served and honoured at all times and to the utmost of his power, keeping himself from wickedness, how will he dare to face him? And he who will be his judge, in what light will he look on him, who has behaved so badly towards him as to be found so much at fault, wretch that he is, and so sluggish of heart that he has no desire to do good?

Great and small alike do the very worst that they can, saving their honour, and they all seem to have agreed and conspired to do it. But everyone's honour is not often preserved by agreement: instead men receive many serious punishments, or death, or great worldly shame. But what is the wretch to think when he appears and enumerates all his sins before that judge, who weighs and judges all things rightly and fairly, firmly and unswervingly? What reward can he expect but a rope to hang him from the grievous gallows of hell? Or else to be taken and clapped in irons, riveted to everlasting rings before the prince of devils, or boiled in a copper, roasted on both sides over coals or on a grill, or held with great pegs, like Ixion,* on keen-edged wheels that devils turn with their claws. Or perhaps he will die of hunger and thirst in the marshes, like Tantalus,* who is bathed continually in the water but can never, however tormented he may be by thirst, bring his lips to the water that touches his chin, for the more he tries, the lower it sinks. At the same time, hunger so overwhelms him that he can find no relief from it and dies, maddened with hunger but unable to pluck the apple that he sees continually suspended in front of his face, for the more he gropes for it with his mouth, the higher it rises. Or else the millstone will roll from the top of the rock down to the ground, and he will roll it up again, ceaselessly, just as you do, wretched Sisyphus,* who were put there to perform that task; or he will try to fill up the bottomless cask but will never succeed, like the Danaïds* who are thus punished for their ancient follies. And you know, fair Genius, how vultures strive to devour the liver of Tityus,* and nothing can deter them. There are many other terrible punishments there, cruel and grim, and it may be that mankind will be put there to endure tribulation in great pain and torment, so that I shall be properly avenged. By my faith, if he were merely merciful, this judge of whom I have spoken, who judges all our words and deeds, then the loans of usurers would perhaps be good and delightful, but he is always just and therefore greatly to be feared. It is an evil thing to indulge in sin.

'I will certainly leave God to deal with all the sins with 19293 which the wretch is tainted; he will punish mankind if he likes. But as for those of whom Love complains (for I have heard his complaint), I complain of them myself as vigorously as I can, and I am right to do so, because they deny me the tribute that all men owe me, and always have and always will, as long as they receive my tools. Go, eloquent Genius, to the host of the God of Love, who toils hard in my service and loves me so well, I am certain, that his noble and gracious heart is more attracted to my works than iron to a magnet. Tell him that I send greetings to him and to my friend, Lady Venus, and to all his barons, with the single exception of False Seeming, so that he may now go and associate with those proud traitors and dangerous hypocrites of whom Scripture tells us that they are false prophets. I also strongly suspect Abstinence of being proud and of being like False Seeming, however humble and charitable she seems.

19325   'If False Seeming is ever caught with such proven traitors again, he will receive no greeting from me, nor will his friend Abstinence. Such folk are greatly to be feared, and Love would surely have thrown them out of his host if he had wished to, and if he had not known for certain that they were so necessary to him that he could do nothing without them. But if they are their advocates in the cause of true lovers, whose pain is thus relieved, then I forgive them their deceitfulness.

19339   'Go, my friend, to the God of Love, and take with you my complaints and protests. I do not want him to make me any reparation, but to take comfort and solace from this news, which should be very welcome to him and calamitous for our enemies. Let him forget the pain and anxiety that we see him suffer. Tell him that I have sent you to excommunicate all those who wish to oppose us, and to absolve those worthy folk who willingly make the effort faithfully to observe the rules written in my book by applying themselves energetically to the task of increasing their families and by concentrating on becoming true lovers. I call all such my friends and I will fill their souls with delight, provided they avoid those vices of which I have spoken and which wipe out every merit. Give them a pardon that will be amply sufficient: not just for ten years, for that would not be worth twopence to them, but a perpetual, plenary pardon for everything they have done, when they make a good confession.

'When you reach the host, where you will be warmly welcomed, and when you have greeted them on my behalf as you know how to do, then announce to them in a loud voice this pardon and decree that I would like you to write down here.' Then he wrote at her dictation, and she sealed it and gave it to him, begging him to go quickly but first to absolve her from anything that might have slipped her mind. 19369

As soon as the goddess, Lady Nature, had made her confession as was lawful and customary, then Genius, her worthy priest, gave her absolution and imposed on her a good and fitting penance, appropriate to the seriousness of the fault he thought she had committed. He enjoined her to remain in her forge and toil as she used to when she had no cause for grief, and to continue in the performance of her duties until the king who has the power to set all things right, to create and destroy everything, should offer some other remedy. 19381

'I will gladly do so, sir,' she said.

'And in the meantime,' said Genius, 'I will make all haste to bring aid to true lovers, but first I must take off this silk chasuble, alb, and surplice. He hung them all on a hook and put on his secular clothes, which were less cumbersome for him, as if he were going to dance. Then, taking to his wings, he flew swiftly away.

THE SERMON OF GENIUS

19409 Nature remained in her forge, wielding her hammers, smiting and forging just as before, while Genius beat his wings and flew without delay, more swiftly than the wind, until he came to the host. But he did not find False Seeming there; he had left in a hurry the moment the Old Woman was captured who had opened the door of the enclosure for me and had helped me progress to the point where I was allowed to speak to Fair Welcome; he had been unwilling to delay and had fled without taking leave. But there is certainly no doubt that he found Constrained Abstinence, who, when she saw the priest coming, prepared as best she could to run after False Seeming in such haste that it would have been difficult to restrain her. For in the absence of False Seeming she would not have allowed anyone to see her confiding in the priest, not if someone had given her four bezants.

19433 There and then, Genius, without further delay, greeted them all as he was supposed to and, forgetting nothing, told them why he had come. I do not intend to recount the joy with which they received this news; I prefer to be concise and to spare your ears, for it often happens that the preacher who fails to be brisk and succinct drives his audience away with his verbosity.

19447 Then the God of Love arrayed Genius in a chasuble and handed him a ring, crosier, and mitre, clearer than glass or crystal. They sought no other ornament, for they greatly longed to hear him read the sentence. Venus laughed continually and could not keep quiet in her joy and gaiety; in order to lend added force to his anathema, when he had finished his speech, she put into his hands a lighted candle, which was not made of virgin wax.

19461 Genius made no further delay, but mounted a great platform, the better to read the text of which we have already given an account, while the barons sat on the ground and sought no other seats. Then he unrolled the document before them and, signalling to them with a wave of his hand, called for silence, while they, who were pleased by what he said, nudged one another and winked. Then they fell silent and listened, and he began the definitive sentence in these words.

'By the authority of Nature, custodian of the whole world, vicar and constable of the eternal emperor who sits in the sovereign tower of this noble city, the world, and who made Nature its minister, to administer all its riches through the influence of the stars (for everything is ordered by the stars, according to the imperial right exercised by Nature); by her authority who has brought all things to birth since this world began, and likewise given them their allotted time for growth and increase, and who has never made anything that had no purpose beneath the heaven that constantly turns about the earth, as far above it as it is below it, never stopping by day or night but turning continuously and incessantly; by the authority of Nature, let all those disloyal renegades, great or humble, who scorn those works by which Nature is maintained, be excommunicated and ruthlessly condemned. But if a man strives with all his might to preserve Nature, keeps himself from base thoughts and toils and struggles faithfully to be a true lover, let him go to paradise crowned with flowers. Provided he make a good confession, I will take the whole burden of it upon myself with all the power at my disposal, and he will take away with him no less a pardon than that.

'It was an evil day for Nature when she gave stylus and tablets to those false folk of whom I have spoken, and hammers and anvils according to her laws and customs, and sharp-pointed ploughshares fit for her ploughs, and fallow fields, not stony ones but fertile and grassy, which need tilling and digging if they are to be enjoyed. The false ones will not till them in order to serve and honour Nature; instead they wish to destroy her by fleeing the anvils, tablets, and fallow fields that she has made so rich and dear, so that things might be continued and Death prevented from killing them.

'They ought to be deeply ashamed, those disloyal ones of whom I speak, who will not deign to put their hands to the tablets to write a letter nor to make any visible mark upon them. Their intentions are extremely evil, for the tablets will grow very mossy if left unused. When the anvils are allowed to go to rack and ruin without a single hammer-blow being struck, then rust can attack them and no sound of hammering or beating will be heard. If no one drives the ploughshares into the fallow fields, they will remain fallow. These people should be buried alive for daring to neglect the tools that God fashioned with his own hand and gave to my lady. He chose to give them to her so that she would be able to make similar ones and so give eternal life to mortal creatures.

19553　　'It is apparent that they are doing a great deal of harm, for if the whole of humanity decided to neglect these tools for sixty years, then no offspring would be fathered. If this is God's will, then it is certain that he wants the world to end, or else the earth would remain bare, to be populated by animals, unless, if he liked, he created new men or revived the original ones to inhabit the earth again. And if these kept themselves chaste for sixty years, they would die out once again, so that he would continually have to remake them, if he was willing to do so.

19569　　'If anyone wished to assert that God in his grace removed desire from one man but not from another, then since God's name is so great and he has never ceased to do good, he must surely want to make everyone the same and to give the same grace to each, and so I come back to my conclusion that everything is destined for perdition. I have no answer to this, unless belief may be interpreted by faith. When they are first created, God has the same love for all, and gives rational souls to men as well as to women; therefore I believe that he wants every soul, not just one, to follow the best path and to come as quickly as possible to himself. So if he wants some people to live chaste, the better to follow him, why would he not want others to do so? What reason would deter him? In that case it would seem as though he did not care if generation ceased. If anyone wishes to reply, let him do so, I know no more about it. Let theologians come and theologize about it: they will never reach a conclusion.*

19599　　'But those who will not use their styluses, through which mortals may live forever, to write on those fair and precious tablets that were not prepared by Nature in order to be left idle, but were lent instead so that all might write on them and so that all of us, men and women, might live; those who have received the two hammers but do not forge as they should, properly upon the proper anvil; those who are so blinded by their sin and misled by pride that they despise the straight furrow of the fair and fertile field; those wretches who go tilling the desert ground where their seed is wasted, and will not plough a straight furrow but overturn the plough, justifying their evil ways on the basis of abnormal exceptions when they decide to follow Orpheus,* who could not plough or write or forge on the right forge (may he be hanged by the neck for inventing such rules for them; he did Nature a disservice); those who scorn such a mistress by reading her rules backwards, who refuse to take them the right way so as to understand them properly, but pervert what is written when they come to read it, may all these be excommunicated and condemned to hell for belonging to that party, and before they die, may they also lose the purse and testicles that are the signs of their manhood! May they lose the pendants from which the purse hangs! May the hammers attached inside them be torn out! May they be robbed of their styluses, since they refused to write with them on the precious tablets fit for that purpose! And unless they use them to plough properly, may their ploughs and ploughshares have their bones broken in pieces, so that they can never be erected again! May all who follow them live in great shame, and may their filthy, horrible sin bring them pain and suffering and lead them to be beaten in every place so that they can be seen for what they are!

'By God, my lords, you who are alive should take care not 19657 to follow such folk! When it comes to the works of nature, you should be livelier than any squirrel, lighter and more mobile than a bird or than the wind. Do not waste this excellent pardon: I forgive you all your sins, provided you exert yourselves in this cause. Be active, leap and dance about, do not let yourselves grow cold or your limbs cool down! Put all your implements to work: if you work hard you will get warm enough.

19671   'Plough barons, plough for God's sake, and restore your lineage. Nothing can restore it if you do not put your minds to ploughing vigorously. Tuck your clothes up nicely in front of you as though to take the air, or go quite naked if you like, but do not get too cold or too hot. Lift the stilts of your ploughs with your two bare hands, support them firmly on your arms and make an effort to thrust the ploughshare straight along the right path, the better to penetrate the furrow. As for the horses in front, for God's sake do not let them slow down, but spur them on harshly and give them the most violent blows you possibly can, if you want to plough deeply. Goad into life the horned oxen that are yoked to the ploughs, then you will be admitted to our bounty. By goading them well and frequently, you will plough better and more satisfactorily.

19697   'When you have ploughed so much that you are weary of ploughing (for things will come to a point where you will need some respite, and nothing can last long without a rest), you will not immediately be able to begin again to advance the work, but do not let your desire flag. On the instructions of Lady Pallas, Cadmus* ploughed more than an acre of ground and sowed the teeth of a serpent. Armed knights sprang from these and fought with one another until all died on that spot, except for five, who became his companions and gladly helped him build the walls of Thebes, which he founded. With him, they positioned the stones and populated his city, which is of great antiquity. Cadmus sowed excellent seed, which was thus of benefit to his people. If your beginning is as favourable, your lineage will benefit greatly.

19723   'You also have two very great advantages to help you preserve your lineage, and if you are not willing to make a third with them, you must be quite mad. You have only one disadvantage: defend yourself valiantly against it. You are assailed on one side, but three champions must be very weak and well deserve to be beaten if they cannot overcome the fourth.

19733   'There are three sisters, if you do not know this, two of whom will support you. Only the third, who cuts all lives short, will hurt you. You should know that Clotho, who

holds the distaff, and Lachesis, who spins the thread, will
sustain you well; but whatever these two spin is torn to shreds
by Atropos.* She seeks to deceive you; she will plough no
deep furrow and will bury all your line; she even has her eye
on you. No worse creature was ever seen, and you have no
greater enemy. Have pity, my lords, have pity indeed! Remember your excellent fathers and venerable mothers! Model
your actions upon theirs, and beware of being a traitor to
your ancestry. What did they do? Pay close attention to it. If
we examine their prowess, we see that they defended themselves so well that they gave you your existence. Had it not
been for their chivalry, you would not be alive today. In love
and friendship they took great pity on you; you should think
of the others who will come after you to maintain your
lineage.

'Do not allow yourselves to be defeated; you have styluses, 19765
so put your mind to using them. Do not keep your arms
muffled up: hammer, forge, and blow, help Clotho and Lachesis, so that if base-born Atropos cuts six threads, a dozen
more may spring from them. Concentrate upon multiplying;
in that way you will trick cruel, cantankerous Atropos, who
hinders everything.

'This miserable wretch, who makes war on the living and 19775
whose heart rejoices in the dead, feeds the blackguard, Cerberus,* who so desires their deaths that he is quite on fire
with lust and would have died, maddened by hunger, had the
jade not helped him. For without her, he would never have
found anyone to feed him. She feeds him continually, and in
order to feed comfortably, the hound hangs on her breasts,
of which she has three rather than two. He buries his three
snouts in her breasts, butting, tugging, and sucking, and he
has never been weaned nor ever will be. He does not seek
to slake his thirst with any other milk, nor does he ask to be
fed with any other meat than bodies and souls, and she heaps
up men and women to cast them into his triple maw. She
alone feeds it, always thinking to fill it, but always finding
it empty, however hard she struggles to fill it. The three
cruel harlots, avengers of evil deeds, watch anxiously for the
scraps. I know all their names: they are Alecto and Tisiphone,

and the third is called Megaera,* who will devour you all if she can.

19809   'These three await you in hell, where those who committed crimes when they had life in their bodies will be bound, thrashed and beaten with sticks, hanged, buffeted, dragged along and manhandled, drowned and burned, grilled and boiled before the three provosts who sit there in full consistory. By means of these tortures, the provosts force them to confess all the crimes they ever committed from the time of their birth. All the people tremble before the provosts, and it seems to me that it would be very cowardly of me not to dare to name them here: they are Rhadamanthus and Minos, and the third is their brother, Aeacus. Jupiter was father to all three, who, according to their reputations, were such worthy men during their lifetimes and upheld justice so well that they became judges in the underworld. Pluto gave them this reward: he waited for them until their souls left their bodies, whereupon they filled this office.

19835   'For God's sake, my lords, do not go there; fight against those vices that Nature, our mistress, told me about during mass. She told me all of them, and since then I have not sat down; you will find that there are twenty-six,* and that they do more harm than you imagine. If you are thoroughly purged of the filth of all these vices, you will never enter the confines of the three strumpets I have named and whose reputation is so evil, nor will you fear the judgments of the provosts, who are quick to condemn. I would gladly recount those vices to you, but it would be superfluous for me to do so. The delightful Romance of the Rose gives you a brief account of them: look them up there if you like, the better to avoid them.

19855   'Concentrate on leading a good life; let every man embrace his sweetheart and every lady her lover with kissing, feasting, and pleasure. If you love one another loyally, you ought never to be reproached for it. And when you have played enough in the way I have recommended, remember to make a good confession so as to do good and renounce evil, and call upon the heavenly God, whom Nature acknowledges as her master. It is he who will come to your aid in the end, when Atropos buries you. He is the salvation of body and soul, the fair mirror of my lady, who would never know anything were it not for this fair mirror. He directs and governs her, and my lady knows no other law. He taught her all she knows when he took her for his chamberlain.

'Now, my lords, I would like you, and my lady's instructions are the same, to learn by heart the whole of this sermon, word for word, just as I preach it (for one does not always have one's book, and it is very troublesome to write). In this way, wherever you go, to fortress or castle, city or town, in winter or summer, you may recite it to those who were not here. It is good to remember the words that come from a good school, and better to repeat them. We may rise considerably in the esteem of others as a result. My words have great virtue: they are a hundred times more precious than sapphires, rubies, or balas rubies. Fair sirs, my lady needs preachers for her law, to denounce those sinners who transgress her rules when they ought to observe and keep them. 19877

'If you preach in this way, I grant and promise you, provided your deeds match your words, that you will never be prevented from entering the fair and verdant park where the Virgin's son, the white-fleeced lamb, brings the sheep with him, leaping ahead over the grass. And after him, on the narrow, tranquil path, so little trodden and beaten that it is all covered in grass and flowers, come the gentle white sheep, no multitude but a select company of gracious, noble beasts, grazing and browsing on the tender grass and flowers that grow there. And I can tell you that their pasture is of so wonderful a kind that the lovely little flowers that appear there in their fresh purity, all new and young like maidens in the springtime of their youth, shining like stars through the tender green grass in the dewy morning, retain the exquisitely fresh and vivid colours of their own natural beauty throughout the whole day; they do not wilt in the evening but can be plucked by anyone who likes to do so in the evening just as well as in the morning. And you may be quite sure that they are neither too closed nor too open, but sparkle through the grass in the perfection of their growth, for the sun that shines there does not hurt them nor consume the dew that waters 19901 them; instead it so sweetens their roots that they are always exquisitely beautiful. I assure you also that, however much the little sheep may graze and browse on the grass and flowers (and they will always be eager to do so), they will never be able to graze so much that the plants are not continually seen to be renewed. What is more, and this is no fable, the flowers and grass are indestructible, however much the sheep may graze on them, nor do the sheep pay for their pasture, for their skins are not sold in the end, nor their fleeces used to make woollen cloth or coverings for strangers. These things will never be taken from them: their flesh will not be eaten in the end, nor will it be destroyed by decay nor overcome by disease. But despite what I say, I have certainly no doubt that the good shepherd who guides them as they graze before him is dressed in their wool. He does not fleece them or take anything from them that would cost them the price of a feather, but it seems good and pleasing to him that his dress resembles theirs.

19971   'I can also relate, if it does not weary you, how night was never seen to fall there. They have but a single day; there is no twilight, nor, for all dawn's advances, does morning ever break, for evening is one with morning and the morning resembles the evening. I can say the same of every hour; this day exists in an eternal moment and cannot turn to night, however night struggles against it. Time is not measured in this fair and everlasting day, smiling in its ever-present brightness. There is neither future nor past for, if I understand the truth correctly, all three tenses are present and the day is ordered by this present. It is not a present that will pass in part and come to an end, nor of which part is yet to come, for the past was never present there, and I can also tell you that the future never will be present, so stable and permanent is the day. For the blazing sun which always shines there fixes the day at a single point, such that no one ever saw so fair nor so pure an eternal springtime, not even in the reign of Saturn, who ruled over the age of gold and on whom his son Jupiter inflicted such injury and torment as to cut off his testicles.

20007   'Now to tell the truth, it is certain that anyone who castrates a worthy man exposes him to great hurt and shame, for the removal of his testicles will, I have no doubt, rob him at least of the love of his sweetheart, no matter how great her attachment to him, and that is without mentioning his great shame and distress. Or if he is married, as he may be, now that things are going so badly for him he will lose the love of his loyal wife, however good-natured she may be. It is a great sin to castrate a man. He who does so robs him not only of his testicles, of his sweetheart whom he loves so dearly and who will never smile on him again, and of his wife: that is the least of it. He also takes from him his courage and the way of life that valiant men should follow, for we can be sure that castrated men are cruel, perverted cowards, because they have feminine characteristics. It is certain that no castrated man has any courage, unless perhaps where vice is concerned, the courage to do some great evil, for all women are brave enough to commit the most devilish acts, and castrated men resemble them in this since they have similar characteristics. And although the one who castrates is neither a murderer nor a thief and has committed no mortal sin, he has at least sinned in that he has greatly wronged Nature by stealing the means of procreation. No one, however much he racked his brains, could excuse him for it. I at least could not, for were I to think about it and go over the truth of it, I could wear out my tongue before I excused him for the dreadful sin and crime that he had committed against Nature.

'But Jupiter cared nothing for the seriousness of the sin, 20053 provided only that he could succeed in getting his hands on the kingdom. And when he had become king and was acknowledged as lord of the world, he issued his commands, his laws, and his statutes, and had his proclamation read forthwith, openly and in the hearing of all, in order to teach people how to live. This was the substance of the proclamation:

"Jupiter, ruler of the world, commands and ordains that 20065 everyone put his mind to achieving happiness. If a man knows what he likes and is capable of it, he should do it, so that his heart may be gladdened." He preached no other sermon, but gave a general permission for everyone individually to do whatever seemed delightful to him, for delight, as he said, is the best thing in the world and the chief good in life, and everyone should desire it. And so that everyone would imitate him and take his deeds as examples of how they should live, jolly Lord Jupiter, who so prized delight, gratified his body as much as he liked.

20085   'Now as the author of the *Eclogues* tells us in his *Georgics** (for he learned about Jupiter's behaviour from Greek books), no one ever ploughed until Jupiter came. No one had ever tilled or hoed or cultivated the ground, nor had the good, simple, peaceable folk ever established boundaries, but foraged together for the good things that came to them spontaneously. He ordered them to apportion the land when no one knew how to claim his share, and he divided it up into acres. It was he who raised evil to such heights that he gave the snakes their venom and taught the wolves to hunt their prey. He felled the honey-bearing oaks and dried up the streams of wine. He extinguished fire everywhere, and made men seek for it with flints: this was one of his crafty, deceitful schemes for tormenting mankind. He created various new arts; he named and numbered the stars; he caused traps and nets and limes to be set to catch wild beasts, and cried the first dogs after them, something no one had done before.

20115   'It was he, the malicious tormentor of mankind, who tamed the birds of prey. He provoked combats on battlegrounds between sparrow-hawks, partridges, and quails, and arranged tournaments in the clouds between goshawks, falcons, and cranes. He made them come to the lure, and in order to keep their favour, so that they would come back to his hand, he fed them night and morning. The young man thus succeeded in enslaving mankind to the cruel birds, for they were the terrible and predatory enemies of those other peaceable birds that men could not catch in the air but without whose flesh they were unwilling to live. So dainty was men's appetite, and so fond were they of these game-birds that they longed to eat their flesh, that is why they became the slaves of the cruel birds.

20136   'It was Jupiter who put ferrets into burrows to attack rabbits and make them jump into nets; he it was who so cared for his own body that he had fish from the seas and rivers scaled, skinned, and roasted, and invented entirely new sauces with various kinds of spices, to which he added many herbs. This was the beginning of the arts, for everything can be conquered by work and by grinding poverty, which is why the people are worn with care. For men's ingenuity is stimulated when they encounter hardship and distress. So says Ovid,* who, as he tells us himself, experienced plenty of good and evil, honour and shame, during his lifetime. In short, when Jupiter set out to govern the world, it was with the sole intention of changing the condition of his empire from good to bad and from bad to worse. He was a very lax manager. He shortened the springtime and divided the year into four parts, just as it is today: summer, spring, autumn, and winter, those are the four different seasons that used to be part of a constant spring. Jupiter wanted no more of that, and when he came to the throne, he destroyed the age of gold and created the ages of silver and later of bronze, for men were so eager to do wrong that they went into a permanent decline. Now the condition of the age is so altered that it has changed from bronze to iron, a cause of great rejoicing to the gods in their halls of everlasting grime and gloom, who are jealous of mankind as long as they see them alive. Tied up in their stables never to be released are the unhappy black sheep, worn out, wretched, mortally sick, who were not willing to follow the path marked out for them by the white lamb, through which they would all have been set free and their black fleeces made white. Instead they took the broad highway that brought them to their present shelter, together with a company so great that it filled the whole road.

'No beast that enters there will bear a fleece worth any- 20191 thing; you could not even make cloth from it, unless it were some horrible hair-cloth with more sharp prickles, when brought into contact with the ribs, than a cloak made from the hedgehog's bristly skin. But if you wanted to card the soft, silky-smooth wool taken from the white sheep and, if you had enough of it, make it into cloth, then emperors, kings, and even angels if they wore woollen cloth, could wear it on feast-days. For you may be quite sure that you would be very nobly clad if you had clothes like that, and that they

ought to be valued especially highly because there are very
few such beasts.

20213   'Now the shepherd who guards the flocks and enclosures
in this fair park is no fool, and, truth to tell, he will not allow
a black sheep to enter in spite of all entreaties. It is his pleasure
to set apart the white sheep who know their shepherd, that
is why they go to him for shelter. They are well known to
him, and all the more warmly welcomed.

20223   'And so I tell you that the loveliest, most compassionate
and delightful of all those worthy beasts is the bounding white
lamb who suffers and toils in order to lead the sheep to the
park. He knows that if any stray from the path and is spied
by the wolf that hunts no other prey, it has only to turn aside
from the way in which the lamb is resolved to lead it for the
wolf to carry it off, defenceless, and eat it alive. No living
creature can save it from him.

20237   'My lords, that lamb awaits you. But we shall say no more
of him now, except to pray God the Father to fulfil his
mother's request and grant that he so lead his sheep that the
wolf may not harm them. We pray him also that you might
not be prevented by sin from disporting yourselves in that
park, which is so fair and lovely, with grass and fragrant
flowers, violets, roses, and all good things. Anyone making a
comparison between the beautiful square garden closed by
the little barred wicket where this lover saw Pleasure and his
people dancing in a ring, and the fair, the utterly and perfectly
lovely park of which I speak, would be guilty of serious error
if he did not make the same comparison as he would between
truth and fiction. Anyone who entered the park, or simply
cast his eyes inside it, would dare swear with certainty that
the garden was nothing in comparison with this enclosure,
which is not square in form but round, and so skilfully shaped
that no beryl or ball was ever so perfectly rounded. What
should I tell you? Let us talk of the things he saw there, inside
and out, but let us speak of them briefly, so that we do not
grow too weary.

20273   'He tells us that he saw ten ugly little images depicted on
the outside of the garden. But if you looked outside this park,
you would find hell and all the demons portrayed there in

their frightful hideousness, together with all the outrageous vices that make their home in hell, and Cerberus, who keeps them all locked up. The whole earth would be there, with its ancient riches and all earthly things; you would behold the very sea, the salt-water fish and all other inhabitants of the deep, the fresh waters, muddy and clear, and everything, great and small, that they contain. You would see the air, the birds, flies, and butterflies, and everything whose voice resounds through the air, and also the fire that surrounds the domains and belongings of all the other elements. In addition, you would see all the lovely, bright, shining stars, both the wandering planets and the fixed stars, all attached to their proper spheres. If you were there, you would see all these things excluded from the fair park, and depicted there with all the clarity of their actual appearance.

'But now let us return to the garden, and speak of the things that are within. The young man tells us that he saw Pleasure leading the dance on the fresh grass, and his people dancing with him over the fragrant flowers. He also saw grass and trees, animals and birds, streams and springs babbling and splashing over the gravel, and the spring beneath the pine, and he boasts that no such pine had existed since the days of Pepin, and that the spring also was of consummate beauty. 20305

'For God's sake, my lords, take care. The truth is that the things in the garden are trumpery toys. There is nothing lasting here; everything he saw will perish. He saw dances that came to an end, and all those who danced them will pass away, as will all the things that he saw enclosed there. For the nurse of Cerberus, that Atropos who refuses nothing and can never be prevented by human conduct from consuming everything when she decides to use her power (and she uses it continually and indefatigably), was spying from behind on all of them, except the gods, if there were any, for it is certain that divine things are not subject to death. 20319

'But let us speak now of the lovely things enclosed within this fair park. I shall tell you about them in general terms, for I would like to end my sermon soon. Truth to tell, I cannot give a proper account of them, for no heart could conceive nor human tongue relate the immense beauty and worth of 20339 the things contained therein,* nor the lovely games nor the great, lasting, true joys experienced by the dancers who dwell within the enclosure. Those who disport themselves there have everything that is delightful, true, and lasting, and this is right, for they draw all these good things from a spring which is precious and salutary, fair and clear, bright and pure, and which waters all the enclosure. From this stream the animals drink who have been separated from the black sheep, and who desire and deserve to enter the enclosure, for once they have quenched their thirst there, they will never thirst again, and will live as long as they please, free from sickness and death. It was their good fortune to enter those gates, and to behold the lamb whom they followed along the narrow way, guarded by the good shepherd who wished to give them shelter with himself. No one who drank once from that stream would ever die. This is not the same spring that the young man saw welling up from the marble stone beneath the tree. He deserves to be mocked for praising that spring, the perilous spring, so bitter and venomous that it killed fair Narcissus when he gazed at his reflection from above. The young man himself, far from being ashamed to admit it, acknowledges and does not hide the cruel nature of the spring when he calls it the perilous mirror and says that he felt such grief and heaviness on gazing at his reflection in it that he has often sighed about it since. See what sweetness he finds in the water. By God, this is a fine spring indeed, where the healthy fall sick! How good it is to turn in that direction so as to look at oneself in the water!

20395   'It gushes out, he tells us, in great waves through two deeply hollowed channels, but I know very well that neither the channels nor the water originate there: everything that it has comes to it from somewhere else.

20401   'He goes on to say that it is infinitely brighter than pure silver. See what tales he is telling you! In fact, it is so ugly and muddy that anyone who hangs his head over in order to look at himself will be unable to see a thing. Everyone goes wild with anguish because he cannot recognize himself.

20409   'At the bottom, he says, are two crystals of such power and radiance that when the rays of the unclouded sun fall upon them, they shine so brightly that anyone looking at them can always see half the things that are enclosed in the garden, and can see the remainder by stationing himself on the other side. But it is certain that they are cloudy and murky. Why, when the sun's rays fall upon them, do they not reveal everything at once? By my faith, it seems to me that they cannot, because of the gloom that shadows them. They are so dark and murky as to be insufficient in themselves for the man who looks at his reflection in them, for their brightness comes from elsewhere. If the sun's rays do not strike them in such a way that they can catch them, they are powerless to show anything. But the spring of which I speak is utterly lovely. Now prick up your ears, and you will hear me tell of wondrous things.

'The spring of which I have told you is extremely beautiful, 20435 and the water, sweet, clear, lively, and so delicious that it has great power to heal sick beasts, wells up continually through three skilfully constructed channels. These are so close together that they all become one, and if you see them all and choose to amuse yourself by counting them, you will find both one and three. You will never find four, but always three and always one, this is a characteristic that they share.

'Never has such a spring been seen, for it wells up spontan- 20449 eously. Other springs do not do this: they take their source from alien veins. This one flows of its own accord and needs no other conduit; it has its own life, more sure than natural rock. It needs no marble stone nor any tree for covering, for the inexhaustible water springs from so high a source that, however tall the tree, the source would be higher. However, as the water courses down, it undoubtedly flows beneath a low olive that stands on the slope, and when the little tree feels that its roots have been soaked by the soft sweet water of the spring I have described, it is so nourished that it grows tall and heavy with leaves and fruit, whereas the pine-tree of which the young man told you never rose so high above the ground nor spread its branches so wide nor gave such excellent shade.

'As it stands there, the olive spreads its branches over the 20479 spring, so that the spring is in shadow, and little animals hide there in the lovely cool shade, sipping the sweet dew that is

spread over the flowers and tender grass in the pleasant cool-
ness. Hanging on the olive is a little scroll bearing an inscription in small letters. To those who lie in the shade of the
olive and read it, it says: "Here runs the spring of life, beneath
the leafy olive that bears the fruit of salvation."* What pine-
tree was ever equal to this? I tell you also that in this spring
(foolish people will find this hard to believe and many will
take it for fiction), there shines a carbuncle more wondrous
than any other marvellous stone. It is quite round, with three
facets, and it sits so high up in the middle of the stream that
its shining can plainly be seen from everywhere in the park.
It is so fair and noble that neither wind nor rain nor fog can
deflect its rays. Know too that the virtue of this stone and
the reciprocal power of the facets are such that each facet is
equal in worth to the other two, and those two are equal to
it, no matter how fair each one may be. No amount of
thought could enable you to divide them, or to join them in
such a way that there is no distinction between them. No sun
illuminates it, for it is of a colour so pure, so radiantly bright,
that the sun that shines upon the double crystal in that other
spring would be dark and murky in comparison. In short,
what more can I say? No sun but that resplendent carbuncle
shines in the park. That is the sun that they have there, more
abundantly radiant than any in the world. It sends night into
exile and creates the everlasting day of which I have told you,
that has neither ending nor beginning and of its own accord
remains fixed at one particular point, without passing through
a zodiacal sign or a degree or a minute or any other fraction
into which an hour could be divided. And it has such marvellous power that as soon as those who go to see it turn
towards it and look at their own faces in the water, whatever
side of it they are on, they are always able to see, and rightly
to understand, all the things in the park and themselves as
well. Once they have seen themselves there, they become
such wise masters that nothing that exists will ever be able to
deceive them.

20549   'I shall teach you another marvel, for that sun's rays do not
hurt or weaken or dazzle the eyes of those who behold them;
instead, their sight finds new strength, joy, and vigour in the

vision of that fair brightness, full of gentle warmth, and of so
marvellous a quality that the whole park is filled with the
sweet fragrance that issues from it. So as not to detain you
too long, I would like you to store just one short observation
in your minds: it is that anyone seeing the form and substance
of this park would surely assert that the paradise in which
Adam was formed in days of yore was not so fair.

'In God's name, my lords, what do you think of the park   20567
and garden together? Judge them rationally, according to
their accidents and substances; declare in good faith which
has the greater beauty, and consider which of the two springs
has the purer, more wholesome, and more potent water. Pass
judgement also on the nature of the channels: which are the
more powerful? Judge between the precious stones, and then
between the pine and the olive that covers the living foun-
tain. I will abide by your judgements, if you will deliver a
verdict that is just, and based on the evidence I have read to
you. For I tell you without deceit that I will not be entirely
bound by your judgement; if you did anything amiss, if you
uttered falsehoods or suppressed the truth, I will not conceal
from you that I would immediately appeal to someone else.
Now, so that you may reach agreement quickly, I will briefly
remind you of what I have told you concerning their great
power and goodness: one of them drugs the living with death,
the other restores the dead to life.

'You may be quite certain, my lords, that if you conduct   20597
yourselves well and do as you ought, you will drink of the
second spring. And to make it easier for you to remember all
my instructions (for a lesson is more easily retained when it
is concisely delivered), I will briefly remind you of everything
you should do. Take care to honour Nature, and toil hard in
her service. If you have anything that belongs to someone
else, give it back if you can, and if you cannot, because you
have spent it or lost it in play, make sure you are willing to
do so when you have means in plenty. Avoid killing, keep
your hands and mouth clean, be loyal and merciful, and then
you will go to the delectable fields, following in the footsteps
of the lamb. There you will live for ever, and drink of the
fair spring which is so sweet and bright and healthful that as

long as you drink of its water you will never die. Instead you will wander gaily over the green grass and the flowers, singing motets, part-songs, and canzonets for all eternity and dancing beneath the olive. But what business have I chattering on? I should put away my flute, for fine singing often becomes wearisome. I might detain you too long, and so I will end my sermon at this point. Now we shall see what you will do when you are perched high up, preaching on the parapet.'

20638   This was Genius' sermon, which brought them joy and solace. Then he threw down his candle in their midst, and its smoky flame spread throughout the world. It was so effectively spread by Venus that no lady could protect herself from it, and so fanned by the wind that the bodies, hearts, and thoughts of every lady alive were permeated by its odour. For his part, Love spread the news of the charter that had been read, with the result that no worthy man ever disagreed with the judgement.

CHAPTER 12

THE CONQUEST OF THE ROSE

When Genius had finished reading, the barons were over- 20653
come with joy (for, as they said, they had never heard so good
a sermon nor since they were conceived had they received
so full a pardon or heard so just a sentence of excommuni-
cation), and lest they lose the pardon, they all assented to the
judgement and replied swiftly and hastily: 'Amen, amen,
fiat, fiat.'*

Once things reached this point, there was no further delay. 20665
All those who approved of the sermon noted it word for word
in their hearts, for it seemed to them very salutary because of
the excellent and charitable pardon that it offered, and they
were very glad to hear it. Genius disappeared, and they never
knew what became of him. Then more than twenty of the
host cried out: 'To arms! No more delay! If we understand
the verdict correctly, our enemies are quite discomfited.'
Then all rose to their feet, ready to continue the war until
everything should be captured and razed to the ground.

Venus was ready for the assault, and was the first to urge 20681
the enemy to surrender. And what did they do? Shame and
Fear replied: 'Venus, that is quite out of the question. You
will never set foot within these walls.'

'No indeed,' said Shame, 'even if I were alone, I would
not be in the least afraid,'

When the goddess heard Shame, she said: 'Back, filthy slut,
what good will it do you to resist me? You will see what a
turmoil everything will be in if you do not surrender the
castle to me. You will never be able to defend it. You!
Defend it against us! By God's flesh you will surrender it, or
I will burn you alive, miserable wretches that you are. I will
gladly set fire to the whole enclosure, and level every tower
and turret. I'll singe your tail for you. I'll burn down pillars,
walls, and stakes. Your moat will be filled in; all the barbi-
cans you have erected will be destroyed, for I will raze them
to the ground, however high you have built them. Fair

Welcome will let us take all the roses and rose-buds we like: sometimes he will sell them, and at other times he will give them away.

20711   'All your fierceness will not stop everyone from rushing at them. Once I have opened the barriers, all without exception will walk in procession among the rose-trees and the roses. In order to deceive Jealousy, I shall have all the meadows and lawns trampled underfoot. I shall so widen the paths that clerks and laymen, religious and secular will all be able to pluck the roses and the rose-buds without delay. No one will be able to hold back, and all will perform their penances there, but there will be a difference between them. Some will come in secret, while others do so openly, but the ones who come in secret will be perceived as worthy men, while the others will be maligned and known as rakes and libertines, even though they have sinned less than some whom no one accuses.

20735   'It is still true that some evil men (may God and our Holy Father in Rome confound both them and their affairs) will abandon the roses in favour of worse pursuits, and the devil who goads them on will give them garlands of nettles. For Genius, on behalf of Nature, has sentenced them and all our other enemies for their base and filthy conduct.

20745   'If I do not succeed in tricking you, Shame, then my bow and my skill are worthless, for I will not appeal to anything else. It is certain, Shame, that I shall never love you or your mother, Reason, who is so harsh to lovers. No one who listened to you or your mother would ever be a true lover.' Venus had no desire to say any more, for she had said enough.

20755   Then Venus tucked up her skirts, a picture of womanly anger. She drew the bow and fitted the brand to the string, then, when it was properly nocked, she brought the bow, no longer than six feet, up to her ear. Then, like the good archer she was, she took aim at a little loophole that she saw hidden in the tower. It was at the front rather than the side of the tower, and Nature had set it very skilfully between two little pillars.

20767   These little pillars were made of silver and were most fair. Instead of a reliquary, they supported a silver image that was neither too high nor too low, neither too fat nor too thin, but whose arms, shoulders and hands were neither excessive nor defective but all fashioned in perfect proportion. The other limbs also were very fair, but within there was a sanctuary, more fragrant than a pomander and covered with a precious cloth, the finest and most noble between here and Constantinople. A reasonable comparison between this and any other image would show that this is to Pygmalion's image as a lion is to a mouse.

Pygmalion* was a sculptor who worked in wood and stone, 20787 in metal, bone, and wax, and every other material that could be used for this purpose. In order to put his great skill to the test (for no one ever had greater skill than he), and to win renown, he decided to make a portrait for his own pleasure. He created an ivory image and took such care over the making of it that it was as lovely and beautiful and apparently as alive as the fairest creature living. Helen and Lavinia* were beautifully fashioned, but they were not born with such fine complexions or such shapely forms, nor had they one-tenth of her beauty. Pygmalion himself stood amazed at the sight of her. As you see, he was not on his guard, and Love bound him so tightly in his nets that he did not know what he was doing. He uttered his grief to himself, but could not stifle his complaint:

'Alas!' he said, 'What am I doing? Am I asleep? I have made 20813 and forged many images whose worth was beyond price, and I have never been overcome with love for any of them. But this one has done me great mischief and made me lose my wits. Alas! Where did this thought come from? How was such a love conceived? I love an image that is deaf and dumb, that cannot move or stir, and that will never have pity on me. How could I have been wounded by such a love? Surely, anyone who heard of it would be utterly astounded. I am the greatest madman in the world! What can I do in this situation?

'By my faith, if I loved a queen, I could at least hope for 20829 mercy because it would be a possibility, but this love is so horrible that it cannot be Nature's work. I am at odds with Nature, who has a bad son in me and who disgraced herself in making me. And yet I ought not to blame her for my insensate love; I have only myself to blame. Since I received the name Pygmalion and could walk on my own two feet, I have never heard of such a love. And yet my love is not so very foolish, for if the texts can be relied on, many have loved more foolishly. Did not Narcissus, thinking to quench his thirst at the bright pure stream in the dense forest, once fall in love with his own face? He had no defence against it and, according to the story, which is still well remembered, he later died of his love. At least I am less mad than he, for I can go to this image whenever I like, and take her in my arms and kiss her, which makes it easier for me to endure my distress, whereas Narcissus could not possess the image that he saw in the spring.

20859   'Moreover, there are many countries where many men have loved many ladies and served them as well as they could without receiving a single kiss in spite of all their toil. So has Love treated me better than these? No, for however uncertain, they had at least the hope of a kiss and of other things, whereas I am denied the hope of such delights, the goal of those who expect the pleasures of Love. When I want to enjoy kisses and embraces, I find my mistress as rigid as a stake, and so cold that when my kiss touches her, my lips are chilled.

20877   'Ha! I have spoken very roughly. Sweet friend, I ask for mercy and beg you to accept these amends, for if you would only deign to look gently and smile upon me, I believe that that would suffice me, for sweet looks and gracious smiles give great delight to lovers.'

20885   Then Pygmalion fell on his knees, and his face was wet with tears. He proffered his gage in reparation, but she cared nothing for these amends. She neither heard nor felt anything about him or his gift, and he was afraid of wasting his effort and his labour in the love of such a creature. Nor did he know how to regain his own heart, for Love robbed him of sense and knowledge, and so he was in great distress. He did not know whether she was alive or dead; he touched her gently with his hands and believed that her flesh yielded to his touch as if it were putty, but it was his own hand that yielded as he pressed.

20901   Such were Pygmalion's struggles, unrelieved by peace or respite. He could not remain in any one mood: sometimes

he loved, sometimes he hated, sometimes laughed and sometimes cried; he was by turns happy or distressed, tormented
or calm. He would dress her in different ways, in robes
fashioned with great skill from soft white wool, from scarlet
cloth or linsey woolsey, from cloth of green or blue, or rich
dark stuff, in colours that were fresh and fine and bright,
richly furred with ermine, miniver, and squirrel. Then he
would take them off again, to see how well she looked in a
robe of silk, sendal, tabby, or other precious stuffs, in indigo,
vermilion, yellow, or brown, in samite, diapered fabric, or
camlet. She might have been an angel, so modest was her
countenance. Sometimes he would attire her in a wimple,
with a kerchief to cover the wimple and the head, but not
the face, for he had no wish to imitate the habit of the
Saracens, who are so full of jealous fury that they cover the
faces of their women with cloths whenever they go into
the streets, so that no passer-by will see them. At other times
he would be filled with a desire to take all these off again and
deck her in braids of yellow and red, green and blue, and in
lovely fine ribbons of silk and gold, decorated with tiny
pearls. Her head-dress would be fastened with a costly net,
on top of which he would place a slender coronet of gold,
with many precious stones in settings that were square with
semi-circles on each of the four sides, not to mention all the
other little stones that clustered thickly round. Two delicate
pendant ear-rings of gold would be fixed in her ears, and two
golden clasps at her throat, to fasten the neck of her dress.
He would pin another clasp to her breast and fasten a girdle
around her waist, a richer girdle than any girl ever wore. He
would hang a purse upon the girdle, a most precious and
costly one, in which he would place five little stones picked
from the sea-shore, fair and round such as maidens find to
play marbles* with. He took great care over her feet, clothing
each of them in a shoe and stocking, prettily cut off two
fingers' length above the floor; not having been born in Paris,
she did not wear boots, for such footwear would have been
far too rough for so youthful a maiden. Then he would take
a pointed needle of pure gold, threaded with golden thread,
and snugly sew up her two sleeves, so that she was even better

dressed. He would bring her fresh flowers, which gay young maidens use to weave garlands in the spring, and balls and little birds and all kinds of novelties to delight young girls. He would make garlands of flowers for her, the finest ever seen, for he gave all his attention to the task. He would slip golden rings on to her fingers and say, like any true and loyal husband: 'Fair, sweet lady, I hereby wed you and become yours, and you mine. I call upon Hymen* and Juno; may they be present at our wedding. I have no need of clerk or priest, nor of any prelate's crook or mitre: those I have named are the true gods of marriage.' Then, instead of a mass, he would sing songs of love's sweet secrets in a voice that was loud and clear and full of gaiety. He would play loudly enough to drown God's thunder, for he had all kinds of instruments, and his hands were more skilful than those of Amphion of Thebes.* For his pleasure he would choose gigues and rebecs,* guitars and lutes; his clocks would chime throughout his halls and apartments by means of cunningly contrived wheels that ran for ever. He had organs that were extremely easy to handle and could be carried in one hand, and he himself would blow and play them, while singing the treble or tenor part of a motet in full voice. Next he would turn his attention to the cymbals, and fife upon his fife and pipe upon his pipes. He would beat his tabor, flute his flute, and drum his drum; he would pluck his citole, sound his trumpet and blow his bagpipes; he would strum and play upon his psaltery and viol. He would take up his musette and work at his Cornish pipes, he would dance and leap and caper, kicking his feet throughout the hall, he would take her by the hand and dance about, but his heart was very heavy, for she would neither sing nor answer him, for all his prayers and exhortations.

21029   Then he would embrace her once again and take her in his arms as he lay in his bed, kissing and caressing her. But it is not very pleasant for two people to kiss each other when they are not both enjoying it.

Thus Pygmalion was tricked by his passion for his deaf image; his wild thoughts provoked in him a mortal fury. He decked her in all the finery he could, for he was solely bent on serving her; but she seemed no less fair naked than clothed.

Now it so happened that there was a famous feast in that country, at which many wondrous things occurred, and all the people held a vigil in a temple of Venus that was there. The young man had great confidence in this, and came to keep the festal vigil in order to find a solution to his love. He complained mournfully to the gods about the love that tormented him. 'Great gods,' he said, 'if you can do everything, please hear my request. And you, blessed Venus, the lady of this temple, fill me with your grace, for you are greatly angered when Chastity finds favour, and I have deserved severe punishment for having served her so long. I repent of it now, without further delay, and I beg you to pardon me. Be merciful to me, be tender and kind and grant, on the understanding that I will flee into exile if I do not shun Chastity from now on, that the fair one who has stolen away my heart and who is so like ivory, may become my true sweetheart, with the body, soul, and life of a woman. If you make haste to do this and I am ever again found to be chaste, may I be hanged, or hewn in two with great hatchets, or may Cerberus, the doorkeeper of hell, swallow me alive and crush me in his triple jaws, or bind me with ropes or chains.'

On hearing the young man's prayer, Venus was overjoyed that he was abandoning Chastity and coming to do her service like a good penitent, ready to perform his penance naked in the arms of his sweetheart, if he could only possess her alive. She sent a soul to the image, which thus became so fair a lady that none so fair had ever been seen in all that country.

After he had made his request, Pygmalion did not remain at the temple but made haste to return to his image, for he could not wait to hold and see it. He ran back at great speed until he reached it. He knew nothing about the miracle, but he had great faith in the gods, and the closer he looked, the more his heart burned and flamed with desire. He saw that she was living flesh; he caressed the naked flesh, he saw the lovely blond locks shining and rippling together like the waves, he felt the bones and the veins all full of blood, and the throbbing movement of the pulse. He did not know

21043

21079

21091

whether it was false or true, and drew back, unsure of what to do. He dared not approach more closely, for he was afraid of being bewitched.

'What is this?' he said, 'Am I being tempted? Am I awake? No, I am dreaming. But I have never had so realistic a dream. Dream? By my faith, I am not dreaming but awake. So where has this marvel come from? Is it a phantom or a demon that has possessed my image?'

21121   Then the maiden, who was so fair and lovely and whose hair was so blond, answered him: 'Sweet friend, it is neither demon nor phantom. I am your sweetheart, ready to receive your companionship, and I offer you my love if you will be pleased to accept it.'

21129   He heard that the phenomenon was real, he beheld the plain miracle, he drew near to reassure himself. Since it was genuine, he willingly gave himself to her as one who was entirely hers. At these words they came together and thanked one another for their love. They gave each other every joy: they embraced most lovingly, kissed like two turtle-doves, and shared great love and great pleasure. Both of them gave thanks to the gods who had done them this courtesy, especially to Venus, who had helped them more than anyone.

21145   Then Pygmalion was happy and there was nothing to displease him, for she refused him nothing that he wanted. If he raised objections, she yielded, overcome by his arguments; if she commanded, he obeyed; under no circumstances would he refuse to gratify her every desire. He could lie with his sweetheart, and she would neither resist nor make complaint. They played such games of love that she became pregnant with Paphus, from whom Fame tells us that the island of Paphos took its name. Of him was born King Cinyras, a good man except on one occasion, and who would have enjoyed every good fortune had he not been deceived by his daughter, Myrrha* the blond, whom the old woman, heedless of sin (may God confound her!), brought to the king in his bed by night.

21165   The queen was at a feast. The king took the maiden in haste, and without any idea that he was lying with his daughter. Here was a strange begetting, when the old woman allowed the king to lie with his daughter. When she had brought them together, the fair Adonis was born of their union, after Myrrha had been changed into a tree. Her father would have killed her when, having had candles brought, he noticed the deception, but this could not happen, because she who was no longer a virgin made her escape quickly; otherwise he would have slain her. But I am too far from my subject and should retrace my steps. You will certainly hear what this signifies before my work is finished.*

I will not detain you for the moment, for I have a different 21185 furrow to plough and must return to my subject. It seems to me, therefore, that one might make the same comparison between the beauties of these two images as between a mouse and a lion, for just as the mouse is inferior to the lion and less to be feared for its physical strength and qualities, so, I tell you truly, was this image inferior in beauty to the one I prize so highly. Lady Cypris* took careful aim at the image I have described, set between the pillars in the very middle of the tower. I found more pleasure in gazing at this than at any place I had ever seen; indeed, I would have fallen on my knees and adored it, together with the reliquary and the aperture. No archer with her bow and brand could have made me abandon my contemplation of it or my desire to enter freely; at least I would have tried my best, whatever the consequences, if anyone had offered me the chance or had simply permitted it.

Concerning these relics of which I have told you, I have 21213 vowed to God that if it please him, and the time and place are right, I will petition for them with my staff and scrip. May God preserve me from mockery, or from anything that might prevent my enjoying the rose!

Venus delayed no longer, but loosed the blazing, feathered 21221 brand upon the people of the castle, to madden them. But I tell you that she shot it with such skill that not one of them could see it, however long they looked.

Once the brand had flown, those inside fell into a panic. 21229 Fire engulfed all the enclosure, and they knew they were caught. All cried out: 'Treason, treason! Alas, alas! We are all dead! Let us flee the country!' And all threw down their keys on the spot.

21237   When that dreadful devil, Rebuff, felt the heat, he fled more quickly than a stag over the heath. None waited for the others, but each one tucked his skirts into his belt and thought only of flight.

21243   Fear fled, and Shame sprang after her, leaving behind the blazing castle; never again would she set any store by the lessons of Reason.

21247   Then came Courtesy, of admirable virtue and loveliness. When she saw the destruction, she leapt with Pity and Generosity of Spirit into the enclosure, to save her son from the flames. They did not refrain because of the fire, but kept going until they reached him.

21255   Courtesy, who was not slow to speak fair words, was the first to address him. 'Fair son, I have endured great grief, and my heart has been very sorrowful because of your long imprisonment. May he who thus confined you burn in the blazing fires of hell! Now, by God's grace, you are free, while the slanderer Evil Tongue lies dead out there in the moat, together with his Norman drunkards, unable to see or hear. You need not fear Jealousy; Jealousy should not prevent you from leading a good life and giving pleasure to your lover in private, especially when she happens to be unable to hear or see what is going on, and there is no one to tell her, and she cannot find you here. The others too, wicked, presumptuous creatures, have been deprived of support and have fled, utterly discomfited: they have all left the enclosure.

21281   'Fair, sweet son, by God's mercy do not let yourself burn here. Generosity of Spirit, Pity, and I implore you in friendship to allow this true lover to make reparation to you. He has suffered long for your sake and has never tricked you, noble as he is, nor played you false. Receive him and all he has: he offers you his very soul. For God's sake, fair, sweet son, do not refuse this offer, but accept it by the faith you owe me and for the sake of Love, who is striving to bring this about and who has invested much energy in the attempt.

21297   'Fair son, Love conquers all; he has all things under lock and key. Virgil himself confirms this firmly and courteously, for if you search in the *Eclogues*, you will find that "Love

conquers all, and we must welcome him.'"* His words are
certainly good and true: he tells us all this in a single line,
and he could have told no better tale.

'Fair son, be kind to this lover, God save you both, and   21307
grant him the gift of the rose.'

'Lady,' said Fair Welcome, 'I will give it up to him most
willingly. He may pluck it while the two of us are alone here.
I should have received him long ago, for I can see that his
love is true.'

I thanked him a hundred thousand times, and promptly
made my way, like the good pilgrim I was, with heart as
ardent, fervent, and loyal as any true lover, towards the
aperture, there to fulfil my pilgrimage. I had laboriously
brought with me my scrip and my staff that was so stiff and
strong that it needed no ferrule when going on journeys. The
scrip was well made of a supple, seamless skin, but I assure
you it was not empty. At the time she made the scrip, Nature,
who gave it to me, had forged two hammers for it with great
skill and care (for it seems to me that no one can do a thing
thoroughly when in a hurry), and Nature was a better smith
than Daedalus ever was. I believe she made them because she
thought I would use them to shoe my horses on my journeys,
and I shall certainly do so if I find it possible, for, thank God,
I know how to forge. I assure you that my two hammers and
my scrip are dearer to me than my citole or my harp.

Nature did me great honour by equipping me with this   21347
weaponry and teaching me so well how to use it that I
became a good and wise workman. She herself had made me
a gift of the staff, and gladly set to work to polish it before I
was sent to school; but she had no interest in making a ferrule
for it, and it was worth none the less for that. Ever since I
first received it I have always had it with me; I have never
lost it, nor will I if I can help it, for I would not part with
it for five hundred times a hundred thousand pounds. It was
a fair gift she made me, and therefore I take care of it. I am
very glad when I look at it and I thank her for her present,
being full of joy and happiness whenever I feel it. Since
then, I have taken it into many places, and it has often
brought me comfort. It is very useful to me, and do you know

how? When I am travelling in some out of the way place, I
stick it into those ditches in which I cannot make anything
out, and I also use it to try out the fords. Thus I can boast
that I need have no fear of drowning, for I am very good at
testing the fords, and at striking the bed and banks with my
staff. Sometimes I encounter streams that are so deep and
whose banks are so far apart that I would find it less painful
and wearisome to swim two leagues along the sea-shore than
to attempt so perilous a passage. I have tried those great gulfs,
and yet I have not been drowned, for as soon as I had tested
them and begun to make my way into them, and discovered
that I could not touch the bottom with a stick or with my
oar, I went around them, keeping close to the bank until at
last I got out. But had it not been for the arms given to me
by Nature, I would never have been able to get out. But let
us leave these broad highways to the ones who are glad to
journey along them, and let those of us who lead a merry life
follow the pleasant pathways, not the cart-tracks but the
charming little footpaths, with gay and joyful hearts.

21405   Nevertheless, there is more to be gained from an old road
than from a new pathway, and more property to be found
there, from which great profit is to be had. Juvenal* himself
tells us that the quickest way to become a man of substance
is to attach oneself to some rich old woman: if your service
is pleasing to her, she will raise you at once to a high station.
And Ovid* gives it as his firm and tested opinion that if a
man is willing to court an old woman, he can expect great
rewards. You can acquire great wealth at once, if you will
indulge in this kind of trade.

21421   But anyone who tries to steal the love of an old woman,
or even to acquire it honestly, once Love has caught him in
his snares, must take care not to do or say anything that looks
like trickery. For these tough and hoary old dames knew
flattery, trickery, and deceit in their youth, long ago, and
since they have been more often deceived, they are quicker
to recognize lying talk than are the gentle maidens who can
listen to flatterers without suspecting treachery, and who
believe falsehoods and insincerities as if they were gospel,
never having been scorched themselves.

But as for the tough, wrinkled, malicious, crafty old crones, 21440
time and experience have made them knowledgeable in the
art of fraud. Flatterers may come and detain them with their
insincere talk, dinning their ears with their efforts to curry
favour, sighing and abasing themselves, joining their hands to
beg for mercy, bowing, kneeling, drenching themselves with
their tears, crossing themselves in order to gain their confidence, treacherously pledging hearts and bodies, property and
service, promising and swearing by the saints who are, have
been, and will be, and deceiving them with words that are
only so much hot air, just as the fowler hidden in the woods
like a thief sets his snare for the bird and calls it with sweet
songs to come to his trap so that he may catch it. The foolish
bird approaches, unable to reply to the sophism which has
deceived him through a figure of speech;* in the same way
the quail-catcher calls the quail to make it jump into the net,
and the quail listens to the sound, draws near, and hops under
the net that he has spread over the fresh, thick grass in the
springtime. But the old quail will not come to the quail-
catcher: she has been scorched and beaten before, for she has
seen other nets in the new grass, and has perhaps escaped
them when she should have been caught. In just the same
way, the old women of whom I speak, who have been
petitioned in the past and deceived by the petitioners, can
recognize treachery from afar, by the words they hear and
the demeanour they see; therefore they are unlikely to entertain such deceptions. Even if their lovers are sincere and
desire the rewards of Love, having been entangled in the nets
that are so exquisitely pleasant, so delightfully burdensome
that nothing is so agreeable as that painful hope which both
pleases and torments them, even then, they are very wary of
being hooked, and listen very carefully to determine whether
or not they are being told the truth. They weigh up every
word, for the deceptions they have suffered in the past, and
which are still fresh in their memories, have caused them to
dread present treachery. Old women always think that everyone is out to trick them.

Now if you decide to subdue your heart to these measures 21509
in order to grow rich more quickly, or if those of you who

find delight there care to obtain this delight, you are welcome
to follow this path in pursuit of pleasure and enjoyment. As
for those of you who desire young women, I will not deceive
you, for I will truthfully repeat to you my master's commands
(and all his commands are good). Believe me or not, as you
will, you do well to try everything, the better to enjoy the
things that are good. Whenever he can get into the kitchen,
the epicurean connoisseur of delicious morsels tries meats of
various kinds, whether boiled in a pot or roasted, marinaded
or in a pastry crust, fried or in a galantine. Having tasted many
in this way, he knows which to praise and which to condemn,
which are sweet and which are bitter. I assure you also, and
there is no doubt about it, that no one can know anything
of good if he has not experienced evil, and no one who does
not know the meaning of honour will be able to understand
shame. No one ever knew what comfort was without first
learning about discomfort: if a man is unwilling to encounter
discomfort and unable to endure it, he is unworthy to enjoy
comfort and no one should offer it to him. The nature of
opposites is that one explains the other: if you want to define
one, you must be mindful of the other, or else you will never
achieve a definition, however good your intentions. Unless
you know both, you will never understand the difference
between them, without which no proper definition can be
made.

21553   I longed to touch the relics with my harness, if I could
carry it, just as it was, as far as the haven, and bring it close
enough to them. Then, having done so much and wandered
so far with my unshod staff, I knelt without delay, full of
agility and vigour, between the two fair pillars, for I was
consumed with desire to worship at that lovely and venerable
shrine with devout and reverent heart. Everything had been
razed to the ground, for nothing could withstand the flames
without falling, although it had suffered no harm. I partly
raised the curtain that screened the relics, and, drawing near
to the image that I knew to be close to the sanctuary, I kissed
it devoutly. Next, I wanted to sheathe my staff by putting it
into the aperture while the scrip hung outside. I tried to
thrust it in at one go, but it came out and I tried again, to

no avail because it sprang out every time and nothing I did could make it go in. There was a barrier within, which I could feel but could not see. When the aperture was first constructed, it had been placed there, close to the edge to fortify it and make it stronger and more secure. I attacked it vigorously and hurled myself at it time and time again, but in vain.

Had you seen me jousting (and you would have had to be very observant), you might have been reminded of Hercules when he wanted to dismember Cacus.* Three times he attacked the gate, three times he hurled himself at it, three times he failed, and sat down wearily in the valley to regain his breath after his gruelling toil and exertions. As for me, when I could not immediately break the barrier, I struggled so hard and with such violence that I was drenched in sweat, and I was, I believe, quite as weary as Hercules, or even more so. However, I continued my assault until I noticed a narrow passage through which I thought I could pass, but first I had to break down the barrier. This tiny, narrow pathway that I have mentioned and through which I sought to pass, allowed me to break down the barrier with my staff and introduce myself into the aperture, but I could not even get halfway in. It grieved me that I could get no further, but I was powerless to go on. Nothing, however, could have prevented me from sliding my staff all the way in. I did so without delay, but the scrip with its pounding hammers stayed dangling outside. This caused me great distress, for I found the passage to be very narrow, and it was quite impossible for me to pass that way. Indeed, if I understood the nature of that path correctly, no one had ever passed that way, for I was the first to do so, and the place was not yet in the habit of collecting tolls. I do not know whether it later favoured others with the same advantages as it did me, but I can tell you that my love for it was such that I could never have believed it, even if it were true: no one lightly suspects a beloved object, however tarnished its reputation, and I do not believe it to this day. I know at least that at that time the path had not been opened up or trodden. Therefore I forced my way into it, for it was the only entrance, in order duly to pluck the rose-bud. And now

21589

I shall tell you how I dealt with the rose-bud. Young sirs, you shall learn what I did and how I did it, so that if, when springtime comes, you find it necessary to pluck the roses yourselves, open or closed, you will go about it so skilfully that you will not fail. You shall hear what I did, and if you know no better way of achieving your object, you can do the same. But if you can negotiate the passage with greater ease, or better or more skilfully, without pain or weariness, then use your own method, once you have learned mine. You will at least have the advantage of my having taught you my technique without taking any of your money, and you ought to be grateful to me for that.

21665   While I was in this cramped position, I had approached so close to the rose-bush that I could have stretched out my hands to the branches and plucked the rose-bud whenever I liked. Fair Welcome begged me in God's name to do nothing violent, and I promised him solemnly, in response to his repeated prayers, to do nothing that was not both his will and my own.

I grasped the branches of the rose-tree, nobler than any willow, and when I could reach it with both my hands, I began, very gently and without pricking myself, to shake the bud, for it would have been hard for me to obtain it without thus disturbing it. I had to move the branches and agitate them, but without destroying a single one, for I did not want to cause any injury. Even so, I was forced to break the bark a little, for I knew no other way to obtain the thing I so desired.

21689   I can tell you that at last, when I had shaken the bud, I scattered a little seed there. This was when I had touched the inside of the rose-bud and explored all its little leaves, for I longed, and it seemed good to me, to probe its very depths. I thus mingled the seeds in such a way that it would have been hard to disentangle them, with the result that all the rose-bud swelled and expanded. I did nothing worse than that. But I was certain of this, that gentle Fair Welcome saw nothing wrong in it and bore me no ill will: instead he submitted and allowed me to do whatever he knew would please me. Of course, he reminded me of my promise, and told me that my behaviour was outrageously improper. But

he did nothing to oppose my taking and caressing and pluck-
ing the rose-bush, with all its branches, flowers, and leaves.

When I saw that I had been raised so high and had so nobly 21713
achieved my aim that my success was no longer in doubt, I
wished to demonstrate my loyalty and gratitude towards all
my benefactors, as a good debtor should. I was greatly be-
holden to them, since thanks to them I became so rich that,
as I can truly affirm, Wealth herself was not so rich. The God
of Love and Venus had helped me more than anyone, and
after them all the barons of the host (and I pray God that he
may never deprive true lovers of their help), and so, in
between the delicious kisses, I thanked them ten or twenty
times. But I did not care to thank Reason, who had wasted
so much effort upon me.

In spite of Wealth, that villainous creature who showed no
pity but refused me entry to the path she guarded (she paid
no heed to the path by which I came here in secret haste);
in spite of my mortal enemies who caused me so many
setbacks; in spite particularly of Jealousy, weighed down by
her garland of marigolds,* who protects the roses from lovers
(much good her guard is doing now!), before I left that place
in which, had I had my way, I would have remained to this
day, I plucked with joy the flower from the fair and leafy
rose-bush. And so I won my bright red rose. Then it was day
and I awoke.

EXPLANATORY NOTES

3   *vision . . . King Scipio*: an allusion to the influential commentary on Cicero's *Somnium Scipionis* by the 4th-cent. author Macrobius.

4   *Lacing up my sleeves*: i.e. to make them fit better.

11   *Alexander's lands*: the empire of Alexander the Great. Other manuscripts have 'Saracen lands'.

12   *sirens . . . sweet voices*: the imagined etymological connection between the adjectives *saines* and *series* ('pure' and 'sweet') and the noun *seraines* is lost in translation.

15   *not yellow . . . nor white*: Lecoy notes that his base manuscript is faulty here. I have translated the authentic version.

19   *uncircled*: the helmet was reinforced by a band of metal.

       sorquenie: a *souquenille* in Modern French is a smock, but here it is clearly a close-fitting garment.

20   *Lord of Windsor*: the king of England, perhaps King Arthur.

23   *Pepin*: the first Carolingian king of the Franks, father of Charlemagne.

       Narcissus: in Greek mythology, a young man of great beauty whom the gods punished for his rejection of the nymph Echo, by causing him to pine away for love of his own reflection.

24   *crystal*: it is clear that there are two crystals at the bottom of the spring, and therefore the use of the singular here has posed a problem for editors of the *Rose*. Lecoy suggests that it can just possibly be justified if the word 'crystal' is taken to refer to the substance rather than to the object.

32   *expound . . . the dream*: both Guillaume de Lorris and Jean de Meun promise explanations or commentaries which never materialize.

       Kay: in Arthurian legend, the foster brother of King Arthur, whose seneschal he became. Usually represented as malicious and sarcastic.

       Gawain: nephew of King Arthur and son of King Lot of Orkney. Usually figures as a model of courtesy and prowess.

33   *ugly things*: this injunction will be remembered by the Lover in his conversation with Reason.

44 *Rebuff*: *Dangiers* in French. The word comes from Latin *dom-iniarium* ('lordship'). I have followed C. S. Lewis in translating it as 'Rebuff'. Another possibility might be 'Resistance'.

52 *warmed many a lady*: Venus appears here as the personification of feminine desire.

53 *Love . . . through his efforts*: an indication that Guillaume intended the Lover to succeed in his quest.

58 *bailey*: the outer wall of a castle.

59 *mangonels*: large catapults for hurling stones.

    cross-bows . . . screw-jacks: i.e. larger and more powerful than the ordinary cross-bow, where the bow-string was pulled back by a lever worked by hand or foot.

62 *constructs . . . negative conclusion*: a number of scholastic metaphors of this kind occur in Jean de Meun's continuation.

64 *I will . . . quickly*: Jean de Meun here quotes Guillaume de Lorris (see ll. 2022–6).

65 *par amour*: the expression means roughly: 'in accordance with the precepts of courtly love'.

66 *Charybdis*: in Homeric legend, one of two sea-monsters (the other being Scylla) which inhabited two rocks between Italy and Sicily.

    excommunicated by Genius: Jean de Meun is here following the 12th-cent. author Alain de Lille, whose *De Planctu Naturae* (The Complaint of Nature) was extremely influential in the Middle Ages. In the *De Planctu*, Genius excommunicates those who commit perverted or unnatural acts. The *De Planctu* is also the source of the oxymoronic definition of love.

68 *On Old Age*: Cicero, *De Senectute*, xii.

72 *Cicero . . . discourses*: Cicero, *De Amicitia*.

76 *hôtel-Dieu*: hospital.

77 *Pythagoras . . . Golden Verses*: Jean de Meun's source for this reference was probably Chalcidius' influential commentary on Plato's *Timaeus* (ed. Waszink, London, 1962, p. 177).

    Boethius . . . service: the *De Consolatione Philosophiae* of the 6th-cent. Roman philosopher Boethius was enormously influential in the Middle Ages. Jean de Meun himself later took his own advice and translated it into French.

    La Grève: an area by the Seine in Paris where goods arriving at the Port de Grève were unloaded.

Saint-Marcel: a suburb of Paris.

80 *Daedalus . . . Icarus*: in Greek mythology, Daedalus was a sculptor and architect who constructed the labyrinth for the Minotaur. Incurring the displeasure of Minos, he made wings for himself and his son, Icarus, to fly from Crete, but when Icarus flew too close to the sun, the wax in his wings melted and he was drowned in the sea.

82 *giants . . . flight*: in Greek mythology, after the overthrow of the Titans, a mighty battle took place between the giants and the gods, in which the gods were eventually victorious.

83 *swan of Socrates*: see John of Salisbury, *Polycraticus*, ii. 16, p. 96, ed. Webb.

and create . . . participate: Lecoy's text apparently reads: 'and never create a fellowship . . .', which makes poor sense.

85 *Saturn . . . book says*: the myth of the castration of Saturn by his son, Jupiter, recurs many times in the *Romance of the Rose*.

86 *Appius*: the story of Appius and Virginia is taken from the *Annals* of the Roman historian, Livy, I. iii. 44–58.

87 *Lucan*: Roman epic poet of the 1st cent. AD, author of the *Pharsalia*.

88 *word . . . lips*: see ll. 2097 ff.

Horace: Roman poet of the 1st cent. BC.

old books: i.e. you are not a classical scholar.

90 *Solinus*: 3rd-cent. author of *Collectaneum rerum memorabilium*.

Apollo's answer: the Delphic oracle.

Heraclitus and Diogenes: Greek philosophers.

91 *Zephyrus*: the West wind.

ambiguous forest: 'bois doutable' in the original is a translation of the Latin 'nemus ambiguum', and means a forest whose nature is uncertain and contradictory.

95 *Seneca and Nero*: the Roman philosopher Seneca was the tutor of the emperor Nero.

96 *our text*: the text referred to is the *De Consolatione Philosophiae* of Boethius.

97 *Claudian*: 4th-cent. Latin poet.

alembic . . . aludel: apparatus used by alchemists for distilling.

98   *Suetonius*: Latin historian of the 2nd cent. AD, author of the
      Lives of the Twelve Caesars.

99   *Croesus . . . Lydia*: Lydia was a country of Asia Minor, lying
      between the Aegean Sea and Mysia. Croesus (*c.* 540 BC) was
      its last king.

101   *Manfred, king of Sicily*: Manfred, the bastard son of the Em-
      peror Frederick II, was killed by Charles of Anjou at the battle
      of Benevento in 1266, while his nephew, Conradin, died at
      the battle of Tagliacozzo in 1268. Charles himself died on 7
      January 1285. These references to contemporary events help
      to date the poem.

102   *Polycraticus*: the best-known work of the English scholastic
      philosopher John of Salisbury (1110–80). For reference to At-
      halus as inventor of chess, see Polycraticus i. 5, ed. Webb,
      1909.

103   *Hecuba*: queen of Troy at the time of the Trojan war.

      Sisigambis: mother of Darius III (336–331 BC), who was con-
      quered by Alexander the Great.

104   *Homer tells us*: in the *Iliad*, xxiv. 527.

      three-card trick: literally: 'strap-folding game', which consisted
      in folding a strap in such a way as to deceive the unwary player
      into imagining that he could prevent it from being unfolded
      by placing his finger in one of the folds.

105   *I left my heart . . . confession*: see ll. 4184 ff.

107   *Almagest*: an important astronomical and mathematical work
      by the 2nd-cent. Greek astronomer Ptolemy.

      Cato's book: Dionysius Cato was the supposed author of the
      Disticha, a collection of moral sayings which enjoyed great
      popularity in the Middle Ages.

108   *Timaeus of Plato*: Chalcidius' translation of Plato's *Timaeus* was
      an important text in the Middle Ages.

109   *integuments on the poets*: the integument is the covering of
      fiction which clothes the deeper meaning of a text. Reason is
      perhaps referring here to the *Integumenta Ovidii*, a well-known
      commentary by John of Garland.

121   *Charlemagne . . . Ganelon's treachery*: according to the 12th-
      cent. *Chanson de Roland*, earliest and most famous of the *chan-
      sons de geste*, Charlemagne's nephew, Roland, was killed at the
      battle of Roncevaus while commanding the rearguard of the

army as it withdrew from Spain. He had been given the command on the advice of his stepfather, Ganelon, who then betrayed him to the enemy.

122 *Ovid*: Latin poet of the Augustan age, whose *Ars Amatoria* suggests amorous strategies very similar to those proposed by Friend.

125 *Pirithous . . . look for him*: in fact, according to Greek legend, Theseus descended to the underworld to help Pirithous to abduct Persephone. The two friends were captured by Pluto, and only Theseus was saved by Hercules.

Fair son . . . poor: Ecclesiasticus 40: 28.

127 *Juvenal*: Roman satirical poet (*c.* AD 60–*c.* AD 140).

130 *sheep's bladder*: a sheep's bladder tied to a stick was used by court jesters.

131 *Aureolus*: this lost work, ascribed to the Greek philosopher Theophrastus, is known to us through the *Adversus Jovinianum* of Saint Jerome and the *Polycraticus* of John of Salisbury.

132 *Penelope*: the wife of Ulysses, a model of feminine virtue.

Lucretia . . . force: the story of the rape of Lucretia by Sextus Tarquinius, son of Tarquinius Superbus, the last king of Rome, is told in Livy, *Annals*, i. 58 ff.

133 *Valerius*: the *Dissuasio Valerii ad Rufinum philosophum ne uxorem ducat*, an anti-feminist work by Gautier Map, was sometimes ascribed in the Middle Ages to the 1st-cent. Latin author Valerius Maximus.

134 *pain and torment*: Juvenal, *Satires*, vi. 28–32.

Phoroneus: this example of Phoroneus, a legendary king of Argos, is taken from Gautier Map.

Abelard: these details concerning the careers of Abelard and Heloise are taken from Abelard's autobiographical *Historia Calamitatum*, and from the letter written by Heloise after reading the *Historia*.

137 *Alcibiades*: 450–404 BC. A pupil of Socrates, famous for his vices.

138 *Virgil*: Roman poet of the 1st cent. BC, author of the Aeneid, the great national epic of the Romans.

Sibyl: priestess of Apollo who guided Aeneas to the underworld (*Aeneid*, vi).

142   *camlet*: a costly fabric.

      miniver: kind of fur.

144   *Greece*: 'Romenie' (Romania) in the original was a name used
      by some historians for the Latin kingdom founded at Constan-
      tinople in 1204 by Baldwin of Flanders.

145   *Arabia or Phrygia*: legendary for their wealth. Rulers of Phrygia
      include Midas and Croesus.

      Triton: a sea-god, son of Neptune.

      Doris and all her daughters: Doris, daughter of the Ocean and
      wife of Nereus, was the mother of the 50 Nereids, or sea-
      nymphs.

156   *Ceres . . . dragons*: Ceres, goddess of plenty, gave to Triptole-
      mus the first grains of corn, together with a winged chariot
      harnessed with dragons in which he was to travel the world,
      spreading the benefits of agriculture.

157   *beech-tree . . . folly*: the pun on *fou* (beech tree) and *fou*
      (mad/foolish) is untranslatable.

159   *I made my will*: at the beginning of his continuation, Jean de
      Meun recounts that the Lover makes a will in which he leaves
      his heart to Fair Welcome (see ll. 4188 ff.).

      Atropos: third of the three Parcae, or goddesses of fate. Clotho,
      the youngest, presides over men's birth and is represented with
      a distaff in her hand, Lachesis draws out the thread of destiny,
      and Atropos, dressed in black, cuts it short.

      confiteor: prayer of confession.

      double ace: the lowest possible score at dice.

161   *Tibullus*: roman love-poet of the 1st cent. BC, as were Gallus
      and Catullus, mentioned a little further on.

163   *finish it*: this passage is our only evidence of Guillaume's author-
      ship of the first part of the *Rose*. It is also extremely confusing.
      The only interpretation that makes sense is that Jean de Meun
      has succeeded Guillaume as writer, but not as dreamer, i.e. that
      Guillaume was unable to finish the account of his dream, and
      that Jean de Meun is now finishing it on his behalf. Otherwise,
      there is a clear contradiction between the sentence beginning
      'Full of fear . . .' and the statement by the God of Love that
      Jean de Meun is not present here. On the other hand, the
      passage undoubtedly suggests that Jean has succeeded Guil-
      laume as writer and as dreamer. At any rate, one effect of this

undermining of the autobiographical framework is to distance the author from his text, and from the opinions expressed in it.

casks . . . always two: see ll. 6783 ff.

Mirror of Lovers: in medieval literature, the title 'Mirror' was given to encyclopedic works or to didactic works that offered advice to particular groups of people.

166 *espoused wife*: see ll. 5505 ff.

170 *syllogism . . . conclusion*: see ll. 4053 ff.

razor of Elenchis: Aristotle's treatise, *De Sophisticis Elenchis*, which dealt with the means of convincing an adversary in argument and divided these means into 13 categories.

Tibert the cat: a character in the *Roman de Renart*.

eleven thousand virgins: according to legend, the companions of the 4th-cent. German saint Ursula.

171 *Sir Isengrin . . . Dam Belin*: the wolf and the sheep from the *Roman de Renart*.

new apostles: the mendicant orders.

172 *Proteus*: in Greek legend, a sea-god who would change his shape in order to avoid those who questioned him about the future.

173 *perjurer*: Prov. 30: 8–9.

wish to beg: for the attack on the mendicant orders which follows, see Introd.

174 *Justinian*: the Emperor Justinian (483–565), codifier of Roman Law.

175 *Work . . . others*: 1 Thess, 4: 11–12.

White Monks . . . canons regular: the Cistercians, the Benedictines, and the Augustinian canons.

176 *hands of this sort*: the drawings of the *manus corporalis* (bodily hand) and the *manus spiritualis* (spiritual hand) appear in certain MSS of the *Rose*, and are clearly required by the text. The second drawing encloses a translation into Latin of the first two verses of Genesis: 'In the beginning, God created heaven and earth. Now the earth was formless and empty.'

177 *he of Saint-Amour*: Guillaume de Saint-Amour, rector of the University of Paris and chief adversary of the mendicant friars.

179 *twenty-third chapter*: Matt. 23: 2–8.

181 *caillou pear*: a late variety, with sweet, granular flesh.

commonplaces . . . equivalences: scholastic jargon.

182 *Eternal Gospel*: published in 1254 (not 1255) by the Franciscan Gerard de Borgo, who claimed that this gospel of the Holy Spirit should supersede the New Testament as the New Testament had superseded the Old. The scandal provoked by the appearance of this work was naturally exploited by the opponents of the mendicant orders.

for so it is called: the *Evangelium Aeternum* (Eternal Gospel) was also known as the *Evangelium Spiritus Sancti* (Gospel of the Holy Spirit).

185 *cameline*: a kind of coarse fabric supposed to be made of camel's hair.

beguine: the beguines were religious women who lived a regular community life but did not take vows. In the 13th cent. they came under the influence of the friars.

186 *brother Saier*: this person has not been identified.

187 *a sophism*: another metaphor taken from scholastic philosophy: see ll. 4053 ff.

197 *Master Algus*: 9th-cent. Arab mathematician.

198 *Plato says*: in Chalcidius' translation of the *Timaeus*, ed. Waszink, p. 18, 16–17.

201 *Pygmalion's image*: this reference is not clear. The story of the legendary Greek sculptor Pygmalion and the statue brought to life by Venus occurs later in the poem.

203 *Saint Lifard of Meung*: abbot at Meung-sur-Loire, home town of Jean de Meun.

Dido . . . Aeneas: the story of Dido and Aeneas is told in the fourth book of Virgil's *Aeneid*.

Phyllis . . . Demophoön: Jean de Meun probably took this story, and that of Paris and Oenone, from Ovid, *Heroides* ii and v.

204 *Xanthus*: a river in Asia Minor.

Helen: the most beautiful woman in the world, wife of Menelaus of Sparta. Her abduction by Paris, son of Priam of Troy, resulted in the Trojan war.

Jason . . . Medea: Jason, son of Aeson, was the leader of the Argonauts, and obtained the Golden Fleece with the help of the sorceress Medea, whom he later abandoned in favour of Creusa.

elegantly attired: the Old Woman's advice to women to make the best of themselves is largely based on Ovid, *Ars Amatoria* iii.

207 *Palinurus*: See Virgil, *Aeneid* v. 833–71.

210 *Ptolemy*: the opinion is attributed to Ptolemy in the *Dicta et gesta philosophorum antiquorum* (ed. Franceschini, *Atti del Reale Instituto Veneto*, 1931, 2, xci, p. 532 (140)).

213 *Vulcan . . . Mars*: Vulcan was the god of fire and of the arts which need fire in their execution, and Mars the god of war.

Absalon: son of King David, the handsomest man in Israel. In the Middle Ages he was regarded as a type of beauty.

214 *written accounts*: see Horace, *Satires*, i. 3, 107–10.

215 *mouth of the net*: the image of the married man as a fish trapped in a net was to become traditional in anti-feminist writing. It was most famously used in the 15th-cent. *Quinze Joyes de Mariage*.

216 *Horace . . . come back*: see Horace, *Epistles*, i. 10.

222 *Argus . . . Juno*: Jupiter changed his mistress Io into a white heifer to protect her from Juno. But Juno persuaded Jupiter to give her the heifer, which she then entrusted to the guard of Argus, a giant with 100 eyes, of which 50 remained open while the other 50 slept. On Jupiter's orders, Mercury succeeded in charming the giant to sleep with the sound of his flute, and cut off his head.

Balenus: supposed author of treatises on magic. We do not know who he was, or even whether he existed.

Circe . . . Ulysses: The sorceress Circe changed the companions of Ulysses into swine when they visited her island on their way home from Troy. Ulysses spent a year with her, forgetting his wife and his country, but ultimately escaped her enchantments.

224 *His mouth was so tender*: i.e. he could not bear the discipline (like a horse which cannot endure the bit).

229 *everything*: including the young man himself.

232 *Reynard*: the fox, hero of the *Roman de Renart*.

234 *the hounds . . . rabbit*: there is an implied pun on the words *connin* (rabbit) and *con* (female genitalia).

235 *Sallust*: Roman historian, author of *Catilina*, from which this quotation is taken (ch. 3).

236 *the text tells us*: Horace, *Ars Poetica*, 333–4.

robe he wears: a reference to religious orders.

237 *Biere*: an old name for the forest of Fontainebleau.

Renouart of the Staff: a character from French *chanson de geste*, specifically from the epic cycle of *Guillaume d'Orange*.

238 *misericord*: a kind of dagger.

241 *Cacus*: the son of Vulcan, half man and half satyr, he stole some of Hercules' heifers and was later slain by the hero.

242 *Cythera*: an island off the southern coast of Greece, the home of Venus (perhaps confused by Jean de Meun with Mount Cithaeron).

Adonis: the story of Venus and Adonis is told by Ovid in his *Metamorphoses*.

246 *Nature*: Jean de Meun's chief source for Nature's 'confession' and the sermon of Genius which follows was the *De Planctu Naturae* of Alain de Lille. This extremely influential work was itself modelled on Boethius' *De Consolatione Philosophiae*.

247 *Hippocrates . . . Avicenna*: celebrated Greek and Arab physicians.

248 *elemental matter*: a particularly pure form of mercury, which was supposed to have combined with sulphur to form all other metals. The aim of the alchemist was to obtain this substance and then to achieve the right combination to produce gold.

249 *spirits . . . bodies*: 'spirits' were volatile substances (sal ammoniac, sulphur, mercury, arsenic) which could be combined with metals ('bodies').

250 *my wit is not equal to the task*: this confession of inadequacy is a rhetorical commonplace.

Euclid: Greek mathematician who flourished *c.* 300 BC.

Parrhasius . . . Zeuxis: celebrated Greek painters and sculptors.

Rhetoric: Cicero, *De Inventione Rhetorica*, ii. 1.

252 *Virgil . . . inconstant*: Virgil, *Aeneid*, iv. 569–70.

Solomon . . . woman: Ecclus. 25.

Titus Livy . . . prayers: Livy, *Annals*, i.9.

256 *Virgil*: *Eclogues*, iii. 92–3.

257 *Scripture*: Ecclus. 25: 30.

Guard . . . bosom: Mic. 7: 5.

260   *heaven*: Lecoy's edition of the *Romance of the Rose* has the
      following note: 'To understand this passage, it must be remem-
      bered that the cosmology of our poet is, in a simplified form,
      the Aristotelian cosmology of homocentric spheres, common-
      place in the Middle Ages. According to that doctrine, the
      universe consists of a set of spheres, one inside the other (eight
      in this case), all of which have the earth at their centre. The
      spheres revolve about the centre, which does not itself move.
      The outside sphere, furthest from the earth, bears the fixed
      stars; as it revolves it carries with it the seven other spheres,
      which are those of the planets. This revolution is from east to
      west. But the seven planetary spheres also move of their own
      accord; each planet has its own particular motion, but all move
      backwards, that is to say, from west to east. The terrestrial
      observer perceives the resultant of these various motions: the
      motion of the outside sphere is slowed down and life is there-
      fore possible beneath it, and the planetary spheres move from
      east to west. . . . Nevertheless, because each of the planetary
      spheres moves in its own particular way, each has its own
      rhythm which is not that of the fixed stars. This is why the
      planets rise and set at different times, and why they seem to
      move with respect to the fixed stars, travelling through differ-
      ent regions of the sky, each according to its own law. (*Roman
      de la Rose*, ed. Lecoy, iii. 164–5, my translation.)

      like a wheel: 'the retrograde motion of the planetary spheres
      slows down the sphere of the fixed stars to the extent that the
      heaven of the stars completes its revolution in one day, or rather
      in approximately one day. In fact, this revolution is slightly
      more than 360 degrees. As a result, the heaven of the fixed
      stars also moves, although very little, and this steady progress,
      however slow, must eventually add up to a complete revolution.
      At that moment, the heaven will be in the condition that it
      was in at the very beginning, in other words (for the Christian
      interpreters of this somewhat unorthodox hypothesis), at the
      moment of creation, and the phenomenon will be repeated
      periodically. . . . This is the theory of the "great year", already
      known in antiquity. Opinion varied concerning the length of the
      great year. Many fixed it at 36,000 years, in which case progress
      would be at the rate of one degree per century.' (Ibid. 165.)

261   *rays of the eyes*: the tactile theory of vision, current alongside
      the emission theory until the early Middle Ages, postulated

that the eye sends out invisible antennae and is thus able to 'feel' distant objects. Jean de Meun seems here to be combining the two theories.

261 *their appearance suggests*: a number of different interpretations of the marks on the moon's surface were current in the Middle Ages. Jean de Meun here follows the explanation given by Albertus Magnus in *De celo et mundo*, ii. 3, 8.

twelve houses: the twelve signs of the zodiac.

262 *Acheron*: the husband of Night. In Greek mythology, a river of the underworld.

harmonies: the theory that the revolutions of the heavenly bodies produced music whose harmonies were the model for our own music was attributed to Pythagoras.

263 *Empedocles*: 5th-cent. Greek philosopher.

Origen: Alexandrian church father (185–254).

264 *free will*: the discussion on predestination and free will which follows is based in essence on Book V of Boethius' *De Consolatione*.

271 *in one direction or another*: this definition of destiny is taken from Boethius IV, prose 6,9.

Deucalion and Pyrrha: the story of Deucalion and Pyrrha is told by Ovid in the *Metamorphoses*.

272 *Themis*: goddess of law and order.

277 *Bacchus . . . Cybele*: deities associated with vineyards, harvest, nature, and earth.

dryads: nymphs who inhabited trees.

sew up their sleeves: to make them fit properly.

278 *Alhazen*: 11th-cent. Arab physician and mathematician.

280 *a good woman*: Ecclus. 26: 1.

of Aristotle himself: in the *Meteorologica*, trans. by Mahieu le Vilain (ed. Rolf Edgren, p. 144).

283 *Scipio once did*: an allusion to Macrobius' commentary on Cicero's *Somnium Scipionis*.

284 *Lady Abundance*: Dame Habundia, leader of witches on their night rides.

286 *author of the Almagest*: i.e. Ptolemy.

Horace tells us: in *Epistles* i. 18, 86–7.

287 *shocking and stupid*: the question of what constituted true nobility was frequently debated in the Middle Ages.

    the wild stag: only nobles were allowed to hunt.

288 *Robert of Artois*: Robert II of Anjou, nephew of Saint Louis,
c. 1250–1302.

289 *Virgil . . . Calabria*: Virgil was associated with Naples in medieval legend, while the notion that the Roman poet Ennius
(239–169 BC) received gardens in Calabria is probably based
on a faulty manuscript of Ovid's *Ars Amatoria*.

    the wooden stick: the cross.

294 *Gods of gods . . . your immortality*: Chalcidius' translation of
Plato's *Timaeus*, ed. Waszink, p. 35.

295 *the wondrous sphere . . . place*: the first known example of this
image, which was to become commonplace, occurs in a 12th-
cent. work entitled *Liber XXIV philosophorum*.

    in the world: Virgil, *Eclogues*, iv. 7–10.

    Albumazar: Arab philosopher and astronomer of the 9th cent.
The passage occurs in his *Introductorium in Astronomiam*.

297 *Ixion*: punished by Zeus for his treachery by being bound to
a fiery wheel of perpetual motion.

    Tantalus: hero who abused his privilege of being admitted to
the table of the gods, and was punished accordingly.

    Sisyphus: legendary king of Corinth, punished for bad faith in
his dealings with the gods.

    Danaïds: 50 daughters of Danaus who married the 50 sons of
their uncle, Aegyptus. To avoid being killed by a son-in-law,
as the oracle predicted, Danaus ordered his daughters to kill
their husbands on their wedding night.

    Tityus: a giant, punished for offering violence to Artemis by
being cast into Tartarus, where two vultures perpetually devoured his liver.

302 *they will never reach a conclusion*: although Genius disapproves
of chastity, he admits that there may be arguments in its favour
on which he is not qualified to pronounce. When it comes to
'sexual perversions', however (in the next paragraph), he is on
surer ground. See Introd.

303 *Orpheus*: legendary poet and musician. He was supposed to
have invented homosexualism after the death of Eurydice.

304 *Cadmus*: legendary founder of Thebes.

305 *Clotho . . . Atropos*: see note to p. 159.

     Cerberus: three-headed dog, guardian of the underworld.

306 *Alecto . . . Megaera*: the three Furies, dreadful maidens whose function was to punish men for crimes such as perjury, murder, inhospitality, and violation of filial duty.

     twenty-six: a reference to ll. 19195–207.

310 *Georgics*: Virgil, *Georgics*, i. 125–46.

311 *So says Ovid*: in *Metamorphoses*, i. 114–27.

314 *no heart . . . contained therein*: see 1 Cor. 2: 9.

316 *fruit of salvation*: the olive-tree represents the cross.

319 *fiat*: 'let it be done.'

321 *Pygmalion*: the story of Pygmalion is told in Ovid, *Metamorphoses*, x. 242–97.

     Lavinia: the wife of Aeneas; her reputation for beauty was established in the 12th-cent. *Roman d'Eneas*.

323 *marbles*: the game of *marteaus* in the original has not been identified.

324 *Hymen*: god of marriage.

     Amphion of Thebes: the son of Jupiter and Antiope. He helped to build walls around Thebes by playing his lyre and causing the stones to move.

     gigues and rebecs: stringed instruments.

326 *Cinyras . . . Myrrha*: the story of Cinyras and Myrrha follows that of Pygmalion in Ovid *Metamorphoses*, x. 298–447.

327 *work is finished*: yet again, the poet promises a commentary which never materializes.

     Lady Cypris: another name for Venus.

329 *Virgil . . . welcome him*: Virgil, *Eclogues*, x. 69.

330 *Juvenal*: *Satires*, i. 38–9.

     Ovid: *Ars Amatoria*, ii. 667–8.

331 *figure of speech*: one of the thirteen arguments enumerated by Aristotle in *De Sophisticis Elenchis*.

333 *Hercules . . . Cacus*: see note to p. 241.

335 *garland of marigolds*: there is a pun on *soussie* (marigold) and *souci* (worry, anxiety).

The Oxford World's Classics Website

www.worldsclassics.co.uk

- Information about new titles
- Explore the full range of Oxford World's Classics
- Links to other literary sites and the main OUP webpage
- Imaginative competitions, with bookish prizes
- Peruse *Compass*, the Oxford World's Classics magazine
- Articles by editors
- Extracts from Introductions
- A forum for discussion and feedback on the series
- Special information for teachers and lecturers

www.worldsclassics.co.uk

American Literature

British and Irish Literature

Children's Literature

Classics and Ancient Literature

Colonial Literature

Eastern Literature

European Literature

History

Medieval Literature

Oxford English Drama

Poetry

Philosophy

Politics

Religion

The Oxford Shakespeare

A complete list of Oxford Paperbacks, including Oxford World's Classics, OPUS, Past Masters, Oxford Authors, Oxford Shakespeare, Oxford Drama, and Oxford Paperback Reference, is available in the UK from the Academic Division Publicity Department, Oxford University Press, Great Clarendon Street, Oxford OX2 6DP.

In the USA, complete lists are available from the Paperbacks Marketing Manager, Oxford University Press, 198 Madison Avenue, New York, NY 10016.

Oxford Paperbacks are available from all good bookshops. In case of difficulty, customers in the UK can order direct from Oxford University Press Bookshop, Freepost, 116 High Street, Oxford OX1 4BR, enclosing full payment. Please add 10 per cent of published price for postage and packing.